Dead Secret

Beverly Connor

W F HOWES LTD

This large print edition published in 2006 by
W F Howes Ltd
Unit 4, Rearsby Business Park, Gaddesby Lane,
Rearsby, Leicester LE7 4YH

1 3 5 7 9 10 8 6 4 2

First published in the United Kingdom in 2005
by Piatkus Books

A CIP catalogue record for this book is available
from the British Library

ISBN 1 84632 466 1

Typeset by Palimpsest Book Production Limited,
Grangemouth, Stirlingshire
Printed and bound in Great Britain
by Antony Rowe Ltd, Chippenham, Wilts.

To my niece, Tonya

ACKNOWLEDGEMENTS

A special thanks to my brother, Charlie, for information about knives; Dr McDaniel; my husband; and my editor Martha Bushko.

CHAPTER 1

Diane squirmed on her belly through the crack in the rock, dragging her backpack behind her on a tether. The crawlway was no more than a slit, as if the cave wall had been pierced through with a giant knife blade. The passage was maybe twenty feet long, barely wider than her shoulders, the ceiling two feet high at its highest, sixteen inches at its lowest – a tight fit. Loose stones scraped through her clothes from her chest to her abdomen and down her back. Of all the places she could be, this was the best – the dark, secret places of a cave.

Despite the cool temperature, sweat dampened her shirt, making it cling to her skin. Her mouth was dry from breathing in dust, and she craved a sip of cool water from the bottle tied to her backpack. Her fingertips felt the edges of the opening at the end of the tight passage. She tugged and squirmed until her head emerged into a larger tunnel running sharply to the right. Diane slithered out of the crack like a cave creature, a small cascade of pebbles and dust following her out and down a gentle slope to where she had room to rise to her hands and knees.

The dual lamps on her helmet illuminated the walls, making round designs of light and shadows on the red-brown rock. Ahead, the height of the tunnel increased. At its end, about three feet above the floor, an irregular opening gaped like the mouth of a shark.

Diane slid into a sitting position, pulled her backpack to her and took a long drink from her water bottle. Her gaze briefly lingered on the distant hole in the wall before she examined the sides of the tunnel, picking out survey stations – line-of-sight points from which to measure direction and distance. This visit, she'd only mark the stations with small tags. She liked to go slow when she mapped a cave – do an open traverse and take only basic measurements the first trip, get a feel for the cave.

It took time to learn a cave. When she finished mapping a section, it became like a good home, a place she knew intimately, yet still holding surprises. Her two favorite times to be in a cave were the first time – seeing everything new – and after she had mapped it and made it home.

A big cave like this one could take years to map. The landowners told her that no one had been through the entire cave. As far as she knew, she was the first to be in the section she was now in.

Diane took another drink of water. She listened for Mike, one of her caving partners, who should have been close behind her, but she didn't hear him crawling through the tunnel.

She turned on her walkie-talkie. 'Mike, the passage I just came through is tight.'

There was a moment of static before she heard his voice. 'Guess I shouldn't have eaten that pizza for breakfast.'

The section of zigzagging tunnels she'd just explored was devoid of any remarkable features but possessed a subtle beauty just from the color and texture of the rock.

Her gaze shifted again to the hole at the end of the tunnel. In another cave she'd crawled through a very similar hole that led into a cathedral room with flowstone draperies rippling across an entire wall, stalagmites that reached the ceiling like the trunks of giant redwood trees, and stalactites hanging like colossal chimes. Diane looked forward to getting to the hole at the tunnel's end.

She took the bright yellow ultrasonic distometer from a pocket on her backpack to measure the tunnel length. The electronic device was more convenient than a tape measure – though she still carried a tape: There were some places that just had to be measured the traditional way.

The floor of the tunnel was covered with breakdown – piles of broken bedrock fallen from the roof – but none were high enough to block her device. She pressed the button and the digital display showed 15.7 feet. She recorded it in her notebook.

The tunnel was three feet tall at its highest, not tall enough to stand in, so she would have to cross the space on her hands and knees. She eyed the breakdown. Not the most comfortable surface to crawl across, but easier than squirming on her belly. At least the knee pads would protect her knees from the sharp debris.

Diane shifted her backpack so that it hung from her side, stuffed the extra tether into one of the backpack pockets, and began the slow advance over the stacks of shaky rubble toward the opening in the wall ahead. She had gone perhaps half the distance when the floor beneath her seemed to shift a little differently with her weight. She glanced down at the angular rocks beneath her and hesitated, unsure what she was seeing.

Between the piles of rock was something strange – an optical illusion. She stopped and stared a long moment, moving her head one way, then another, studying the images. Looking through the space between several of the rocks was like looking through a View-Master – three-dimensional. She thought she glimpsed the tip of a stalagmite. With an electric flash of insight, she realized she was not seeing an illusion, but looking through to another chamber below her, and she was held up only by a jumble of rocks plugging a hole.

'Oh, shit,' she said out loud.

She moved a hand to her shoulder to turn on her walkie-talkie. The rocks shifted again.

'Mike,' she said, 'I'm in trouble.'

4

'I'm not far behind you. What's the problem?'

'I'm on top of some breakdown that has plugged an opening to a lower level. There's no floor under me.'

'Okay. Don't move. Let me get you in sight.'

Mike was one of the geologists who worked in her museum, and he was the best caving partner she'd ever had. Diane heard the scraping and heavy breathing as he crawled through the slit. So much adrenaline was pumping through her system it was hard not to take flight. She tried to stay completely still, though her heart was pounding so hard that she felt like it could shake the stones all by itself. Just shifting her weight to access her walkie-talkie had made the rocks beneath her move, grinding against each other as they labored under her weight.

If she stretched out on the rocks, would that even out the pressure her body was exerting on them? It might, but moving into a prone position might also be enough to cause the rocks to fall. Diane's gaze darted around, looking for the edges of the hole, hoping the entire floor of the tunnel wasn't false. Couldn't be, her mind told her. The rocks couldn't be suspended in a large hole. The logic gave her a moment of relief.

Suddenly with the next breath, the rocks fell from beneath her. Diane hurled her weight toward the closest wall and grabbed for the rim of the opening. Her fingers clenched the lip of the hole as her backpack fell to the end of its tether, snatching at the joints in her shoulders, jerking at her grip. She held on to the ledge. Her body, weighted by her backpack, swung above the black void.

Her arms ached after just seconds of hanging. Her gaze searched the rock for a better place to grip, but luck had been with the first hold her hands had found. There was none better.

'Hold on.' She heard Mike's hammer pounding somewhere behind her, driving an anchor bolt into the rock.

Diane wanted to tell him to hurry. She knew he was working as fast as he could, but her hands were cramping and each breath was a struggle, her ribs stretched tight by the weight of her hanging body. She tried not to think about falling. Jerky flashes of her headlamps reflected fleeting glimpses of the cavern floor below. It would be a twenty-foot drop or more – not necessarily far enough to kill, but far enough to break more than a few bones.

Don't think about that. Think about holding on.

She heard Mike working with the rope, tying it off.

'*Hurry,*' she whispered.

'Almost there,' he said.

She must have whispered louder than she thought.

The backpack felt as if it were filled with lead. She felt her grip slipping. If she fell and landed on her feet, she'd break her legs, but her skeleton could still absorb most of the shock of the fall. Still, spine and hip injury would be almost inevitable.

Don't think about falling, she rebuked herself. *Think about hanging on to this damn rock.*

'I can't reach you,' said Mike. 'I'm going to toss you the rope. Grab it. You'll swing back this way, so hold on tight.'

She leaned her head back slightly so that the rope fell between her face and her arms. Diane didn't hesitate; she grabbed the rope with one hand, then the other. As soon as she released her grip, her body swung across the opening. The rope caught on the rim of the hole beneath the anchor, sending her under the ledge and slamming her into the thick face of rock dividing the upper chamber from the cavern.

Her backpack whipped back and forth below her like a frantic pendulum. She held tight as Mike tried to stop the swinging.

When the swinging stopped, Diane didn't move for a long moment. She grasped the rope and breathed deeply, rejecting the pain caused from slamming into solid rock.

'You okay?' Mike peered over the edge at her.

'Nothing's broken, as far as I can tell.' She looked up at him and then down at the cavern floor and the length of the rope below her. 'I think I have more strength to climb down than up.'

'Okay. Let yourself down easy. I'm going to secure the rope a bit more.'

Diane lowered herself, hand over hand, until she reached the bottom of the chamber. Her feet were unsteady on the loose rocks. She sat down and untied from around her waist the line that tethered her backpack to her. Fortunately, nothing had dropped out of it. She stretched her muscles and fingered her rib cage. She'd be sore tomorrow, but right now she seemed fine.

From where she sat, she could see Mike setting another anchor bolt, securing her means of escape. He then placed a pad under the rope to keep it from fraying where it came in contact with the rock.

'Thank you,' she shouted up to Mike.

'No problem.'

Mike was a geologist at the museum where she was director and was working on his Ph.D. at Bartram University. He was a good friend and caving partner, and professed an attraction to her that left her a little unnerved, mainly because he was so much younger than she. But lately, to her relief, he had been seeing Neva, a fellow caver and a member of the crime scene lab that Diane also directed. And if Diane was any judge of body language, Mike and Neva had become close.

Diane thought to herself that while she was down here she might as well make good use of the time. She took her distometer, a notepad and bottle of water from secure pouches on the side of the backpack.

As Mike worked above, Diane picked her way

8

out of the worst of the breakdown and examined the chamber she'd discovered, or perhaps, she thought wryly, that had discovered her. She glanced around and saw that she was standing almost in the middle if it. She measured to the wall ahead – twenty feet, three inches. She turned and measured the opposite direction: nineteen feet, seven inches – thirty-nine feet, ten inches long. Its width was eleven feet shorter. The height to the rim at the top of the chamber was thirty-two feet. Good thing she didn't know that while she was hanging by her fingernails.

The twin headlamps on her helmet threw round pools of light on the several stalagmites that stood like sentinels around the room, tall and straight, casting their shadows on the wall behind them. The tallest was perhaps twenty feet. The thought that she might have fallen atop any one of them made her cringe.

Other than the entrance she had accidentally created at the top, the chamber had only one other egress. About twenty feet from the floor on the wall of the cave was a rounded opening leading to what looked like a tunnel. She scribbled down some notes.

'Ready to climb back up?' yelled Mike.

'In a minute.' Diane walked around the room, examining everything.

'That's what I like about you, Doc. You don't let a little thing like a near-death experience keep you from having a good time.'

Diane had hardly heard him, however. The hair on the back of her neck prickled. In her dim peripheral vision she saw the figure of someone crouching behind one of the stalagmites.

CHAPTER 2

Diane drew a shallow breath, focused her light full on the figure and discovered that it was not crouching but slumping, its back against the wall, long dead. She walked carefully to it, examining the floor each step of the way, then dropped on her haunches next to the body. What lay before her were the mummified remains of a male, judging from the prominence of his brow ridge and jaw, clad in the rotted remnants of a plaid shirt and jeans turned almost the color of the surrounding rock. With the partial disintegration of his soft tissue, he had collapsed and reclined in a fearful repose, his head leaning back against the wall and turned slightly, his mouth gaping, his thin lips stretched open, showing yellowed teeth.

She saw glimpses of dry skin and bone through his shirt. One hand rested in his lap, and the other lay beside him on the floor. They were balled into fists. A helmet lay upside down beside him along with a canteen. She retrieved her digital camera from her backpack and snapped several pictures from different angles and distances.

'Damn, Doc. What was that I said about you knowing how to have a good time? You find the creepiest things.' Mike was standing beside her. Diane had been so engrossed in her find that she hadn't heard him descend into the chamber. 'Is that what it looks like – a mummy?'

'Yes,' she said. 'Natural mummification. The tissues have been partially preserved by the dry air of the cave.'

Mike squatted beside her, looking at the crumpled remains. 'Wonder what happened to him. Did he get lost? Lose his light? Fall? He probably didn't come in the way we did. How did he get in here?'

'Don't know.' Diane snapped a picture of his helmet. 'What I need you to do is take our mapping notes to the surface and figure out what county we're in and call the appropriate coroner.'

'Coroner?'

'The county coroner has to be notified when a body is found.'

'You going to work this as a crime scene?'

'That's for the coroner to decide. Until then, I can't touch him.'

'But you're dying to look at him, aren't you?'

Diane smiled. 'I am looking at him.' She stood up. Mike rose with her, and Diane turned toward him, careful not to shine her headlamp in his eyes. 'I appreciate your being quick with the rope.'

'Sure. I've had to hang from my hands before, and it's dicey if you're not used to it. You okay?

12

You crashed pretty hard into the rock wall.' He looked up toward the hole in the roof.

From their vantage point she could see the thick walls of the hole surrounded by a thin lip that had at one time been a too-thin floor that had collapsed countless years ago.

She looked down at her hands. Faint abraded lines of blood etched her palms and fingers. 'My hands are going to be sore for a while. I imagine my body's going to ache too.'

Mike took one of her hands and examined the palm. 'Now, how many caving trips has it been that I've told you, you need to put on your gloves?'

'I know, I know. I just like the tactile feel of the cave.'

'Yeah, well, you're going to be feeling the tactile sensation for several days.'

Diane stretched her sore muscles and groaned. Damn, she was going to be in just great shape when she and Frank, her detective boyfriend, went on vacation tomorrow. *Better remember to pack the Ben-Gay and heating pad*, she thought.

'Is everybody okay?' Neva leaned over the edge of the hole in the ceiling. 'We heard you on the walkie-talkie and came as quickly as we could.'

'We're fine,' Diane yelled up at her. 'Thanks to Mike's quick rope-tying skills. Be careful of that hole; there might still be some weak spots up there. Where's MacGregor?'

'He didn't think he'd fit down that narrow

tunnel. Frankly, I think he was right. It's a tight squeeze.'

Dick MacGregor was a member of the caving club and, most important to Diane, he was a relative of the owner of the land where the entrance to the cave was located. That fact was enough for her to put up with his annoying personality traits and have him as one of her caving partners. He wasn't fat, but he was stouter than Mike, Neva and Diane – and there were some close places he wouldn't fit into without becoming stuck.

'Neva, would you climb down here with me? Mike's going back to the surface with MacGregor.'

'So,' said Mike with a grin, 'you *are* itching to have a go at the skeleton.'

'Mysteries, particularly cave mysteries, always interest me.'

'I thought so,' he said as he stepped through the rubble and made his way to the rope dangling from the hole in the ceiling.

Diane noted that he'd tied a series of loops on the rope to aid in climbing back up.

'How stable is the lip of that hole?'

He looked up. 'It'll do for now.'

'Can you bring more lights?' said Diane.

'Sure. Want me to contact someone at the crime lab for you?'

'Ask David or Jin to bring a kit, but tell them to wait outside. I think you had better bring it in.'

Diane was director of the RiverTrail Museum of Natural History in Rosewood, Georgia. The

14

successful use of the museum's forensic anthropology lab in the solution of a number of local homicides had caught the attention of Rosewood's mayor and police chief. As a result of political manipulations by Rosewood city officials, a crime scene unit had been set up on the third floor of the west wing of the museum, with Diane as its director also. All in all, it was an interesting world she lived in. However disparate the combination of museum work and crime fighting might seem, she found it helpful for the crime lab to have access to the abundance of museum experts. The talents of the crime scene unit had even come in handy when the museum acquired an Egyptian mummy. A museum and a crime scene lab turned out, to everyone's surprise, to be a good, if odd, fit.

David and Jin were members of Diane's crime scene crew. Jin was in his twenties, half-Asian, and came from New York, where he'd been a criminalist. David had worked with her at World Accord International when the two of them were human rights investigators. Neva, a former police officer, came to her from the Rosewood Police Department. The three of them made up Diane's crime scene unit. But David and Jin weren't cavers, and Diane didn't want them inside a rugged cave like this one.

Mike began his ascent, easily climbing the rope hand over hand. When he cleared the top, he and Neva exchanged a few quiet words, and then she started down the rope.

Diane had been surprised that Neva wanted to take up caving again after her true near-death experience in this very cave system. Being wedged in a crevasse between rocks, with gravity pulling her ever tighter into the squeeze, had been a frightening experience. But Neva showed a remarkable determination to get over the trauma. She was wide-eyed and pale the first few times back in a cave, but she stuck with it. Diane wondered if it was as much for Mike as for caves.

'What's up?' Neva looked up at the opening until the light disappeared with Mike down the tunnel. She grinned, and Diane watched her face change as she turned her head and spotted the remains.

'My God, that's not anyone we know . . . ?'

'No. This guy's been here a very long time.'

'What happened to him?'

'I don't know. I can't see enough of his bones to tell, but I'd bet he broke a limb, probably a leg. Looks like he was a caver. Has a helmet with a carbide lamp, a canteen, and I just noticed a backpack sticking out from under him. But I haven't seen any rope. I don't know of any caver who would venture this far into a cave without rope.'

'Novice?' Neva said, squatting to look at the mummy and his artifacts.

'Maybe, but novices usually bring rope – sometimes not enough of it, but they usually have it.'

'What do you want me to do?'

'We can't touch the body until the coroner arrives, but we can do a grid search of the floor.'

16

'What about the breakdown?'

'We'll get Mike to help with some of it.'

'You're kidding. You're going to look under the rocks?'

Diane surveyed the piles of rocks on the floor. 'We're not going to move them all, but I'd like to see if anything is under the rocks that just fell. You take that end; I'll start at the wall with the opening.' She gestured toward the hole in the opposite wall. 'We'll meet in the middle.'

Diane and Neva made their way to opposite sides of the room, but instead of searching the floor, Diane looked up at the opening in the wall.

'I think he fell from here,' she said. Her words reverberated across the cavern. She doubted Neva could make out what she'd said, Diane waved her away when she saw Neva's headlamp turn in her direction.

Diane rubbed a hand over the rough texture of the wall. It was about twenty feet to the opening, not a bad climb. She examined the wall, mentally noting hand- and foot-holds. Piece of cake, like climbing a ladder. She keyed her radio. 'Neva, I'm going up top to the opening here. You can continue searching the floor, or wait for me, whichever you prefer.'

Diane pulled her chalk bag from her pants pocket, dusted her hands and felt for the first two holds – a crack in the rock face in which she slipped the fingers of her right hand, and a protrusion she grabbed with the other. She proceeded up the face of the cliff, making sure every hand-hold and foothold was stable before she moved to the next, always using her hands for balance and her legs to push upward.

Diane liked solo climbing. She enjoyed being free of the ropes, but she always brought a climbing harness just in case she came across something really deep and interesting in the cave.

When she reached the opening, she pulled herself over the bottom edge, stood up in the newfound tunnel and viewed the cavern from this new vantage point. The scene was beautiful. Illuminated by her headlamps, the varied hues of red, orange, ivory and silver rock had a golden glow. The icy-looking stalactites and stalagmites with their pointed peaks and knobby textures looked like spires from some Middle Earth kingdom. Diane found the unearthly appearance ironic – nothing was more of the earth than a cave.

She turned her attention to details of the tunnel. Her first thought on examining the rock face she'd just climbed was that Caver Doe, as she dubbed him in her mind, had fallen the twenty feet from this tunnel to the cavern floor. The rock wall had a concave dip in it under the entrance, so that if he had been walking down this passage without paying attention, he would have run out of floor before he ran out of sides. From this vantage point at the top, that seemed a viable hypothesis.

There was little breakdown on the floor of the

tunnel near the opening. Nothing to trip over. As she studied the walls, she saw something angular jutting from the rock near the bottom of the wall. It wasn't rock. She knelt and examined the object – a railroad spike. Its presence puzzled her for a moment; then she realized that it might have been a crude anchor bolt, used to secure a rope. Caver Doe's equipment was old, predating all the modern gear that she had.

Several inches above the spike she discovered a gash in the stone wall. She put a hand in the gouged-out place, poking around in the hole, feeling its shape. In the middle of the gash was a smaller hole. *Interesting.*

A new hypothesis formed in her mind. Caver Doe had set his railroad spike in the top hole, tied his rope to it, and started over the edge. The spike had pulled out of the wall when he put his full weight on it – causing him to fall. If they found a railroad spike on the floor of the cavern, that would support her idea.

But what of the spike that was set – his caving partner? Surely he hadn't been caving alone. Then . . . why wasn't he rescued?

CHAPTER 3

Diane pondered various hypotheses of how Caver Doe might have come to his end, turning the ideas over in her mind, trying them out in various scenarios. She knew it was pointless at the moment, since she had not examined the remains, but she couldn't help herself.

She turned away from the chamber and faced the other end of the tunnel. The terminal height of the passage at the point it opened into the cavern measured fifteen feet, and the width was about twenty-five feet. The walls, a light tan streaked with many hues of brown, were patterned with large scallops, some nearly a foot in length, and dug into the stone with such repetition and consistency they looked almost man-made.

The limestone rock made of calcium derived from skeleta, shells, and the secretions of a host of marine life was literally the bones of the earth. She rubbed her fingers over the rock surface – a surface seemingly too hard to have dissolved in a little acidic groundwater. But it had, and that was the wonder of it. Slow-moving, slightly acidic water long ago in the time before man had dissolved this sinuous passage through the lime-stone. Diane raised a bare hand above her head and paused. There was no air movement.

She decided to follow the tunnel, even though she was without a caving companion for the moment. If she stayed on the main path, taking no detours, entering no mazes, it would be all right.

Adrenaline still electrified her body from her near fall. She was hyperalert as she walked, step-ping over the rubble that littered the silt floor, examining the pathway, the ceiling.

At the first gentle curve in the tunnel she stopped and looked back, viewing where she had just traversed. It was a habit she'd developed so she could always recognize passages from any direc-tion – a safeguard against becoming hopelessly lost and having to be rescued.

Diane knew she probably should go back while she could still see the glow from the chamber dimly illuminated by Neva's light. When she rounded the bend the chamber would be out of sight. Was she going to be cautious or adven-turous? She compromised and called Neva on the walkie-talkie.

'I'm going to follow this tunnel.'

'Should you be doing that alone?' said Neva.

Diane had drilled into Neva never to cave alone or go off alone, at least not for any great distance.

'I'm only going to the end of the tunnel. Not any farther. You stay in the chamber. Don't go anywhere until Mike and MacGregor get back. And keep in touch.'

'Will do.'

She shined her light on the curve of another bend just ahead. She pointed her distometer and measured the distance – 16.3 feet. It was indeed promising to be a long, sinuous tunnel.

On the floor of the winding passage she found no objects that might have been dropped by Caver Doe. Nothing. Not even footprints. That seemed odd. Even with the years of dust settling in the cave, there should be some ghost of a footprint left. Perhaps all traces of his passing had been covered by the breakdown. In many spots it was like gravel. She looked back where she had just come. Her footprints on the silt were actually very light, and in some places where the bedrock showed through the silt floor, there were none. Okay, maybe the absence of evidence of his passing was not odd, but interesting.

What was it Mike had told her about meanders? Flowing water left a greater amount of silt on the inside of bends where it slowed down. She squatted down at the turn in the bend and examined the heavy layer of silt. No footprints, but there were wavy smears and striations, as if someone had dragged or wiped something over the surface. The markings in the silt were so slight that they might have simply been products of her imagination – seeing evidence where there was none. She took her camera from a pocket on her pack and snapped a picture of it anyway.

She stood up and was about to continue on when her light caught the reflection of something in a slit between two large rocks. She squatted to examine the sparkle. It was silver, tiny, and had the smooth, rounded, shiny look of something man-made. She moved some of the silt from around it, revealing a thick wire loop-looking object. She grasped it between her thumb and index finger. It shifted slightly, but was stuck. *Must be attached to something bigger and held in place by the rocks,* she thought.

Diane dug between the rocks with her finger and felt a rounded edge. A button? Caught between the rocks when someone was wiping footprints from the surface of the silt? Or was her imagination making a mystery out of a simple caving accident?

Her digging had partially freed it. If she could just turn the object sideways she could get it out. Her fingernail caught it and swiveled it around on its edge. Diane grasped it and pulled it out, trying not to touch anything but the edges.

It was a button. Metallic – silver with the letters A.S.C. over an eagle with spread wings. Military button? On the reverse side was a thick wire shank – the part that Diane had first caught sight of. She laid the button on top of a rock near its original location, photographed it, made notations in her notebook of the spot where she had found it, and stuffed the camera and notebook back in her pack.

Diane searched her pockets for something suitable to put the button in and came up with a Ziploc bag. She sealed it so that enough air remained inside to reduce contact with the button, though it probably wouldn't matter anyway. The passage of time and the conditions had most likely resulted in the destruction of anything that might have been clinging to the surface of the button. But you never knew. She put it in the backpack and proceeded down the tunnel. She stopped at the next bend and examined the silt and found no other marks in the dirt.

'Dr Fallon.' The radio squawked a string of static syllables.

'Neva?'

'Just checking in. I found a railroad spike.' Even with the static, Diane could hear the puzzlement in Neva's voice.

'That's great. Mark the place where you found it.'

'Sure thing. Out.'

Diane followed the tunnel, watching the floor, the walls, the ceiling. It was like a gently waving avenue, not too cluttered, big enough to drive a car through with room to spare. The light shining off the uneven, rippling walls, and the distant outline of the oval cross-section, made the passage look like a vortex funneling her to some mysterious destination. It was a close call, but at this moment the mysteries of the cave held more allure to her than the remains back in the chamber. She wished that her caving partners were here so she wouldn't have to stop when the tunnel ended.

Just ahead a pile of breakdown with rocks the size of boulders littered the way. Beside the pile she found another passage, a side branch. The entrance was small; she would have to duck to get through it. From her vantage she could see that it sloped steeply upward and the passageway was strewn with large boulders – negotiable, but they didn't look stable. She scanned the walls around the entryway. Above the opening, almost at eye level, she saw a smudge. It was so faint she almost missed it, but it was definitely an X.

Smiling to herself, she grabbed her camera from the pack and snapped a picture. This was confirmation of her expectation that previous explorers, perhaps Caver Doe, had marked their path. In her notepad she made sketches and drew an X to mark the spot. This would definitely go on their caving itinerary. She was willing to bet this new tunnel led to another entrance aboveground. She didn't remember Mike or any members of her caving club mentioning other caves or entrances in the area. She grinned. New discoveries were what cavers lived for. Returning her notebook and camera to their backpack pockets, she squatted to examine the floor around the opening for artifacts.

Other than the mark on the wall, it looked as if no one had ever been there. She stood up and continued down the main passage. It was an easy traverse, and she wasn't taking any detours, so she decided to see where the tunnel ended. She picked her way around the jumble of rocks at the side tunnel's entrance and then walked down the path toward the next bend in this ghost river. She tried to imagine the water flowing through here aeons ago. The image in her mind would make a good visual display for the museum, she thought. She wondered if she could get footage of an underwater river for the video terminals at the museum geology exhibit.

Around the curve the tunnel forked. Diane felt a vague disappointment that her solo exploration was ended, but she'd already decided that she would stop when she got to the end of the main tunnel. She wished that caves weren't so dangerous, because she loved to explore them alone.

She examined the walls around the irregular entrances of the fork. No marks. Nothing. The larger of the two passages slanted upward. She shined her headlamps just inside. The walls were close together and, like the first offshoot passage, it was littered with large boulders.

The other tunnel was even smaller, almost a squeeze. She would fit, but she would have to go sideways. Diane leaned inside just enough to see around a rock that partially blocked the way. The passage slanted downward at a steep angle. She had the impression it was twisted around like a corkscrew. She stopped for a moment, holding her breath. She wasn't sure, but she thought she heard a sound, like white noise or flowing water. The sound was just at the edge of her hearing, like a whisper she wasn't sure she even heard.

The temptation to follow was almost more than she could resist – just a little way down the tunnel, she could always turn back and still find her way – but Diane ducked out of the entrance before the siren call became too tempting. She took another look around the two branch tunnels and snapped a picture before she started back toward the chamber.

Returning to the chamber through the tunnel was faster, since she knew the route and the lay of the rocks. As she rounded the last bend back, she saw a light from a helmet. For a moment she thought Neva had climbed up the wall, and Diane was about to chastise her – Neva was new to caving and Diane had warned her never to go it alone. But here Diane herself was – alone. She smiled inwardly.

When the figure grew closer she saw it was Mike. He had a deep crease between his brows, and with the light and shadows on his face, it was hard to read his expression.

'Are you all right?' His words sounded tight. 'I was surprised to find you had gone off by yourself.'

Diane was a little startled at his level of concern. 'No farther than we've strayed many times. I stuck to this main tunnel.'

She started to say something more, but realized

that he was worried. It was disturbing to witness an accident, and though her fall had turned out all right, she could have been seriously injured. Mike was as shaken by it as she.

'I'm fine, really.'

His face split into a smile. 'Yeah, I would've done the same thing.'

'Did you find the coroner?'

He nodded. 'The entrance to the cave is in Hall County, but according to the mapping we've done so far, it turns out the chamber containing the body is across the county line in Lumpkin County. The Lumpkin County coroner is a man named Brewster Pilgrim. Great name, huh? He said that he "would not dream of interfering with a cosmos that allowed a forensic anthropologist caver to discover human bones in a cave" and that you should "have at it." Just send him the paperwork.'

Diane laughed and realized just how tense she still was from the mishap. She'd forced it out of her mind, made light of the seriousness of it, but her muscles remembered, and the relief of laughing brought a dull ache to her head. She absently rubbed her temple.

'I've got some aspirin,' said Mike.

'I'm fine, really.'

'The coroner's sending a deputy to make it official. I got hold of Jin,' said Mike. 'He's bringing what you need from the crime lab. MacGregor's waiting outside the cave for him. I'll go back up and get your equipment when it arrives.'

'Good job. I'll have to start paying you out of the crime lab budget before long.' They stood looking at each other, their headlamps making a pool of light surrounding them. 'How is Neva doing?' asked Diane after a pause.

'She's happily searching a grid pattern of the chamber floor. She showed me the railroad spike she found. Said you seemed happy about it, but she wasn't sure why. When I climbed up I saw the spike in the wall and the place where it looked like one was pulled out. You thinking that's what caused his fall?'

'It's likely. At first, however, I thought he might not have been paying attention to the floor and walked out into thin air.'

'There is a drop there that could be a hell of a first step. Find anything else up here?'

Diane fished the bag with the button out of her pack. 'I found this wedged between two rocks.'

Mike looked at the button, then down at the rock-strewn floor of the tunnel and back at Diane, his eyes wide. 'I thought Neva was a detail freak. There's thousands of rocks here. How could you possibly find that little thing between two of them?' He took the plastic bag from her and peered at the button. 'I think you pulled it off your shirt.' Diane was wearing an open plaid flannel shirt and a white tee underneath. Mike handed her back the plastic bag and tugged the button side of her flannel shirt. 'Nope, they're all here . . . Hey, this is a guy's shirt.'

'You don't recognize it?'

He looked closer. 'Yes, it's my shirt. The one I gave you last month when you got yours all mucked up. So you're wearing my clothes. This means I'm making progress.' He grinned broadly.

Diane suddenly felt self-conscious and wished she hadn't brought the shirt's history to his attention. 'You said it was too small for you and that I could keep it. Besides, I understand you and Neva are dating.'

'You interested in my love life, Doc?'

'Just making conversation.'

'We've gone out a few times. We're good friends and I like that.' He let go of her shirt.

'It's a good caving shirt. Don't take it as a proposition – or wishful thinking.'

He put his hand on his chest. 'Doc, you're always cutting out my heart.' He gave her a crooked smile.

'You look all broken up,' she said with her best poker face, cuffing him lightly on his chest and starting back to the cavern.

'Find anything interesting down the tunnel?' asked Mike.

Diane stopped. 'Several things.'

'Why don't you show me while we wait for Jin to get here?'

'I really need to get back and help Neva search the cavern for any dead-caver clues.'

'Will it take long to show me?' Mike nodded his head in the direction Diane had just investigated.

'No, but . . .'

'I'll help with the search when we get back.'

'All right, but let me check in first.' Diane put the button back in her pack and shifted the pack so that the walkie-talkie clipped to it was near her shoulder. 'Neva, how are you doing?'

'I'm fine,' she replied. 'I kind of like this cavern. And I have someone here to keep me company. He's a little old for me, but he's a great listener, lets me do all the talking.'

'That's my girl,' Mike said, mostly to himself.

Diane grinned. 'Take a break. I'm going to show Mike a couple of things and I'll be there to help you finish.'

'I don't need a break. I'm fine.'

'All right but don't tire yourself out. We'll be there in a few minutes.'

'No problem.'

She turned to Mike. 'When we finish here, would you go to the entrance to meet Jin? I don't want him coming into the cave. He's never done any caving that I'm aware of.'

Mike nodded, and Diane watched the light from his duel headlamps dance up and down on the walls.

She led the way, backtracking to the first offshoot tunnel. They picked their way through the rubble to the opening.

'Here.' She pointed at the mark above the entrance. 'There's no way to know who made it, but it could have been made by our guy to find his way back.'

31

'You're thinking there has to be another entry point,' said Mike, leaning forward to get a close look at the faint X over the entrance.

'Maybe. Until we made the new hole in the roof of the cavern this may have been a separate cave with its own entrance, unconnected to the cave we came in – unless, of course, one of the passages connects them up somewhere else.'

Mike squatted and examined the rocks around the mouth of the entrance, moving some of the rock, touching the silt and sand with his fingers. Then he stood and stepped through the opening. Diane followed directly behind him, the passage so narrow that they fit only single file. The tunnel was filled with tight meanders between huge boulders and uneroded protrusions from the wall of the cave. Some of the boulders were caught between other rocks as if they had tumbled down the passage.

'I don't like this,' said Mike. 'I'm thinking they marked the opening to tell them not to go here. It looks too unstable. Some of the rocks at the entrance have been thrown out from a recent rock slide. Be easy to get trapped if one of these big guys shifts—'

His voice was cut off by a grinding rumble above them.

CHAPTER 4

Mike turned and put a hand on Diane's back just as she sprang toward the tunnel entrance. A cloud of dust and pebbles suddenly surrounded them, blinding them. Diane kept running, hoping her feet would hit solid ground and not the rocks littering the floor. She sensed Mike right behind her. Her next footfall landed on an angular rock and she started falling. She put her arms in front of her to break the impact but was caught by Mike's arm around her waist. He carried her for one step; then she regained her footing. They ran out of the tunnel entrance veering sharply away from the path of the rocks. The change of direction and uneven rocky floor threw them both off balance, and the momentum sent them sprawling to the cave floor. By good fortune, they landed mainly on silt and missed the sharp, jagged rocks. Dust bellowed from the opening, followed by a small avalanche of rocks. Mike still held her around the waist.

'Glad to see I've still got adrenaline left; how about you?' said Mike, sliding his arm away.

'I'm good for another scare or two.' Diane

struggled to her hands and knees. Mike rose, pulling her up with him, and they moved away from the dust.

'Okay, so X means keep out,' he said.

'It does now.' Diane bent over, coughing the dust out of her lungs.

'You okay?' Mike choked as he spoke, and he started coughing too.

'A little beat up, but otherwise fine.' Diane examined the fresh scrapes on the heel of her hands and rubbed her shoulder where it hit a rock. 'I've never had two close calls in one outing. I don't have *one* close call very often.'

'Sometimes things happen. That's why we don't cave alone.'

'What happened here, do you think?'

Mike shrugged. 'One of the boulders lost its foundation for some reason and gravity took over, sending it crashing into another boulder, and suddenly we had an avalanche.' He shrugged again. 'Could have been caused by small seismic activity, sonic boom, who knows . . . like I said, it looked unstable. Wouldn't have taken much. Judging by the rocks around the entrance, I'm guessing this has happened before.'

'The entrance looks blocked now,' Diane said, staring at the mouth of the offshoot tunnel still shrouded in a thin fog of dust.

Mike's light flickered. He tapped it with his finger. 'We'd better do a lamp check.'

They checked out each other's headlamps to

make sure nothing was broken or loose. During the check, Diane noticed for the first time with some alarm that there was blood on Mike's face.

'You're bleeding,' she said, pointing to the corresponding spot on her own face. 'You sure you're okay?'

Mike pulled a handkerchief from his pocket, wiped his chin and looked at the small smear of blood. 'This is nothing. I've had worse spills . . . Hell, I've had worse cuts shaving. You said you found some more tunnels at the end of this main one? Why don't we have a look before we go back?'

Diane hesitated. 'Sure, it won't take long.' She led the way toward the end of the main tunnel.

'It's not dangerous, is it?' Mike quipped.

Diane's radio squawked.

'I heard a noise; is everything all right?' It was Neva.

'We're fine,' said Diane. 'Just a little rockfall in one of the offshoot tunnels. No damage done. Is everything okay there?'

'Yup. I'm almost done.'

Diane felt a pang of guilt. She'd left Neva to search the entire chamber by herself.

As if sensing her guilt, Mike laughed and said, 'Neva's really having a good time. Nothing like a nice big cavern to knock around in for a while to get your confidence back. Neva loves caves but is still a little scared of them, with good reason – she had a really close call.'

Diane winced as she thought of how close Neva came to dying in this very cave system.

'I think having something focused to do is helping her get over her fears,' said Mike. 'Her eye for detail is amazing. The girl must have been a killer on an Easter-egg hunt. Of course, if you found that tiny button among all these rocks, you weren't too shabby either. What is it about you crime scene types? Got some kind of locator gene?'

'It's all in knowing how to look – and also luck,' Diane pointed to the split end of the tunnel. 'I'd like to explore those passages the next time we come,' she said. The two openings looked like huge dark eyes staring unblinkingly at them as they approached.

'The high road and the low road,' said Mike as they stood next to the openings.

Diane noticed that, like her, he was drawn to the one that led down. He stepped through the entrance and looked down. Diane stood behind him, very still, listening.

'You hear that?' said Mike.

'I thought I heard something when I was here before. You hear it too?'

'Like flowing water, maybe? It's hard to say.' He grinned at her. 'Interesting.'

'I'd like to investigate, but I don't want to leave Neva alone any longer.'

'No. But we can come back next weekend,' said Mike. 'What do you say?'

'I'm leaving for a two-week vacation in the

mountains tomorrow. How about in three weeks? Can you wait that long?'

'Doc, I can wait for you forever.' Mike grinned. 'But we're going to have a little problem with MacGregor. He can't get though the squeeze, and right now I can't see an alternate route to the cavern.'

Diane stepped back out into the main passage. 'We'll figure something out. Maybe more members of the caving club can join us and we can split up and look for another entrance to the cave system.'

'Good idea. There must be another way in.'

As they walked back to the cavern, Diane kept an eye out along the way for any clue that might have been left behind by their mummy friend. She saw nothing. But it was only luck that she had found the button. There were thousands of rocks littering the tunnel from one end to the other that could be hiding something.

They rounded the last bend and came in sight of the cavern. Neva's lights illuminated the cavern, casting the large stalagmites and stalactites in a dim, shadowy golden glow. Diane stopped a moment to look.

'Breathtaking,' said Mike.

'It's one of the reasons I love caves,' said Diane. 'So many gorgeous views.'

They walked to the opening, and Diane climbed down the wall first. It took her several minutes to get back down. Mike, more experienced at rock climbing, made the descent in less than half the time.

'A button,' said Neva, holding the bag and

peering at the silver disk. 'David will be happy with this. Did you know he's constructing a button-recognition database?'

Mike raised his eyebrows. The expression on his face was obvious: He was wondering if maybe David had too much time on his hands.

'David lives for databases,' Diane said.

'And recognition algorithms,' added Neva.

'But buttons?' said Mike.

'Well, we have a button that needs recognition,' said Diane.

'I found a rope among the rocks by the wall over there.' Neva pointed to a pile of rubble not far from where Diane and Mike had climbed in and out of the opening. 'It's pretty rotten. Our guy here ate Moon Pies.' She held up two wrappers, then dropped them in an evidence bag.

'Early energy bars, I guess,' said Mike. 'Jin ought to be here by now. I'll go meet him.' Mike made his way across the rubble to the rope hanging from the chamber above, ready to climb up.

'Hi, guys!' The voice came from above them, and they all looked up to see Jin peering down from the hole in the ceiling.

Dammit, Diane thought as the image flashed through her head of him traipsing over rocks and across ledges, oblivious to the dangers. 'Jin, you were supposed to stay outside,' she yelled up at him. 'How did you get here?'

'Dick MacGregor brought me as far as that really narrow tunnel. You guys do this all the time?'

'You didn't answer my question. What are you doing here? This is not a cave for a novice. You've never been in a cave.'

'Come on now, Boss. You don't expect me to hear a story about you finding mummified remains in a cave and just stay outside the door. I got my hiking backpack, extra flashlights and batteries, a bota bag of water, and a hard hat. I'm good to go.'

Mike looked over at Diane. 'I'll go up and help him down.'

Mike climbed the rope and lowered Jin's duffel bag, a crime scene kit, and a large backpack on a frame. Diane noticed a spray of dust come down with the equipment. She looked up at the ceiling but didn't see any loose rocks. Must be dust and rocks left over from her fall, she thought. She heard Mike warn Jin of the instability of the rocks around the hole as Jin climbed down after his equipment.

Close to the bottom, Jin jumped off the rope and dusted off his hands. Diane and Neva gawked at him. He sported a construction hard hat and a shirt and jeans that were several sizes too big for his thin frame.

'What do you have on?' said Neva. Diane tried to suppress laughter.

Jin grinned and looked down at his pants, lifting them up by the pockets and turning them loose, letting the rolled-up cuffs fall around his running shoes.

'Well, see, when I got here, I was wearing shorts and a tee. Your guy Dick told me that I would get cold down here in the cave, and he loaned me some clothes he had in his car.'

'Make sure you don't trip on the cuffs,' said Neva. 'There's a lot of rocks around here to fall over.'

'Jin,' said Diane. 'Since you are here, you are to do everything we tell you. We'll be carrying a lot of stuff getting out of here, and it won't be easy.'

'Sure thing, Boss.'

Jin didn't look the least contrite to Diane. He shined a flashlight around the cavern with a happy-to-be-here look on his face.

Mike climbed down the rope. More dust fell from the hole.

'Jin make it okay?' It was Dick MacGregor calling on the walkie-talkie. 'He had a lot of stuff with him.'

'He's here in fine shape,' Diane replied, using her radio. 'The equipment looks pretty good too.'

'I told him I didn't think he could drag all that stuff through that tunnel.'

'It's all here,' said Diane. She glanced at the pile of stuff Jin brought with him and was surprised he managed to get it through the narrow tunnel.

'I gotta go wait for the deputy outside the cave,' said Dick. 'He's got some kind of paper for you to sign.'

'Thanks, Dick. I appreciate your help.'

'Sure. Always fun to go caving with you guys.

You never know what we'll run into. Went caving all my life and never had near the adventures I've had with you guys.'

'Glad we've been able to provide you with new experiences,' said Mike into his walkie-talkie, grinning at Diane. 'You think the deputy has had time to get up there yet?'

'Probably waiting for me outside now. I'll go see.'

Jin's duffel bag carried several battery-powered lanterns that he had padded with bubble wrap. They positioned them around the chamber. The duffel also contained a body bag. Jin grabbed his crime scene kit and walked with them to the mummified remains.

'I wonder what happened. Fall through that hole, you think?' asked Jin.

'No,' said Mike. 'Diane made that hole when she fell through the ceiling.'

Jin looked at the two of them, wide-eyed.

'I managed to hang on to the ledge until Mike rescued me,' said Diane.

'Jeez, Boss, you could have broken something.'

'Fortunately, I didn't. Our guy may have been trying to descend a rope from that opening over there.' Diane pointed to the high opening in the cavern wall. 'And the railroad spike the rope was anchored to came loose and sent him crashing to the cavern floor.'

'Bet he broke something,' said Jin.

'I'm sure he did,' said Diane. 'Jin, you and Neva

process his body. Neva, pack the evidence and take pictures. I'm going to move some of these rocks that I dislodged from that hole in the ceiling and look at the floor. Work as fast as you comfortably can.'

Jin and Neva busied themselves while Diane surveyed the rock pile. Mike had moved some of them from around the bottom of the rope to give them a place to stand. Diane didn't know if there might be anything under the fallen rocks, but prudence dictated that she have a look.

'You want some help?' asked Mike.

'I hate to ask you to do this.'

'That's all right. Helping with a crime scene makes my résumé look more interesting. No one has to know that all I did was move rocks.'

It was a bigger job than Diane had anticipated, but they cleared a good portion of the fallen rocks, stacking them to the side.

Diane stood tall and stretched her muscles, she looked up and scanned the ceiling. 'I'm a little concerned about the ceiling,' she said.

'I saw the dust falling,' said Mike. 'I believe it's from the newly opened hole. I haven't seen any larger rocks breaking away. Before everyone climbs back up, I'll reposition the rope so that it doesn't put pressure on the rim of the hole.'

She took a flashlight and examined the newly revealed floor. She found nothing.

'That was a lot of work with nothing to show for it,' she said.

'Maybe this will show something interesting,' said Jin. He stood next to the cave wall beneath the tunnel opening with a squirt bottle in one hand. 'I'll need to turn off all the lights in a minute.'

'No!' yelled Diane and Mike simultaneously.

CHAPTER 5

Neva looked up from the evidence bags and moved to stop Jin.

'Tell me you didn't spray anything on the rocks,' said Mike.

Jin raised his eyebrows and stared at him for a moment, then at Diane. 'We almost always check for blood. I didn't think—'

'We don't contaminate caves. The ecosystem here is fragile. I should have told you not to bring any chemicals,' said Diane.

Jin looked around at the barren landscape of rock and speleotherms. 'I didn't know. Who would have thought?'

'The fauna can be very small – microscopic,' said Mike.

'And we can't leave anything toxic that other cavers might get into,' said Diane.

Jin wrinkled his face. 'Didn't think of that.' He glanced at Mike, who was staring at him with a disapproving frown. 'I haven't sprayed anything. We're safe.'

Mike nodded, then gave him a crooked half smile.

'Good. Then I don't have to dangle you over a bottomless pit.'

'Well, that's a relief,' said Jin. 'I'm not wearing my Spider-Man underwear.' He grinned at Mike, then looked at Diane. 'I saw some suspicious dark stains that might be blood,' said Jin. 'I'll take samples and photographs. We can map any pattern that way.'

'I have something here.' Neva had donned a pair of latex gloves from the crime kit and was examining what looked like a slip of paper. 'I think it might be a photograph, but it's been soaked through – with blood maybe.'

'Really?' said Jin. 'Let me see.'

Diane and Jin walked over and peered at what appeared to be a dirty brown square piece of paper in Neva's hand. Neva shined her flashlight through it.

'I think I see a shape,' said Neva. 'Maybe a person.'

'Maybe,' agreed Diane. 'We'll clean it up at the lab. If we're lucky, it will have a name on the back. Good find.'

Neva dropped the paper fragment into an evidence bag she retrieved from the crime kit and set it in the row of bags containing evidence that had been collected so far – more than Diane expected.

Jin returned to his soil samples. Diane slipped on a pair of gloves and helped Neva put the mummified remains of Caver Doe into the body bag. With his body fluids gone and only skin and bone remaining, he was light, but he was fixed in a sitting position, so they had to lay him on his side in the bag.

'Do you know how long he's been here?' Mike peered into the body bag. 'He looks a little like that Egyptian mummy you have at the museum – if it weren't for the clothes.'

Diane shrugged her shoulders. 'Perhaps between thirty and a hundred years.' She zipped up the bag. 'We'll know when we analyze the evidence.'

Neva let out a breath. 'He's been sitting a long time waiting for someone to find him.' She gave the body bag a pat. 'Poor fellow.'

Jin squatted beside a dented, discolored brass lamp setting with collected evidence. 'He had a carbide lamp. Do they still make them?'

'Most definitely,' said Mike. 'I have several.'

'Many cavers still use them,' Diane said.

'Really?' said Jin. 'Interesting. Well, this one looks old.'

Neva stood, stretched, and began packing up the evidence in the crime scene kit. 'I'll bet we can get something from the Moon Pie wrappers. And heaven knows what's in his backpack. Maybe he kept a journal while he was waiting.' She grinned. 'He had to do something to pass the time.'

'Probably just sat and groaned,' said Mike, still staring at the closed body bag. 'Depending on how he landed, he could have been in a lot of pain.'

While they discussed the last days of Caver Doe, Diane studied all the objects littering the cavern. They looked incongruous amid the columns of stalagmites and stalactites. 'Now we have to haul this stuff out of here.'

Mike came over to her side. 'I've been thinking about that,' he said. 'We can hoist the stuff up to the cavern above and divide it among us.' He lifted Jin's huge backpack. 'You were only going to be here a few hours; why did you bring such a big backpack? What do you have in it?'

'Flashlights, space blanket, bedroll, food, dishes, duct tape, first-aid kit, binoculars, emergency shelter . . .'

'Emergency shelter?'

'It's the stuff I take on long hikes. I thought some of it might be useful in a cave.'

Mike laughed. 'We'll have to teach you how to put it in a smaller pack.'

'It was kind of hard dragging it through the tunnels,' admitted Jin.

Diane winced, trying not to think of the speleotherms he may have damaged with the huge metal frame on his pack.

Mike climbed up the rope to the chamber above while Diane and her crew packed up the lamps and evidence. Now the cavern was illuminated only by Diane's and Neva's headlamps and Jin's flashlight.

Diane's eyes hadn't yet adjusted to the loss of light. Everything in her peripheral vision was a dim shadow. It was like closing a door, leaving the cave as it should be – deep and dark.

At the sound of hammering from above, Jin looked up. 'What's he doing?'

'Probably putting in pulleys to make it easier to haul this stuff back up.'

Jin paused. 'You mean he carries pulleys around in his backpack, but he scoffed at my emergency shelter?' He grinned, showing a row of even white teeth.

'We work on rope a lot, so we carry a lot of rope gear,' said Diane.

They had moved all their things near the rope. Diane glanced up just as Mike peered down from the hole.

'Stand back,' he yelled. 'I'm dropping a rope.'

Diane tied the metal case of the crime scene kit to the end of the rope, and Mike quickly hauled it up. The duffel bag and the lamps were next, and then Jin's backpack.

While Mike was hoisting the backpack, Diane made a rope harness for the body bag. She tied the harness to the hoist rope and Mike lifted it up through the hole. All that was left was Diane, Neva and Jin.

Jin looked up the long rope and over at Diane.

'There's no disgrace in using the loops in the rope as hand- and footholds if you need them. That's what they're for,' said Diane.

Jin gave her a sideways look. 'You say that as if you don't have to use them when you climb.'

Diane smiled at him. 'Here's some chalk,' she said.

Jin dusted his hands, put his flashlight in his belt and started up. He did better than Diane expected. Mike grabbed his arm at the top of the climb and helped pull him over the ledge. Neva was next. She had a more difficult time. She was strong, but it took a special set of muscles to climb a rope, and she struggled to get to the top and over the ledge. When Neva was up, Diane chalked her own hands and climbed up the rope with only slight discomfort.

It was crowded in the small chamber with all four of them and their supplies. Now they had to get through the narrow passage dragging Caver Doe and all their paraphernalia.

'I called MacGregor and asked him to meet us on the other end of this passage to help carry some of this stuff,' said Mike. 'He'll get a kick out of helping carry the body.'

'Yes,' said Neva. 'It'll give him something to talk about – for months, maybe years.'

Diane decided that she would take the lead out of the tunnel and Mike would bring up the rear. She went through, pulling both her and Jin's backpacks. The metal frame on Jin's pack scraped the rock wall all the way through the tight tunnel. She emerged almost in MacGregor's lap.

'Hi! Need help getting the stuff out?' Dick MacGregor was sitting outside the narrow tunnel eating an apple. He stuffed the unfinished snack in his backpack.

'Yes. We could use your help,' said Diane.

Neva's headlamp was visible as she squirmed through the narrow passage, dragging the crime scene kit and her backpack behind her.

Diane tried to tune out the scraping sounds of the hard metal crime scene case.

'Is the deputy outside?' she asked.

'Oh, yeah. Me and him have been talking. He said the sheriff wasn't going to like the coroner giving you the body. But, heck, what was he going to do with it anyway? I mean, I think the coroner was right – finders keepers. You going to put him on show with the other mummy at the museum?'

'We're going to find out who he is. He may have relatives from around here. You ever heard stories about anyone getting lost in a cave?' asked Diane as she helped Neva out of the tunnel with her load.

MacGregor scratched his scruffy dark beard. 'No . . . come to think of it, I never did. I'll ask my cousin. It's his family's land. They might know.'

Jin came tumbling out, pulling Caver Doe in the body bag behind him. They were in a small room devoid of any formations. It had an irregular dome shape and walls a light color similar to the big tunnel where Diane had found the button. It was a cozy room, almost like a bubble between the narrow crack they just came through and the twisting passage they were about to enter.

They waited several minutes for Mike.

'What's keeping him?' asked Jin.

'He's getting the rope,' said Diane.

'Oh, yeah. Isn't it heavy carrying around all that rope?'

'Can be, but it's good to have it when you need it.'

Finally Mike came through, pulling Jin's duffel bag and his backpack with his coils of rope tied to it.

'Why don't MacGregor and Jin carry the body bag?' Mike said to Diane. 'I can take the crime scene kit and Jin's backpack. Neva can carry your pack, and you can carry the duffel bag.'

Diane nodded in agreement. She and Mike were the most experienced cavers, and he had given the heaviest loads to himself and her.

'Can't believe there's a dead body in this bag,' said MacGregor. 'You don't think it's anybody we know, do you?' His voice had a sudden tone of concern in it.

Diane shook her head. 'No, this guy's been here a long time.'

It took them three times as long to get out of the cave as it had to get in, loaded down as they were. Several times they had to stop and nego-tiate through squeezes, taking off their load and pulling it behind them or pushing it in front of them.

A loaded caravan through a cave wasn't as much fun as simple caving. Diane felt relieved when they first emerged into the outdoors, but she quickly wished she were back in the cave. It was hot, especially compared to the cool cave. With her long-sleeved caving attire, it wouldn't take long to get uncomfortably hot. But there was the deputy to talk to first.

He sat on the bumper of his Lumpkin County patrol car with his arms folded in a manner that Diane had seen young children do when they were in full pout mode. Dressed in navy-blue pants and a short-sleeved shirt, the deputy looked to be in his early forties and had wavy blond hair and the beginnings of a potbelly.

'You know, I have other things to do than sit around here all day. Which one of you is Diane Fallon?' His gaze took in all of them, as if one of the males might have been named Diane.

'I'm Diane Fallon.'

'You could have come out and signed this paper and I could have been on my way.'

'I'm sorry, Deputy' – she looked at his name-plate above his shirt pocket – 'Deputy Singer. I would have if I could. But I'm here now and I'll be glad to sign the coroner's papers.' Diane smiled at him, hoping she wasn't showing the amusement she felt at listening to him complain.

The deputy shoved some wrinkled papers at her.

'Got a pen?' asked Diane.

The deputy breathed a heavy sigh and handed her the pen from his shirt pocket.

Diane took the papers and laid them out on the hood of his car.

'Now just a minute.' The deputy sprang toward

his car and grabbed a notebook from the back-seat. 'Use this. I don't want you scratching my car.'

As she wrote, Deputy Singer looked over her shoulder and told her what the sheriff was going to think of all this. His breath smelled of garlic and onions.

Mike opened the back of his SUV, took soft drinks from his cooler and passed them around, handing the deputy a Coke. Deputy Singer took it and muttered a thanks and went on with his harangue between sips. Diane had a feeling he'd been mentally rehearsing it while he was waiting. Mike gave her a 7-UP and popped the tab for her. It was cold and felt good going down her throat.

Diane took several long gulps before retuning her attention to the paperwork. She glanced up and saw Mike leaning against his vehicle with an arm around Neva's neck, sharing a Coke with her, the two of them sporting amused expressions as they watched her deal with the deputy.

'Yes, sirree, Sheriff Burns is going to have a talk with Pilgrim. I don't know what he was thinking, giving all this to Rosewood, like we can't take care of our own. Who does Rosewood think they are anyway? Atlanta? Too big for your britches, I'd say.'

Diane let the deputy get the ire out of his system. She'd learned from her former boss, who was a career diplomat, that sometimes letting people have their say defused their hard feelings.

'I'm sure he thought the sheriff had more important things to do than fool with some incident that
happened maybe fifty or sixty years ago,' said
Diane.

'Fifty or sixty years ago? That long, huh? You're
right about that. Probably don't even have a next
of kin still living. Just be a waste of time. I guess
ol' Pilgrim thought you all had the time to waste,
with your fancy equipment doing everything for
you.'

'I imagine so.' Diane smiled and handed him
the papers.

'Tell Sheriff Burns I'll give him a call, and thank
you for waiting for us. I know it was an inconvenience, but I appreciate it.'

'Just doing my job. It's what they pay me for.'
He slumped toward his patrol car, got in, and
drove off with a spin of his wheels, kicking a cloud
of dirt and grass on them.

CHAPTER 6

'Pleasant fellow,' Neva said, turning to MacGregor. 'Bet you had a good time with him out here, Mac.'

'Oh, that's just him. My cousin said he was like that as a kid – like everything puts him out. I tried to get him in a good mood for you guys, but I guess I failed.'

Diane couldn't suppress a chuckle; neither could Mike or Neva. Diane looked at her watch. It was almost three o'clock. If she hurried she'd have time for an extra-long soak in the tub before her date with Frank. She and the others got their clean clothes out of the car. The guys went behind Mike's SUV to change.

Dick MacGregor had built a blind just into the woods for Neva and Diane to change behind. The blind was at the base of a hillside with thick woods all around, and it included a bench. For all his annoying habits – talking incessantly, humming *The Twilight Zone* theme song every time they passed through the twilight zone of a cave, telling bad jokes – MacGregor was actually a kind and considerate person. She and

55

Neva both appreciated the place he had built for them.

Diane sat down on the bench, pulled off her boots and wiggled her freed toes. Neva sat down beside her and began unlacing hers.

'This was certainly an eventful caving trip.' Neva kneaded her foot before she took off her jeans and put on a fresh pair. She slipped her bare feet into running shoes that didn't look much cleaner than her caving boots. 'How are you doing – you know, after the almost fall?'

'A little sore.' Diane stretched her muscles, bending down so that her head touched her ankles and stretching her back. It felt good.

'That had to be scary,' said Neva.

Diane sat up. 'It was. But when something like that happens, as you know, you put all your energies into hanging on. I was lucky that Mike was there to throw me a rope.'

'How do you get rid of the fear?'

'You don't. It's kind of like pain – you just work through it.' Neva was silent for a moment, as if contemplating what Diane said. 'You appear to be working through your fear of caving pretty well,' said Diane.

Neva nodded and smiled. 'Mike's been a big help. He's a really great guy, although . . .' She smiled and lowered her voice, as if he might be lurking around listening. 'Sometimes he's a little stuffy.'

Diane was surprised. 'Mike, stuffy? How?'

Neva took off her dirty shirt and slipped a clean tee over her head. 'He's a vegetarian and mostly likes classical music. And when he starts talking about geology . . . I mean, he thinks folded rocks are so interesting. I never knew you could fold rocks, but Georgia apparently has a lot of them.'

'I knew he liked classical music. He used to date a violinist in a string quartet.' Diane slipped on a pair of clean blue jeans.

'Did he? One thing I like about Mike is that he never talks about his ex-girlfriends, and he's apparently had a lot.'

'Oh?'

'At least, a lot of girls seem to know him.'

Diane knew that when Neva was first assigned by the Rosewood Police Department to Diane's crime scene unit, she had been afraid of Diane. She had come a long way to be able to share girl talk with her.

'I can imagine. He's a great-looking guy.'

'And smart. He's the most educated guy I've ever dated. In my family, when I went to the police academy, you'd have thought I was going to Yale. Mike knows a lot of stuff. Sometimes I have no idea what he's talking about.'

'Neither do I when he starts talking geology. You and I aren't geologists. But you know a lot of stuff he doesn't. The whole area of evidence collection and forensics, for example. And your artwork.'

'That's true.' Neva nodded. 'You know those

little animals I do from clay? He loves that. I gave him one I did of a mustang.'

'Mike admires talent.'

Diane pulled her shirt off over her head and reached for her blouse – crisp white with an embroidered neckline.

Neva stared at Diane's rib cage. 'My God, did you get that when you fell?'

Diane looked down at her ribs. A large patch of skin had started to turn blue. 'Must have been when I grabbed onto the rope. I swung into the wall pretty hard.'

'It looks sore.'

Diane fingered the bruise and made a face when it smarted. 'It is a little tender. I'll put an ice pack on it when I get home.' She pulled the blouse over her head. 'This has been quite an eventful trip.'

'I'll say. Do you think the sheriff will let us process the evidence?'

'I imagine he'll go along with the coroner.' Diane scooped up her dirty clothes, rolled them up and tucked them into her pack, and walked with Neva to the vehicles. Diane climbed in hers and started the engine. She waved at Neva and MacGregor as they climbed into Mike's SUV.

The next order of business was to get the body of Caver Doe logged in and secured in the museum forensic lab until arrangements could be made for the autopsy. That job was made easier by a call on her cell phone from Sheriff Burns as she drove back to Rosewood. As she had suspected, the possibly fifty-year-old case of Caver Doe did not rank as a priority in Sheriff Burns's pressing case-load. He was more than happy to let Diane arrange the processing of the body.

Diane scrolled down her cell phone address book to the number for Lynn Webber, the medical examiner for Hall County, and got Lynn on the phone.

'Well, hello, Diane Fallon. What can I do for you?'

As soon as she spoke in her deep South Georgia accent Diane visualized Lynn's dark, well-coiffed hair and manicured nails. Lynn didn't look like a medical examiner until you saw her elbow-deep in the bowels of a cadaver.

'I have a special situation here, and your expertise immediately came to mind.'

'Flattery usually works with me, but this sounds like a problem.'

'No, really, this could be a welcome break from what we usually see.' She explained the circumstances and the condition of Caver Doe to Lynn.

'You have the most experience with mummified remains of anyone in the area, so I'd like you to do the autopsy.' Diane said. 'And the entrance to the cave is in Hall County, so technically, it could have been your body – sort of.'

'I looked at the MRI of the Egyptian mummy for your museum. That is the extent of my experience.'

'Yes, and that gives you much more experience than anyone else around.'

'A fifty-year-old mummy?'

Mike blew his horn as he passed her on the road. He was a much faster driver than Diane.

'Fifty, sixty, seventy. We don't know the exact age. But his Moon Pie wrappers look pretty old.'

Lynn laughed. 'This isn't a joke, is it? Did that Brewster Pilgrim tell you to call me?'

'No, this is legit.'

'Okay, send him over. You want your mummy stripped when I'm finished, I guess?'

'Yes, please. And . . . thanks, Lynn.'

'You tell Brewster that if this is a joke, payback's a bitch.'

It took about twenty minutes for Diane to deliver the body to the hospital morgue where Lynn worked, and another twenty minutes to check it in with the attendant on duty. By the time the mummy was safely inside his drawer Diane was more than ready to be in her small Rosewood apartment soaking in her large claw-footed tub.

Just as Diane had anticipated, the bubble bath was soothing and relaxing. She would have preferred warm water, but with the bruises on her midsection, she opted for a cooler soak. She was leaning back in the tub when she heard Frank's knock on the front door. He had a rhythmic knock he did with his knuckles before he let himself in with the key Diane had given him. And he always called out when he entered.

'Diane, it's me.'

'I'm in the tub.'

'That sounds nice. Let me put the food down and I'll join you.'

She smiled to herself as she heard him rattling around in the kitchen and then his footfalls coming toward the bathroom.

'You look all relaxed. Hard day at the cave?' He sat on the edge of the tub and dipped his hand in the water. 'A little cool. How long you been soaking?' He shook the bubbles off his sleeve.

'I'm about ready to get out.'

Frank Duncan was a detective in the Metro Atlanta Fraud and Computer Forensics Unit, where he investigated everything from white-collar and computer crimes to identity theft. They had dated before she went to South America to work for World Accord International looking for and excavating mass graves. When she returned to take over directorship of the museum, she had been surprised to discover that his blue-green eyes still made her quiver when his smile made them crinkle at the corners and sparkle – like they did now.

'We have the rest of the evening and two full weeks,' he said.

'I am *so* looking forward to being in a mountain cabin with you, and no dead bodies, blood spatter, or fussy board members.' Diane relaxed back in the tub, feeling content and peaceful in the cool water, glad Frank was here.

'I brought some Thai food for dinner. Thought we could eat in the living room, look out your picture window, listen to music and . . .' He let his words drift off as he sloshed the water back and forth with his hand. Diane sat up in the tub and smoothed the water out of her hair with her hands. Frank took the towel she had folded and laid on the counter and opened it up. 'I can help.'

Diane pulled the plug in the bathtub, stood up and reached for the towel. 'Great, I'm in the mood to be waited on.'

'Diane, what happened?' Frank held on to the towel as he stared at the blue bruise that covered the length of her left rib cage.

'It's nothing. I bumped into a wall in the cave.'

'It's not nothing, and you don't get a bruise like that bumping into a wall.'

'I was hanging on to a rope at the time – it was swinging. Look, it's just a bruise. I get bruises all the time when I'm caving.'

'I see you naked on a fairly regular basis and I have never seen you bruised up like this.'

Diane grabbed at the towel. Frank wrapped it around her and helped her dry off.

'There's not much to tell, really.'

'When you say there's not much to tell, I know there's a story lurking. What happened?'

'I fell through some loose rocks . . . an ordinary caving mishap.'

'Fell through some loose rocks, hanging on a rope? I'm not getting a picture of this. You are going to have to draw a little better.'

Damn. Diane could see she was going to have to tell him. The last thing she wanted to hear from Frank tonight was a lecture on the dangers of caving. Noncavers just didn't understand the allure of caves – and it wasn't like she had accidents every weekend. 'At least let me get dressed.'

'Is that necessary?' He drew her close.

Later, Diane, in faded jeans and a tee, sat on her sofa cross-legged, finishing her chicken-and-cashew-nut dinner. Frank sat on the other end enjoying a dish of spareribs in peanut curry sauce. Brahms's 'Waltz in A-flat' was just finishing on her CD player.

Frank took the plates to the kitchen and came back with a cup of coffee for each of them. 'Okay, now that you've had time to think out your story, are you going to tell me how you got that bruise?'

Diane should have known he wouldn't forget. She explained how the rocks were caught in the hole, creating a false floor, trying to make it sound like nothing. In fact, the near miss had rattled her, but she found ignoring it was more effective for her peace of mind than dwelling on it. What nagged at her the most was not as much the near fall, but the fact that she had overlooked something dangerous.

'Mike was there with some rope,' she said.

'That's why I cave with several people. We watch one another's backs.'

'But for a while you were hanging by your fingers?'

Diane stared at the stereo. She had put some Beethoven sonatas on low. She was wondering now if she should turn up the volume and drown out the conversation. She glanced at the remote and sighed. 'Yes. But when you climb rocks you develop strong hands.'

'Right. How far would you have fallen?'

'Not that far. I'm not sure,' Diane said as she took a long sip of her coffee and made a grab for the remote. Frank, apparently, anticipated her move and grabbed it first.

'Yes, you are. You map caves. You have that little laser gadget with you. Don't tell me you didn't measure the height of the chamber once you were in it.'

'Okay. Thirty feet.'

'Thirty feet! God, Diane, that could have killed you.'

'Probably only broken some bones. But I didn't fall. Look, most of the time caving is uneventful, in terms of actual danger. This was an unusual trip.' She glared at him directly in his eyes. 'Frank, I love caving. I'm a good caver, and a safe one.'

She decided not to mention the rock slide. That wasn't even a near miss. They got out of the tunnel in plenty of time . . . sort of.

'This is actually a fairly tame cave so far. But

what was interesting was what we found in the chamber,' she said.

Frank raised his eyebrows. 'What did you find?'

'A mummified caver who wasn't as lucky as I was. Looks like he probably broke some bones and couldn't get out.'

Frank shook his head. 'Do you have some kind of compass that points you to dead bodies?'

'I think he got into that chamber from another entrance no one knows about. We may have discovered a connection to an entirely different cave. That kind of discovery is important to us cavers.'

'What good luck you had your crime scene people with you.'

'Wasn't it? We got a call out to Jin and he brought the crime scene kit. We found quite a few things that may have belonged to the deceased. There's no indication so far of who he might be. We're calling him Caver Doe.'

'Caver Doe . . . nice. How long do you think he was down there?'

'The body was pretty well desiccated, and he had an old carbide lamp with him. Several decades, I'm thinking – maybe from the fifties, maybe earlier. I won't know until I examine him.'

The telephone's sudden ring was shrill compared to the music that had just been playing. Diane wasn't going to pick it up. But a glance at the caller ID told her it was Gregory.

Gregory Lincoln was Diane's former boss at

World Accord International. He had seen her through the tough time when her adopted daughter was murdered in South America. Even though now he was back in his home in England and she in the States, they had kept in touch and talked at least once a month.

'Diane, this is Gregory.'

'Hi, Gregory, it's good to hear from you. It must be in the wee hours of the morning there. Is everything all right?'

'Just fine. It's not too far beyond midnight. I do some of my best work at this time.'

'How's your family?' Diane smiled at Frank. He leaned back on the sofa and took one of Diane's feet and began to massage it. Frank had a knack for massage. She forced her mind back to what Gregory was saying.

'Marguerite is fine. The boys are in the United States. They went to space camp this summer. Got this thing about wanting to be astronauts. And how's your museum faring?'

'We inherited an Egyptian mummy, so now everyone thinks we're a real museum.'

Diane heard him chuckle. Gregory had the sort of low, throaty laugh that made you want to laugh along with him.

'You don't say. A real Egyptian mummy. You'll have to send pictures. Marguerite loves mummies.'

'I will. He was unwrapped, but we managed to get our hands on the amulets that were in his

66

original wrappings. Our Web site has pictures. I'll e-mail you the URL.'

'Your museum is the reason I called. I'm afraid I volunteered you to a friend. I hope you don't mind.'

'Volunteered me?'

'Your expertise. He's sending you the bones of a witch.'

CHAPTER 7

'The bones of a witch?' said Diane. 'Did I hear you right, Gregory?'

Frank lifted his brow, gave her that okay-this-is-interesting look of his, took her other foot and began kneading tender spots on the bottom of it.

'Perhaps I should have said the bones of an alleged witch. This is going to take a bit of explaining.'

'I'm all ears.'

'There's a charming little museum here in Dorset we like to visit with the boys. It's really more like the old cabinet of curiosities. It's housed in this charming sixteenth-century cottage. John Rose is the proprietor. He's collected a lot of odd bits of the cultural and natural history from around here. I think he barely makes a living at it. One of his main attractions is a skeleton called the Moonhater witch.'

'Moonhater witch?' Diane raised her eyebrows at Frank and he returned a quizzical look of his own.

'Legend has it that the skeleton was found in Moonhater Cave – the name, I believe, refers to smugglers. Anyway, the stories say the witch was killed by a young man. Seems he stabbed her with some sort of magical sword, but not before the witch had turned his bride into a pillar of salt.'

'Fascinating story, but I won't be able to tell him if she was a witch.' She grinned at Frank, who, from his knitted brow and upturned lips, was anxious to hear the other end of the conversation. She retrieved her foot and leaned her back against him before the faces he was making caused her to burst out laughing.

Gregory chuckled. 'I don't think he expects that. John doesn't believe in witches. Legends aside, he would like to know something about his skeleton.'

'I'll be glad to look at the bones. But tell me, there are plenty of forensic anthropologists in the UK; why—'

'Is he sending it across the ocean? That's where the story gets a little more bizarre.'

'It gets more bizarre?'

Frank began massaging her shoulders and neck. *He is really is good at this*, thought Diane as she moved her shoulders under his grip.

'There are two other parties interested in possessing the bones. One party is the owner of Moonhater Cave. It is one of several caves in the area that are tourist attractions. It has the pillar of the unfortunate girl.'

'The pillar of salt she turned into? It's in the cave?'

Frank stopped and turned so that he could see her face. His eyes twinkled the way they did when he was about to hear the punch line of a joke. Diane smiled at him and pointed to her shoulders. He rolled his eyes and resumed kneading her muscles.

'Yes. It's actually a rather large column formation that had the good or bad luck, depending on your perspective, to have a vague resemblance to a woman. The image has been enhanced by the creative use of a chisel and sandpaper. Whoever it was did quite a good job, actually – subtle, made good use of the natural form of the stone for her flowing gown.'

'And the cave owner wants the bones back to go with his statue.'

'Yes. Sort of keep the family together.'

'Who's the other party?' asked Diane.

'A handful of Druids or Wiccans. Marguerite tells me there's a difference, but I don't know what it is. They claim the bones are of an ancestor. Of course, given that they found a descendent of nine-thousand-year-old Cheddar Man, that very well could be true.'

'Cheddar Man was found somewhere near you, wasn't he?'

'Close. In Somerset, actually, in Cheddar. Somerset also has a cave with a statue of sorts, only this one is of a witch who was turned to stone by a monk. There are bones associated with it too – which are owned by a museum in Somerset. The Somerset cave owner is trying to get those bones back. Probably where the Moonhater Cave owner got the idea. Caves with stories are rather popular here.'

'So he thinks the Druids – or Wiccans – or this other cave owner might try to steal them?'

'He's afraid they might. The Wiccans involved are some kind of outcast coven, or whatever, it seems. They threatened John with black magic – something that's prohibited by the Wiccan home office, apparently. Anyway, John feels his bones would be safer if they were examined in the U.S., and I told him I'd help. So . . .'

'Sure, I'll help.'

'Great! John will be delighted. I thought you would, so I took the liberty of telling him to go ahead and send them. They are already on their way. John said he'll call. He wants to talk with you before you actually do the analysis.'

'Does he know if the bones were actually found in the cave?'

'No.'

'I'll need samples of soil from the cave.'

There was a pause for a moment. 'A sample will be sent along to you shortly with the bones.'

'Why does it sound like there is a story there?'

'Because I collected the sample. Marguerite and I went on a tour of the Moonhater Cave. And I surreptitiously collected a sample from the floor. Marguerite said I was disgraceful. The owner has some strict rules about carrying things out of the cave, but she provided the distraction – quite shameful, really.'

Diane laughed out loud at the image of the very proper Gregory and his wife on a mission, stealing dirt from a cave. 'How did Mr Rose acquire the bones?'

'Bought them from a family who had them in a box in their basement for about a hundred years – that is, they were in the basement for a hundred years.'

'Was the story of the provenance written on the box?'

'No. It was handed down. So you see, the whole thing's rather iffy, John is actually glad now that the bones have no provenance. It strengthens his case – not that he really has anything to worry about.'

'Gregory, it sounds interesting. I'll look forward to examining them.'

'I think so. Thanks for helping out. I'll let you get back to whatever you were engaged in. Oh, how is David?'

Gregory liked to keep track of his former employees. Especially the ones who worked for him at the time of the massacre that killed Diane's daughter and many of their friends at the mission in South America.

'He's doing fine. You know he's doing crime scene work for me.'

'He's okay with that?'

'Yes. We've put several criminals in jail, and David has found that satisfying.'

'That's good. I think about all of you a lot. And you and your fellow, Frank, are fine?'

'Yes. We're going on a vacation tomorrow for two whole weeks.' Diane put a hand over Frank's as she talked about him.

'Good for you! He must be something special to be able to pull you away from work.'

'He is indeed.' Diane squeezed his hand. 'Good to hear from you, Gregory. Take care.'

Diane hung up the phone and turned toward Frank. 'That was Gregory.'

'I gathered. Your side of the conversation was interesting. Sounds like you have another body from a cave to look at? A witch?' Frank grinned at her.

'That's what he said – a witch with a story.' Diane related Gregory's side of the conversation to Frank's chuckles.

'Pillar of salt. It sounds rather biblical. You know,' he said without losing his smile, 'it seems to me that a lot of people die in caves.'

Diane kissed him rather than go where that conversation was leading.

The next two weeks passed by in a relaxing blur of fishing, hiking and cuddling up with Frank. Diane was surprised at how easy it had been to let go and just enjoy being on vacation. Frank seemed to have just as easily been able to let go of his job. That was a good sign, she'd thought several times. They enjoyed each other's company. Only occasionally did she find her mind wandering to Caver Doe and the witch bones – she couldn't deny she was intrigued. Unfortunately Diane had to cut her vacation short by one day. Andie, Diane's office manager at the museum, had called and told her that Helen Egan, the grandmother of Diane's friend and mentor, had died and that the funeral was scheduled for Sunday.

Diane arrived back at her office on Sunday morning rested and happy that the museum was still standing and the crime lab was not overflowing with unprocessed evidence. In fact, it looked as if they didn't need her. She wasn't sure if that was a good or bad thing. She smiled and sifted through the stack of clippings Andie had cut from the papers while she was gone. She found a two-week-old front-page story about the mummified caver they had found, along with everything Diane had told the deputy. She noted with satisfaction that they didn't have any pictures.

Yesterday's paper lay on top of her cluttered walnut desk. The headline across the front page read: *Helen Elizabeth Price Egan, 1891–2005*. Most of the front page was taken up with the story of Vanessa Van Ross's grandmother, who had died at age 114. Diane and some of the museum staff were going to her funeral later in the morning.

Vanessa Van Ross was the most prominent member of the museum board, RiverTrail's most generous contributor, and Diane's mentor. Diane stared at the photograph of the young Helen Elizabeth, wondering if she had any idea she would go on to live a hundred years after it was taken.

74

Andie Layne, Diane's administrative assistant, came bopping in with two cups of steaming hot tea, put one in front of Diane and sat down in the chair opposite her desk.

'Good to have you back. You and Frank get a lot of fishing in?'

'Sure did. He taught me how to fish for trout. A lot more active than sitting in a boat with a pole. We had a great time.'

'So you think you guys will ever get married?'

Diane took another drink of tea, hoping Andie didn't see the grimace on her face. Life with Frank would be great, and he had certainly hinted that they should marry, but Diane was convinced that they got along so well because they saw each other so little. They were never in each other's pockets, tripping over each other's feet, or irritated by each other's idiosyncracies.

'Things are going well the way they are,' muttered Diane.

Fortunately, Andie didn't linger on the subject, but went dancing on to the next thing on her mind.

'Neva told me about the caving trip you guys had. Wow. Exciting.' She pointed to the newspaper clipping peeking out of the folder, sipped her tea and swung her legs back and forth. 'That mummy you found – you think it was an accident or murder?' Her thick auburn curls shook as she talked in her animated way, and she looked delighted at the thought of murder.

'Accident is the most likely scenario.' Diane sipped her green tea. It tasted like Andie had squeezed an orange into it.

Andie looked over at the photograph on the wall of Diane descending on a rope into the vertical entrance of a cave. 'I just don't see how you all can go down into a cave like that. I would be terrified.'

'It's fun. You kind of have to like dark, closed-in places.'

Diane glanced at her e-mail as she listened to Andie. Nothing urgent. Andie had answered and filed away most of her messages while she was gone. She could also see that Kendel had handled the rest. Life had gotten easier in the museum since she'd hired Kendel Williams, her assistant director.

Between Kendel and Andie, her absence was hardly noticeable. That is, if she didn't look at the stack of queries from her curators – requests for larger budgets, more room, and all the assorted concerns they invariably had.

'I understand it's really beautiful inside a cave. I've seen pictures . . .'

'Sometimes caves are beautiful; sometimes they're pretty ugly. Depends on the cave. But every cave has its own magic. This one we've been mapping's pretty nice. Very large, with a variety of formations.'

'Neva said you almost had a bad fall. That sounds scary.'

'Sort of. Mike threw me a rope, so it ended well.

We did find the lost caver because of it.' That was how Diane handled the question about her fall when it came up – made light of it, praised Mike, and diverted attention elsewhere. So far, with everyone except Frank, it had worked.

'The lost caver. That sounds forlorn, doesn't it?' Andie stared for a long moment at the photograph of Diane hanging on the rope, then laid a folder on Diane's desk. 'These are the letters that need your signature. But you can wait till after the funeral. Wow, a hundred and fourteen. Imagine that. After she became a teenager, she lived another hundred years.'

'It is amazing to think about. Vanessa has had her grandmother a long time. This must be hard on her.'

'If I'm gonna live that long, I'd hate to live most of my life as an old woman,' Andie said.

'Spoken like a youngster,' a soft voice behind her said.

They looked up to see Vanessa Van Ross standing in the doorway wearing a dark blue silk suit. Her silver hair was swept up in her usual French twist.

Andie turned bright red. 'Mrs Van Ross, I am so sorry . . . I didn't mean . . . I . . . I'm so sorry.'

The older woman put an arm around Andie's shoulder. 'That's all right, dear. I tell my doctor the same thing every time I see him. They've been able to put a man on the moon for over thirty years, but they still can't make me look twenty.'

Andie was a little consoled. 'May I get you some tea?'

'No, thank you, dear. I just came to ask Diane if she would ride with me to church. The children are taking Mother. I love them all dearly, but right now the three of them are too much.'

'Certainly. Would you like to go now?'

She looked at her watch. 'It's a little early. I thought I'd just enjoy the museum until it's time to leave. You go about your business. Maybe I will take a cup of tea.'

Andie hurried off to make a cup. Diane led Vanessa into the private sitting room adjacent to her office.

'Feel free to stay in here if you like. I just need to check in with the crime lab.'

As she spoke, raised voices – between Andie and someone whose voice Diane didn't recognize – filtered in from Andie's office.

'I demand you allow me to see her now,' the disembodied voice said. Diane and Vanessa raised their brows at each other.

'I suppose I'd better go see about this. Andie will be in with your tea shortly.'

CHAPTER 8

Diane walked through her office and into Andie's, where she stood with her arms folded, literally barring the door. Two women were facing Andie, one about her age, the other maybe twenty years older. It was the younger who threatened to go through Andie to get to Diane's office; at least it had been a young voice.

What struck Diane first about her was that she was purple. She had hair dyed black with burgundy highlights, wore low-rise dark-purple jeans with glitter in the fabric, and a light purple cami covered by a darker purple cotton blazer. On a silver chain around her neck hung an amethyst crystal about the size of the woman's little finger. She also wore purple eyeshadow and lipstick. Odd as it might seem, she actually looked good.

The other woman had no particular matching color scheme. She wore a plain navy cotton-blend pantsuit with a stark white shirt. Her red hair was streaked with gray and, Diane noticed when she turned her head, stuffed into a sloppy bun on back of her head. Several strands had escaped and now hung down on each side of her face. She wore no makeup to camouflage her drooping eyelids and slight jowls.

'Can I help you?' asked Diane.

The young purple woman looked surprised, as if she never really expected to see the person she was asking for.

'I'm Caitlin Shanahan. This is Charlotte Hawkins. We've come to speak with the head of the museum.'

'I've come a very long way to see Diane Fallon,' said Charlotte Hawkins.

Caitlin Shanahan had a Midwestern American accent. Charlotte Hawkins's was British. Diane thought she knew who they were.

'I'm sorry,' said Andie. 'They somehow slipped through security. I told them the museum was closed today.'

'It's all right, Andie, I'm Diane Fallon.' She led them into her office. 'I only have a little time this morning, but please sit down and tell me what you've come about.'

The two of them sat in the stuffed chairs that faced Diane's desk. The younger woman, Caitlin, spoke first.

'Charlotte just came from England. She has asked my coven to help her reclaim the bones of her ancestor.'

'Coven?' *This ought to be good,* thought Diane.

'I'm a Wiccan. Charlotte is a Druid. Though not the same, we share a kindred spirit . . . if for nothing else than that we are both misunderstood minority religions.'

80

'What do you want with me?' asked Diane, although she suspected she already knew.

'Annwn is my ancestor,' said Charlotte. 'We know that her bones were sent here from the Rose Museum in Dorset.'

Diane raised her eyebrows slightly, surprised that the witch had a name. It intrigued her. She wondered if it was her real name, or just families filling out the legend over the years. 'Exactly what are you asking of me?'

'That you give the bones back so that I can take them home and bury them properly.'

'Surely you must know that I can't do that.'

Charlotte tucked her stray locks of hair behind her ears, leaned forward, and looked earnestly at Diane. 'People of goodwill can do anything,' she said.

'Wouldn't you agree that my goodwill should extend to those who entrust items to me?'

'So you do have them?'

'Actually, I don't know whether I do or not. I just got back from a two-week vacation. I really don't know what may have arrived during my absence. So our conversation may be moot.'

'Can you check to see if you have them?' asked Charlotte.

Diane looked at her watch. 'Not right now. I'm leaving soon.'

Caitlin stood and leaned on Diane's desk. 'Look, I told Charlotte that in this country we place value on ancestral remains. I explained to her about the Native American Graves Protection and Repatriation Act.'

'NAGPRA does not apply here. We know they are not the bones of a Native American,' said Diane.

'I'm making an analogy. Work with me. We have the act because many of us over here place value on returning remains to their descendants.'

'Nevertheless, I could not give them to you if I were to have them. And Miss Shanahan, please sit down.' To Diane's surprise, Caitlin did as she was told.

'Why can't you give them to me?' asked Charlotte.

'You know there is another claimant. What if he walked in and asked for them and I gave them to him?'

'He's not related.'

Diane was actually glad they came to see her. It was a good opportunity to learn about some of the lore surrounding the bones. 'Why do you think they are the bones of your ancestor?' she asked.

'The story of Annwn has been in my family for generations,' said Charlotte, holding her arms wide, as if that would encompass all her ancestry. 'She was a Druid, she was accused of being a witch, and she was murdered in a cave.'

'Why do you think these specific bones are hers?' asked Diane.

'How many bones of witches in caves can there be?' Caitlin was getting exasperated.

Diane had the impression that if Caitlin knew where the bones were, she'd make a break for them.

'Apparently more than one,' said Diane.

Caitlin looked over at Charlotte, who nodded in agreement with Diane. 'There's another set of bones from Somerset said to be those of a witch that were discovered in a cave,' she said.

'You're kidding . . .' said Caitlin.

'Why do you think these bones and not the others are your ancestor?' Diane asked the question again.

Diane heard the door open in the next room – Andie taking Vanessa her tea.

'The story is different. In the case of the Somerset bones, the alleged witch was killed by a monk through some kind of ritual . . . She was supposedly turned to stone.' Charlotte waved a hand as if dismissing the story.

'Wasn't Annwn turned into . . .' began Caitlin.

'Salt?' said Diane.

'No,' said Charlotte. 'Some people say Annwn turned some woman to salt, but that's not what happened.'

'But the stories from the two caves sound very similar – stone, pillar of salt. How do you know it's not just one story with several variations?'

Charlotte sighed heavily. 'Annwn was a Druid artisan. She was deceived by her husband and his Roman lover, the daughter of a government official. They lured her into a cave, and while she

83

talked with her beloved, the Roman woman crept up behind her and stabbed her in the back. The pillar of salt was probably a Christianized addition to the story, influenced by the biblical story of Lot's wife. The story I just told you has been in my family for generations. No one was turned to salt. I mean, you can't really do that.'

'I think it's obvious,' said Caitlin. 'The bones are her ancestor.'

Diane stared at both women for a moment, then slid open the bottom drawer of her desk and took out a sealed packet, opened it, walked around her desk and stood in front of Charlotte.

'Will you give me a sample of your DNA?'

The two of them looked at her as if she'd asked them to pee in a glass. Diane pulled a swab from the kit.

Diane smiled. 'I'll take it from your cheek. Doesn't hurt.'

'Why?' asked Charlotte, her mouth turned down into a frown.

'If we can get some usable DNA from the bones then there's a chance we can tell if the bones are truly your ancestor.'

Charlotte looked over at Caitlin. Both stared at Diane as if she were pulling some kind of trick on them.

'It's my understanding,' she said, 'that the Druids were scholarly people.'

'We are,' said Charlotte.

'A positive result would strengthen your case.'

'What proof do I have that you won't manipulate the data?' asked Charlotte.

'I'm a person of goodwill.'

Charlotte still hesitated. Caitlin was on the verge of telling her not to do it. Diane could see the suspicion in her eyes. Maybe if she gave them a little information, it might ease their suspicions.

'I was asked to take a look at the bones to find out what I can. Mr Rose wants to know everything he can about the skeleton. You say you are a relative. This is a possible way to prove it.'

'I suppose I have no choice.'

'You always have a choice. This is simply the only way I know of supporting your claim.'

'Or dismissing it,' said Caitlin.

Diane suspected that Caitlin was more interested in the protest than the disposition of the bones.

Diane looked at Charlotte. 'If she is not a relative, then you don't want to claim her, do you?'

'She's someone's relative,' said Caitlin. 'She should be treated with dignity.'

'She will be. I treat every body I examine with dignity.' Diane put her forearms on her desk and leaned forward. 'Look, this is the way I communicate with people who have died long ago. I read what is written in their bones. I respect the information that they tell me.'

'Go ahead,' said Charlotte. 'I'm trusting you to tell me the truth.'

She opened her mouth and allowed Diane to

take a swab from the inside of her cheek. Diane sealed the swab in its pouch, went behind her desk, labeled it and locked it in the bottom drawer.

'Thank you. I assure you I will tell you the truth when I have it. I have no interest in doing otherwise. Now I'm going to have to leave. I'm attending a funeral.'

'I'm sorry,' said Charlotte. 'Not someone very close, I hope.'

'I'm close to her family.'

'A death in the family is very sad.'

'Yes, it is. However, she was a hundred and fourteen when she died, and we also have reason to celebrate her life.'

'I didn't know people could live that long,' said Caitlin. 'Imagine.'

'It is hard to imagine,' said Diane, rising to show them out the door.

Vanessa was sitting on the couch in the sitting room that adjoined Diane's office, sipping the tea that Andie had brought her. 'That was very strange. I confess, Andie and I sort of eavesdropped.'

'I'll say,' said Andie. 'I thought they were going to run over me. They're witches?' She hesitated. 'Sorry, couldn't help but listen.'

'Wiccan and Druid. As I understand it they're not the same, and neither is necessarily a witch. Anyway, it was interesting. I don't know if I can discover if the story goes with the skeleton, but it'll be fun working on it. Andie, did we get a package from the Rose Museum in England while I was gone?'

'Yes. The paperwork is in your in box. Mr Rose said in the letter that he doesn't want you to start until you speak to him. There were also some pretty cool photographs with the paperwork – this statue in a cave. I thought you'd like that. Do you really think you can get DNA from the skeleton? I had the idea from reading the paperwork that the skeleton is really old, like *really* old, like over a thousand years.'

'I don't know if I can get any usable DNA or not. It will certainly be interesting if I do.'

Vanessa stood up. 'I suppose it's time. I have to tell you, I'm dreading this. People from all over are coming. Even the governor is sending someone. It is going to be a long funeral. Gram would hate it.'

CHAPTER 9

Diane gazed out the window of Vanessa's limo as they pulled up in front of the First Presbyterian Church. It was a huge structure built with granite from Georgia. The rock, blue when it was freshly quarried, had weathered to a dark bluish gray after ninety-two years of exposure to the elements. Helen was twenty-two years older than the church. Her daughter was two years older than the ninety-two-year-old structure. Odd and somehow comforting, thought, Diane, that people could be older than this stone edifice.

The central sanctuary had tall stained-glass windows in shades of blue and green and was flanked by two medieval-looking towers. The parking lot was to one side and was already filling up. Vanessa was right: A great many people were there – many more, Diane guessed, than her grandmother had known. But as Vanessa said, this was the price for being from a prominent family and for living way past a hundred.

Vanessa asked Diane to sit with her and her family – five generations of them beyond Helen

Egan. The family members smiled at Diane and patted Vanessa's arm as they sat down.

As Vanessa held on to her hand, Diane realized that her mentor was probably mourning the loss of her only grandmother, but also of Milo Lorenzo, the museum founder. Vanessa had said good-bye to him here also. It was Milo who had hired Diane. The museum was his life's work, the center-piece of all his creative endeavors, and he died much too young of a heart attack before it was finished. Diane was supposed to be the assistant director, but thanks to Vanessa and to Milo's will, she became director with all the power that Milo had designed for himself. But more than the visionary of the museum, Milo was the love of Vanessa's life, and Diane could feel the loss flowing from her like a current of electricity as she sat silently on the hard wooden pew.

The church was filling up quickly now. Diane looked behind her at the people. She spotted Korey, her head conservator, Mike, Andie and Kendel sitting together. They must have come together from the museum. She saw most of the board members either seated or entering the church. Some who caught her eye nodded. The mayor was there; so were the chief of detectives and the police commissioner. She spotted several businessmen from Rosewood and Atlanta whom she knew because they were large contributors to the museum. Attendance was a who's who of Rosewood and beyond. Diane put an arm around

Vanessa's granddaughter, eight-year-old Alexis Van Ross, who had come from the pew in front of her and slid in beside her.

The service began. Diane hoped it would be a short one. The minister was a young man full of hope and awe that someone he knew had lived such a long life. It was not a sad service. It was filled with references to the great events, inventions and changes Helen had witnessed in her many years.

As Diane listened to the minister's words, she had the unexpected realization that she had not had a memorial service for her daughter, Ariel. Her thoughts brought tears to her eyes, and she blinked to try to keep them at bay. Why had she never done that? Because, she thought, answering her own question, she did everything she could to avoid dealing with the fact that Ariel was dead. Diane fingered the locket at her throat. She absently pulled Alexis to her, and the little girl leaned into Diane and put her arms around her waist.

Before Diane realized it, the ushers were at the end of the pews to let the family file out of the church first. When Diane stood, it was a relief. She was glad the service was over. She held Alexis's hand and walked out with the family.

'Just the cemetery now and it will be over.' Vanessa patted Alexis's blond curls. 'You know, I'm going to put it in my will that I don't want a funeral. I'm not sure I agree with this final goodbye ritual.'

Right now Diane agreed with her. The limo drove up and the driver opened the door for Vanessa, Diane and Alexis. Alexis had bonded with Diane ever since she'd been given a private tour of the museum.

'Can I spend the night at your house sometime?' she asked.

'Alexis . . .' said Vanessa.

I would like that, thought Diane. 'Sometime,' she said. 'I'll talk to your mother in a few weeks; how will that be?'

Alexis was the farthest generation from Helen Egan – her great-great-great-granddaughter. Diane wondered if the little girl understood just what an amazing thing that was.

Rose Street Cemetery wasn't far from the church. Diane could already see the tops of the larger monuments. It was an old cemetery, fifty years older than Helen Egan. It seemed fitting. Helen Egan would be buried beside her husband, who had died half a century earlier than she.

The limo driver drove them to the plot, now covered with a tent under which were rows of chairs for the family. Diane didn't want to sit through another service. She told Vanessa she was going to stand with her people from the museum.

'Of course, dear.' Vanessa looked around at the cars pulling onto the shoulder of the small roadway. 'I can't believe this many people came to the cemetery. What could they be thinking?'

Vanessa cocked her lips into a half smile. 'Come, Alexis. It won't be long now.'

Diane walked to where Andie and the others were standing.

'Hey, Dr F.,' said Korey. 'Want a ride back with us? We brought the minivan.'

'Probably so. Let me talk to Vanessa when the graveside service is over.' She stood between Andie and Korey as people gathered around and listened to the final words.

The ceremony was very short, to Diane's relief. When it was over, they all stood in a line of people waiting to express their condolences to the family.

Vanessa was speaking to the mayor and a tall man with dark salt-and-pepper hair as Diane approached. The mayor frowned when he saw Diane, but quickly recovered. She guessed he had just remembered that she was now a friend and not a foe. She hadn't really spoken with him since an argument resulting from his urging that the museum be moved. She didn't really want to speak with him now, but there he was.

'I hear a lot of good things about the . . . museum,' the mayor said.

Diane knew he almost said 'crime scene lab,' but realized at the last minute that this wasn't the venue to talk about it.

Diane nodded and muttered, 'We do our best.'

'Ah, you must be Diane Fallon.' It was the tall, distinguished-looking man beside the mayor. He looked like a politician too. 'Vanessa has told me much about you.'

'This is Steve Taggart,' said Vanessa. 'His mother and father are old acquaintances of my parents.' She pointed to an elderly man with sparse white hair and a silver-headed cane, and a slim silver-haired woman with him. They were talking to Vanessa's mother and a friend of Diane's.

'We think Steve's going to be one of Georgia's next senators in Washington,' added the mayor.

Steve Taggart extended his hand, and Diane shook it. 'I'm thinking about running. Talking to my family about it. One doesn't run alone; unfortunately, it's a family affair.'

'Indeed,' agreed the mayor.

Diane smiled and nodded, wondering if they would notice if she turned and ran. Unfortunately, her way was blocked by a throng of people closing in on the family. Vanessa, apparently with the same idea, wandered away to speak to a young couple, leaving Diane with the mayor and the Taggarts.

'My father's been wanting to meet you,' he said. 'He's wild about your new Egyptian exhibit.' Steve Taggart stepped a few feet over to a small group of people and escorted an elderly gentleman to Diane. 'Dad, this is the director of the museum. My dad's Emmett Taggart . . .'

'Of course,' said Diane. 'Mr Taggart is one of the museum's supporters . . . among many other things, I understand.' Diane shook his hand and he held on to it, placing his other hand on top.

'Dad believes in giving back to the community. Something he's drilled into all of us since we were old enough to sit up and listen.' Steve Taggart was already making his political speeches.

As Steve Taggart spoke about his father, Diane noticed that the elder Mr Taggart seemed to have an unpleasant odor. She caught just a whiff, but her cheeks suddenly burned with embarrassment for him.

'Wonderful exhibit.' The elder Taggart shook her hand as he spoke. 'That mummy and all those trinkets that he was wrapped with – so interesting. This is my wife, Rosemary.' The older woman nodded at Diane. She seemed more curt and standoffish than the rest of her family. 'And this is my grandson, Robert. He's my daughter's son.'

Robert was shorter than his politician uncle, but a lot like him, except with auburn hair. He had the same black eyes and broad-toothed grin. As Diane made small talk with the Taggart family, she heard Kendel, Korey, Mike and Andie talking to Vanessa, who hugged each of them. Diane didn't realize Vanessa knew Mike and Korey that well, then remembered that she was prone to making night-time visits to the museum just to look around by herself, and both Mike and Korey often worked late.

The only other time that Diane had seen Korey in a suit was at formal museum functions. He usually wore T-shirts and Dockers. Today, however, he had on a suit, and his long dread-locks were gathered up and tied in a low ponytail down his back.

'We're real sorry, Mrs V.,' said Korey. 'Bekka's mother's in the hospital. She wanted you to know that she would've been here . . .'

'Tell her that's all right; we understand and hope her mother gets better soon.'

Bekka was one of the anthropologists at the museum. She was making a record of Helen Egan's 114-year history and had spent a lot of time with her. Diane was sure she hated missing her funeral.

Diane herself was wishing she could escape as she listened to the voices expressing condolences and making light banter. Mr Taggart kept going on about ancient Egypt and burning mummies for firewood, and did they really do that or was Mr Twain pulling everyone's leg.

'He was pulling our leg. He was the only one who ever mentioned that practice, I believe.' Diane had to remind herself that Mr Taggart, as well as being a prominent humanitarian and businessman, was a major contributor to the museum, and that his enthusiasm was a good thing.

'And you, Mrs Taggart, are you a fan of ancient Egypt?' asked Diane.

'The trinkets were lovely.' Rosemary Taggart's voice had not lost any of its strength; it was smooth and strong, like her skin. Mrs Taggart had good genes. 'I enjoy the shells and the gems in the museum. Some of the other things are not to my taste.'

Diane smiled, wishing she hadn't asked. She glanced at Vanessa, who was being approached by a man Diane suspected was from the governor's office. Vanessa smiled and held out her hand, and the man took it in both of his. Vanessa turned her head slightly and looked toward Andie, Kendel and the other members of the museum group. Vanessa's face froze.

Diane followed Vanessa's gaze to the museum employees. They were all staring at Mike, who had a look of confusion and pain on his face. He fell to his knees.

CHAPTER 10

Diane pushed through the crowd of people hurrying over to Mike. A middle-aged man was trying to help him to his feet, but Mike was resisting. The whole scene looked odd, but she couldn't see what was wrong.

'Mike, buddy,' she heard Korey say as he knelt beside him. 'What's the matter?'

Pain arced through Diane's foot when someone stepped on it as she attempted to push through a clump of people. When 'excuse me' didn't work, she tried gently pushing the person away. She apparently had pulled a tricep muscle at the gym this morning climbing the rock wall, for she felt a twinge in her muscle.

'Move it, dammit,' she said, not meaning to say it as loud as she did, but it got the person's attention. They muttered, 'Sorry,' and moved.

Mike was still on his knees, leaning forward with a hand on the grass. The man – Diane thought she recognized him as a local businessman – was still trying to help Mike up, and Korey was arguing with him.

'Something's wrong, man. Let him go.'

'He just fell, needs a little help up.'

'Mike?' Diane knelt beside him opposite Korey. She put a hand on his back and immediately pulled it away. Her palm and fingers were bright red.

'He's hurt,' said Diane. 'Korey, help me get his coat off.'

The man let go of his arm. 'Is that blood?'

Diane ignored him as she and Korey pulled off Mike's dark suit coat. She heard several people gasp at the large wet red stain on his white shirt.

Korey looked wide-eyed. 'Jesus, buddy, what happened?'

'I don't know. I just feel funny,' whispered Mike.

The blood was near the right side of his waist and was seeping down into his pants. Diane carefully pulled up his shirt and looked at his wound.

'Someone call nine-one-one. Mike, I want you to lie down on the grass here and stay calm,' Diane said. *What the hell happened?*

Diane heard Kendel giving directions. She must have already been calling.

'What is it?' asked Mike, as Diane helped him lie on his side.

'You've been stabbed.' Diane tried to keep her voice calm. All the organs and vessels in his lower back that could have been cut ran through her mind, and it frightened her.

'Stabbed? Jesus. How?'

'Just lie down. Help is coming.'

There was no blood on the front of his shirt,

but she pulled it up just the same and checked him for any more wounds.

'Korey, stay with him.' She pulled a handkerchief from Mike's suit coat and put it over the wound. 'Put some pressure here. If the blood soaks through . . .'

'Got it covered, Dr F. I took the first-aid training for our department.'

Diane had sent all the docents and a staff member from each department to take courses in first aid. She was glad Korey was the one who had gone from the conservation lab.

'I'm going to talk to the chief of detectives,' she said, and Korey nodded.

'Take it easy, buddy; we have help coming,' said Korey.

Diane stood up. Andie and Kendel knelt beside Mike, covering him with his coat. Diane headed for the chief of detectives, stopping first next to Vanessa's son when she saw little Alexis standing with her parents, looking scared. Vanessa's son looked at her hand and gave her a handkerchief to wipe off the blood. Her hand shook as she took it. *Who would do this – and why?* The fear that settled in the pit of her stomach made her nauseated. *Dammit, get yourself under control.*

'What happened to him?' he asked.

'He was stabbed.'

Vanessa sucked in her breath.

'Take Alexis and your family home,' continued Diane. 'Don't talk about this with one another.

The police will want to ask you individually what you remember. But for now, get your family home.'

He nodded and began to collect his family.

Diane took a deep breath and tried to find the objectivity she had at any other crime scene. She took her cell from her pocket and dialed her crime scene lab as she scanned the crowd and the cemetery. David Goldstein, one of her crime scene specialists, answered, and Diane briefly explained what had happened.

'What? At the cemetery?' said David.

'I want you and Jin to come and take a look around. There've been a lot of people here, so I doubt you'll find anything right around where Mike was standing, but look behind the trees and large monuments in the area. Someone may have been standing, waiting for an opportunity.'

'How is Mike?'

'I don't know. He's conscious.'

'What about Neva?'

'She's not at the funeral. I think she's at home. Would you call her?'

'Sure. You all right?'

'I'm trying to hold on. Come as quickly as you can.' Diane folded her phone and slipped it into the pocket of her jacket.

Douglas Garnett, the Rosewood chief of detectives, was asking all the people to go sit in their cars until someone could come talk to them. But news of what had happened was running through

100

the crowd like an electric current, and people were already hurrying to leave. Andie and Kendel were making sure the exiting crowd gave Mike a wide berth.

'What can we do to help?' Diane heard Steve Taggart ask Garnett.

'Take your family to your car and wait for the police. Encourage others to do the same. Someone will come and interview you just as soon as we can get them there.' Garnett was looking out over the crowd of people leaving.

'Most of their names will be in the guest book,' said Diane. 'But I doubt our perp signed it.'

'What kind of nut comes to a funeral and stabs someone?' said Garnett. 'Does this guy – Mike – have enemies?'

'Not that I know of. It seems like only a nut would take a chance like this.'

'Just when I thought perps couldn't surprise me anymore . . .' He shook his head. 'I called the squad. Police and detectives will be on their way. What about an ambulance?' asked Garnett.

'One of my staff called nine-one-one. I'm going to ride with Mike to the hospital, if they let me. I want my crime scene people to come down here and look around. I thought Neva might want to meet us at the hospital. She and Mike are dating.' Garnett nodded. Diane let out a deep breath. 'I also told the Van Ross family to go home. I'm sorry. I was thinking of the kids. I did instruct them not to talk among themselves.'

'Just as well. I think most of our people are going to go home anyway. The mayor and the governor's man already left.' He paused, then asked, 'Did you see anyone suspicious?'

'No. I've been scanning the crowd.' Diane shrugged in frustration. 'There are just so many people I don't know.'

At the sound of the ambulance she left Garnett to attend to the policing and she hurried back to Mike, who was trying to get up off the ground. Korey was still applying pressure to the wound, and Andie had a hand on Mike's shoulder, trying to keep him still. Kendel went to wait for the ambulance so she could lead the paramedics to Mike.

'I'm feeling better,' Mike said.

'The ambulance is here,' said Diane. 'Stay where you are.'

The ambulance parked on the grass shoulder of the roadway, and two paramedics hurried with their equipment to where Mike lay, shooing everyone out of the way. Korey stood back, blood dripping from his hand. Chief Garnett came forward and offered him his handkerchief.

The female paramedic, a black woman who wore her hair in waves tight against her head like a twenties blues singer, took Mike's blood pressure and nodded to the male who began hooking him up to a drip.

'What happened?' she asked.

'Someone stabbed him,' Diane told her.

'At a funeral?'

'We don't know who or why,' said Diane.

'What's the world coming to?' She looked in Mike's eyes with a light. 'Can you talk to me, baby?'

'Sure, what would you like to talk about?' His voice was husky, and words trailed off at the end.

She smiled at him. 'Do you have any allergies?'

'No.'

'What's your name?'

'Mike Seger.'

'Okay, Mike Seger, we're going to take you to the hospital and you're going to be just fine.'

As they loaded him onto the stretcher, Diane gave instructions to Korey and the others to go back to the museum after they talked to the police.

'May I ride with him to the hospital?' asked Diane.

'And you are?' asked the woman.

'Yes, she can,' whispered Mike, reaching out his hand, which Diane grasped.

'My name is Diane Fallon,' she said as she walked down to the ambulance with them.

'Oh, the museum crime scene lady,' said the male paramedic, a blond-haired, blue-eyed guy who looked too young for the job, but Diane noticed that he was efficient and sure in everything he did. 'Sure you can ride.'

Diane was surprised and grateful as she climbed in the back that he recognized her. She tried to stay out of the way as much as she could in the tiny space.

'He's looking good,' the woman told her.

She must see how terrified I am, Diane thought. She hoped Mike hadn't noticed. She reached out and stroked his hair. 'Good thing you stay in such great shape.'

It took under ten minutes to get to the hospital. They carried Mike in, and Diane went to the waiting room.

The room had a shabby look to it, no doubt from years of use by thousands of people. The vinyl chairs were brightly colored either red, blue, green or orange. A large blond-wood coffee table with a pile of magazines sat in the center. She rifled through the magazines on the table, looking for something that might hold her interest long enough to pass the time. She picked up the same magazine twice and put it down. Her head was starting to hurt right in the middle of her forehead. Finally she went outside and called Frank on her cell.

'Hey, babe. I was just trying to get in touch with you. My partner's meeting with a Rosewood detective today. He called me and said someone was stabbed at a funeral. Was it the one you went to?'

'Yes. It was Mike.'

'My God. Your caving partner Mike? How is he?'

'I don't know. The doctor hasn't come out yet. Frank, what kind of maniac stabs someone at a funeral, of all places?'

'I don't know. I'll come over when I get home. You doing okay?'

104

'I'm fine. All that adrenaline's keeping me going, but I think it's about to wear off. I'm getting a terrible headache.'

'Try not to worry. Mike's a strong guy. Let me know when you find out something.'

'I will. I think I see Neva's car pulling into the parking lot. I'll talk with you later.'

Korey, Andie and Kendel pulled in beside Neva. They all piled out of their vehicles and headed toward Diane.

'I thought I told you guys to go back to the museum.'

'We were going to, but decided we'd rather be here,' said Andie. 'Heard anything?'

Diane shook her head. 'No, but it hasn't been that long.' She turned to Neva, who was looking at her with wide, tear-filled eyes. 'He was conscious and very coherent the whole time. He even joked with the paramedics. He's going to be all right,' Diane said with more conviction than she felt.

'If he's joking, that's good.' Neva tried to smile. 'Mike's really healthy.' She nodded as if agreeing with herself. 'He'll be fine.'

'David and Jin arrived before we left the cemetery,' said Andie. 'They want us to call when we know something about Mike.'

'Let's go sit down,' said Diane. She put an arm around Neva's shoulders and led them all to the waiting room. With the excitement wearing down, Diane was starting to have more aches and pains.

There was a dull throb in her foot as well as her tricep muscle, and her head was getting worse. She was glad to sit. She dug in her purse for a couple of aspirin, spotting a water fountain. The pills were hard going down. She took several more sips of water before she went back to the others.

'You okay, Neva?' Diane asked, sitting back down in her red chair.

Neva nodded. 'This is just so weird – and scary. Makes me wonder if it's some serial perp who's going to start showing up in public places stabbing people.'

'If he does,' said Korey, 'it shouldn't be too hard to catch him. I mean, how often would he be able to get away with something like that?'

'None of us saw a thing,' said Andie.

'We weren't looking,' said Korey.

All of them sat in the colorful chairs and did the magazine shuffle that Diane had finally given up on, opting to stare at the rainbow-colored carpet instead.

'Did you have a chance to look at your witch this morning?' asked Korey. They all looked toward Diane with anticipation.

'No, but she has had visitors.' Diane told Korey, Neva and Kendel about the Wiccan and the Druid. They all listened with rapt attention, as if glad for the least distraction. Andie added a description of Caitlin's shades of purple.

'And they actually thought you'd give the bones to them?' asked Kendel.

'Apparently that was their hope,' said Diane.

They all lapsed into silence after that. Diane was lost in her thoughts when the waiting room's double swinging doors opened and a doctor in scrubs emerged.

CHAPTER 11

The doctor was a man about Diane's age. He spoke to the nurse at the information station, and she pointed to Diane. She, Neva, Andie, Korey and Kendel all rose in one motion, as if connected, and walked over to him.

'We're friends of Mike Seger. I'm Diane Fallon, his employer. We were with him when this happened. Can you tell us his condition?' asked Diane.

'I'm Dr Nolan. The knife nicked a vessel and his colon, but he's going to be all right. He lost a lot of blood, but I didn't have to transfuse, and that's good. He should be able to go home in a few days if he progresses as well as he is now. I understand this happened at a funeral?' The doctor looked at them as if expecting them to tell him he had been misinformed.

'Yes. We don't know who or why. First thing we saw was Mike falling to his knees.'

Chief Garnett came through the waiting room doors and joined them, introducing himself to the doctor.

Diane had expected a detective to show up soon. She wasn't surprised that the chief himself was taking the lead. It had become a high-profile case, not because of the victim, but because of where the crime had taken place. At least Mike would get their undivided attention.

'Can you tell us anything about the weapon?' he asked the doctor.

'It cut clean like a scalpel – very sharp. Given the depth of the wound, however, whatever kind of weapon did this, it was longer than a regular scalpel.'

'Has he said anything?' asked Garnett.

'No. He's in recovery now, just coming out of the anesthesia.'

Chief Garnett took hold of Diane's upper arm, and she yelped at the sudden pain. Garnett quickly withdrew his hand and looked down at his palm. He frowned at her.

Damn, that hurt, she thought. She must have torn the muscle.

'You're bleeding.'

Diane shook her head. 'It's Mike's. My arm is just sore because I pulled a muscle at the gym this morning.'

The doctor walked around her and looked at the back of her arm. 'I don't think so. That blood looks too fresh. Let's get your jacket off and take a look.'

The doctor and Garnett slid the jacket off her shoulder. She heard Andie and Kendel gasp.

Diane felt his fingers on her upper arm just beneath the short sleeve of her blouse.

'You have a deep laceration in your arm.' He turned to the nurses' station. 'Nurse. We need to get Ms Fallon into an examination room.'

Diane looked at the expressions of surprise on all their faces. She imagined it matched her own. She handed Andie her purse and asked her to give her insurance information to the receptionist. She tried to look at her arm.

'Let's not move too much. You're starting to bleed again,' said Dr Nolan. 'Chief Garnett, this looks like a scalpel wound. I wouldn't be surprised if it was done by the same weapon.'

The nurse led her to the examination room, then helped her change into one of those embarrassing backless hospital gowns. She had Diane lie down on the examination table on her good side.

A few minutes later, the doctor came in, washed his hands, then slipped on a pair of latex gloves. He examined the wound. She flinched several times as he palpated the area on the back of her arm.

'Sorry,' he said. 'I'm trying to be as gentle as I can.'

What the shit is this about? she wondered. Since hearing that Mike was out of danger, her fear had been replaced by anger. *Dammit, who in the hell goes to a funeral and stabs people?* She wondered if anyone else was stabbed.

The doctor stepped around the table and stood where she could see him.

'We need to irrigate the wound before I can sew

110

it up. It's going to be uncomfortable, but nothing you shouldn't be able to handle.'

'I'm fine. I just want to get this over with and go home.' Diane suddenly remembered the pills she'd taken. 'I just took a couple of aspirin.'

'That's probably why it started bleeding again.'

'Why didn't I feel anything?'

'You felt nothing?'

'A twinge when it happened. I just thought I had injured a tricep when I was rock climbing at the gym this morning. I often pull muscles when I'm climbing. But I didn't feel like I had been stabbed.' Diane felt incredulous that this had happened to her. She could imagine how Mike must feel.

'Probably all the adrenaline in your system's been giving you some pain protection. When did you first feel the twinge?'

'Just after I saw Mike fall to his knees at the cemetery. I was pushing through the crowd to get to him. I remember someone stepped on my foot, and right after that I felt a sharp pain in my arm. As I said, I thought it was a pulled muscle.'

Dr Nolan moved to the end of the table and examined her feet.

'There's no bruising. Flex your toes. Does that hurt?'

'Just minor soreness. It wasn't that hard. It was just pinned to the ground for a moment.'

'Any other pains or sore spots anywhere that you didn't have before?'

'No, nothing else. Just the arm and the foot.'

'We'll get you fixed up. I'll come back when the nurse has cleaned your wound. Is your tetanus up-to-date?' Diane nodded. 'Good. I'm going to give you some powerful antibiotics,' he continued. 'And we'll have to take precautionary blood tests for possible infections, but I don't see any reason you can't go home right away.'

'I'd like to see Mike before I leave.'

'He should be awake by then. Now this is going to sting . . .' The doctor stuck in the needle to numb her arm.

Damn, she was pissed at whoever did this.

Neva and Korey were waiting for Diane when she walked back into the waiting room after the doctor had stitched her muscle and skin back together. She was surprised anyone was still there. It seemed like it had taken several hours. Neva said she had taken Kendel and Andie to the museum and had come back.

'What did the doctor say?' asked Korey.

'Just a few stitches and minor muscle repairs. They're letting me go home. How is Mike?'

'Mike's doing okay,' said Neva. 'He had me go to his apartment and bring him some things. I left him asleep, but if you'd like to go see him he may be awake. I'm going to stay the night . . .'

'Don't worry about coming to work tomorrow morning. We'll call if we need you.'

*   *   *

Mike was asleep when she, Neva and Korey entered his room. Diane and Korey turned and started to leave.

'Hey, guys.'

Diane turned around. 'You awake?'

'More or less,' Mike said, sounding a little groggy. 'I think we must have really pissed someone off in an earlier life. Neva said you were getting sewn up.'

Diane shrugged and sat down in the chair Neva had pulled up for her. 'The doctor said I'll live.'

Mike moved and winced in pain. 'What the hell happened? Who's doing this?'

'I don't know. Do you want me to call your parents?'

He shook his head. 'They were so worried when I was shot; I'll tell them myself when I'm not feeling so out of it.'

'Do you know of anyone who doesn't like you?'

'Enough to stab me? No. That detective – Garnett – asked the same thing. Graduate school can be cutthroat, but not literally. Besides, that wouldn't explain why they went after you.'

Diane deeply hoped that this was not somehow her fault, that it had nothing to do with the crime scene lab. She would never forgive herself if it did.

'Hey, Doc. Don't look so glum. This isn't your fault.'

It was as if Mike had read her mind, but she guessed he had merely read her face.

'How are you feeling?' she said.

'Actually, pretty good. Got me hooked up to some sweet painkillers. But I don't think I'll be able to go caving this weekend.'

Diane gave him a weak smile and lifted her arm. 'Me either.'

'They have to test my blood,' he said. 'They said the knife might have been contaminated with other blood or something . . .' He let the sentence trail off and looked at Neva. She kissed his forehead.

'I know,' said Diane. 'Mine, too.'

'Shit. I hate that son of a bitch,' said Mike.

'We'll get through this.' She grasped his hand and squeezed it.

Mike looked at her and smiled. 'Sure, we will.'

'I'm going home and getting a long night's sleep. I'll come by in the morning before I go to the museum,' said Diane.

'Don't worry about me, Doc. I'll be fine.'

'You take care, buddy,' said Korey.

'Sure. Nothing can happen to me in the hospital, right?' He laughed weakly as they went out the door.

Korey drove Diane to her car at the museum parking lot. 'I'll take you home and pick you up in the morning,' he said. 'It's not out of my way.'

'Thanks, Korey, but I can drive. Look, I appreciate your staying at the hospital so long. It must have been boring.'

'No problem. Glad I could be there for you guys.'

'See you tomorrow.' Diane got out of his car and into her SUV. It felt good to be going home.

She drove slowly, not quite trusting the use of her right arm, relieved when she pulled into the parking space in front of her apartment building. The building was a huge old Greek Revival house subdivided into apartments.

She wished it had an elevator as she climbed the stairs to her apartment. Just as she got inside the phone rang. She picked it up.

'Hey, it's me,' said Frank. 'How's Mike doing?'

'Good. They expect a full recovery. I spoke with him before I left.'

'That's a relief. Look, babe, I'm sorry but I've got to stay in Atlanta for the next couple of days. We have a development in a case.' Frank worked in Atlanta, but lived in Rosewood, and he often stayed in Atlanta when he was working on a case instead of making the ninety-minute commute. She couldn't blame him.

'Sure. I'd like to get to bed early, anyway.' She hoped the depth of her disappointment didn't sound in her voice.

'I know this has been a rotten day. I really wanted to be with you tonight.'

'Don't worry about it.'

'I'll see you day after tomorrow for sure and take you out to dinner. We'll do a movie.'

Maybe we'll bring dinner and a movie home, she thought. Somehow she couldn't imagine feeling any better in a couple of days than she did now.

'I'll look forward to it,' she said, trying to force some enthusiasm into her tone.

'Take care,' he said, and was gone.

She didn't tell him that she had also been stabbed. It would only make him feel worse about not being there. She decided to take a Percocet and go to bed early.

Diane awoke feeling just as angry as she had when she went to sleep. Her arm hurt, and it pissed her off that she was going to have to get a series of blood tests to make sure she didn't catch anything nasty from the knife. Damn that guy.

She wanted to call Garnett and see if he was making progress, but it was only six and he was most likely still at home. On top of all the other worries about herself and Mike, Diane also felt guilty, and she wasn't sure why. But a free-floating sick feeling had come on her like a constant pain in her stomach. 'Get a hold of yourself,' she said out loud to her empty bedroom.

She took a bath, taking care not to get the bandage wet, got dressed and drove to the hospital, eating a nutrition bar on the way. She wanted to see how Mike was doing, and she also wanted to ask him a question that had been nagging at the back of her mind since her near fall in the cave.

A nurse was just carrying out his breakfast tray when she entered Mike's room. He was alone and sitting up with several pillows behind him.

'Hey, Doc.' He grinned at her.

'You look good,' she said, pulling up a chair. He actually looked better than she felt. The sight lifted some of her depression.

'I'm doing okay. How's your arm?'

'Sore, but mending. Where's Neva?'

'She went home to get a shower. She'll probably be back any minute. She stayed here all night sleeping in that chair.'

Diane was silent for several moments, feeling a little foolish for her concerns about the cave, trying to come up with some small talk.

'Got something else on your mind, Doc?'

'Mike . . .'

'Uh-oh, that either sounds like we're breaking up or I'm getting fired. Since we aren't going together and technically I work for the university . . .'

Diane smiled. 'It's something that's been nagging at me since I nearly fell in the cave, and I need your opinion. Was I reckless? As I was crawling through that tunnel, my mind was on the new opening . . . I lost track of the moment. You can't do that in a cave.'

'No, but we all have. Reckless? No. You're like me. Safety is automatic. You just didn't recognize the danger. While you were off on vacation enjoying yourself, I did some experiments on a piece of wood with a hole drilled in it. I poured gravel on the board to see if the rocks that got caught in the hole made any recognizable pattern.'

Diane raised her eyebrows. 'How scientific of you.'

Mike smiled, showing his dimples. He tried to stretch and winced from the pain. 'Son of a bitch.'

'You okay?'

'Yeah, just a little pain. If I get my hands on the guy who did this . . . Shit. Anyway, the experiment – I thought maybe we could recognize the formation if we ever ran across one again.'

'Can we?'

'Maybe – if all we saw was the plug. The rocks shift toward each other when they get stuck. You can sort of recognize it. But with other breakdown on top of the plug, the pattern was hard to see.' He shook his head. 'You weren't reckless. What brought this on?'

'It was just something I was thinking about.'

Mike squinted his eyes at her. 'There's something else that's bothering you.'

'Just trying to make sense out of things. Why us?'

'I've been thinking. You know, there is one person who would like to do us both in.'

Diane lowered her eyes, then brought her gaze back up to Mike's intent look. His light brown eyes still looked sleepy, but he had a strength in his voice just now when he talked about a killer that got away, almost taking their lives with him – the one who left Neva to die.

'I've thought of him too. But he's dead. He has to be.'

'Does he?'

'Yes. There's no way he could have survived. I believe that.'

'Is that why you scan the parking lot every time you leave the museum? I've seen you. I do it too.'

'It's a good habit to get into.'

'It's just a thought I had, trying to figure out who could be so damn mad at both of us. You're right, though – he's probably dead. I can't imagine how he could have possibly escaped the cave, wounded like he was and with no light.'

'I'll mention it to Garnett.' Diane stood. 'I need to let you get some rest.'

'Wait. There's something else I'd like to talk to you about while I'm laid up here looking pitiful and after having saved your life two weeks ago.'

Diane laughed out loud. 'This sounds like you're going to ask a really big favor.'

'It's a proposal.'

CHAPTER 12

Diane's eyebrows rose a fraction. 'A proposal?'

'Business,' Mike added.

'Okay, shoot.'

'It's a job proposal, a rather unusual one. I've got it written out, but I don't have it here. I'll ask Neva to drop it by your office. However, I'll tell you about it.'

Diane moved the chair closer to Mike's bed and sat back down. 'I'm listening. What is your unusual proposal?'

'Can I have a drink of water?'

A glass of ice water was sitting on the stand next to his bed. She helped him take a sip from the straw.

'Can I do anything else for you? Get you an extra pillow?' She felt helpless watching him lie there.

'I'm okay, really.'

But Diane had seen him push the button that gave him his intravenous painkiller. She sat back down and leaned forward.

'I'm listening,' she said.

'I've been asked by a biotechnology and

pharmaceutical research company to search out and collect extremophiles.'

'Extremophiles?'

'Organisms that live in the most extreme environments on earth, conditions that would kill other creatures. Some grow in very cold or extremely hot temperatures, some in very high- or low-pH environments, and some live under high pressure or in high salt concentrations, and others have very limited nutrient needs.'

'And they want you to find these . . . organisms? What does this company want with them?'

'Extremophiles have some very interesting characteristics. For example, you know that polymerase chain reaction test you guys do for the DNA in blood?'

'Uh-huh. It replicates small samples of DNA to increase the amount we have to work with. We don't do it here. We send our samples to the GBI lab in Atlanta, but sure, I know what it is.'

'Did you know the Taq DNA polymerase used for the reaction originally came from *Thermus aquaticus*, a bacterium found in the hot springs of Yellowstone National Park?'

Diane blinked. 'Really? I had no idea,' she said, feeling oddly abashed. 'Jin is more up on this than I am. He has a particular interest in DNA testing.'

'Does he know that for some other PCR applications, Taq DNA polymerase isn't as useful because it lacks proofreading? It doesn't have the ability to detect and remove replication errors.'

Diane shrugged and smiled at Mike, who was clearly having fun. 'I'll ask him.'

'The DNA polymerase from *Thermococcus litoralis* has an enzyme that has very promising proofreading capabilities. The point is that some of these extremophiles are like little engines that do really cool stuff.'

'It sounds to me a lot like nanotechnology.'

'Interesting you should say that. Some researchers are looking at extremophiles as a model for nanotechnology. Extremophile research has a lot of branches – medicine, environmental cleanup, food preservation and lots more. The characteristics that allow them to survive in extreme conditions are sometimes very useful for other kinds of work.'

'Fascinating, I agree. But your Ph.D. is in geology. What do they want with a geologist?'

He gave her a lopsided smile. 'Some extremophiles live inside rocks.' He laughed. 'I think I'm getting silly. This painkiller is feeling really good. Is my speech slurred?'

'Not much more than usual,' said Diane.

Mike clasped his chest with both hands. 'Oh, now I've been stabbed through the heart. Seriously, sometimes locating extremophiles in their natural habitat is a geologic problem. That's part of what geomicrobiology is about. But it's mainly my skill set they are interested in – caving and rock climbing. Extremophiles live in remote, hard-to-get-to places – like ice caves and inside volcanoes. They need someone like me. I've climbed a five-fourteen rock face.'

The surprise must have shown on Diane's face, the way Mike grinned broadly at her. She knew Mike was good, but they always had relatively easy climbs in the caves they visited. She could do a five-seven, a five-eight or -nine in a pinch. Only a handful of elite rock climbers could handle a rock face with a five-fourteen degree of difficulty – it required an enormous amount of skill and strength.

'Have I impressed you, Doc?'

'You've impressed the hell out of me, Mike.'

She didn't think it possible, but his grin got even broader and a little more lopsided.

'I've sure been working hard at it.'

Diane suddenly felt a pang of sadness. Mike was an extremely talented and intelligent individual, and a genuinely nice guy. All that would be gone had he died. Twice now he'd almost been killed when they were together.

She fingered the locket that hung on a chain around her neck. It contained a photograph of her and her daughter. Diane wondered what Ariel would have become had her bright light not been extinguished so soon. Her eyes filled with tears.

'You okay, Doc?'

Diane blushed and hoped that Mike didn't notice that as well as the tears. 'Yes . . . it's . . . I was just thinking about my daughter. Now you – twice – and Frank getting shot last year, too. It seems I'm not a lucky person to be around.'

'Doc, none of what happened to any of us was your fault. This time we were at a funeral, for heaven's sake. Who knew?' He reached out his hand and Diane took it. 'Thanks for riding with me in the ambulance. I have to tell you, I was scared.'

'Me too.'

She squeezed his hand, let it go, took a tissue from the box on his nightstand, and blotted the tears from her eyes.

'I'm sorry. Please tell me more about your proposal. Where does the museum come into it?'

'That's the unusual part. The company wants me to work for them on a job-by-job basis – kind of open-ended contract work. This proposal is really an application for a job in the museum – an official job. Right now I work there because of my assistantship in the Geology Department at Bartram, and that won't last forever.' He took a deep breath, and it looked to Diane like his eyes were drooping. 'In the written proposal, I've got several ideas for exhibits for the museum.'

He stopped for a long moment and closed his eyes. Diane was about to leave when he spoke up suddenly.

'What I was thinking is that I could work part-time at the museum with enough hours to get insurance and benefits. I would continue to do the duties I do now. When I'm off working for

Extreme Research, I can also collect rocks, minerals, fossils, whatever, for the museum, and make videos of some of our explorations. I think an exhibit on extremophiles, for instance, would be popular – I outlined a plan in the paper.'

'It's an intriguing proposal.'

'Does it work for you?'

'I like it. I'll need to think about it. When do you need to know something?'

'No deadline, but sooner rather than later, if possible.'

'I'll give it serious thought, Mike. It's a good idea,' she said. 'But now I really should let you get some rest.'

Diane stood just as Neva came in the door bearing flowers and a bright smile. She set the flowers across from Mike's bed and went to his bedside.

'You're looking good. How do you feel?' She bent over to kiss him on his cheek, but he turned his head and kissed her on the lips.

'Thanks for the flowers. They are for me, aren't they?'

'No. Your doctor's really cute. They're for him.' She kissed him again.

Diane was relieved to see Mike's interest in Neva. His attraction to Diane had become more of a joke between them than anything serious, but seeing that he genuinely liked Neva put her at ease.

'How's your arm?' Neva asked Diane.

'Sore, but that's all. I'll see you guys later. I'm going to the museum.'

As Diane was leaving, three young women came into the room and gathered around Mike. They looked like graduate students, she thought. She noticed that Neva started to back away, but Mike held on to her hand.

Diane met Korey coming into the museum along with a throng of visiting children and two tour buses. It was good to see the museum crowded and noisy.

'Begging you're pardon, Dr F.,' said Korey. 'Why aren't you at home taking it easy?'

'If I get to feeling bad, I'll go home. There's just so much to do in the museum and the crime lab.'

'That's why you have all those people working for you.'

'I know, but I've been gone for a couple of weeks . . . I get uneasy leaving things that long.'

Korey grinned and waved as they parted company at the stairwell and he went up to the conservation lab on the second floor. Diane continued on through the double doors to the private office of the museum. Several of her staff gathered around when they saw her, and expressed their concern about her and asked about Mike. Diane held out her arm to show them that it was still functional and that she would live, and she gave them a short briefing on Mike's condition.

Her chair felt good when she finally sat down

behind her desk. The first thing she did was call Kendel and Andie to her office.

'Andie, Neva is bringing by a proposal from Mike. Make a copy and give it to Kendel.' She turned toward Kendel. 'I'd like your opinion on it as soon as you have a chance to evaluate it.'

Kendel nodded. 'Sure. Mike always has good ideas.'

After catching up with Kendel and Andie, she walked upstairs to the labs. Her arm was throbbing, but she didn't want to take painkillers if she could get by without them.

In her osteology lab two boxes sat on a metal table. The tag on one told her it was from Lynn Webber, the Hall County medical examiner. That would be Caver Doe. Lynn had autopsied the mummified body and had her diener strip the bones of the dried flesh so that Diane could examine them. Lynn's report said the probable cause of death was infection from a compound fracture of the tibia exacerbated by kidney damage consistent with a vertical-height fall. Lynn noted that at this point the manner of death looked like an accident, but she couldn't be sure.

The second box was from England – the Moonhater Cave bones. On top of the box was a large envelope with photographs of the bones, the cave, and the so-called salt maiden. The salt maiden was obviously a carved stalagmite. She wondered if the part of the story about turning a woman to salt was added much later, when someone saw what looked a little like a face in the cave formation. It would be interesting to hear all the various stories about the cave and the bones.

She took the Moonhater photographs and the Caver Doe medical examiner's report into her office and sat down behind her desk. This office, unlike her other one in the museum, was stark, almost bare of personal items. The pale off-white walls and green slate floor did little to warm up the room. She had hoped the burgundy sofa and chair and walnut desk furniture would add something to the atmosphere, but it was a room much like the watercolor of a wolf hunting in the wild she had hanging on one wall – lean and efficient-looking.

Diane picked up the phone and called the crime lab a few doors away and asked David and Jin to bring her up to speed on what they'd been doing while she was on vacation – and whether they had discovered anything at Mike's crime scene. She didn't look forward to that part. Her arm continued to throb.

CHAPTER 13

Jin bopped into her office, pulled the burgundy stuffed chair up close to her desk and sat down. David sat down on one end of the sofa and propped his feet up on the other end. He rubbed the top of his bald head as if that would make his hair grow back.

'How come I don't have one of these in my office?' said David.

'Because you don't have an office,' said Diane.

'Oh, yeah, that's right. I have a cubicle with maggots.'

'You are welcome to use my couch if you leave your maggots behind.' Diane flashed him a grin, then took a deep breath. It was time to get started. 'Where are we with the cemetery stabbings? Do we know anything about the perp? Were there any more vics?' She said it as if she didn't know the victims, as if she herself weren't one of them.

'We've kept in touch with Garnett. As far as we know you and Mike are the only two,' said Jin.

Why? wondered Diane. *Why the two of them?* 'Did you find anything at the site?'

'*Nada*,' said David. 'Not a damn thing. If he was lurking behind one of the monuments or a tree, he wasn't drinking, eating, smoking, chewing gum or tobacco, spitting or spewing blood – or at least he left no evidence if he was doing any of those things. We found a bracelet with a broken clasp, but it turned out to belong to one of the mourners, and Garnett cleared her. She was eighty-seven and not given to homicidal mania.'

Diane smiled briefly. 'So where does that leave us?' she asked.

'As far as the crime scene, nowhere,' said David. 'Neva brought us Mike's clothes and your jacket. We've processed them. The fibers that we found on Mike's clothes are from the museum van. Your coat only had fibers from your office chair, Mrs Van Ross's clothes and the limo.'

'So that's no help,' mused Diane. 'Do we have anything?'

'The doctor said that the weapon you and Mike were stabbed with was as sharp as a scalpel, had a double edge and was at least six inches long,' said David. 'My guess is it's an expensive knife – or rather a dagger, since it was double-edged.'

'Why do you say it was expensive?' asked Diane.

'Because you can't sharpen cheap steel as sharp as the knife that stabbed you and Mike was.'

'So that's something.'

'He's probably proficient with it,' said David.

Diane raised her eyebrows and leaned forward. 'How so?'

'Because, relatively speaking, he did minimal damage,' said David. 'An unsteady hand could have been much worse on the two of you. The doctor said Mike's cut showed no evidence of rocking inside the wound, and it came out on the same plane that it went in. That's a steady hand.' David made an underhanded stabbing gesture. 'The angle was slightly upward – about five degrees from a level plane. He wasn't taller than Mike. I'd say about the same height, maybe slightly shorter, but not by much.'

Diane pinched the bridge of her nose, forcing herself to visualize Mike being stabbed, trying to get an image of the event. David was right: The guy had to be proficient to do it quickly and not be seen.

'You okay with this, Boss?' asked Jin.

'Yes. I'm all right. Go on.'

'Your jacket had a slice almost equal to the length of your wound,' said Jin. 'The knife went in; he sliced down and withdrew. All very neat.'

Diane winced at his description. She saw both David and Jin grimace as well.

'So what can we infer – he's proficient with a knife and had no intention of killing, just maiming?'

'I can't say he had no intention of killing Mike,' said David. 'He could easily have died.'

Diane cast her eyes upward to stop the emotion that was threatening to spill tears into her eyes. If David and Jin noticed, they said nothing.

'So all we know for sure is that he had an expensive knife and knew how to use it.'

'That's about it,' said Jin.

'It's a help. Did you tell Garnett all this?'

Jin nodded. 'We keep him up-to-date.'

Diane was surprised at how much they had gotten done in just a few hours. 'Good work. Okay. How about the other cases you processed while I was on vacation?

One by one, Jin and David reported on all the pending cases and where they were in the process. When they finished, she complimented them on their thorough work and then asked about Caver Doe.

'He's not a priority, but did you have time to work on his effects?'

Both David and Jin bobbed their heads. 'Oh, yeah,' said Jin. 'He was wearing a plain green plaid flannel shirt, but some really cool jeans. Levi's, pre-1936.'

Diane could see that Jin was dying to tell her about them. She waved a hand at him. 'You have the floor,' she said, knowing he'd certainly take it.

Jin stood. 'Caver Doe's jeans had a back cinch.' Jin turned and pointed to the back of his jeans – which did not have a cinch – and looked over his shoulder at Diane. 'The back cinch was a little minibelt that tightened the waist. They were called waist overalls back then, not blue jeans.'

Jin turned to face Diane. David sat up on the

sofa, resting his forearms on his thighs and leaned forward, listening.

'His jeans also have a crotch rivet.' Jin started to point, but stopped as a flush crept over his face. 'Well, never mind. The crotch rivet and the back cinch were removed during World War Two to save on metal and fabric and never used again. That dates them to before the Second World War.

'In 1937 the company changed the way they sewed the back pockets, so the material would cover the rivets. That was because the cowboys complained that the metal rivets scratched their saddles – they were marketing to cowboys, and cowboys were particular about their saddles. Caver Doe's jeans also had suspender buttons. All that puts them before 1937. Now, what Caver Doe's jeans didn't have was a red label.'

Jin turned and pointed to his left rear pocket, where a red Levi's label was sewn, then faced her again, and for a minute Diane didn't know if he was going to sit back down or break into a dance. Instead, he walked closer to her desk and looked earnestly at her.

'I checked and there was never a red label sewn on Caver Doe's jeans. The company started sewing the red label in 1936 so Levi's could be recognized at a distance. Caver Doe's jeans did have belt loops. Those were first added in 1922.'

'So the time line for the jeans is between 1922 and 1936,' said Diane.

'Yep.' Jin sat back down and leaned forward in

the chair. 'I found a lot of animal hairs on the jeans.'

'That's interesting . . .' Diane winced in pain. Her amusement at Jin's demonstrative explanation of Caver Doe's jeans had relieved Diane from some of the pain in her arm, but it was back – sharp pains, as if the knifer were stabbing her over and over again.

'What's wrong?' asked David. 'You don't look well.'

'A little pain. I didn't want to take any medication until I got home tonight.'

'Take a pain pill. Jin and I'll take you home when you want to go.'

'I wanted to start on Caver Doe's bones this afternoon.'

David got up and went around to Diane's small refrigerator hidden behind a walnut cabinet, took out a bottle of water and handed it to her. 'Take a pill.'

Diane fished out the bottle of extra-strength Tylenol rather than her prescription Percocet, took out a pill and downed it with a long drink of water. 'David, it's a good thing you are a friend.'

'I know,' he said. 'It lets me get away with a lot.'

'What kind of animal hairs did you find on the jeans?' Diane asked.

'*Sylvilagus floridanus, Sciurus carolinensis, Equus caballus* and *Canis familiaris*,' said Jin.

Diane wrinkled her forehead. 'So we have rabbit, squirrel, horse and dog. What color horse?' asked Diane, smiling at Jin.

134

'Brown,' said Jin, grinning back at her. 'The dog was black. The horse hair was clustered on the seat – looks like Caver Doe rode bareback and didn't wash his jeans before going caving.'

'We think he hunted squirrels and rabbits,' said David. 'I suppose those were his all-purpose jeans – hunting, riding, caving. The lantern's kind of nice too. It's circa nineteen-thirties or -forties. We're still looking into that.'

'You'd better tell her about the book,' said Jin.

'It was a perfectly reasonable purchase. We've bought many more expensive things,' David protested.

Diane looked from Jin to David. 'You bought something?'

'A used dog-eared book on railroad-spike collecting, for seventy-five dollars,' Jin said.

'Seventy-five dollars?' said Diane. 'For a book on railroad spikes?'

'We didn't have a database of railroad spikes,' said David. 'It was perfectly reasonable to get a book to start one. I couldn't help it if the only one was out of print and rare.'

'Do we really need a database of railroad spikes?' asked Diane.

'We have two spikes in this case.'

'And he read where last year someone used one as a murder weapon in Nevada,' said Jin in a mock defense.

'I'll admit there's not a lot of call for it, but you never know what information a case will hinge on.'

Diane shook her head. 'Okay. So what about the button? We do have a database on buttons, as I recall.'

David's grin was so big that both Jin and Diane laughed at him.

'Our button, it turns out, is rare. And it gives our time line a new date – provided the button actually has some connection to Caver Doe, which is really a long shot, because there were no finger-prints and nothing whatsoever to connect it to the caver, except that they were both in the cave.

'Although our jeans may date from the thirties, our button dates from the forties. It's a silver-plated plastic officer's-uniform button specially commis-sioned for the newly authorized Army Specialist Corps. The buttons were never used because the secretary of war unauthorized – or whatever it is they do – the ASC before it went into effect. The only people to have them besides the manufac-turer were the Philadelphia Quartermaster's Department and a few colonels.'

'I'm surprised,' said Diane. 'I had no idea you would get that much from the button.'

'How much is it worth?' asked Jin.

'Couple hundred, maybe,' said David.

'Damn,' said Jin.

'It's very rare.'

'Tell her about the backpack,' said Jin.

'The backpack was rare?' said Diane.

David shook his head. 'No. It's a World War One U.S. Army backpack. It's what was in it. He had a lot of candles and matches, of course, and get this – a Mickey Mouse flashlight.'

'A Mickey Mouse flashlight?'

'Made by USALite. Shows Mickey Mouse walking in the dark with a flashlight. It dates to 1935. About ruined, though. It used two D-cell batteries, and they leaked all in it. It's a shame; it was a cool light. He had extra batteries and they leaked too. The battery acid got all over a couple of handkerchiefs, the matches, and some candles.'

'What about the picture?' asked Diane. 'It was pretty soaked with blood and body fluids, as I remember.'

'We photographed it in different kinds of light. I'm working on cleaning it,' said Jin. 'Did you know that Korey has some of the same document-cleaning agents that we use?'

'Yes,' said Diane. 'The museum occasionally does the same kind of restorative work that we do here in the crime lab.'

'I just thought it was kind of interesting,' said Jin.

'Anything else?' asked Diane.

'Caver Doe had a wad of cash in his pocket,' said Jin.

Diane raised her eyebrows. 'Oh?'

'They were stuck together. I'm cleaning them. The bills I can see are ones, so I don't think it's going to be a lot of money.'

'He also had a pencil and a key in his pocket,' said David. 'The key looks like it belonged to something small, like a box. Didn't see any strong-boxes while you were in the tunnels, did you?'

'No. I guess we'd better keep an eye out when we go back. Is that it?'

'That's all we know so far,' said Jin.

'You know,' began David, 'Jin, Neva and I thought we'd like to have a crime scene section in the museum with displays on what we do . . . like the bottle reconstruction we did at the bar fight crime scene – how it's like the potsherd analysis the archaeologists do.'

'A crime scene section in the museum? You're joking, aren't you?' The medicine hadn't kicked in yet and her arm was still throbbing. It was too early in the day for her to feel so bad now. She took another sip of water.

'No, Boss,' said Jin. 'You're always getting flak because we're housed in the west wing here. Why not show people what we do? It doesn't have to be gruesome.'

'Frankly, I'd never thought about that,' admitted Diane. She had always worked hard to keep them completely separate – with the exception of occasionally using the museum staff as consultants to the crime lab.

'Jin's right,' said David. 'People would find trace analysis interesting, and they wouldn't be so averse to our being here.'

'I'll give it some thought.'

'And we could make some of our more innocuous databases available on a computer,' added David. 'Not AFIS, CODIS or anything like that, of course.'

'Some of David's databases that we don't use that often,' said Jin, 'like buttons and railroad spikes, maybe feathers. Feathers are nice. You know, makes us not look so . . . gruesome – just really weird.'

'We would only be able to use the databases that are ours,' began Diane, when there was a muted knock on her door.

'Yes?'

Neva entered. She nodded at David and Jin, but the uneasy look on her face worried Diane.

CHAPTER 14

Jin jumped up and gave Neva his chair. 'Mike okay?' he asked.

Diane held her breath as Neva answered.

'He's doing good.' Neva's hair was falling from the clasp that held it up in its casual twist. She smoothed the freed locks behind her ears. 'They got him standing up. I just came here to check in; then I'm going home to get something to eat, take a shower and change clothes.' Neva smoothed her wrinkled shirt with her hands as she settled into the chair. 'I'm going to spend the night at the hospital. He doesn't really need me to, but he insists on not telling his parents until he's well, and I think someone needs to be there.' Her gaze darted from David to Jin, then to Diane, as if waiting for permission.

'I'm sure he'll appreciate having you there,' said Diane.

Neva's downturned mouth and wrinkled brow looked to Diane as though she still had something to say, but was waiting to be alone with Diane and did not want to ask the others to leave. David's and Jin's eyes met Diane's for a fraction of a

140

second before the two men headed for the door. They were almost out when Jin turned and asked Neva if she'd heard from the company that made Moon Pies.

Neva's lips curved up in a small smile as she twisted around toward them. 'It's from the nineteen-forties. They sent me a chart and pictures of all their wrappers since 1917. Another database for David.'

'Yeah,' said Jin, 'a Moon Pie database. I'm going to enter it into a contest for the least-used database of all time.'

David rolled his eyes and pulled Jin out the door with him.

'Is Mike really okay? You look worried,' said Diane.

Neva nodded. 'They got him up and he walked around his room for a few minutes. He's stiff, sore and really pissed at the guy who stabbed the two of you. The nurses said he's doing great.'

Neva didn't say anything more, just sat in the chair looking small and uncomfortable.

'What's on your mind, Neva?'

'This is really hard. I always keep confidences. I do. I'm good at that. But . . .' Tears welled up in her brown eyes and she looked like a doe about to make a run for it.

Diane came around her desk and led Neva to the couch. They sat half-turned so they faced each other. Diane rested her injured arm on the back of the sofa.

141

'But what?' she asked.

Neva took a breath. 'Mike's being sexually harassed.'

Diane didn't know what she had expected Neva to tell her, but that wasn't even on the list. She stared at Neva, openmouthed and speechless for a moment.

'What?'

'He asked me not to tell anyone, especially you.'

'Why especially me?'

She shrugged. 'He might be afraid you'd think less of him.'

'He should know better than that. Who's doing it?'

'Look, I know this is a bombshell I'm handing you, but please don't tell him I told you. He'll never trust me again. It's just that Mike's a really nice guy and deserves better – and now this has happened to him.'

'Who's harassing him? Someone here?'

'Sort of, but mainly at Bartram University. Dr Lymon, the geology professor.'

That it was Dr Lymon also surprised Diane. Dr Annette Lymon was part of the faculty-exchange arrangement Diane had with various departments at the university – faculty serving as part-time curators in exchange for office and research space. It was a great money-saving system for the museum, which didn't have a lot of money but did have a lot of space. Mike was Dr Lymon's graduate assistant.

'Is he doing anything about it?'

Neva shook her head. 'He's a guy, so he doesn't believe anyone would take it seriously. But when he turned her down, he lost his assistantship.'

Diane felt fire rise to her face. The wound in her arm tingled from the heat in her skin. 'I didn't know he was losing his assistantship. When did this happen, and why doesn't he file a complaint? He's not shy.'

'She came on to him about a month ago. She's a professor. He's a student. He says it doesn't matter, that he can always sling hash until he graduates, and anyway, she's not on his committee – whatever that means.'

'It means she doesn't get to judge his dissertation.'

Diane thought for a moment. As she recalled, Annette Lymon was Mike's major professor. Then she remembered that he had changed the focus of his dissertation from sedimentary structures – Lymon's expertise – to crystallography several months ago, and changed major professors. Even though that predated the harassment by several months, Diane wondered if it was connected.

There was something about Dr Lymon that Diane remembered – last month she expressed a desire to step down from her museum post, which was a relief to Diane. It had been clear to her that Dr Lymon didn't enjoy working at the museum, even though it virtually doubled her research space. Plus, the manager for the geology collection had come to Diane and complained about Lymon's work on several occasions since Lymon arrived – something managers rarely did.

'Last month? Was that the first time?' asked Diane.

Neva nodded. 'It was completely out of the blue.' Her eyes narrowed to slits. 'She grabbed him by the crotch and propositioned him. Then she got really upset when he turned her down.' Neva leaned forward. 'It's not just that. She came up to me in the parking lot and told me I'd better watch out, that Mike abused his last girlfriend. I didn't believe her and told her so. Mike shows no signs of being an abuser. My cousin married one, and I know what they're like. Even when they're trying to make nice, I know what they're like.'

'You're right, it's not true,' said Diane. 'I know what she's referring to, and I also know it wasn't Mike. He was trying to help the victim – as was I.'

'I didn't tell Mike what she said, but if she's spreading it around . . .'

'I'll take care of it.'

'I know it's asking a lot, but can you do it without letting Mike know I told you about the harassment?'

Diane nodded. 'I'll fix it.'

She rubbed her aching arm. As she tried to find a comfortable position in which to rest it, Neva's eyes grew wide with what looked like fear. Diane checked to see if she was bleeding.

144

'What if it was her?' said Neva.

'What do you mean?' asked Diane.

'Everyone around here knows Mike thinks you're great. What if she's jealous of you two and she's the one who stabbed both of you? I just now thought of that. There has to be a reason that you two were targeted, and I've been racking my brain trying to figure out something that makes sense.'

Diane couldn't imagine Dr Lymon wielding a knife and disappearing like the Shadow, but Neva had a point.

'I'll discreetly check into it. Don't worry, Neva. Go and be with Mike and put this out of your mind. It's something I can fix. If you need to be late in the morning or take a day off, that's all right. We can call you if we need you.'

Neva nodded and gave Diane a weak smile.

Diane said, 'I'm going to have to tell David about the harassment, because I need him to do some investigating. He'll keep your confidence.'

Neva made a face. 'David? He doesn't exactly . . . well . . . have a lot of finesse dealing with people. I mean—'

'Not in his personal interactions, but I assure you, he can slither around in an investigation and you never know he's there . . . kind of like our elusive museum snake.'

David's having any finesse obviously surprised Neva. 'Okay. Thanks. Really, thanks. This is so unfair, and I've been worried about what to do.' She stood, still looking uncertain. Diane imagined she felt guilty for breaking a confidence. 'I've got some work to do in the lab,' said Neva as she was leaving. 'Then I'm going back to the hospital.' She went out the door, Diane hoped feeling better than when she came in.

When Neva left, it was suddenly clear to Diane that she needed to do two things. First, she picked up the phone and called Kendel.

'Kendel, something has come up. I don't want to rush you, but have you seen Mike's proposal yet?'

'Neva brought it by early this morning. I've just read it, and I like it. I like Mike, too. He did a great job on the Journey to the Center of the Earth exhibit. The new exhibits he's proposing are cutting-edge stuff. He has my vote.'

'Okay, thank you, Kendel. Get with the accountant and work it out so that he has benefits.'

For her second task, Diane called David and asked him to meet her in her osteology lab. She arrived before him, and while she waited she opened the box containing the stripped skeleton of Caver Doe that Lynn Webber's new diener had processed. He had wrapped the skull and each long bone in bubble wrap and put all the hand and foot bones in small boxes. He'd arranged the vertebrae in a separate box and wrapped each rib in thin paper. What surprised her was not so much his meticulous handling of each bone, but that he had separated out the hand and foot bones in boxes labeled left and right. Not easy, unless you happened to be a bone person. Diane began by laying out the bones in anatomical position. Because of his meticulous labeling, it went quickly.

Diane heard the door open and looked up to see David. 'Nice wrapping,' he said, walking up to the table.

'Yes, it is. I've received bones from medical examiners with many different kinds of packaging, but I've never before had them individually wrapped, labeled and divided into left and right.'

David gave a short laugh. 'He sided the bones for you?'

Diane didn't know if the medicine was finally taking effect, or if it was the cathartic effect of good humor, but she felt better, and the pain in her arm was gone.

'Yes, he did. He even stacked the ribs together in order. Got it right too – side and all,' she said, then looked up from the bone she had just laid down. 'David, I need you to investigate something – confidentially.'

David cocked an eyebrow. 'Okay.'

She told him Neva's story and of her sudden concern that Dr Lymon might be the cemetery stabber.

David whistled. 'You need to tell Garnett.'

'Yes, I do, but I can't right now. That's why I'm asking you to investigate.' She unwrapped the two sides of the pelvis and held them together in front of her. A glimpse told her it was a male

147

pelvis – narrow pelvic basin, narrow sciatic notch. She set them down on either side of the sacrum.

'Sure. I'll do it,' David said. 'But just allow me to play the devil's advocate for a moment, because I know how you like me to be your moral anchor. Aren't you afraid that Garnett will accuse you of a conflict of interest – protecting the museum by conducting your own investigation?'

Diane picked up a tibia with a compound fracture mid-shaft. 'No. The museum wouldn't be hurt by this. I'm protecting the confidentiality of Neva and Mike – employees of mine. I have no knowledge that Dr Lymon is the perp. If you uncover evidence that she is, we'll take that to Garnett.'

David stared at the bone in Diane's hand. 'That break looks like it hurt,' said David.

'It did. Tibias often break through the skin because the shinbone is so close to the surface. According to Webber's report, he got an infection from the wound.'

David wrinkled up his face. 'Poor fellow. Okay, I understand you have no direct knowledge of Dr Lymon's guilt, but bear with me. It's a lead . . .'

'Perhaps. As I said, if it turns out to be, we'll tell Garnett.' Diane set the tibia down and lifted the skull from its nest on the doughnut ring.

David stroked his chin. 'What do you want me to do?'

CHAPTER 15

Caver Doe's clean bones looked like ivory ornaments on the shiny silver table. All of them were present – every bone in each hand and foot, the small hyoid bone from the throat, all the tiny bones of the ear. The diener had done a superior job in preparing them. Diane made a mental note to call and thank Lynn Webber and praise her assistant. To use her own words, flattery went a long way with Lynn.

David stood with his hands in his pockets studying Caver Doe, waiting for instructions as Diane collected her calipers, forms and pen and set them on the table in preparation for the examination. She stuck her forms in her clipboard and looked up at him.

'I want you to investigate Annette Lymon. I want to know if she could have stabbed Mike and me or if she could have had it done.'

'Do you think she could have?' he said.

'You want to start with a preconceived notion of what I think?' said Diane, putting a hand on the dome of Caver Doe's skull.

'I'm not starting with a preconceived notion. I'm

149

investigating. You're the first witness. She's someone you are acquainted with.'

Diane laughed and felt another rush of the sublime brain chemicals that soothed her body and cleared her head. She was glad she had opted for the Tylenol and not the Percocet.

'I can't see her acting with the finesse it took to stab both of us without our knowing it and then getting away clean. I've been going over the faces at the funeral in my mind, and I didn't see her. I would have recognized her. So would Mike. On the other hand, I wasn't really looking at the faces.' Diane stopped working and thought for a moment. 'Lymon is a good bit shorter than Mike and a couple of inches shorter than me. Not the right height, judging by the angle of Mike's wound.'

David seemed to ponder that for a moment. 'Would she know how to hire it done? Would she know those kind of people? I know that is rather extreme, but . . . would she?'

'I doubt it, but I don't know that much about her personal life or her background. Maybe she recruited a graduate student to do it.'

'Is it that easy for professors to get their students to commit murder for them?'

Diane laughed. It was starting to sound ridiculous. David chuckled with her. 'I wouldn't have thought so,' she said. 'But who knows what hold she may have on someone. When I was in graduate school, there were a few crazy students.'

David's face sobered. 'This harassment – Mike's

probably not the first. You can't keep it a secret. You know she'll do it again.'

Diane stared at the blank form on the clipboard as if it had an answer for her. She nodded. 'I know. I haven't decided yet how to handle it. I need information and time. And first I want to know if she was involved in the stabbing.'

'You can't protect everyone by yourself. I like Neva too, but . . .'

'I can protect people here, and I will.' She said it so vehemently that David was startled. She put the calipers and clipboard down on the table with a clink.

'What's up with you?' he said.

Diane pressed her lips together and looked away. 'First Ariel and all our friends at the mission were slaughtered, then Frank was shot last year, now Mike's been hurt – again. Except for now, all connected with people I was investigating, so who is the common denominator for all of them?' She turned and stared at David as if daring him not to say it was her.

'The common denominator is men who are willing to kill to get what they want,' said David. 'Not you.'

'It feels like me. I know I can't fix everything, but I can help Neva and Mike. And I can control what goes on in my museum.' She paused a moment, putting a hand to her forehead. 'Mike gave me a dynamite job proposal. He didn't tell me he needed the job because he had lost his assistantship. I gave the proposal to Kendel. She likes it too, so I'm going to hire him.'

David smiled. 'Have I told you lately that I appreciate your hiring me?'

'Yes.'

'Well, I do. We've brought more people to justice in the short time I've been here than we ever did working in human rights, and that's been very healing for me.'

Diane understood how he felt. When they worked in human rights investigation, they collected mass amounts of evidence, but rarely were they able to take anyone to court.

'It's been cathartic for me too.'

David smiled at her. 'I'm sure Mike will appreciate a job here as much as I do.'

'He'll be half-time. His Journey to the Center of the Earth display looks like it will be a big success. The advertising is going well. Early response indicates it's likely to be just behind the dinosaurs and the Egyptian exhibit in popularity. It's projected to bring in enough extra revenue to pay his salary. He's earning his keep.'

'I didn't think you would hire him if he couldn't do the job,' said David. 'Like I know you didn't hire me simply because I'm a friend.'

'I know. It's just . . .' She shrugged.

'Just what?'

'Nothing. I need to get back to these bones.'

'Jin and I are going down to the restaurant a little later for lunch; you hungry?'

'Thanks. I've got some yogurt in the fridge in my museum office. I don't feel like much more than that.'

'Look, I'll take you home tonight if you need to take any stronger medication. Is Frank coming over tonight?'

'No. He's still in Atlanta on a case.'

David started out the door. 'I'll start tomorrow morning on Lymon. I know Garnett's detectives are questioning Mike's associates in Geology. They may have picked up on something. I'll wheedle information out of them.'

'Thanks, David.'

'Sure.' He headed for the door, turned as if to say something, but hesitated. Finally he simply said, 'I'll let you know when I have something.'

Diane focused her attention back to the bones lying on the metal table, forcing everything else out of her mind. She actually knew a lot about Caver Doe just by the things he had with him when he died. She just didn't know who he was. Nor did she know why he wasn't rescued, and the question nagged at her.

She picked up the skull and traced her fingers over his frontal bone. Caver Doe had a gracile forehead, more so than when she saw him covered with dried flesh in the cave. If his frontal bone was all she had now Diane would have thought that he was a female. She picked up his mandible and fitted it to the skull and looked at his face. Straight on, it looked like a female skull. His chin had the roundness of a female's. That was not so uncommon. Not every male had a prominent brow ridge or square jaw. But the placement of other markers – nuchal crests, the zygomatic process, the mastoid process – pointed to male.

She ran a finger along his teeth, counting his dentition. The dental formula for an adult human was two, one, two, three. Two incisors, one canine, two premolars and three molars – the number of upper and lower teeth on one side, thirty-two in all. Caver Doe's third molars, his wisdom teeth, had not yet erupted, which probably meant he was under twenty-five.

His teeth were uneven – the incisors slightly turned and overlapping, the molars crowded. Had the wisdom teeth erupted, there would have been little room for them. Caver Doe had fourteen gold fillings.

Diane set down the mandible, picked up her calipers and measured all the craniometric points on the face, recording them on her clipboard. Her stomach growled just as she put the skull back down on the doughnut ring. Her arm started to throb again.

She put down her calipers. Yogurt wasn't going to be enough. She called the museum's restaurant and asked them to deliver a turkey sandwich, potato chips and Dr Pepper to her museum office. She took off her lab coat and went down to the first floor. The museum was filled with visitors and noise. She always found that satisfying. She stopped in front of the dinosaur room and watched a group of children having their pictures made by the brachiosaur. She smiled and continued down the length of the museum to her office. The restaurant had just delivered the sandwich to Andie when she arrived.

'You doing okay, Dr Fallon?' asked Andie.

'Fine . . . a little sore.' Diane was getting a little tired of people asking if she was okay, but knew they were just being kind and concerned. She hoped she didn't sound short when she answered. 'I'm going to eat lunch in my office.'

'I won't put anyone through unless it's an emergency.'

'Thanks, Andie.' She carried the sack from the restaurant into her office lounge and set it down on the table. After putting on a CD of Native American music, she sat down to eat, listening to the peaceful sounds of flutes and drums. Better than drugs, she thought as the harmonic strains took her to a quiet place in her mind.

The food and music had remarkable restorative powers. Diane felt much better after lunch. She went back to the lab, put on her white coat and resumed working on Caver Doe. She picked up each rib, examined and felt along the shaft for any nicks that might have been caused by a weapon. She gently squeezed the ends of the ribs toward each other to check for fractures. Nothing. Tomorrow she would put them under the dissecting microscope and examine them again. Ribs were one of the best places to look for marks left by weapons. Gunshots and knives to the torso could hardly miss them.

Diane gave the vertebrae a quick look. Most were in good condition, what she expected for a young person. Two of the lumbar vertebrae showed minute signs of a compression fracture, probably from the fall. He would not have been paralyzed, but his back would have hurt like hell. His right tibia was broken, and his right calcaneus – his heel bone – and talus – ankle bone – had compression fractures. He had no fractures on the left side of his body. She checked his arm bones and hands. His right side navicular, one of the carpal bones of the hand, was crushed. The end of his radius where it articulated with the navicular was also fractured with forward displacement – a Smith's fracture.

Judging by the bones, it looked like he'd fallen, landed on his feet, favoring his right side, then fell backward, catching himself with his hands, again favoring his right side and fracturing his wrist. When he sat in the cavern in pain, Diane wondered if he pondered the foolishness of caving alone. Or did he sit waiting in the darkness, expecting help to arrive?

Or was he with someone? Did his caving partner have some accident on the way to get help, or was Caver Doe deliberately left there to die, with all traces of his partner wiped away, leaving only a lost button behind? Or had Diane imagined the faint lines in the silt? Maybe, but she hadn't imagined the button.

Her pain came creeping back, so she decided to pack it in and go home early. It was only six o'clock and she was exhausted. She'd just locked the door of her lab when her cell phone rang. She looked at the display.

'Hey, Frank.' Diane walked down the hallway from her lab leading to the dinosaur overlook.

'Diane, why didn't you tell me you'd been stabbed too? I had to hear it from my partner.' The annoyance in Frank's voice was clear, even over the cell phone.

'How did he know?'

'He heard it from the Rosewood police. Don't change the subject.'

No secrets around the police department, thought Diane. She had forgotten that Frank said his partner was working with a detective here. 'I didn't want you to worry,' she said. 'It's not serious.'

'I heard that you had several stitches.'

'Yes, but I was treated and released.'

'What am I going to do with you?' His voice was softer, more concerned.

Diane smiled into the phone. 'What did you have in mind?'

'Don't change the subject.' He paused. 'It'll be late when I get home. I'll come over.'

'That's why I didn't tell you. It's over an hour's drive. Stay in Atlanta.'

'I'll see how things shake out here.' There was a pause, but she could hear him breathing. 'Are you all right?'

'Yes. Frank, you know that because they didn't know where the knife had been, I had to have blood tests – you know, for hepatitis and other stuff . . .'

'When I heard what happened, I assumed you would. A couple of years ago I got bitten by a man I was arresting.' He laughed. 'You wouldn't think white-collar perps would do that kind of thing. He was HIV-positive and I had to go through those tests. Don't worry. We'll get through it fine. It's just a precaution.'

Diane stood on the third-floor overlook to the dinosaur room, trying to think of something to say to Frank that would put his mind at ease and at the same time attempting not to tear up over his kindness. 'I was just leaving work, on my way home.' The words sounded choked.

As she spoke, she looked across at the hallway connecting to the opposite overlook. Dr Annette Lymon had just rounded the corner facing Diane and went into the staff lounge. She usually worked for an oil company in the summers, so Diane was surprised to see her. But it was nearing the start of fall term at Bartram, so perhaps she had just gotten back. In any case, Diane was surprised to see her in the museum.

'Try not to worry,' he said. 'I'll see you tonight – it may be late. Call me when you get home.'

'I will.'

Diane slipped her cell back in her pocket, walked around the overlook and headed down the hallway to the lounge. By the time she reached the doorway, she'd rearranged her face into a welcoming smile that she hoped didn't look as fake as it felt. She didn't want to alert Lymon that she was under investigation, but she did want to stop the rumor that Mike had abused his former girlfriend.

Annette Lymon was standing in front of the candy vending machines, rattling one of the knobs. She raked her hands through her auburn hair to get it out of her face. She was a lean woman with toned muscles and a tan from spending time outdoors. She appeared to Diane to be in her forties, but Diane found the older she got, the harder it was to estimate age – at least in a living person. Dr Lymon wore a white shirt with the sleeves rolled up to her elbows, and brown trousers. To Diane she looked vaguely as if she might have been going horseback riding.

'Dr Lymon,' said Diane. 'I'm glad I saw you.'

Annette Lymon looked at her and frowned, then smiled thinly, smoothing out the lines around her lips. 'Yes, I needed to speak with you too. But, please, what did you want?'

The woman looked haggard, her face drawn. She smelled of cigarette smoke. Diane hoped she had been doing her smoking outside. Probably so, because if the collection manager had ever caught her smoking in the museum, she'd definitely have told Diane about it.

'Neva, one of my crime scene specialists, came to me with a disturbing story you told her about Mike.' Diane paused and watched Dr Lymon's lips turn up in what looked like gratification.

'I was concerned about her welfare.'

'And I wanted to thank you for your concern and put your mind at ease.'

'Oh?'

Diane measured her words carefully. 'I have personal knowledge of the circumstances of his last girlfriend. Mike was not abusing her. I know for certain who was. Mike tried to help her; so did I.'

Annette Lymon's lips turned down again. She gave the knob on the machine another jerk and a candy bar dropped into the tray.

'I thought it was important for you to know that,' finished Diane.

Lymon grabbed up her candy. 'Did you? Well, I'm glad. I hated to think that of him.'

'You needn't. Mike is a fine young man.'

'I had to terminate his assistantship.'

'Is that so?' said Diane. It was an effort making sure anger didn't show on her face. Even so, her own words sounded harsh to her ears. Dr Lymon didn't seem to notice, for she went on talking without missing a beat.

'He just doesn't work as hard as he should, and there are others who really need the assistantship who will do the work.'

'I'm surprised to hear that. I've heard nothing but good things about Mike from the geology collection manager.'

'She's female, isn't she? Females tend to like Mike.' Dr Lymon eyed Diane up and down.

Please, you can be more subtle than that, thought Diane as she smiled grimly at her. 'Everyone likes Mike. Males and females. I've gotten reports of his work not only from the collection manager, but from the exhibit planners and other staff as well. I pretty much know who in the museum works and who doesn't. His work on the Journey to the Center of the Earth exhibit has been exemplary.'

'But that's just play, isn't it? It's not real geology, and that's his problem.'

'It's instructional work and research, the kind of work we do here. However, we don't need to argue the merits of research versus fieldwork. You wanted to see me about something?'

Dr Lymon glared at Diane a moment before she spoke.

'Yes. I've been appointed head of the Geology Department.'

'Congratulations.' Diane's smile was getting harder to maintain.

'I'm going to be making some changes. This . . .' She made a broad gesture with her arm. 'This relationship the department has with the museum isn't working out for us as well as it has for you, I'm afraid, so I'm cutting it out of next year's budget.'

'I'm sorry to hear that.'

'The extra lab space is nice, of course, but splitting my time between two labs just makes more work. And the office space is terribly small. I'm sorry to inconvenience you, but it's the best thing for the Geology Department.'

'I understand completely. It's not an inconvenience for us.'

'I didn't want to leave on bad terms.'

Throughout the conversation, Diane tried to gauge whether Annette Lymon was the type of person to knife someone. It struck her as odd that not once during the conversation did she mention Mike's being in the hospital. Maybe she didn't know, but the news was all over the museum.

It was a good place to end the conversation; there were suddenly several voices in the hallway, and it looked like they were about to have company.

'We almost had him the other day.'

Diane recognized the voice of Spence Mitchell, the herpetologist. He rounded the corner with Jonas Briggs, the archaeologist, and Sylvia Mercer, the zoologist, and came face-to-face with Diane. He stopped abruptly and smiled weakly, rubbing a nervous hand over his bald head. Diane knew he dreaded seeing her.

'I was just telling Dr Mercer and Dr Briggs that we almost had our snake.'

Against Diane's better judgment, she had allowed the herpetologist to put in a live exhibit when the museum opened last year. Unfortunately, one of the live exhibits, a black snake, *Elaphe obsoleta*, had escaped and taken up residence in the museum walls and cabinets, showing himself at inopportune times.

'Almost?' said Diane.

He shrugged as if to say, *Almost is as close as we've gotten so far.*

'What I don't understand,' said Diane, 'is why he doesn't go outside.'

'Well, uh, I'm not sure.' He smiled brightly. 'But I'll bet we don't have any rodents in the museum.'

'Small compensation.' As Diane spoke to the herpetologist she noticed Dr Sylvia Mercer eyeing Dr Lymon, who had just grabbed a Coke from another machine and was now hurrying out of the lounge.

The herpetologist nodded at Diane and backed away toward the candy machine, followed by Jonas, who was laughing. Sylvia Mercer stopped in front of Diane.

'I need to speak with you. I should have sooner. Can we talk somewhere?'

CHAPTER 16

Diane led Sylvia Mercer to her osteology lab office. Sylvia flexed her hands, rubbed them together and sat down in the stuffed burgundy chair.

'I haven't seen this office.' Her gaze traveled around the sparsely decorated room, finally resting on the watercolor of a gray wolf. '*Canis lupus,*' she said in almost a whisper, as if she were practicing her memory of taxonomy. 'That's a very nice watercolor.'

'Thank you,' said Diane. 'It was painted by a friend.'

Sylvia was a zoologist from Bartram University and one of the part-time curators. She was a slender woman, athletic and energetic, though this evening all her energy seemed to be of the nervous kind. She was wearing her lab work clothes – jeans and a T-shirt – and had her midlength brown hair tied back in a ponytail. Since she'd helped Diane solve the murder of Frank's friends by helping excavate and identify a mass grave of animal bones, she and Diane had become friends of sorts.

'You wanted to talk to me about something?' Diane said.

She hoped she hadn't sounded curt, but she was tired and her damned cut was hurting again.

If Sylvia noticed her abruptness she didn't let on. She seemed to be searching the room for something to talk about. There was nothing else for her eyes to rest on but the gray wolf, and Diane thought she was going to mention it again, perhaps tell her something about wolves in order to avoid whatever topic had brought her here. Instead, Sylvia finally brought her gaze back to Diane.

'I'm very ashamed of what I'm about to tell you.'

'Sylvia, you've never been shy or reticent. You're acting like my herpetologist. Did you lose a snake?'

Sylvia smiled briefly, then reverted to a frown again. 'I wish it were that simple. It's something I should have come to you about when it happened.' She took a deep breath, as if about to dive into cold water. 'One evening about a month ago I was out of microscope slides. I knew Mike always keeps plenty, so I walked up to the geology lab. I arrived there just in time to see Annette grab a handful of Mike's most private parts.'

Diane arched an eyebrow.

'Poor guy, he was as stunned as I was,' said Sylvia. 'Fortunately, they didn't see me – or maybe it wasn't fortunate. She would have stopped if she had known I was there. He tried backing away, but she apparently had a good hold on him through his Dockers and he was backed up against the cabinets. He, uh, asked her to let go, but . . .' Sylvia's gaze darted around the room again. 'This is just shit; I hate this.'

'Tell me what happened.'

'Mike was quite restrained. He could have knocked her on her ass. Anyway, he asked her what the hell she was doing. She told him to not look so shocked, that this was the kind of thing guys dream about, and to come home with her and she would show him the best time he'd ever had.' Sylvia looked away for a moment and shook her head. 'Mike told her he was seeing someone. She told him she didn't want a relationship – these are her words – she just wanted a "good, hard fuck." That clearly was the last straw for Mike. He grabbed her wrist and jerked her hand away and told her that what she was doing wasn't appropriate. Man, she got angry, I mean *really* angry. I couldn't make out everything she said, but it sounded like she said he owed her.' Sylvia let out a deep breath. 'I was appalled, but I didn't report her, and I'm ashamed of that.'

Diane leaned forward with her elbows on her desk. 'Why didn't you?'

'She's got tenure and is better connected than I am. Frankly, I was scared. I rationalized that Mike was a guy and it wasn't a big deal for guys – and I felt sorry for her.'

That surprised Diane. 'Sorry for her? Why?'

'Did you know her husband? Ransford Lymon, bigwig in chemistry?'

'I've never met him.'

'He ran off with his twenty-four-year-old graduate student about three months ago. Up until then, Annette thought he was a devoted husband. It turned out he'd been planning his escape for months. Got a position at a university in California, had everything in place before he left with his nymphet and their bank account. Annette was beside herself. She canceled her work with the oil company this summer. For a month she barely left her house. I've never heard of her doing anything like this business with Mike before, and believe me, Bartram is a hotbed of gossip. I think she just wanted to stop feeling old and used up, and there was Mike and that crooked, dimpled smile of his.'

Sylvia stopped talking a moment. Diane thought she was about to get up and leave, the way her hands were perched on the arms of the chair, but instead she slumped forward, looking defeated.

'I know this is hard,' said Diane.

'Hard and embarrassing.' She shook her head. 'I had convinced myself that Annette just felt safe with Mike because she knew him so well, and that it was harmless. Then I heard she pulled his assistantship. God, the sleepless nights I had over that.'

'Why didn't you come forward then?'

'Same reason. Annette is a member of the tenure approval committee for the university. I had the support of my department, but I needed hers.'

'And now?'

'And now I have my letter of tenure. It arrived today – and there's Mike in the hospital. He's had so much bad luck in the past few months – getting shot, stabbed, sexually harassed, losing his assistantship. And with all that, he is always cheerful. I'd made up my mind to come forward even if I didn't get tenure. I'm so sorry I didn't do it sooner.'

Diane was sorry too. But she didn't say it. 'I appreciate your telling me now.'

'Maybe something can be done about his assistantship. I know it's already been awarded to someone else, but . . .'

'I think things will work out.' Diane started to ask her if she thought that Annette Lymon could have stabbed them, but stopped. She'd put David on the task, and he had his own ways of investigating. Asking questions now would only interfere.

Diane stood, and Sylvia rose with her. It was then that Sylvia noticed Diane's bandaged arm. 'Are you hurt?'

Diane rubbed her upper arm. 'Whoever stabbed Mike got me too. Apparently the knife was so sharp that neither of us noticed it at first.'

'Oh, my God. I hadn't heard. What kind of maniac is out there? It makes me afraid to walk to my car.'

'I think it was just some nut at the funeral. But you should ask one of the security guards to walk you to your car. They don't mind.'

Diane walked to the door with Sylvia and again locked her osteology lab, retracing her steps back across the overlook and past the staff lounge. At the elevator she met Jin and David getting off.

'You want me to take you home?' asked David. 'I'll drive your SUV and Jin can follow in mine.'

Diane thought for a moment. She could drive, but her arm hurt and she was tired, and it would be an opportunity to tell David about her conversation with Sylvia. 'Yes, if you wouldn't mind.'

She looked at her watch. It was just after eight. It was too late to go by the hospital to visit Mike. Too bad; she was looking forward to telling him of her decision to accept his proposal. It would have to wait until morning. On the way to her house she told David about Sylvia's confession.

'That lets Neva off the hook,' said David. 'Now that you have heard the story from another source.'

'She'll be relieved.' Diane sighed. 'Maybe this is the first time Dr Lymon has done such a thing. Maybe it was triggered by her husband leaving.'

'That's possible,' said David. 'You still want this investigation to be on the QT?'

'Yes. For now let's keep it that way.'

Diane was getting drowsy sitting in the passenger seat of a moving vehicle. If she laid her head back, she'd probably fall asleep. Her thoughts kept going to her bed at home and the crisp, clean sheets she'd put on that morning.

'Are the detectives making any headway in the

funeral stabbings?' Diane realized as she said it that she still talked about it as if she weren't one of the victims. David chuckled. She supposed it did sound funny.

'No. But I imagine it'll take a while to talk to everyone who attended the graveside service.' David pulled up to the curb in front of Diane's apartment, and Jin pulled in behind them. David looked up at the old building. 'Why don't you move and get away from your creepy neighbors?' he said.

Diane followed his gaze. 'But that means I couldn't entertain you with stories about them.' She opened the door and started to get out.

'I'll walk you to your door,' said David. He stopped abruptly and looked at Diane. 'Did your neighbors go to the funeral?'

Diane returned David's look of dawning apprehension. Her elderly neighbors' hobby was attending funerals – even funerals of strangers.

'I don't know. They must have. It was the type of funeral that would be of interest to them. You know, they like to give a running critique of funerals to anyone who will listen.'

'Maybe I'll visit them tomorrow,' said David. 'Unless you'd rather speak with them?'

'They don't really like me. They may open up more to you. But I don't know if they came to the graveside service afterward.'

'I'll find out.'

David walked Diane up the staircase to her

door. Just as she was about to put in the key, it opened. Diane was startled. David stepped in front of her.

'Hey, guys. Uncle Frank asked me to come and spend the night. I brought pizza, in case you're hungry. It's warming in the oven,' said a very familiar young voice.

'Star,' said Diane. Star, Frank's adopted daughter, stood in the middle of the room grinning happily.

'I'll leave you guys to your pizza,' said David, putting his hand over his heart and shaking his head.

'Thanks, and thank Jin for me,' Diane called after him. She stepped inside the apartment, then locked and bolted the door behind her.

'You sit down and rest,' said Star. 'I'll get the pizza.'

Diane didn't have the heart to tell her she wasn't hungry and that all she really wanted to do was go to bed. Frank had adopted Star when her parents, who were his best friends, and younger brother were murdered. The police had thought Star had killed her family, and Diane had helped clear her. Though now his daughter, she still called him Uncle Frank like she always had when her parents were alive. Diane's latest contribution to Star's upbringing was the somewhat rash offer to take her to Paris and buy her a new wardrobe if she would go to college for at least one year and make a 2.7 grade point average. Star, who

171

just a few months ago was adamantly against going to college, would be starting at Bartram in the fall.

'It was nice of you to come over,' said Diane.

'It'll be fun. Like a slumber party. We'll stay up and you can tell me all about how you got hurt. How's Mike? He's the real cute guy, isn't he?' Her dark eyes sparkled.

'We have a lot of real cute guys at the museum. But yes, I think you met him on one of your visits. He's a geologist.'

'Yeah, rocks and stuff,' Star said over her shoulder as she disappeared into the kitchen.

Diane collapsed on the couch and leaned back against the pillows, listening to Star knocking around in the kitchen.

'I started to look for some music,' Star called. 'I hope you don't mind; I just looked in the stereo cabinet, not your personal stuff. All I could find was classical. Do you have any good music?'

Diane laughed to herself. 'I'll see what I can find.' She located a CD of Ray Charles and put it on the player.

'Okay, now see, that's good.'

'I'm glad you like it. You going to take music appreciation next fall?'

'You're real funny – like I'd ever think that classical stuff was good.' Star came in carrying a dish with three pizza slices and a Dr Pepper for Diane.

'This is a gracious plenty,' said Diane, looking at the large slices, and Star laughed.

'We can eat the leftovers for breakfast. That's the best thing about pizza: You can eat it anytime, cold or hot. I hope you like pepperoni, sausage and mushrooms.' Star left, came back with her own plate, and sat down on the floor at the coffee table across from Diane.

'It is good,' said Diane after taking a few bites. 'Did you pick it up on your way over?'

'Yes. It's Calystos. My favorite.'

'You need some money?'

Star shook her head. 'You're going to be buying me a whole bunch of expensive clothes. I can spring for pizza.'

'I'm glad you're taking a positive attitude toward school.' Diane took a bite of pizza, realizing that Star's positive attitude was going to cost her plenty. She smiled to herself.

'My friend Jessica suggested that maybe we could go to Italy to get some shoes. I've been saving money. What do you think?'

'That's possible. I have a friend in England. I thought we could visit him and his family while we are across the ocean.'

'That'll be fun.' Star took a bite of her pizza and washed it down with a drink of Dr Pepper.

'Your hair looks good,' said Diane. 'New cut?'

'Jessica did it. She's pretty good, isn't she?'

Diane reached across the coffee table and put a hand on Star's dark hair. 'Nice to see it all one color for a change.'

Star giggled. Diane liked seeing her happy. Star

was still having a difficult time dealing with her feelings of guilt over her parents' death. Diane understood those dark and aching pains that kept yelling into your brain – if only you had done something different; if only you could go back and do things over. Frank said that Star still cried at night when she thought he couldn't hear. Diane understood that too. Her pillow was soaked with thousands of tears. She was lost in that thought when the telephone rang. Diane jumped.

'I'll get it,' said Star. 'Uncle Frank wants me to take care of you.'

Diane started to protest, but Star was already to the phone.

'Hello . . . Who?' Star put a hand over the mouthpiece and turned to Diane. 'Do you want to talk to a Susan Abernathy?'

Diane reached for the phone. Something heavy formed in the pit of her stomach. Her sister, Susan, almost never called her. There would have to be a dire emergency for her to phone.

'Susan?'

'Diane, I've been trying all week to reach you. Don't you answer your messages? I had no idea what the name is of that museum you work for, and I don't know your cell phone number.' Susan made it sound like Diane had been avoiding her on purpose.

'Susan, what's wrong? Has something happened to Mother or Dad?'

'Yes, something has happened,' Susan snapped.

'It's a nightmare. You have to come to Alabama tonight.'

Diane's heart was beating hard against her chest. She and her parents were all but estranged, but the thought of something happening to them filled her with fear.

'What is it, Susan?' Diane tried to sound calm.

'Mother's been sent to prison for robbing a bank.'

CHAPTER 17

Diane expected to hear that her mother or father was ill, had been in an accident, had disappeared or had died. She had not expected to hear that her mother had robbed a bank.

'Susan, is this some kind of joke? It's in very poor taste. It's late and I'm tired.'

'Diane, it's not a joke. Have you ever known me to joke? Mother's been arrested. Dad is beside himself. He's so upset he can't go in to the office. You know about this kind of thing. You'll have to come.' Her sister sounded frantic.

'I'll . . . I'll leave tomorrow,' stammered Diane.

'You have to come now.'

'I can't.'

'Why not? What's more important? Dammit, Diane, you have to get on a plane and come right now.'

'I had a medical procedure done yesterday. I can't come right now, but I'll leave as early as I can tomorrow morning. Mother's had a bail hearing, hasn't she? Are you at the house? Can I talk to her?'

'No, she's not out on bail. I already told you, she's in prison.'

'Is Dad there?'

'He went to bed early. I made him take a sleeping pill. We've both been trying to get you. Why don't you ever check your messages?'

With the funeral and the stabbings Diane had forgotten to look at her answering machine. *Damn.* 'I just got back from a two-week vacation. Why didn't you call the museum? They would have gotten in touch with me.'

'I couldn't remember the name of it.'

'You could call information and ask for the museum in Rosewood. There's only one.'

Diane heard Susan expel her breath in the exasperated way she did when they argued. It meant that she wasn't going to listen to anything Diane said on the subject.

'But that doesn't matter; I'm here now,' Diane said. 'Tell me what happened.'

'Mother didn't come home last Tuesday. We've been frantic, calling hospitals, friends, the police, everywhere we could think. We thought she'd been kidnapped. She finally phoned this morning – from federal prison! They told her she robbed a bank!'

Diane ran her fingers through her hair, and the effort brought a pain to her arm. She winced.

'Well, that's ridiculous,' Diane said. 'Why do they think it was her?'

'I don't know. We can't find out anything. The

177

police are witless and uncooperative. This is just awful.'

None of this was making sense. 'What did Mother say?'

'She's just as confused as we are.'

'What does her lawyer say?'

There was a long pause. *Surely,* thought Diane, *they have a lawyer.*

'Alan is trying to find out something,' Susan said.

'Alan? Alan who? Not Alan Delacroix?' Diane shot up off the sofa and paced back and forth.

'Yes, and don't you start anything. You know he's been friends with Mother and Dad forever. He's always been like a son to them.'

'I didn't know he was in Birmingham.'

'Yes, he is. Dad helped him get a job with a law firm down here.'

What a cozy little family, thought Diane. Her parents, her sister and her ex-husband.

'He only does wills and estates,' said Diane. Alan would be a fish out of water in criminal court.

'Alan is a good lawyer.'

Diane let it go for now. Arguing with Susan was a waste of time and energy. She sat back down on the sofa. 'I'll call tomorrow and let you know when to pick me up at the airport – you can pick me up, can't you?'

'Of course.'

'Has she been arraigned? Do you know when she goes to trial – anything?'

'She's not going to trial. They took her straight to prison. There's not any talk of a trial.' Susan sounded exasperated. 'Are you listening to me?'

'What? Susan, what country did she get arrested in?'

'Here, of course. Diane, you ask such absurd questions sometimes.'

'They can't put you in prison without a trial.'

'Alan thinks she got caught up in this Homeland Security thing.'

'Are you saying they think she's a foreign terrorist?' Diane was completely bewildered now. For the life of her she couldn't imagine anyone in their right minds thinking her sixty-five-year-old, upper-middle-class mother was a bank-robbing terrorist. She was beginning to wonder if Susan had started drinking.

As she talked to her sister, Diane watched Star eating her pizza and listening to the conversation. Her dark eyes were as large as saucers. Diane thought that must be the way she looked too.

'I'm not saying anything. I'm telling you what's happened.'

'Susan, they can't send her to prison without a trial.'

'They can. It's in that new Homeland Security act.'

'The act doesn't give those kinds of powers, Susan.'

'Oh, so you know what it says.'

'I know about anything that concerns human rights. I still keep up with the law in that area.'

'You always think you are so smart. Well, you're not. I'm telling you what has been going on with Mother and you're over there smugly saying it didn't happen, but it did.'

Diane felt her face getting hot and her jaw aching as she clamped down on her teeth. 'Dammit, Susan,' she yelled into the phone. 'Listen to yourself. Nothing you've said so far has made any sense. That's why I'm skeptical.'

Star's eyes got really wide as she stared at Diane.

'Alan says there are several ways they can put you in prison without a trial. He believes they are holding her as a material witness to a bank robbery that the government thinks was done by terrorists.'

Diane shook her head, though Susan couldn't see it. 'That doesn't track.'

'"That doesn't track"? What does that mean? Just because Alan thought of it? It's the only thing I've heard that makes any sense.'

Diane pinched the bridge of her nose, glad she hadn't taken any Percocet or she'd probably wake up in the morning thinking she had dreamed the whole thing. 'I'll make sense of it when I get there.'

'God, that is so typical of you. You think you are the only one in the family with any brains and we have to wait for you to tell us what's going on.

Just because you couldn't stay married to Alan, you think everything he says is wrong. Well, Gerald agrees with him; so does Dad.'

'It's not a matter for a majority vote; it's a matter of facts. And we don't have all the facts.'

'I hate it when you get like this. Let me know when to pick you up.'

'I will. Before you hang up, do you know where Mother is being held?'

'In Montgomery. Tombsberg Prison for Women.'

Diane's heart froze. Tombsberg was one of the most overcrowded facilities and had the most deplorable conditions of any prison in the country.

'I'll be in Birmingham tomorrow as early as I can.'

'Wow,' said Star when Diane hung up the phone. 'I've never heard you yell at anybody.'

'Unfortunately, that's the way my sister and I usually interact.'

'I'm glad I don't have . . .' Star didn't finish, and her happy face suddenly collapsed into grief. 'I didn't mean that.' Large tears welled up in her eyes.

Diane knelt beside Star and hugged her. 'It's all right, Star. I know what you meant. You can still love and miss your brother without grieving forever.'

Star sobbed for a moment and then pulled away. 'I sometimes forget and then I feel guilty. Jay was good. I was the one doing bad things, and he's the one who got killed.'

Diane smoothed Star's hair and put a hand under her chin. 'It wasn't your fault.'

'It feels like it is.'

'I know that feeling. I feel the same way about my daughter . . . if I had just gotten her out of the country.'

Star wiped her eyes with the heel of her hand. 'I'm sorry about her. Uncle Frank said she liked music.'

'She did like music.' Diane's eyes teared. Frank must have told Star about the special CD of her favorite music Diane had made for her. Diane rubbed her eyes with her fingertips. All she needed was for the two of them to sit there crying.

'Tell me about your sister. Is she older or younger than you?' Star asked quickly.

'Older.'

'You're a little sister? You don't seem like a little sister.'

'Well, I am. By three years.'

'Sounds like the two of you don't get along.'

'We don't.' Diane walked back around to the couch, sat down and took another bite of her pizza. It was cold.

'Did you fight when you were kids?'

'Yep. She and her friends were always tormenting me. But I was faster, stronger and smarter than they were. Susan liked to get into trouble and blame it on me. It worked for a while.'

'What?'

182

'I started collecting evidence. Jeez – I'd forgotten about that.'

'What did you do?'

'I think I was eight; Susan was eleven. She and her friends were getting into Mother's makeup and jewelry, as usual. She told Mother that I was the one who spilled powder all over her dresser and dented up her lipsticks. What she didn't know was that time I'd gotten my dad's brand-new camcorder, hid in his closet, and filmed them. When Susan blamed me for the mess she and her friends had made, I popped the cassette in the VCR.' Diane laughed. 'You should have seen her face.'

'So they punished her instead if you,' said Star.

'Yes, they did punish her for lying. But they made an appointment for me to see a child psychologist.'

'You? Why you?'

'What I did scared them for some reason. The psychologist told them I was simply bright and inventive and that they shouldn't worry.'

'That was good. So you became a crime fighter early. I'll bet you that stopped your sister dead in her tracks.'

'It slowed her down, and my parents didn't automatically believe her like they did before. But they didn't really trust me either after that. Taping her just offended their sensibilities.'

'So it wasn't too good for you growing up?'

'It wasn't bad. I spent a lot of time at my

grandparents'. I was my granddad's fishing buddy. He's the one who took me to my first caves.'

Diane was surprised how easy it was to talk to Star about her family. Maybe because Star seemed to find comfort in the fact that Diane had similar problems communicating with her parents as Star had when hers were alive.

'Where did you grow up? Uncle Frank said you were from here in Rosewood to start with.'

'Yes. We moved to Tennessee when I was about twelve. They didn't move to Birmingham until after I was in college.'

Star sipped her drink and started another slice of pizza. She didn't take her eyes off Diane as she fired questions at her. 'What does your dad do?'

'He's a stockbroker.'

'Is he rich?'

'Probably. They live in a wealthy section of Birmingham.'

'They sound nice. Uncle Frank's family's real nice, too. We went out to visit them at Christmas. It was fun.'

'I've met them. They are nice.'

'When you lived in Rosewood, did you know Uncle Frank?'

'No. I'm sure we were in the same elementary school, but I didn't know him.'

'So are you and Uncle Frank going to get married? I'd be your daughter then.'

Diane got up and collected her leftovers. 'It feels like you're my daughter now.'

The ring of Star's laughter followed her into the kitchen. 'You aren't going to answer me, are you?' she said.

'Nope.' Diane came back to the living room. 'I'm going to head to bed now. Do you mind?'

Star shook her head. 'No. Uncle Frank said you'd probably turn in early.'

'You can watch TV if you like. Just don't stay up all night.' Diane started to get some bedclothes for the sofa, when she spotted them on a dining room chair.

Star followed her gaze. 'I hope you don't mind. I got them out before you got here.'

'That's fine. The sofa makes a bed. I'll help you pull it out.'

'I'd rather sleep on it like it is.'

'Okay. Don't stay up late.'

Diane called David and told him she had to go out of town on a family emergency and that he was in charge of the crime lab. When she hung up, she called Kendel and told her she would be gone a couple of days and to go ahead with setting up the position for Mike. With that finished, she took a shower, making an effort not to get her bandage wet – no easy task – and it took her three times as long. She selected a thin nightgown. Even at its end, the summer was still hotter than usual for North Georgia. Just as she slipped the gown over her head and was about to climb into bed, Frank's characteristic knock sounded at the front door; then she heard his key in the lock.

'Anybody home?'

'Uncle Frank, you're back.'

Diane put on a robe and walked to the living room. 'I didn't expect you, but I'm glad you're here.'

Frank was putting an overnight bag on a chair. 'I made an effort to wrap things up as soon as I could. How's it going? Star made you crazy yet?' He winked at Star, who made a face at him.

'She's good company.'

'We've had a really interesting time,' said Star. 'Diane's sister called. Her mother's been arrested for armed bank robbery.'

Frank stood holding his shaving kit under his arm, staring from Diane to Star, as if waiting for Diane to contradict her absurd statement.

'I know,' said Diane. 'That's how I was when Susan told me. I don't understand it.'

'Armed robbery? Your mother?'

'As unlikely as that sounds, she's apparently in prison,' she said, smoothing back her still-damp hair. 'I'm glad you're here. Maybe you can make some sense out of what Susan was trying to tell me.'

The dining table sat in a corner just outside Diane's efficiency kitchen. Frank pulled out a chair and sat down. Diane sat opposite him. Star heated Frank several slices of the pizza, then joined them at the table, propping her chin up on her hands, apparently content to listen quietly.

The whole conversation between her and her

sister didn't take long to relate. When Diane finished, Frank sat silently eating his pizza and washing it down with Dr Pepper. He set down his glass.

'There's another reason they would take her to prison without a trial or bail,' he said.

CHAPTER 18

'What reason? How could they legally put her in prison without a trial?' Diane asked.

'If they thought she already had one.'

'Why would they think that?' she asked as she rubbed her upper arm, hoping to knead the ache out of it.

'A couple of possible reasons. One could be that somebody stole her identity. Someone got her Social Security number, and when they were arrested, instead of giving their own name and number, they gave your mother's.'

'But wouldn't something come out in a trial? People would recognize her.' Diane was having a hard time wrapping her brain around this whole situation. Nothing made sense.

'The real perp could have pled out – no trial, no witnesses called – then escaped,' said Frank. 'She wouldn't have to worry about being caught, because the outstanding warrant would be for your mother.'

'But what about fingerprints?'

'When they picked up your mother they

wouldn't necessarily have a reason to check her prints. She probably confirmed her name and Social Security number. So with the right name and Social Security number, maybe the approximate age and appearance, she goes back to prison.' Frank took another bite of pizza.

'But the prison personnel would recognize that it wasn't her – the guards would know, wouldn't they?'

'Depends on how long since the real perp escaped and the circumstances of the escape. They may never have seen her. What prison is she in?'

Diane hated to say the word. 'Tombsberg.'

'Damn. That's a bad place. It's so overcrowded they may not have noticed the difference in appearance. The real perp may have picked your mother because she had a passing similarity and that was enough to fool the guards.'

'This makes much more sense than what Alan came up with.'

'Alan? Would that be the ex-husband Alan?'

'That would be him,' said Diane.

'You were married before?' said Star. 'Really? Why did you divorce him?'

'Not now, Star,' said Frank.

'But—'

'You said there are a couple of ways they could hold her without a trial,' said Diane.

'Someone could have hacked into the Justice Department computer files and changed the name and Social Security number of someone already in the system, or could have made up a record and slipped it into the database, so when the police did a warrant check, there was your mother's name.'

'Who could do that – and how?' asked Diane. 'Aren't government files hackproof?'

Frank smiled and took another bite of pizza. 'Nothing's hackproof for a determined hacker. However, the easiest way is to pay off someone on the inside who has legitimate access to the computer files. As to why . . .' Frank shrugged. 'Aren't your parents well-off; doesn't your dad work in high finance – stockbroker or something? Perhaps the motive lies there.'

'How do I get her out?'

'Your parents are in Birmingham, right?'

'Yes.'

Frank stroked his chin a moment. 'There's this criminal lawyer – Daniel Reynolds. He's expensive, but he earns his money. Get an appointment with him right away. He'll make them look at the fingerprints. You find out which bank she was supposed to have robbed, the date, and if it was actually robbed. I'd go with you, but I can't get any more time off. I can take you to the airport in the morning, though.'

Diane laid a hand on his arm and squeezed. 'Thanks, Frank. I really appreciate all this.'

'It's what I do.' He slid his arm from under her hand and grabbed hold of it. He looked around and saw the couch made up with bedsheets and a pillow. 'Guess we had all better get some sleep. I'll take the couch and you and Star can have the bed.'

'No,' said Star. 'I have dibs on the sofa. It's not like I don't know you two probably sleep together – occasionally. I can handle it. I'll be in college this fall. What you think we'll do when we go to Paris, all get separate rooms?'

'So,' said Frank, 'you are planning on making the grade.' He winked at Diane.

'Of course. I can do it. I plan on being the best-dressed person in Rosewood. Now what's this about an ex-husband?'

Before Diane left for the airport, she and Frank stopped by the hospital to see Mike. The third-floor hallway wasn't crowded. An orderly pushed a breakfast cart with squeaky wheels down the hall. A young girl with a pained expression on her face was walking down the hall looking at the floor, her IV in tow. Monitors beeped and chirped at the nurses' station. Diane didn't like hospitals, and she'd been in this one a lot in the past year.

She and Frank met Neva coming out of a doorway labeled VENDING MACHINES carrying a soft drink and a can of juice. Her dark strawberry-blond hair, down from its usual casual twist, hung just below her shoulders. She had deep circles under her eyes.

'Hi, Neva. You've met Frank.'

Neva nodded. 'Yes. At the opening of the Egyptian exhibit. Hi.'

'How are you and Mike doing?'

'I'm fine. Mike's already itching to get out of here. Considering he's just healed up from that gunshot wound, he's really doing great. Some of the nurses remembered him.' Neva gave a half-hearted laugh. 'I'm having a hard time convincing them that he's really the kind of person who avoids violence.'

Neva started to lead them to Mike's room, but Diane pulled her aside and leaned close to her ear. His room was just a door away, and she didn't want to chance her voice carrying into his room.

'You're off the hook. Sylvia Mercer witnessed the episode and voluntarily told me about it last evening at the museum.'

Neva's eyes grew wide. 'Really? She saw it?'

'Yes. And heard it.'

She took a deep breath. She looked as if she had been holding it since she first spoke with Diane. 'You don't know how relieved I am.'

'I'll have to talk to Mike about it. I just wanted you to know first.'

Neva nodded and they all walked into his room. He was sitting up in bed reading a copy of the *Journal of Geomicrobiology*.

'You look good,' said Diane. The color was back in his face, but the sight of him in a hospital bed was incongruous, despite the fact that this wasn't the first time she'd seen him wounded and laid up. Mike was meant to be active. He had chosen a profession that by its very nature required activity. Even his hobbies were physical.

'I feel great. I'm planning to bust out of here soon.' He paused, looking behind her. 'Hi, Frank.'

Frank grinned at him. 'Hi. Sorry to hear about your attack.'

'Lots of nuts out there, and they seem to be able to find me real easily – Doc here, too.' He turned his head back to Diane and motioned toward her arm with a question on his face.

'Sore,' she said in response.

'I'll bet. You don't know how much you use that tricep muscle until it's all stove up,' Mike said.

Diane curled her arm up and back as if lifting a weight. 'It'll be a while before either of us can go caving.'

'Damn, don't I know it,' said Mike. 'I was looking forward to following that water sound.'

Diane looked at the flowers that lined his room, walked over and smelled one of the roses. 'You have lots of admirers.'

He laughed. 'Looks like it, doesn't it? Lots of them are from people at the museum. That huge vase full over there is from Dr Mercer. That was nice. I hardly know her.'

Diane sighed heavily, and then went over to his bed so she could see his face. 'When the doctor gives you the okay, you can report to work at the museum.'

It took a fraction of a second for Mike to catch on, but when he did, his face broke into a wide smile. 'You accepted my proposal.' He turned to Frank. 'Work proposal.'

Frank chuckled. 'I gathered.'

'It's part-time,' said Diane. She handed him an envelope. 'This is your salary. It's the best I can do. I hope it's acceptable.'

Mike tore open the envelope and looked at the slip of paper. Diane watched his mouth spread into a broad grin. 'This is great. Look, thanks. Really. I appreciate this.'

'You are now the new curator of the geology exhibit.'

His mouth dropped. 'Curator? But Dr Lymon—'

'Dr Lymon was made head of the Geology Department at Bartram.' Mike frowned. 'She severed the relationship between the Geology Department and the museum. She said it wasn't working for them. That left me with an opening for a curator. Fortunately, you had that great proposal. Kendel really liked your ideas,' she added.

'I don't know what to say. Thanks for trusting me with the responsibility. I wasn't expecting this.'

'According to the collection manager, you've been doing all the work.'

'Wow – curator.'

Diane paused. 'There's something else I need to talk to you about.' She turned to Neva and Frank.

194

'Do you two mind letting me speak with Mike alone?'

Mike face wore a puzzled expression as he watched Frank and Neva dutifully file out of the room.

'Dr Sylvia Mercer came to me last night and told me a disturbing story of something she witnessed.'

Mike glanced over at the vase of flowers and back at Diane. 'Dr Mercer?'

'Yes. This is likely to be very uncomfortable for you, and I'm sorry, but it happened in my museum and I have to deal with it.'

Mike looked startled, almost as if he were about to be fired just after he had been hired. 'What?' he asked.

Diane related almost verbatim the story that Dr Mercer had told her. She stopped and stared at Mike, waiting for him to respond.

Mike was quiet for a moment. 'Well, that explains the big bouquet of flowers and the card saying she was sorry.'

'She was very sorry. Like I said, she was ashamed to tell me.'

Mike shook his head. 'She needn't feel bad.'

'Why didn't you tell me?'

'It was between me and Dr Lymon. That wasn't why you decided to hire me, was it?' He looked down at the envelope as if it weren't a prize after all.

Diane shook her head. 'You should know me

195

better than that. I made the decision before I talked with Sylvia. I can afford to hire a groundskeeper for a favor, but I have to have curators who are qualified.' She gestured toward the paper and winced when the back of her arm stung from the quick movement. 'Everyone you've worked with has given you glowing recommendations. I know your work. The Journey to the Center of the Earth exhibit is terrific. I passed your proposal by my assistant director and she's enthusiastic. No, Mike, you earned the position. I only wish it could be full-time.'

His frown turned to a grin. 'This will work out better. I'll have time to work on my dissertation.'

'Good. Okay, now, David will probably come to interview you.'

Mike rearranged himself in his bed, as if to get more comfortable. 'David? Your crime scene guy? About the stabbing? I thought the police were handling that.'

'They are. This is a discreet investigation that I hope can stay that way. But it has to be done. You understand that upon hearing about Dr Lymon's actions, I had to put her on the list of suspects.'

'Dr Lymon?'

'She has motive – at least in your case.'

Mike was quiet for several moments, looking out the window. 'Perhaps in yours too,' he said, looking back at her.

'What do you mean?'

'Something she said to me after the . . .' He paused, leaned his head back on the pillow and closed his eyes for just a moment. 'After the episode. She thought you and I were . . . well, you know.'

'I see.' Diane wondered if anyone else in the museum thought that she and Mike were having an affair.

'I don't know why she thought that, really. I told her she had it all wrong. That we just do caving. But . . .' He shook his head. 'I know she had a hard time when her husband left her, and she's always been kind of mean, but I really can't see her going postal on me.'

'Frankly, neither can I. That's why I hope the investigation can stay discreet. David won't go to the detectives unless he finds something.'

'You're being very nice to her.' He stretched out his hand for his water on the stand beside his bed, but it was just out of his reach. Diane handed it to him and he took a sip.

'Too nice, perhaps,' she said. 'Do you know if you're the only one she has approached in that way?'

Mike shrugged and set the water down. 'I haven't heard anything. It came as a surprise to me. I don't know what came over her. I never got a hint that she had any kind of feelings for me at all, much less sexual ones.'

Mike's room phone rang and Diane went to get Neva and Frank as he answered it.

'It's for you,' said Mike, when Diane came back in. 'It's David.'

Diane took the phone. 'David, what's up?'

'A nasty situation. Jin's on his way over to pick up Neva,' he said.

CHAPTER 19

'You have a crime scene?' asked Diane.

'Yes, we do. Unfortunately, it's Neva's house. The police couldn't get in touch with her so they called here. Jin is coming to help me process it. I want Neva to see what's missing. I'm at her house now and I'm a little concerned. It's tossed and ripped up pretty bad, and they spray-painted some pretty vile things on her walls – *"stupid fucking bitch"* – stuff like that. Her neighbor saw her door open this morning when he went out for his paper and he noticed that it was still open when he was leaving for work. He went to the door to check on her and found this.'

Diane was stunned. 'I'll give her the news. Did anyone see or hear anything?'

'No witnesses so far. The police are canvassing the neighborhood right now.'

Diane hung up and turned to Neva. 'Jin's coming to pick you up.'

'Crime scene?'

Diane nodded and took a deep breath. 'Neva, it's your house. It apparently happened last night.'

199

Neva's eyes grew wide and she looked from Mike to Diane. Mike reached out and took her hand.

'My house? What did they do?'

'David's there now. He says it's vandalized pretty bad. And . . .' Diane hesitated. 'Whoever it was spray-painted some ugly things on your walls. I just wanted to prepare you for that.'

'Why?'

'I don't know, but we'll find out. Jin and David are going to process it. David only wants you there to tell him if anything is missing.'

'But . . . can't I?'

'That's the way it has to be. They'll do a good job.'

Neva put her free hand to her face, pinching the bridge of her nose. Diane could see she was trying not to cry. Diane was thinking, *What if she had been home?*

'You can stay at my apartment tonight,' said Diane. 'I don't want you to stay in your home for now.'

'You can stay in mine,' said Mike.

Frank had been listening quietly to the exchange between Diane and her staff. 'Actually, I think you should stay at my house until yours is cleared up,' he said, surprising them all. He smiled. 'You'll like my daughter, and Diane can vouch for my character.'

Neva glanced back and forth between Diane and Frank, confusion written on her face.

'I don't want to be an alarmist,' said Frank, 'but I don't like the math. Something has happened to Mike, Diane and now you. I don't know if they are related, but if someone wants to get at you physically, he'd think to look at your boyfriend's place, and maybe at your boss's apartment, but not my house.'

Mike lifted his eyebrows and gave Frank a crooked smile.

'It makes sense,' he said – rather reluctantly, Diane thought. She couldn't help notice the amused glint in Frank's eyes at Mike's discomfort.

Neva nodded and looked at Diane. 'If you think it's best.'

At that moment Jin came in, looking his usual happy self. 'Hi, guys. How you doing, Mike?'

'I'm thinking about trying to get out of here today.'

'No,' said Neva. 'Mike, I'll be all right.'

'I know, but if you'd been at home . . .'

'But I wasn't.' She bent down and kissed him.

'We'll see she stays safe,' said Jin. He turned to Neva. 'You ready?'

She nodded and started out the door with him. She paused and looked back at Mike. 'I'll call when I know something.' Her shoulders slumped, and she appeared vulnerable and frightened.

Diane felt uneasy about having to go out of town. She wished she could trust her family to do what needed to be done. She'd like to call and tell them how to proceed, who to contact, but she feared they were completely helpless in the face of the criminal justice system.

'I have to go to Alabama, Mike. It'll be only for a couple of days, I hope. Don't worry about reporting to work until your doctor says you can. I mean it.'

Mike nodded absently. 'You know there are bullies in her neighborhood that Neva's had to pull off some of the younger kids a time or two.'

'I'll remind Neva to tell David,' said Diane. 'If you think of anything else, let David know. He's in charge of the crime lab while I'm gone. Kendel is in charge of the museum, if you have any questions. She's very happy I hired you. She's already approached the exhibit designers with your extremophile plan.'

'I can't wait to get out of here and start on it.' He smiled, but his enthusiasm was weakened. 'Frank, take care of my girl.'

'I'll take good care of both of them.' Frank gave Mike one of what Diane called his prankish smiles.

'That's funny,' said Mike.

'Seriously. Neva'll be safe.' Frank fished a card and a pen from his pocket. 'I'm writing my home phone and my cell phone on my card. If you need anything, give me a call.'

Mike took the card and looked at it and then back up at Frank. 'Thanks.'

'You're welcome. Do what the doctors tell you. I know it's frustrating, believe me. But you're no good to anybody if you don't take care of yourself first.'

Diane took Mike's hand and squeezed it. His hands were rough from the heavy calluses he had developed rock climbing, and even ill he had a strong grip.

'Listen to Frank,' she said. 'I expect a lot of work from you when you recover.'

He smiled, but his eyes still looked worried. Diane left feeling sorry for him.

'He'll be all right,' said Frank as they reached the elevator.

'I know. It's just that . . . that I'm beginning to feel like some kind of bad-luck charm to everyone around me.'

The elevator doors opened and they stepped in. Frank put an arm around Diane's shoulders and pulled her to him. 'I know, but that's not how it is. If Mike thought you were such bad luck, he wouldn't still be interested in you.'

'He isn't, really. It's become sort of a game.'

'Oh, he's interested.'

'You enjoyed yourself inviting Neva to stay at your house, didn't you?'

'I am genuinely concerned about her.' Frank grinned. 'Playing with Mike's head was just a bonus.'

They walked out to the parking lot. As Frank started the engine and put his car in gear, Diane laid a hand on his arm. 'Do we have time to run by Neva's? It's on the way.'

'Sure. What's her address?'

Neva lived on a dead-end street in a neighborhood that was a combination of blue-collar and student housing. Two police cars were parked in front of her white frame house. Across the street a small crowd had formed. Half of them looked like students. Diane got out of the car and scanned the faces. A young woman, stout and squarely built, dressed in cutoffs and a tank top, yelled from the crowd.

'My house was robbed and I can't get the police to even come and take my statement. One of their own gets robbed and you'd think it was the president's house.'

Diane heard a couple of people shout their approval and someone else tell her to shut the fuck up. Frank and Diane ignored them and walked up to the porch.

'Neva,' she called.

Neva came to the door. 'They've done the porch and front entry. David's processed a walkway though the house. You can come in.'

Diane had been in Neva's house several times, picking her up to go caving. Neva liked to call her decor 'early attic.' Her furniture was a combination of hand-me-downs from her parents and inexpensive furniture from Wal-Mart and secondhand stores. Nonetheless, it had a style to it. Neva had an artist's eye for decorating. It shocked Diane to see it now.

The sofa and stuffed chairs were slashed and the filling pulled out. Everything had been sprayed

204

with a swath of black paint. All the chairs were overturned. On the wall over her sofa the words *stupid fucking bitch* were painted in red and black paint. The sentiment was repeated in the bedroom, where her mattress and pillows were also slashed.

'They did a number, didn't they?' said Neva, surveying the ruins of her home. 'Whoever it was spray-painted my clothes in the closets and drawers. I must have really pissed somebody off.' She blew her nose with a Kleenex and dried her eyes with another.

The glass shelves that used to stand against the wall were shattered. Among the shards of glass, Neva's collection of polymer clay animals that she sculpted were lying in fragments.

David came in from the kitchen and stood beside her. 'Notice anything funny about the glass shelves?'

Diane knelt and looked at the broken glass. Frank stared over her shoulder. She glanced at the overturned frame that once held the shelves and back at the pattern of broken shards.

'Whoever it was took the shelves apart, laid them on the floor, and stepped on them.'

David nodded. 'That's what it looks like. The police can't find anyone who heard anything. From the look of the place, you'd think all her neighbors were stone-deaf. But if you look closer at everything he or she did, you'll see that the perp was quiet, deliberately going from room to room breaking things without making much noise.'

A chill went up Diane's spine.

The ride to the airport was unexpectedly calming. Diane hated Atlanta traffic, even as a passenger. It was either moving really fast en masse, or at a dead standstill waiting for a wreck to be cleared. It was fast and crowded today, but sitting talking to Frank in the confines of his car was a comfort.

'It will probably be easier than you think to get this mess with your mother sorted out,' said Frank. 'I'll do what I can from this end. I have some contacts in Alabama, and I'll ask them to take a look at their files.'

'I really do appreciate this, Frank. I'm glad you know about this kind of stuff.'

He reached over and squeezed her hand. 'Me too,' he said.

Diane watched the landscape passing by for a moment – the houses, apartments, businesses, all the places where people clustered – all the places where they hurt each other.

'You know, sometimes I think about getting out of the crime business again. I get so tired seeing the work of evil people, but lately it's like . . .' She paused again, looking at the distant horizon. 'Like it wouldn't do any good. The evil's spilled over into my life – following me to funerals, following my family. There are just too many criminals in the world.'

'I know what you mean,' Frank said. 'Most of the people I deal with are just greedy, but they have no conscience whatsoever about screwing up someone's life, stealing money from people who need it the most. And even when I catch the bad guys, I usually can't restore what's been taken. I had a case of identity theft not long ago. Caught the guy, but the victim killed himself because he thought everything he had was gone. The tragedy was, I got back his money, just not soon enough. It turned out the same guy had scammed him before.' Frank shook his head. 'The perp's attitude was that the guy was just too stupid to learn and was better off dead. I would like to have arrested the guy for murder.'

'At least you could put him in jail for a while.'

'We have a good ADA. In the past, juries have wanted to let white-collar criminals off – they can always afford good lawyers. But this ADA's really good at making the jury walk in the victim's shoes. They end up feeling like if they let him go, their life savings are next.' Frank put his hand on the back of Diane's neck. 'How's the arm feel?'

'Sore as hell.'

Frank had helped her change the bandage the evening before. It was healing well, but still red and sore-looking. She hated the perp every time she moved her arm.

'You know,' she said, 'all in all, despite the crime, I like my life. I love the museum, the people who work for me; I like solving puzzles. I'm really enjoying working on Caver Doe's bones.'

'Yeah, I like the museum too – I even think Mike's a good guy.'

Diane laughed. 'You know, he's always been appropriate with me.'

'I don't doubt it, but there is nothing like that secret love for an unattainable woman.'

'You sound like you speak from experience.' Diane looked over at Frank and could see his smile spread across his face.

'When I was nineteen, home from college for the summer, this couple moved in next door. She was just the most beautiful woman I had ever seen – long black hair, green eyes, long legs. It was love at first sight. The hardest part was keeping my brothers from finding out how I felt. I'd never have heard the end of it.'

Frank turned the car onto the road leading to the airport terminal. 'I can't even remember what the husband looked like, but I remember her. I mowed their lawn, did chores, anything, just to catch a glimpse of her. It was a wonderful summer.' He drove up to the dropoff area. 'I have to let you out and go to work. I hope that's all right.'

'I'll be fine.' She leaned over and gave him a kiss. 'So unattainable women inspire desire in young males. Is that what you are saying?'

'More or less.'

Diane started to get out of the car. Suddenly she turned back to Frank. 'She didn't remain unattainable, did she?'

Frank didn't say anything. He only gave her an amused smile that made his eyes glitter.

'I've got to hear about this when I get back.'

'Have a good trip. Give me a call this evening.'

Diane retrieved her bag from the backseat and headed inside the Atlanta airport. She dreaded this trip.

CHAPTER 20

Had she been feeling better and had more time, Diane would have driven the five hours from Rosewood to Birmingham. But she didn't have the time, nor could she face the traffic through Atlanta or driving for that many hours.

The flight was not a lot better. It was short, but turbulent. The five-year-old sitting behind her kicked her seat the whole way. She turned around once to say something to the mother, but saw that she was young, alone and barely holding herself together. Diane smiled at her and said nothing. By the time the plane set down at the Birmingham airport, Diane was nauseated.

From the air, downtown Birmingham reminded Diane of one of those 1950s photographs of any steel-mill city, though the furnaces were gone now, along with all the enterprises connected with them. Everything about Birmingham was downsized and laid-back compared to Atlanta. The airport was postage stamp-size compared to the Atlanta airport, and not nearly as hectic. Diane had heard it said in Georgia that Birmingham was 120 miles and fifty years away from Atlanta. Alabamians said that the road to hell ran through Atlanta. Truth on both sides, she thought. For her personally, it was like a trip back in time.

She collected her bag from the overhead compartment and walked with the other passengers down the long passageway past security to where she hoped to see Susan waiting for her. She searched the crowd for her face.

'Diane. Over here.'

Susan stood in back of the waiting crowd, waving her arm. She looked just as Diane remembered her – conservative tailored dress, shoulder-length brown hair parted on the side with the ends turned under. A contrast in every way to Diane's slacks, blazer and short-cut hair.

Diane walked around the escalators taking passengers to the luggage pickup and over to her sister. The hug was perfunctory, their cheeks barely touching. Diane felt awkward. She wondered if Susan dreaded the arguments that would come as much as she did.

'Susan, I hope you didn't have to wait long. We were late taking off.'

'No. I had to be here anyway to bring the kids to the airport. We sent them to stay with Gerald's sister until this is cleared up.'

Diane was disappointed. 'I'm sorry I missed them.'

Susan's mouth stretched into what she probably thought was a smile. 'They wanted to see you too. Especially Kayla. She'll be starting college next fall.' Susan fished an envelope from her purse. 'She wrote you a letter and wanted me to give it to you. She was hoping maybe next summer to get a job at the museum.'

Diane smiled, glad to have something she could offer, glad her niece wanted to work at the museum. 'Sure. There are several jobs she'd like. Is she wanting a museum career?'

'No, she wants to be an archaeologist. Gerald and I are trying to talk her into something more useful, but kids can be so impractical.' Susan turned toward the escalators. 'Baggage claim is downstairs.'

'I have everything in here,' Diane said, holding up her duffel bag.

'Is that all? We need you to stay awhile and help us with this.'

Susan continued talking as they walked out of the airport terminal and crossed the street to short-term parking. 'I'm glad to get out of there. I just don't like being in the airport longer than I have to. There's all kinds of people in there that I don't like near me.'

Diane let that pass. 'I'll stay as long as I'm needed. I'm hoping we can get Mother out quickly.'

'We all hope that, but Alan says—' Susan stopped suddenly. 'This is my car.'

She pushed the remote and unlocked the door of a Lincoln Town Car. Diane put her bag in the rear seat and buckled herself in the front seat.

'I have an appointment with a criminal lawyer this afternoon,' said Diane. 'I thought the two of us could go.'

Susan was backing out of the parking space, but stopped abruptly, throwing Diane against her seat back, hurting her arm.

'Shit, Susan, what are you doing?'

'Mother is not a criminal!'

'No, she isn't. But she is in the criminal justice system, and we have to get her out of it. That calls for a criminal lawyer. Let's not argue about this.'

Susan drove the winding circular exit lane through the parking deck out to the street. 'We thought with your contacts in the State Department you could help learn what this is about. Have you called them?'

'No. We first need to find out why she's being held. The State Department probably has nothing to do with it.'

Susan sighed heavily. Diane hated that sound.

'And I suppose you have a theory?'

'Yes, a couple. I've talked to a friend who's a detective in the Metro Atlanta Fraud and Computer Forensics Unit. He believes she may be a victim of identity theft.'

'That's stupid. Her credit cards weren't stolen.'

'No, but her identity may have been. It's like, say I'm caught for shoplifting, and when I'm arrested I give them your name and Social Security number. I could just not show up for trial and they would go looking for you.' A scenario

213

that at the moment sounded rather appealing to Diane. 'I believe something like that may have happened to Mother.'

Susan didn't say anything, and Diane knew that meant her sister found her argument persuasive but didn't want to admit it.

'Susan, we can go at it from both angles. Alan can follow his theory, I'll follow mine, and maybe between us we can get Mother out. This isn't a contest. The goal is to get Mother back.'

'That sounds reasonable,' admitted Susan. 'You said on the phone that you had a medical procedure. How are you?'

'I'm doing okay. A little sore. I was stabbed in the arm.'

Susan looked over at her, then back to the road. 'Well, if you insist on dealing in crime . . .'

Diane had decided on the plane that the best way to get through this visit with her family was to say as little as possible and stay focused on the task at hand.

'I was at the funeral for one of Rosewood's most prominent citizens,' Diane said.

'I read about that in the paper.' Susan gasped. 'They said a student was stabbed.'

'That's true. I didn't know I was also stabbed until later. The, uh, knife was very sharp.'

'God, what's the world coming to?' said Susan. She turned a corner sharply, and Diane held on to the handle above the door for support.

'That's what we've been asking ourselves,' Diane

214

said, keeping her mouth firmly closed about Susan's driving.

Diane's sister drove to Mountain Brook, one of the wealthy suburbs of Birmingham populated by new money in old mansions that were layered on wooded hillsides above narrow, winding quiet streets whose curbs were lined with expensive automobiles. Her parents' home was a large rock-faced structure that looked like an English manor. Susan lived next door in an equally large brick home built a century ago by a steel tycoon. She drove up the steep, winding drive to the garage and parked the car.

'You'll be staying at Mother and Dad's. I've made up the guest room for you. We're all having dinner there this evening – including Alan. I hope that's not a problem.'

'No. Whatever all of you feel comfortable with.'

Susan gave another one of her exasperated sighs. 'It's not about our comfort. Alan is a friend of the family and is Mother and Dad's lawyer.'

'That reminds me,' said Diane. 'We have an appointment in an hour and a half. Do you want to go with me, or do you want me to handle it?'

'I'll go with you. Like you said, going at it from two directions won't hurt. Dad went in briefly to the firm today. He'll be home in an hour or two.'

Diane got out of the car and grabbed her bag from the rear seat. 'I'll just freshen up a bit and we can get started.'

*　　*　　*

Daniel Reynolds's office was over the mountain in downtown Birmingham. They made it with five minutes to spare and were ushered straight into his office by a young woman. Reynolds was sitting at a large dark-wood library table stacked with files. His desk was much older, with scrollwork around the sharp edges. Both looked antique. The desktop held pens, a pad of paper and a telephone. All the office walls were lined with glass-enclosed bookshelves filled with law books. There was no computer visible in his office.

Reynolds himself looked like he belonged out West working cattle. Not because of what he wore – he had on a silver-gray dress shirt and gray suit pants with dark gray suspenders, his suit coat thrown over the back of his chair. It was his rugged face that made him look like a cowboy, that and his wiry steel-gray hair. He stood and held out his hand. Diane and Susan shook it in turn and introduced themselves.

'One of you is from Georgia?' He gestured to two chairs.

'That's Diane,' said Susan. 'She lives in Rosewood, Georgia.' She sat down, holding her purse in her lap, and fidgeted with the strap. 'I live in Mountain Brook. My husband is in business with my father. They have a brokerage firm here in Birmingham – Fallon and Abernathy. Diane . . . Diane has several jobs.'

Diane suppressed a smile. Susan made it sound like she worked at McDonald's during the week

216

and Waffle House on weekends. 'I'm director of the RiverTrail Museum of Natural History, as well as the director of the Rosewood Crime Lab and the Aidan Kavanagh Forensic Anthropology Lab.'

'You do indeed have several jobs. There's got to be a story in that.'

'There is. A long one.'

Diane and Reynolds smiled at each other. Susan was clearly out of her comfort zone. Diane would have liked to reach out and take Susan's hand to give her some measure of solace, but she knew the gesture would not have been welcome.

'So what can I do for you ladies?'

Susan gave Diane the I-dread-this look, but said nothing.

'We've had a rather odd thing happen to our mother,' said Diane. 'She was picked up by federal officers last Tuesday and put in prison. We are having a hard time discovering why. So far we have only speculation. The authorities have said it was for robbing a bank, but little else.'

'They suspect she robbed a bank? Could she have?'

'Mr Reynolds, this is a woman who won't wear white shoes after Labor Day because she thinks it's against the law. No, she wouldn't have robbed a bank, not now or at any time in her life.'

'She doesn't think white after Labor Day is illegal,' sputtered Susan. 'It's just in bad taste.'

Reynolds's homey, pleasant smile spread across his face. 'I see. When does she come to trial?'

'She doesn't get a trial,' said Susan. 'They've already put her in prison. They said she won't get out until her time is up.'

'Your mother is a natural-born citizen of this country?'

'Back for ten generations,' said Diane.

'Twelve generations,' said Susan.

'Then they can't do that. If they arrested her, they have to give her a speedy trial.'

'Even with the Homeland Security laws?' asked Susan.

'Even then.'

'Well, that's what they did. She was sent directly to prison.'

'Then there must be something else going on.'

'The family lawyer,' said Susan, 'that is, the lawyer who handles their finances, thinks that she was witness to a bank robbery and is being held as a material witness as part of this Homeland Security thing.'

Reynolds nodded, then spoke directly to Diane. 'Is that what you think?'

'No.' She explained in detail what she believed may have happened, including the possibility that a hacker could have been involved.

When Diane finished, Reynolds turned to Susan. 'With due respect to the family attorney, I think identity theft is more likely. She didn't get a trial because the authorities believe she's already had her day in court. My guess would be she was picked up on a fugitive warrant.'

Susan looked deflated. 'Our mother, a fugitive? This is all so embarrassing. I was supposed to have an interview with Garden Grace's Kindergarten today. I had to cancel, and now I'm afraid that Christopher will never get in. There's such a long waiting list, you know.'

'Kindergarten?' said Diane.

'The right kindergarten is important,' said Susan. 'It gets the child off to the best start right away. I don't know what they'll make of this.'

'Why don't you send him to Switzerland? They have excellent schools and a stiff language requirement. That'll be important when he joins Dad and Gerald's firm,' said Diane, deadpan. She immediately wished she had just bitten her tongue. This wasn't the place to make fun of Susan.

However, Susan looked at Diane as if she were serious. 'I really don't want him that far away from home.'

Diane turned back to the attorney. 'Mr Reynolds, our mother is very much like my sister, and she is in Tombsberg Prison for Women.'

'I understand,' he said. 'I'll get on it right away. I just need to get some information from you.'

CHAPTER 21

Susan seemed to be more optimistic when they left Daniel Reynolds's office. Diane noticed that the lines between her sister's eyes were smoothed out and she didn't look so tired. His easygoing, competent nature most likely won her over. Diane guessed that he was probably very good with juries.

They stepped from the office building onto the sidewalk. It had just started to rain. Susan had parked out on the street, so they didn't have far to walk. They hurried to the car, and Diane slid into the passenger side and buckled her belt.

'Your car smells new.'

'It is. Gerald bought it for my birthday. Dad will probably be home by now.'

They were both quiet as Susan drove. Diane relaxed in the soft leather seat. So few road noises penetrated the passenger compartment it would be easy to lean her head back and drift off to sleep – she felt so tired. Diane closed her eyes.

'What did you mean that Mother is like me?'

Diane jerked awake. There was a tone in Susan's

voice that sounded like suspicion, like she wanted to make sure Diane didn't have a joke with Reynolds at her expense.

'I meant that Mother isn't the kind of person who should be in prison. He could see that you clearly aren't the criminal type. I was trying to tell him that Mother isn't either.'

Diane wasn't entirely truthful. What she had wanted to convey to him was that her mother was naive, like her sister, and it was imperative that they get her out of Tombsberg Prison as quickly as possible.

'Oh.' Susan paused for a moment, intently watching the traffic. 'I'm glad you're here. Dad and I have been beside ourselves, and . . . well, frankly, I felt Alan was taking too long to get anything done about getting this mess resolved.'

Ah, the first crack in Alan's armor. Maybe Susan would stop believing that Diane's ex-husband had hung the moon. Diane decided to be nice, sensing that disagreement would make Susan turn around and defend him.

'Alan's very good with finances. It's just a different world from the criminal justice system,' Diane said. Fortunately her cell rang then, saving her from having to heap any more praise on her ex. She looked at the name on the display and smiled broadly. It was as if the sky cleared and the day was going to be sunny after all.

'Hi,' she said to Frank.

'Hey, babe, how are you doing?'

'We just saw Daniel Reynolds. I feel better about the whole thing.'

'He's good. I've seen him in action – up close.' Frank chuckled; then his voice became serious. 'I have some news. I looked up your mother's arrest warrant in the federal system. It was there with her name, address and Social Security number.'

'How did you know her Social Security number?'

'I'm a detective.'

Diane could almost see him smiling on his end of the phone. 'That's right, how could I forget?' she said.

'Okay, it says she robbed the Bessemer Branch of the First Southern Bank of Birmingham on June fifteenth, 2004. She was captured just over a month later, on July sixteenth. Plea-bargained and escaped on the way to prison.'

Diane looked over at Susan. 'That just didn't happen. I'm sure Mother will know what she was doing on those dates. She keeps a diary.' Susan nodded in agreement at the mention of the diary as she stopped at a red light. 'Did you find anything else?' asked Diane.

'Yes. There are several interesting things about the warrant. The dates cluster – both months start with J, all the dates are numbered in the teens. When people make things up, they tend to unconsciously stick to patterns. It's something about the way the brain works. It won't convince authorities there, but it's a tell for me when I'm looking at documents. The thing that should convince the authorities, though, is that I haven't been able to find an incident report of the robbery, a bail report, or any of a host of other paperwork that should be on file and isn't.'

'Frank, that's good. That's really good, isn't it?'

'It is. I sent the fingerprints and mug shots via e-mail to your crime lab for them to check the fingerprints – that'll be faster than if I try to do it here – more discreet, too. David should be calling you soon with the results. I'm expecting that the fingerprint images were lifted from some felon's file and won't be your mother's. I'm also betting that if they look for the actual physical paper file, there won't be one – her record will turn out to exist only on computer.'

'This should make it easy to get her out, shouldn't it?'

'I think Reynolds will be able to take care of it without much of a problem, provided nobody gets pigheaded, which sometimes happens when bureaucrats are told they've screwed up big-time.'

'Do you think they can discover who created the bogus records?'

'I don't know. They naturally will not want me looking inside their computer system, so it will be up to their experts. The easiest way for the perp to have done this is to have someone on the inside. I'm sure they'll be looking into that possibility.'

'I'm really grateful, Frank.'

'It was easy. No one tried to do a really slick job of this. It was just enough to get your mother picked up and sent away. She wouldn't have even been sent to prison if they'd done the proper checks.'

'I owe you one.' She smiled into the phone as she said good-bye and hung up.

'That sounded like good news,' Susan said.

'It was. I'll explain in a minute, but first I need to call Reynolds back.'

Just as she started to dial, her phone rang again. This time it was her crime lab.

'David?'

'Hey, Diane, how's it going? Your arm still attached? How about your mental health? Personally, I think relatives ought to be against the law.'

'Everything's working fine, so far,' she said.

'Frank sent me some prints. I ran them through AFIS. They belong to a Jerome Washington, who's doing time for armed robbery of a convenience store.'

'That's music to my ears.'

Diane looked at Susan and gave her a thumbs-up. Susan pulled off the road and parked the car.

'I need you to send the information to a lawyer here in Birmingham. I'll get his fax number and then call you right back,' Diane said. 'Did you get a chance to look at the mug shots?'

'Yup,' David said. 'They're clearly fake. The head

has been glued over the background and the number has been pasted over that. Easy to see when you get down to the pixel level.'

Diane let out a sigh of relief and smiled at her sister. 'What's going on at your end?' she asked David. 'How is Neva?'

'She's really pissed. I don't blame her. She told me she's staying at Frank's tonight. That's a good idea. Someone has it in for her.'

'You and Jin keep on the lookout, too.'

'Always. As you know, I'm paranoid, and I'm training the others well.'

Diane laughed. 'Thanks, David. I'll call you back in just a minute.'

She grabbed a pen and paper from her purse, called Reynolds's office and relayed everything that Frank and David had given her.

'What's your fax number? My crime lab is going to fax the fingerprints and an analysis of the altered mug shots to you.'

'You work fast, don't you, girl?' Reynolds laughed as he read her his fax number.

'It helps to know the right people,' she said.

'I hear you there. I believe we can get your mother out by tomorrow. In the meantime I'll try to get her moved to a private cell. My assistant has gone to the bank to find out if it was actually robbed. Since apparently it wasn't, she'll get an affidavit from the manager. You and your sister go home and relax. I'll call you in the morning.'

'Thanks for getting on this quickly.'

'The only thing that gets under my skin worse than injustice is stupidity, and we seem to have both here.'

When Diane finished talking to Reynolds she called David with the fax number. Susan started the car again and pulled out into the traffic. 'All that sounds like good news,' she said.

'Reynolds thinks he can get Mother out tomorrow,' Diane said.

'Are you serious? Alan said that his contacts told him it could take months.'

'Alan probably approached those people by saying something like, "What are the chances of getting someone out of a federal facility who's been picked up as a material witness in connection with terrorists?" I'm sure Alan didn't doubt his own initial analysis of the situation and framed all his questions based on that.'

Susan sighed. 'That is a little like him. Gerald isn't fond of Alan.'

Diane was completely surprised by Susan's admission.

'Gerald has always struck me as a no-nonsense kind of guy. I imagine you have to be, in his business,' she said, trying to both agree with Susan and to not strike a chord that would set her sister off into defensive mode. It was a game she had learned to play when they were children. The way it usually played out, however, was that Diane would get tired of it and lose her temper, and all her careful phrasing was for nothing.

'Gerald is very levelheaded. I don't know what Dad and I would have done without him these last few weeks.'

'I'm sure he and Dad are going to be relieved at the news we're bringing home. Reynolds is going to have Mother moved to a single cell tonight.'

'What does that mean? Isn't she in a cell now?'

'I haven't been completely frank with you, Susan.' Diane decided to go ahead and tell Susan about the prison their mother was in. She didn't want it to be a complete shock to Susan when her mother told them about her experience in the prison. 'Tombsberg is one of the worst facilities in the country. It's severely overcrowded and riddled with disease. Most of the inmates are housed in a dormitory – young and old together. She probably has a bunk in with several hundred others. She'll need to disinfect herself when she gets out, and she'll have to see a doctor. The place is rife with *Staph* infection, HIV, and sexually transmitted diseases.'

Susan sat driving in silence, her eyes never leaving the road. Diane noticed tears rolling down her cheeks.

'I'm sorry,' said Diane. 'I didn't want to worry you.'

'What if this has changed her?'

'It will have. Let's just hope she can get her old self back. It'll help if she sees a therapist. Would she be willing to do that?'

'I don't know. Let's not tell Dad about that. Not right now. Let's just tell him that we think she'll be coming home.'

'Okay. I'll follow your lead on that,' Diane said, acknowledging that her sister understood their parents much better than she did.

They turned and drove up the winding drive of their parents' home. A Lincoln not unlike Susan's was parked in the garage. Next to it was a silver-blue Jaguar.

'That's Dad's car,' Susan said as she pulled in behind the Lincoln. 'The Jag belongs to Alan.' She pulled down the visor, looked in the mirror and carefully dried her eyes. She took out a compact and lipstick from her purse, smoothed her makeup with a little powder and applied color to her lips. 'We have a good life here. Why would anyone do this to us? We haven't hurt anybody.'

'I don't know. There's a lot of mean people in the world. Just as I was leaving to come here, someone broke into the home of one of my employees and trashed everything she owned. I have no idea why.'

'How do people get like that? I just don't understand.'

'I'm not sure there is any understanding it, Susan.'

Diane hadn't visited her parents in a couple of years. Not since she had returned from South America. Not since they had shown no sympathy whatsoever when Diane's daughter died, simply because Ariel was not born to Diane, simply because she was a native South American Indian. That memory cut through Diane like a sharp knife.

They got out of the car and she followed Susan into the house.

CHAPTER 22

'Diane, dear, it's good to see you,' her father said. Nathan Fallon, Diane's father, rose from his chair as they entered the den to give a hug and kiss to her cheek.

He looked much as he had the last time she'd visited. Hardly aged, but he did look tired. His hair was silver only on the sides, as she remembered, and he was still slender and well dressed as ever in an expensive suit. It was a warmer reception than she usually got. Her family weren't huggers. He held her at arm's length and looked her over.

'You look good. It's been too long. You need to come visit more often.'

'Hello, Diane, it has been a long time.'

Diane just noticed Alan Delacroix, her ex-husband, sitting in one of the stuffed chairs in the den. He wasn't aging as well as her father, but it had been more than a decade since she last saw him. Alan had the dark hair and dark eyes of his mother's Irish side of the family more than his father's French side. His once-black hair was now salted with gray, and his former leanness had given

way to an added twenty-five or thirty pounds. The
one thing that hadn't changed about him was that
his smile still looked like a badly disguised smirk.
What had she been thinking all those years ago?

'Alan. Yes, it has been a long time.'

The den was her father's favorite room. He
called it the library because of lawyer's bookcases
on one wall. Practically everything in it was made
either of dark cherry wood or leather. He and Alan
had been sitting on chocolate-colored leather-
upholstered chairs. The dents in the seats of the
matching ottomans said that both had had their
feet up.

Diane liked the room. She didn't like seeing Alan
in it. It wasn't so much that she harbored any ill
will toward Alan – she was the one who had
wanted out of the marriage – but because in the
divorce Alan had gotten custody of her family.

'You look well,' said Alan. 'A little tired, perhaps.'
His compliments always came with a barb. He
had changed very little.

Susan stood, looking uncomfortable. Diane
wondered if her sister was afraid she would 'start
something' as she called it. Her father simply
smiled.

'Alan has some good news,' he said. 'He has an
appointment with a contact in the Justice
Department to talk about Iris's situation.'

Alan beamed as he looked from Diane to Susan.
They both opened their mouths to speak but were
interrupted by the entry into the library of Susan's

husband, Gerald Abernathy. He put an arm around Diane's shoulders.

'You look great,' he said, kissing her cheek. 'You don't live that far away. We need to see more of you. Susan and I've been thinking about bringing the kids to visit your museum.'

'I'd like that,' said Diane. Susan smiled thinly, and Diane wondered if they had ever had a conversation about visiting her.

Gerald's hairline had receded a little more since the last time Diane had seen him. His square-built body seemed as active as ever, the way he flitted from Diane to Susan to give her a peck on the cheek. Diane noticed Alan frowning at him. He probably didn't like Gerald interrupting his big announcement.

'As your father was just saying, I have an appointment with someone from the Justice Department to talk about Iris.'

'We think Mother will be getting out tomorrow,' said Susan abruptly. 'It's what we've been doing all day, Diane and I, arranging it. Well, Diane mostly.'

Their father stared at them, openmouthed. 'What? Tomorrow? How do you know? How can that be?'

Alan looked crestfallen. Gerald grinned.

'Diane has a detective friend who looked into it, and we consulted a lawyer who specializes in that kind of thing.'

'The only hangup might be if some of the people

in charge get defensive about the mistake,' said Diane just as her cell phone rang. She quickly pulled it out of her purse, and checked the display to see who was calling before she answered.

'It's Daniel Reynolds, the lawyer,' she told them before answering. 'Yes?'

'Dr Fallon,' he said. 'Just wanted to keep you up-to-date. My assistant has confirmed that the bank was not robbed, and has obtained an affidavit to that effect. I received the fax on the fingerprint and mug-shot photograph analysis. After looking at those materials, I filed an emergency petition for a writ of habeas corpus with a district federal judge requesting his expedited review of the false evidence and release of your mother. Based on my testimony to him, the judge has ordered the immediate move of your mother to a guesthouse on the prison grounds. I've sent the judge the documents and fully expect an order for your mother's release to be issued tomorrow morning. She should be able to come home until a hearing can take place to clear this all up. Could you meet me at my office in the morning at eight? We can drive down to Montgomery.'

Diane didn't say anything for several seconds. 'Yes . . . yes, we'll be there. Thank you, from me and my family. Thank you.'

'We have some persuasive evidence. I don't expect any delay from the Feds or the officials at Tombsberg. They know they are in a world of trouble.'

Diane thanked him and put her phone back in her purse.

'We're going to pick Mother up tomorrow morning. They're moving her to a guesthouse tonight.'

'I don't believe it,' said her father. He looked at Alan. 'I don't understand.'

'Mother was a victim of identity theft,' said Susan. 'Or someone hacking into the police computers – one or the other. Isn't that right, Diane?'

'Yes. Right now it looks like someone hacked into the Justice Department computers and created a fugitive arrest warrant in her name.'

'How? Why?' asked her father.

Glenda, the housekeeper who had been with her parents since they moved to Birmingham, came in and announced dinner.

'Hello, Miss Diane. It's good to see you home. It's been a while. I put you in Mrs Fallon's Yukon room, as she likes to call it. It's my favorite. Real cozy.'

'Hello, Glenda. You haven't aged a day since I last saw you.'

'It's all them Botox injections,' she said, laughing. 'But did I hear right? Is Mrs Fallon coming home?'

'You did, indeed, Glenda,' said Diane's father. 'I think we'll have some champagne after dinner. This calls for a celebration.'

'Yes, it does, Mr Fallon. This has been just the

craziest thing I've ever heard of. It's no wonder we have such a high crime rate: The police don't know nothing,' Glenda said as they all walked out of the room.

The dining room was the same as Diane remembered – stucco walls colorwashed in shades of gold, a dark-pine sideboard with terra-cotta tile inlays, a polished dark-pine dining table and chairs with tapestry-covered seats. The still-life of grapes, apples and pears above the sideboard was new. It was a room with warmth and seemed so opposite to her family, Diane thought.

Diane realized that she hadn't eaten all day and was starving. She sat down eagerly and heaped her plate from the platters of food passed to her. Over a dinner of roast lamb, new potatoes and grilled asparagus, Diane and Susan took turns explaining what happened.

'The fingerprints they used in her fake file belong to a Jerome Washington. They also made fake mug shots,' said Diane.

'Alan, I thought your people were telling you that it had something to do with Homeland Security?' said her father.

'That's what the indications were,' Alan said. He forked a piece of meat and stuck it in his mouth, perhaps to forestall the expectation of further words.

Diane noticed that Alan had a lot of color in his face this evening. He was sullen throughout the meal. No one but she and Gerald seemed to notice. Once, Gerald looked at Alan, then at her, and winked. Diane hadn't realized that she had an ally in her brother-in-law. It also surprised her how much Susan seemed to enjoy showing Alan up. She would never understand her family.

'This is the best news we've had in . . . I can't even remember how long,' her father said. 'How did you find out what happened? What made you think it was identity theft or hacking?'

'A friend of mine, Frank Duncan, is a detective in the Metro Atlanta Fraud and Computer Forensics Unit. He deals with identity theft all the time.' Diane told them what he had found. 'Just about the only reason they would put her in a place like Tombsberg without a trial is if they thought she had already had one.'

'These days,' began Alan, 'they are sending lots of people to prison without a trial. About all they need is suspicion or grounds to detain you as a material witness.'

Diane was shocked that Alan knew so little about current law. But he'd probably never set foot in a criminal courtroom. He knew only about laws concerning trusts, wills and anything to do with money. Still, she thought to herself, surely he should know better. She suspected he got his knowledge of criminal law from television.

'Not American citizens,' said Diane. 'And there would have been a process she would have gone through. They wouldn't just throw her in prison. Besides, Mother would have remembered if she had witnessed a bank robbery.'

'I didn't say she actually witnessed a robbery. I only said that the authorities may have thought she had. That is the only way it all made sense. We all know that she couldn't have robbed one herself.'

'Well, what matters now,' said her father, 'is that Iris is coming home.'

Diane wanted to say that something could still go wrong, but she didn't want to ruin his happy mood. At any rate, if everything didn't exactly go as planned, it would only delay the release for a few days. And she had a feeling that Daniel Reynolds had put the fear of God into the prison officials.

'Who would do such a thing?' said Gerald. 'And why, for heaven's sake? What was to be gained?'

'I've been thinking about that,' said Diane's father. 'The market has been down lately. You remember the Wolcotts were very unhappy with the performance of their portfolio. Very unhappy. They lost quite a sum of money. Money makes some people do strange things.'

'The FBI, the Bureau of Prisons, and the federal marshals will all come out of this looking bad,' said Diane. 'They will want to know who got into their files.'

'I agree,' said Gerald. 'But enough about all that for now. Like you said, Nathan, this is the time to celebrate. Diane, tell us about the museum. It's a large operation, isn't it? Annual budget in the millions?'

Diane described the dinosaurs, the Egyptian exhibit, the elegant rocks, butterflies, seashells, the huge paintings of dinosaurs on the walls containing hidden unicorns in each one, the nature trail, the restaurant and even the museum store.

'Christopher loved the collection of model dinosaurs you sent him for Christmas,' said Gerald. 'Especially that big – what do you call it – brachy-something?'

'Brachiosaur.'

'Yeah, that's it. He really liked that one. Carried it around by the neck all the time.'

'And what is your position in the museum?' asked Alan.

'She's the director,' said Susan.

'The director?' her father said. 'Isn't that wonderful? I'm proud of you, Diane.'

Diane had been estranged from her family so long, she'd forgotten they didn't really know what she did for a living.

And his response surprised her. She had never recalled that her parents had expressed pride in what she did. She was always doing things that were so opposite of what they wanted. She grew up thinking that it was her grandparents' job to be proud of her.

'Director. Impressive,' said Alan.

'I suppose you like not having anyone to answer to,' said Susan.

'Oh, I'm sure she has a board to answer to,' said Alan. 'That's the way museums are set up.'

'Actually,' said Diane, 'the board answers to me.'

'What? You have them intimidated?' said Alan.

'No. The governance of RiverTrail Museum is set up differently than most. The board is advisory. All final decisions are mine. A man named Milo Lorenzo, the founder of the museum, wanted it that way.'

'I know him, don't I?' said Diane's father. 'Wasn't he a teacher at the college in Rosewood? Didn't you take some advanced something-or-other there when you were in sixth grade? Went back a few summers to take courses after we moved, if I recall.'

Diane was shocked that her father remembered that small a detail about her from so long ago.

'History,' she said. 'He was a professor. I took his history course and some others during the summers in a special program.'

'As I recall, he was rich,' said her father.

'Yes, he was. He endowed the museum very well. He didn't like the idea of committees making decisions. So he set up the museum the way he wanted it. He was to be the director, and hired me as assistant director. Unfortunately, he died suddenly, but all his power went to me when I stepped into the position.'

'You must like that,' said Alan. 'Absolute power.'

'Not absolute, but close.'

Diane was getting uncomfortable with the conversation. Alan was turning it into something about her personality. She searched for another

subject to talk about, but everything she liked –
caves, bones, even science fiction – was a red flag
for either Alan or her family. She settled on
another subject.

'We have a new geology exhibit opening in a few
months. It should be very popular with the kids.
It's designed to look like they are traveling down
through the layers of the Earth.'

'Gerry would like that,' said Susan. 'He's crazy
about rocks.'

'Then you need to come to the opening. We
always have a gala to celebrate a new exhibit.
Usually black-tie. It's a lot of fun.'

The phone rang in another part of the house.
The ringing stopped abruptly as the housekeeper
picked it up.

'Oh, Mr Fallon,' she said as she came running
in with the phone. 'It's Mrs Fallon. She's on the
phone.'

CHAPTER 23

While her father talked to her mother on the phone, Diane wandered onto the terrace with a cup of coffee. Alan followed.

'You've done well for yourself,' he said.

'Yes, I have. I have a good life.'

Diane tried to remember living with Alan. She couldn't really – not the day-to-day life they shared for eighteen months. Just events. Arguments. Regrets. Nothing to make a scrapbook of. Nothing she wanted to remember.

'If we'd stayed together, we'd be married seventeen years next month,' he said.

'Where's your wife?' asked Diane. She had noticed that she was conspicuously absent, but just assumed she didn't want to dine with her husband's ex-wife.

'We're separated.'

'I'm sorry.'

It was twilight and still hot. Diane would have taken off her blazer, but hadn't wanted to explain her bandage. She sat down at the wrought-iron table with her coffee, trying to think of some polite

way to tell Alan to go away. But he sat down opposite her. In the coming darkness he looked younger
and handsome. He had always been a good-
looking man and had always known it. Alan had
the upbringing of an only child with doting
parents.

'I loved you,' he said. 'I really did.'

'No, you didn't.'

Even in the shadows, she could see the flush rise
in his face.

'Don't tell me what I felt.'

'When we were married you wanted to change
everything about me. I had too much desire to
get an education. I was too adventurous. I had a
smart mouth, and my hair was too short. There
was nothing about me that you liked.'

'I just wanted you to be happy.'

Diane felt her face getting hot and the anger
rising. After all these years, he could still goad her
into an argument. 'I was happy doing all those
things you didn't like. You wanted me to be happy
doing what you wanted me to do. That just wasn't
me.'

'If you had just tried . . . You didn't try.'

'Do you have any idea how that sounds? God,
Alan. Why are we having this conversation? You
know, in the divorce papers there was this line
that said our relationship was now like we had
never been married. Our marriage is history and
should stay that way.'

'You never really loved me, did you?'

That was the way their arguments always went. Alan would ignore Diane's response and go on to the next thing he wanted to take issue with. Alan could certainly suck the joy out a celebration.

'Don't, Alan. It's been seventeen years. Let it go.' *Surely*, thought Diane, *he doesn't want to get back together*. 'I did try. I tried for a year and a half, but I wasn't going to give up graduate school. I wasn't going to give up caving. I might have relented on the hair. All we did was argue. We both were miserable.'

She suddenly felt like making a dash for the door. She rose and started back into the house.

'Dammit, Diane, can't you just listen for once?'

Alan grabbed her arm. His fingers pressed hard against the tender incision. Searing, crippling pain shot through Diane's arm. Bile rose in her throat.

'You're hurting me,' she cried out. 'Let go.'

'Don't be silly. I can't be hurting you.'

The lights to the terrace suddenly came on. Susan and Gerald rushed through the patio doors.

'Stop,' said Susan. 'She's injured.'

'Dammit, man. Let her go,' said Gerald. 'Look at her face. She's about to pass out.'

Alan let go and Diane started to sink. Gerald put a chair under her.

'Shit, that hurt,' she said.

'Let me see if he broke the stitches.' Susan helped her take off the light cotton jacket she'd worn over her short-sleeved shirt.

'This is a long cut, Diane,' said Susan, looking

through the translucent bandage at the line of stitches. 'It looks like it was deep.'

'The doctor said it was to the bone. I had to have some muscle repair.'

'I didn't realize,' sputtered Alan.

'You did,' said Diane, 'because I told you that you were hurting me.'

'It didn't make sense that my grasp was hurting. How was I to know?'

'It's weeping,' said Susan. 'But the stitches look intact.'

'Alan, that kind of logic is exactly the reason we are not married.' Diane's arm throbbed. She turned to her sister. 'I see Dad coming. Help me on with my jacket. We aren't going to mention this.' She bored a hole through Alan with her gaze.

'There you are,' said her dad, coming through the patio door. 'I talked to your mother. She's in a cottage on the prison grounds. As you can imagine, she is greatly relieved. She suffered so much in there.' His voice broke.

'Sit down, Dad,' Susan said as she guided him to a chair.

'They had her in a dormitory with five hundred other women. Five hundred. Some were ill and vomiting. They have elderly people in with young people. Many of them were vicious. She said one woman died during the night and they couldn't get a guard to come and see about her until noon. It was awful. Just awful. Someone is going to pay for this. Alan, I want you to start a lawsuit immediately.'

'I'll look into it.'

'Don't look into it. Do it!' he snapped.

'Of course. That's what I meant,' Alan sputtered.

They skipped the champagne. The joy at getting her mother out of prison was dampened by the knowledge of the frightful conditions. Diane knew what to expect, but hearing it from her father was still sickening. Alan had the good sense not to say that prison was not supposed to be Club Med, as he had often voiced in the past.

Diane excused herself early, telling her father that she was tired from the flight.

'I understand. I'm going to bed myself. We have to get up early and get Iris away from that place. I tell you, they are going to be sorry they picked on a Fallon.' He kissed her cheek and headed for his room. 'God, I'm tired,' he said, going down the hallway.

Alan went home, and Diane hoped it would be the last time she saw him. He apparently couldn't bring himself to apologize for hurting her. An apology would be an admission of guilt, and that was simply beyond his ability to accept.

'I'll go up with you and dress your arm,' said Susan.

Diane was suprised. There weren't that many times during their childhood that they had acted sisterly toward each other. But something had changed between the time she talked with Susan on the phone yesterday and now.

They walked up the stairs and down the hall to

what Diane's mother called the Yukon room. The centerpiece of the room was a huge pine bed covered with a duvet of red-and-hunter-green plaid and littered with fleece pillows. All the furniture was rustic, from the dresser to the table and chairs in the corner. It was a cozy room.

Susan rummaged through the bathroom for fresh bandages. 'Is it still hurting?' she called from the bathroom.

'Unfortunately it is. I'm going to take a painkiller tonight, so please call me in the morning when you get up.' Diane took off her jacket and her blouse.

'I'm going to put some Betadine on the wound.' Susan frowned at Diane. 'Are you telling me that this didn't hurt when it happened?'

'I felt something like a pulled muscle. It was crowded, and my attention was focused elsewhere.'

Susan left for a couple of minutes and came back with a bottle of Betadine and some cotton pads.

'I still can't believe Alan grabbed you like that,' Susan said as she sat down next to Diane on the bed. 'Diane, when you were married to Alan, did he . . . was he . . .'

'Abusive? No. He tried to be controlling.'

'Mother and Dad should have told him that wouldn't work.'

Diane smiled at her. 'Alan's main deal was pouting when he didn't get his way. That didn't work either. I was happiest when he wasn't talking to me. He also liked to try to wear me down until I agreed with him. He was like a dog with a bone trying to get me to drop out of graduate school. I could dig my heels in when I'd a mind to, so we argued constantly. He locked me out of the bedroom once for some reason, thinking that would be a deterrent to my disagreeing with him. I was very happy on the couch,' Diane said with a laugh as she swiveled her body sideways slightly so that Susan could reach her arm.

'Why did you marry him?' Susan asked.

Diane felt her sister blot the incision with a cotton pad soaked with Betadine. It was cool on the hot wound.

'Alan proposed. It was Mother and Dad's wish that I accept. I wanted them to approve of something I did, so I accepted. It was a big mistake, and I regretted it immediately.'

Susan taped a fresh sterile pad on Diane's arm. Diane turned back toward her and noticed how worn-out her sister suddenly looked.

'Diane, I need a favor,' she said after a long, awkward moment. 'I know we haven't gotten along . . . ever, I guess. But you've always been good to my kids. You remember their birthdays and Christmas. You write them letters. Kayla loves getting letters from you.'

'What's the matter, Susan? Has something happened?'

'Something. Yes. Something happened. I made

247

a terrible mistake, and I don't know what to do. I need you to speak to Gerald. He respects you.'

'I didn't think anyone in the family respected me.'

'Do you think that, really?' Susan looked at the painting of a moose at the edge of the woods that hung on the wall opposite the bed. 'You're the smart one. Everyone respects that.'

Yes, the smart one . . . and Susan's the pretty one, Diane thought. That was how Diane's mother described her children. Diane guessed her mother was trying to tell people that each had her own special qualities, but what it had always sounded like to her – and she guessed to Susan too – was that Diane was the ugly one and Susan was the dumb one.

Susan must have been thinking the same thing. 'Prettiness fades with time,' she said. 'I didn't realize that when I was young, and if that's all you have . . .' Susan looked down at her hands and twisted her wedding ring on her finger.

'Would it do any good for me to tell you that is not all you have and that you are plenty smart . . . and still pretty? What's this about, Susan?'

'Last New Year's Eve, Alan and I kissed. It was nothing. I don't know why I even did it. But that's all it was. Honest. We never went beyond that one rather silly kiss.'

'Did Gerald see it or something?'

'No, Alan' – she spit his name out like it tasted bitter – 'Alan told Gerald this morning.'

'Why?'

'I know you think Alan is a good financial lawyer, but he isn't. Dad had to find him a job because he was fired from the firm where he worked before.'

Actually, Diane didn't think Alan was a good lawyer. She had just been trying to soften her remark about Alan's not being a criminal lawyer. 'Fired? I thought he would have been a partner,' she said.

'No. We all thought it was a raw deal . . . jealousy, infighting. Mother and Dad think the world of him, so Dad got him a job with the firm that Fallon and Abernathy use. Alan's made some mistakes with their accounts. He told the partners that Gerald is the one who gave him the information and told him how he wanted things handled. Gerald found out this morning and called him. They had a row, and that's when Alan told him. Now Gerald thinks we . . . that we had an affair. I swear we didn't. That's why we sent the children to his sister's. We didn't want them to witness us sorting this out.'

'I'll tell Gerald that I believe you, if you think that will help.'

'Do you?'

'Believe you? Yes.'

'Why?'

'I have experience with people who lie.' Diane didn't say that one of the people she had experience with was Susan herself when they were children, and

249

that Diane knew exactly when Susan lied and when she was telling the truth.

'Gerald is a good man, and I don't want a divorce.'

'Is that what Gerald is threatening?'

'He hasn't come out and said it, but . . . Alan really rubbed his nose in it.'

'I'll talk to him tomorrow.'

'I appreciate it, Diane. I'd better get back. I don't want Gerald to think that I'm . . .' She left the rest unfinished.

Susan kissed Diane's cheek as she left for home. Her family got downright affectionate during times of stress. She realized that she hardly knew them. Perhaps that was her fault. She could be as stubborn and intransigent as they in her opinions. On the other hand, they had never understood how much Diane loved her daughter. That lack of empathy was hard for Diane to forgive.

Diane undressed and tossed her clothes over the back of a chair. She put on her nightgown, fished a paperback of *Foucault's Pendulum* out of her duffel bag and crawled into bed. Her eyelids were heavy, but she was looking forward to continuing what she started on the plane – and getting her mind away from current events.

Something caused her to jerk awake. The book had fallen to the floor. That was probably what woke her up. She picked up her cell and looked at the display. After eleven. She got out of bed, retrieved the book and turned out the bedside lamp.

She had one knee back up on the bed when she heard soft footfalls in the hallway. On the carpeted floor the sound was only a whisper, but Diane had a good ear for faint rhythm. Her father, probably. He was the only other person in the huge house. And when she and Susan were little, he would look in on them before going to bed. She started to call out, but instead she picked up her cell phone, moved away from the bed and secreted herself in the closet, looking out through the space between the louvers.

Okay, now what was she going to say to her father – *I've been personally attacked so many times that I automatically run for cover at the sound of footsteps?* She put a hand on the door to push it open, but stopped when she saw a shadow come into the room. Her father would have knocked – unless he was just checking. The shadowed form passed through rays of moonlight from the window. It was Alan.

CHAPTER 24

Diane held her breath for several seconds and slowly let it out. A sick knot formed in her stomach. What was he up to? Her father was downstairs and too far away to call. She could dial 911. She started to, holding her hand over the phone display to hide the light, but she hesitated. She knew instinctively that Alan would say she had invited him to her room, and her father would probably believe him. She would have caused an uproar at one of the worst times in their lives. She stayed her finger, but held the open phone.

'Diane,' Alan whispered in the darkness.

Diane watched as he approached her bed and stood looking down at the crumpled sheets. He glanced for a few seconds toward the open bathroom door. Diane readied herself for an approach to her hiding place. But his gaze didn't linger on the closet. He turned around and retraced his steps, stopping at the chair where she had thrown off her clothes. Picking up her camisole, he held it to his face and breathed in. Diane raised her eyebrows and her phone camera. She had clicked several pictures by the time he put down her clothes and walked out her bedroom door.

What was he doing? Diane stayed in the closet for several moments, waiting for him to come back. When he didn't, she stepped out and breathed a sigh of relief. She suddenly thought of her father downstairs. What if he was making his way down to him? What if he had suddenly turned into a maniac?

Diane grabbed her robe and dashed across the room, cautiously looking out the door and listening. She heard his footsteps going down the stairs and ran on tiptoe in the opposite direction down an alternate set of stairs to get to the first-floor hallway – where her father's room was. At the bottom landing, she listened for steps. It was quiet. Leaving the concealment the stairs provided, Diane walked down the hallway toward the kitchen end of the house. Was that a door slamming? She ran to the kitchen and into the utility hallway that connected to the garage, following the noise. At the end of the hall through the window she saw a flash of light, like headlights turning down the drive. She ran to the living room and looked out at the lit driveway just in time to see Alan's car turn the curve.

'Okay, that was weird,' she said to herself.

'What's weird, dear?'

Diane whirled around.

'Dad.'

So much for her good ears. She hadn't heard

him at all. He stood in the doorway to the living room, looking out the windows, probably searching for whatever she was looking at.

'I saw a flash of light – like a car.'

'You didn't see that from your room?'

It was more of a question than an accusation.

'No.'

What was she going to say – *I'm down here protecting you from Alan gone mad?*

'I had a slight headache and I came down to get some aspirin. The bottle in my bathroom is out-of-date. I thought Glenda might keep some in the kitchen.'

'I believe she does. If not, I have some in my bathroom.' He smiled at her. 'Cars sometimes use our drive to turn around in. No reason for alarm.'

She followed him into the kitchen, where he reached up into one of the dark oak cabinets and retrieved a bottle of aspirin.

'These are no good; they're children's aspirin. Glenda probably takes one of these every day. Oh, here's another bottle.'

He handed it to Diane and she jiggled a couple out into her hand, wondering what she was going to do with them. She was caught now. Why had she said that? If she took them, they would probably cause her wound to bleed or weep. But she couldn't tell her father about that, so she had to do something with them.

'Maybe you need to eat an apple or drink a glass

of milk. It's not good to take those on an empty stomach,' her father said.

'Would you like me to pour you some milk, too?'

'That might help. I can't sleep either.' He sighed. 'I keep thinking of your mother in that place.'

'I know, Dad. But she's safe now and we'll have her out tomorrow.'

Diane turned to take a carton of milk from the refrigerator and dropped the aspirin into the pocket of her robe. She poured two glasses of milk and they sat down at the kitchen table. She pretended to put the aspirin in her mouth, then took a drink of milk, feeling like a kid who had done something wrong and was hiding it from her father.

'That's one good thing about your crime work: At least you know your way around the system. I'm afraid poor Alan was out of his depth. He's a financial lawyer, you know.'

Her crime work. Diane and the case of the secreted aspirin, she thought. 'It was a friend who helped the most. Frank Duncan.'

Her father puckered his brow. 'How do I know that name?'

'We date.'

'Oh, I think I remember something about him. A good man?'

'A very good man. He's a detective in Atlanta. Does mainly white collar crimes. When I told him about Mother, he knew right away what might have happened.'

Her father looked very sad. He stared at the milk, not drinking. 'You know,' he said, 'I can't help thinking that this may have been my fault.'

'Your fault? How?'

'The market's not been good lately. Some of my clients have had losses. Of course, if they'd just stayed the course . . . But some of them blame me.'

'I doubt it has anything to do with that,' said Diane, though such a motive had crossed her mind too. 'That's a rather severe reaction for an investment downturn.' She took a drink of the milk.

'You know, sitting in front of a computer doing mischief . . . that's a pretty safe way to get even with someone. You don't have to even leave home, you don't have to worry about confronting anyone, you just hit a few buttons and wreck someone's life.'

'It's trickier than that in this case. The police don't take kindly to people hacking into their system, and it may have left an electronic trail they can backtrack.'

'Then why did they take such a risk?' He shook his head. 'Diane, you need to come home more often. Get to know us. Let us get to know you again.'

'I know, Dad. I will.' She searched for a change of subject. 'Susan tells me Kayla would like a job in the museum next summer.'

'Yes, she said that. I didn't realize until this evening at dinner that you actually run the museum. That's a big job.'

'There's a lot of satisfaction in it. I learn new things all the time.'

Her father had run out of things to say to her, too. He fingered his glass and downed the rest of his milk.

'I guess we'd better get some sleep. Maybe the milk will help. Just put the glasses on the sink. Glenda will get them tomorrow.'

Diane walked with him to his door and went up the back staircase to her room. She locked her door and put a chair under the knob. Then she checked the window to make sure it was locked, even though she was on the second floor and she doubted that Alan could climb anything.

She got into bed and turned on her bedside lamp so she could look at the photos of Alan she had taken with her camera. They were too dark. She knew they would be, but perhaps the brightness and contrast could be improved. David could do wonders with bad photographs, though she had doubts that there was anything here to work with. She e-mailed them to her computer at the museum and then sent an e-mail to Jin, telling him where to find them and asking him to see what he could do with them. She also sent an e-mail to David and told him to check out Alan Delacroix for an alibi. It had occurred to her that maybe it was Alan who had stabbed her. Though she didn't know why he would stab Mike. Jealousy, perhaps? But how would he even know Mike? Could Alan have been stalking her?

It took a few minutes to send the photos and write messages to Jin and David using the buttons on the handset. When she finished, she flipped her phone closed, put it under her pillow and went to sleep.

Tombsberg Prison for Women looked like a cheap cinder-block fort in the middle of a field of dead grass. It was surrounded by a chain-link fence topped by razor wire.

The prison was built just after World War II and meant to house only four hundred inmates at most. The current population hovered around two thousand and was little more than a warehouse for women prisoners. Tombsberg didn't have any educational programs, rehabilitation programs, occupational programs or any other activities to occupy the prisoners' time. It was riddled with disease, and medical care was better in third-world countries. On any list of prisons, Tombsberg would rank at the bottom.

Diane and her family arrived in the early morning. Gerald drove. Diane's father had sat beside him in the front seat while Susan and Diane sat in back. They followed Daniel Reynolds's car through the gates and into visitor parking and got out of the car. Diane stretched her aching muscles. She longed for a good run.

'Oh, God,' said Susan. 'This is terrible. I can't believe Mother is in this place.'

'The warden knows we're coming,' Reynolds said. 'We'll have to do some paperwork, but it shouldn't take long.'

They all made their way to the warden's office and waited while Reynolds and his assistant made arrangements for Diane's mother to be released. The waiting room looked as cheaply constructed and decorated as the rest of the place. They sat uneasily for two hours on dingy lime-green couch and chairs, hardly talking.

Finally the door opened and Diane's mother stepped through, escorted by Daniel Reynolds. A guard closed the door behind them. She ran to Diane's father as soon as she saw him. The look on her mother's face reminded Diane of what she had seen in the faces of refugees.

'Oh, Nathan, I can't believe this nightmare is over. It's been so horrible.'

Diane's mother was usually well dressed and well coiffed. Her dark-brown-and-silver hair was now pulled back in a bun at the back of her neck in a way she would never wear it. Her clothes looked like she had slept in them for a week – they had probably been rolled up in a bag and returned to her just before their arrival, to wear in place of the orange prison coveralls.

Iris Fallon hugged Susan and Gerald, then Diane last. 'Your father tells me you are the one to thank for getting me out of here.'

'I had help from a detective friend who discovered the falsified records and recommended we go to Mr Reynolds. Mr Reynolds is the one who got you out.'

Diane's mother went to the lawyer and took

his hands in hers. 'I don't know how to repay you.'

He grinned. 'I take checks.' They all laughed. 'Seriously, I'm glad to help. This is just a terrible miscarriage of justice.'

They left without any apology from the warden and without looking back. On the way out to the car Reynolds asked Diane who it was who recommended him. When she told him it was Frank, Reynolds smiled.

'Frank Duncan. I've had him on the stand before. So he recommended me, did he? One of the toughest people I've ever cross-examined. He knows his stuff.'

'Apparently he thinks the same about you.'

Diane's mother didn't even want to stop to eat. Diane tried to talk her into going first to the doctor to get checked out, but she said she'd make an appointment later.

'I just want to get home,' she said. 'I just want to get home.'

They drove the two hours back to Birmingham. Glenda had a huge meal waiting for them, but the first thing her mother wanted to do was take a shower and change clothes. As they waited for her, Diane managed to subtly herd Gerald out to the patio. She was not looking forward to this, but with Alan's recent behavior, she had even more reason to try to keep their marriage intact. She took a sip of wine and bit her lower lip before she began.

CHAPTER 25

'Susan told me about what the two of you are going through right now,' said Diane.

'What we are going through? Nice way of putting it. How about what Susan is making me go through? I suppose she wants you to talk to me.' Gerald looked at his wineglass, turning it in his hand as if examining the ruby-red color. 'She wants you to convince me they weren't having an affair, is that right?' He took a drink.

She sat down on the low rock-garden wall. Gerald sat down beside her. 'I don't believe she was having an affair.'

'You're her sister. What else would you say?'

'You know we don't get along. I was surprised she took me into her confidence enough to ask me to help.'

'I guess it shows her desperation.' He took another sip of wine.

'Desperation doesn't mean guilt.'

He looked over at Diane, his jaw set, his face like granite. 'Why do you believe her, Diane? Can you tell me that?'

'I've spoken with enough liars in my time to pretty much be able to pick them out. Susan's a bad liar; she always has been. I know her, and I know when she's lying and when she's telling the truth. She's telling the truth.' Diane took a drink of her wine. It was sweet – a little too sweet. 'Gerald, it was just a kiss.'

Gerald's laugh was without any mirth. 'She said it wasn't even a good kiss.'

'I can believe that. Alan never was very good.'

Gerald chuckled again. This time he seemed to mean it. Diane laughed with him. 'You don't like him, do you?' he asked.

'No. I never have. Gerald, I know this has to hurt like hell, but it was New Year's Eve, for heaven's sake.'

'It wasn't a New Year's kiss; even Susan admitted that.'

'It probably wasn't. I'm sure everyone was drinking. I've noticed that Susan is feeling like she's getting older these days and less attractive. I'm sure that had something to do with it. Just forgive her and move on.'

The afternoon air was smothering in a way that only Southern climates could pull off. The rain the day before made it steamy. Even with fall approaching, it still felt like summer. The heat never left the South quickly.

'It's not that easy,' said Gerald.

Diane looked over at Gerald. 'Is it harder than disrupting your children's lives?'

'It wasn't my doing that got us here.' His voice was filled with emotion.

'Nevertheless, you are now the one with the power to stop it.' Diane took another sip of her wine. 'Don't let Alan do this to you.'

Gerald set set his wineglass down on the wall. 'You should come around more often, Diane. You're the only one in the family I can talk to sometimes. Is Alan the reason you don't?'

'Part of the reason, but not all of it. There were some things said about my daughter that are hard to forget.' Diane touched her locket.

'Your daughter? Oh . . . look, Diane, I suppose I'm as guilty as the others. I'm really sorry. Honestly. I would like to have met her.'

'Ariel was very bright. She spoke three languages and was working on a fourth, and she was only six. To her, learning a new language was like learning a song. She loved music. Ariel was very special and very precious.' Diane's eyes teared up. 'This is what she looked like.' Diane showed him the locket with their pictures in it.

'Cute little girl. It looks like the two of you were dressed alike.'

'We were.'

'I don't think any of us appreciated what you went through, and I'm sorry for my part.'

Diane snapped the locket closed. 'You are the first person in the family to express that.' She paused, and there was an awkward silence between them. She wondered if he yet understood what

Ariel meant to her. 'I also have another reason I want you and Susan to patch things up.'

'What's that?'

'I'm concerned about Mother and Dad. I'm afraid that Alan might have excessive influence over them and that he's going off the deep end.' Diane took another sip of wine and swallowed hard. 'Alan came into my bedroom last night.'

Gerald jerked his head around to Diane. 'What? What did he do? He didn't . . .'

Diane shook her head, 'This is going to sound really strange, and all I can say is that I've been gun-shy lately. I heard footsteps outside my door and I hid in the closet. He came in, called my name, stared around the room and left, after sniffing my clothes.'

Gerald made a face. 'Good heavens, did you tell Nathan?'

It was a relief to be able to talk to Gerald about Alan. Her parents were so upset when she divorced him, she felt the whole family was against her. 'No. I didn't tell Dad. I don't want to introduce another issue with everything that's going on. Dad is very fond of Alan.'

'Tell me about it. I sometimes wonder if Alan isn't really his son.'

Diane smiled. 'I doubt he would have let me marry him.'

'Yeah, right. I sometimes forget,' said Gerald, chuckling.

'God, Gerald, don't put that thought in my

head.' They both laughed. Diane noticed dark clouds in the sky and wondered if they would have another shower.

'I understand,' he said. 'But really, you need to tell your father about last night. That had to scare you.'

'It did, but they have had enough to worry about. They need a break.'

'I agree. It's been pretty awful for all of us, especially when we didn't know where she was.' He shook his head. 'Susan was a wreck. She tried to hide it for the kids, but . . .'

'Just keep an eye out for Alan. Has he mentioned me at all?'

'No, not really. Sometimes in passing, and I'm afraid nothing complimentary.'

'I just can't imagine what last night was about. I had to ask someone from my crime lab to investigate him. He's made himself a suspect.'

Gerald frowned. 'You don't think he could have stabbed you?'

The edge of the rock wall cut into her legs, so Diane stood up and smoothed out her slacks. 'Honestly, I doubt it, but I have to check. I'll do it discreetly.'

She thought of her discreet investigation of Annette Lymon. Stressors could cause people to do some amazing things, and she seemed to have a lot of stressed-out people around her. Diane saw her mother through the glass doors of the patio returning from her shower.

'Let's go eat lunch.'

Diane and Gerald walked into the dining room from the patio. Susan looked up expectantly. Diane smiled at her. She didn't know what to tell her, except that she thought that the conversation had gone well. Gerald walked over to Susan and whispered in her ear. Susan turned to Diane with a horrified look and mouthed, *Alan?* Diane nodded. Susan grasped Gerald's hand and they walked into the dining room. Glenda was serving a feast for lunch – grilled salmon, ambrosia salad and grilled summer squash.

'It's a relief to have you back, Mrs Fallon.'

'Thank you, Glenda. This looks delicious,' Diane's mother said as she sat down heavily, sighed and spread her napkin in her lap.

They ate in silence for several minutes. One or the other of them would occasionally try to make small talk. Suddenly her mother broke down and started sobbing.

'Iris,' said Nathan Fallon, reaching over to put an arm around her shoulders. He looked helpless.

'I just don't know how I'm going to face everybody.'

'With indignation and a sense of dark humor,' said Diane.

Everyone looked at Diane, as if no one had expected her mother's question to be answered and was surprised that she had. Diane felt that what her mother needed was some practical advice.

266

'Mother, most everyone will take their cue from you. If you act ashamed, they will treat you as if you have something to be ashamed of. Be frank and indignant about what happened to you and outraged that such a thing could be allowed to happen. Accept no guilt or shame whatsoever.'

'Good advice,' said Gerald.

'You might want to write an article for the newspaper,' said Diane. 'Let everyone know what can happen to a perfectly innocent, law-abiding citizen.'

Her mother shook her head back and forth. 'I couldn't.'

'I can write one for you and let you read it. If you are comfortable with it, send it in as a human-interest article on the perils of relying too much on computers without proper safeguards.'

Her mother moved her fork around in her vegetables. 'I don't want anyone to know.'

'They will find out anyway, but the knowledge will be passed on in whispers behind your back. Making it public knowledge takes the power away from gossipers. When you talk to people about it, sprinkle in some humor here and there. People react favorably to people who can laugh at themselves in the direst situations.'

'What could possibly be funny about any of this?' said Susan.

'I don't know,' said her mother. She tried to eat a few more bites of her food, but ended up putting down her fork. She looked at Diane. 'You mean

267

something like, "I had to leave before I could get my prison tattoo"?'

Diane laughed out loud. 'That's funny.'

Neither of her parents was known for their sense of humor, and her mother had made a joke. Susan and the others laughed, too. Diane was relieved to see it.

None of them did justice to Glenda's terrific meal, and all of them apologized to her. Susan and Gerald went out on the terrace to talk. Diane sat in the living room visiting with her parents, trying to steer clear of all the argument traps she usually fell into. That was made easier because both of them were more subdued in their opinions today.

Then her mother said, 'You know, dear, Alan is still very fond of you.'

Diane started to open her mouth to give some sort of noninflammatory reply, like *I could tell by the way he sniffed my clothes*, when her phone rang. Whoever it was, she felt grateful.

'Excuse me.' She looked at the display. 'It's the museum. I need to take this.'

It was actually David. Diane walked into another room and flipped up her phone to answer.

'David, hello.'

'Sorry to bother you at your parents' home.'

'No bother.' She felt like giving him a raise for getting her away from her family. 'You called at a very fortuitous moment. Did you get my e-mail? It was rather abbreviated because I did it by phone.'

268

'Yes, I'm getting on it. The reason I called is to tell you that the crime lab and your osteology lab were broken into. They stole several things out of the crime lab, including a couple of microscopes and some of Caver Doe's things. They also stole the skeleton from England that was in your bone lab.'

Diane's face flushed with anger – not only at the thieves, but at her security guards. How could they let this happen? 'When?' she asked.

'Last night around three A.M.'

'I'll leave here as soon as I can make arrangements.'

'That'll be a relief. I don't like cutting your visit short, but frankly, we've suddenly got bodies piling up.'

Diane told her parents that there was an emergency at the crime lab and she had to get back.

'Oh, no,' pleaded her mother, 'With everything that's happened, couldn't you stay a little longer? I've just gotten to see you after all this time. We haven't really had time to visit. I'm still so—'

'Surely, Diane,' said her father, 'someone else can handle matters for a few days. We need you here with us right now.'

Diane could feel her guilt index rising. 'I'm sorry to leave sooner than I expected. But with the authority I have at the museum also comes the responsibility. Something very serious has happened involving a break-in at the crime lab and the loss of evidence entrusted to me. I simply have to get back to take charge of the investigation.' *Besides*, she thought, *we'll only start arguing after a few days, and then I won't be out of your hair fast enough.*

'But what about your mother?' asked her father.

'Daniel Reynolds will do everything that needs to be done. It's all legal procedures and paper-work now, and I'm no help with that. She's in the best of hands. And Susan is right next door. She was a big help when we were at the lawyer's office.' That wasn't exactly true, but complimenting her sister was bound to get her some credits with them.

'You don't have to leave right this minute, do you?' asked her mother.

'No. I'll stay tonight and leave tomorrow morning on the first available flight.'

'Well, that's something, at least,' said her mother. By the tone in her voice, Diane could tell she was hurt, and frankly, Diane couldn't blame her. It was callous to leave so soon after her ordeal. But Diane had to see about the crime lab and the museum. She thought about asking them to come with her and visit, but dismissed that idea. She wouldn't have time to spend with them, and that would also hurt their feelings. There was no way to win.

'I'll drive you to the airport in the morning,' said Susan.

Considering the condition everyone was in, Diane might as well have gone back to Georgia that afternoon. Despite everyone's wanting to hear about her mother's experience, Iris was simply too exhausted after her ordeal to carry on a conversation. She kept dozing off and finally went up to her bedroom shortly after dark.

Diane's father was fidgety, worrying about her mother, and didn't seem to know what to do with himself. He appeared to be blaming himself for not being able to help her mother sooner, while not really understanding what had happened or why. He seemed very concerned that he was somehow responsible.

Susan and Gerald were distracted by their own problem that needed to be resolved, and they made their excuses and left while Diane's mother was napping.

The only absolutely positive event of the evening was that Diane was saved from having to see Alan again. He was uncharacteristically absent.

When she and Susan pulled away from the house the next morning, Diane's mother and father stood on the steps and waved good-bye to her. Her father stood with his arm around her mother's shoulders, trying hard to be strong. Her mother had tears in her eyes and leaned her head against her father's chest.

On the way to the airport, Susan told her that Gerald had been easier to talk to about 'the event,' as she called it. Diane must have had some influence with him. And probably for the first time in her life, Susan expressed gratitude. Diane was surprised that she could have a positive influence on the family. That alone would have made the trip worthwhile.

Susan was as disturbed by Alan's behavior as Diane. 'Do you think he's flipped out?' she asked.

'I don't know. Just keep an eye on Mother and Dad.'

'That'll be hard. Alan is in and out so much. Gerald thinks Alan would like for Mother and Dad to take both of us out of their will.'

'I hadn't thought of that.' The idea chilled Diane. She knew her parents had a lot of money. For someone like Alan, money was a tremendous temptation. 'That's scary, but they would never disinherit us – you, anyway,' said Diane.

'I don't think he would actually do anything to them. Do you?' asked Susan. 'Threaten them in some way?'

'Probably not. But I'm glad though that you and Gerald live next door,' she said.

'Me too.'

Susan dropped Diane off at the curb, and she rushed to the ticket counter with just enough time to get her ticket, pass through security and catch her flight.

CHAPTER 26

No matter what was awaiting her at the museum, Diane was relieved to be home. She had taken the airport limo service from the Atlanta airport to Rosewood and a taxi to her apartment, arriving there before ten A.M. When she walked in the door, she felt like kissing the floor. Instead, she took a quick shower, got dressed and called Kendel.

'I'm in Rosewood. David called me about the break-in. Is anything missing from the museum?'

'Good to have you back,' said Kendel. 'No, the museum proper is just fine. I had security double-check everything here, and nothing seems to have been taken.'

'I'll be in shortly and you can brief me on anything I need to know.'

Diane hung up, then called David and told him she was coming in. He told her that Chief Garnett and the head of security for the crime lab were coming over to meet with him.

'I'll be there as soon as I can.'

After David, she dialed Frank's cell phone and was relieved when he answered immediately. She really wanted to hear his voice. 'Hey, babe. You back?'

'Yes. And I'm so glad to be here.'

'How were things in Alabama?'

'Interesting.'

'That sounds like that Chinese curse – "May you live in interesting times."'

'It was something like that. Mother's home and safe. You had a lot to do with her release, and I wanted to thank you. I'll fill you in on the details later.'

'I didn't do anything but look up a few things, but I'll accept your gratitude,' he said. Diane smiled into the phone.

'Guess you heard about the break-in while I was gone. Looks like it's going to be a busy day. Maybe we can get together for something restful.'

'I think I can come by tonight. Not doing anything urgent right now. How's your arm?'

Diane flexed her arm. 'It's healing. Not quite as sore. You, Star and Neva get along?'

'We had a good time. Neva and Star played Monopoly and watched DVDs. Can you believe it? Mike's leaving the hospital today, and Neva's going to stay with him. There's been no news on who trashed her place.'

When Diane hung up the phone she had the sudden feeling she was late for something. It had been just three days, but it felt as though she'd been gone a month, and there were going to be too many things for her to catch up on. She headed out the door. In the hallway she met Mrs Odell. The woman must have video surveillance, thought Diane.

Veda Odell was a pencil-thin woman with a long, dour face. The color of her hair and eyes matched and were sort of a gray-brown, almost the color one got when mixing all the colors together. Her skin was milky white and paper thin, showing blue veins. The Odells were a retired couple who had a love of funerals and an allergy to cats.

'That boy David Goldstein came to see us. He said he works for you. He's a nice boy. Very interested in our opinion of the Egan rites. Not many young people care about funerals these days.'

'No, I don't imagine they do.'

'He asked us what we thought of the funeral.'

'I told him that you and your husband are experts,' said Diane.

Mrs Odell had a smile as thin as her body, but satisfaction shined in her gray-brown eyes. 'Marvin and I gave him quite an education, I can tell you. Told him what a proper funeral should be like. Showed him our collections. Not many people get to see them.'

Collections of what? Diane wondered, but knew better than to ask. David ought to have an unusual report.

'Thank you for giving your expert opinion. It should be a great help in our investigation.'

Diane made her escape down the stairs and out to her car. As she drove to the museum, she couldn't get the Odells out of her mind. *Collections of what?*

The beautiful Gothic nineteenth-century three-story granite structure that was the RiverTrail Museum of Natural History came into view as she turned off the street onto its main drive. The sight made her smile every time she saw it. She hoped it was the same for everyone who visited it. The parking lot was full, including several tour buses – another sight she quite enjoyed.

Diane went to her museum office first to make a call she dreaded.

'Good to have you back, Dr Fallon,' said Andie. 'The place is exciting, as usual. David has Detective Garnett – I think that's his name – at the crime lab.' Andie's usual excited demeanor was ratcheted up a notch.

'Thank you, Andie. I'm going over there in a minute, but I need to make a call first. Do you have the file on the Moonhater witch bones?'

'Sure. I guess you hate telling the guy his bones were stolen.' Andie handed her the file.

'More than you know.'

Diane looked at her watch and figured out the time difference. He should be there and awake, she thought. She dialed John Rose's museum number.

'Mr Rose, this is Diane Fallon.'

'Dear Dr Fallon. I'm so glad we have been able to connect. I've been out of town, and I understand that you have too.'

'Yes, I have. Mr Rose, I am so sorry to have to

tell you this, but someone broke in here and stole your bones the night before last. We are doing everything we can to recover them. I can't tell you how sorry—'

'No, dear lady, it is you who are owed an apology. And I sincerely do apologize.'

Diane was taken aback. *Had he come to get them?* she wondered. No, of course not. He wouldn't have broken in – and stolen other things too.

'I don't understand,' she said.

'The bones are safe. I wanted to tell you before they arrived that the bones I sent were those of a roe. I suspected something like this would happen. I heard Charlotte Hawkins was traveling to the United States, and I just knew she would try to steal my bones, or that Dean Denning would. He is the owner of Moonhater Cave.'

Diane was speechless. She didn't know whether to be relieved or angry. 'Well, Mr Rose, I don't quite know what to say.'

'I can well imagine. And I am very sorry to have played such a trick on you. I well intended to talk to you sooner, but I had to be out unexpectedly. I do want you to look at the genuine bones, please. Sir Gregory says you are the best. The real ones will be arriving at your door within the week by special courier.'

'All right. At least I now have some possible suspects. We had some other things taken as well.'

'Oh, dear. I've let you in for a spot of trouble indeed, haven't I? Please forgive me.'

'That's all right. I'm just glad they aren't missing. I'll let you know when your bones arrive.' Diane paused a moment. 'Did I hear you say Sir Gregory?'

'Yes. He was knighted just last week.'

'He didn't tell me, but he was never one to talk about his own achievements.' Nevertheless, Diane felt a little hurt that he didn't share his news with her.

'That's him. Very nice fellow. Wonderful family.'

Diane cradled the phone and sat a moment, shaking her head. At least she should be grateful that the witch bones had not been stolen. She pulled a card with Charlotte Hawkins's local address on it out of her desk drawer and slipped it into her pocket.

'Andie, I'll be in the crime lab. Call me if you need me.'

'Will do,' said Andie as Diane went out the door.

The crime lab was on the third floor of the west wing of the building. The room was a warren of glassed-in work-spaces outfitted with all the modern forensic equipment for various kinds of microscopic analysis, gas chromatography, spectral analysis, electrostatic detection and computer analysis. The computers held national and international databases for fingerprint and DNA identification, as well as databases for fibers, shoe prints, bullet casings, tire treads, paint, hair, cigarette butts and several others that David had added. In addition, the computers had software that matched, categorized, imaged, mapped and correlated all manner of data. The lab also had bug-rearing chambers. The crime lab was a separate entity from the museum, though Diane often consulted with the museum when she needed an expert on such things as pollen analysis, soil analysis or animal identification.

David, Chief Garnett and Lane Emery, head of security for the crime lab, sat at the round metal table in a corner of the lab.

'I was beginning to wonder where you were,' said Garnett, looking at his watch. He slid his hand over his salt-and-pepper hair.

Diane ignored Garnett's cross tone. She was rather cross herself. 'Tell me what happened,' she asked Emery.

The head of crime lab security looked to Garnett as if for permission. Diane hadn't hired him – the Rosewood police had – and he looked to Garnett as his boss. Diane didn't like that, but so far it hadn't been a battle she wanted to fight. She suspected that that would now change.

'Mr Emery, tell me what happened,' Diane repeated in a firmer tone.

'Oh, sure. At three sixteen A.M., someone bypassed the security system and broke into the crime lab. They hit Lee Carey, the night receptionist, with a stun gun and chloroformed him. Did the same with one guard, Joe Rich, and stole two microscopes, along with a box of evidence – I'm not sure what was in it.' He looked at David.

'The box contained railroad spikes, the Moon Pie wrappers, the rope and the Mickey Mouse flashlight from the cave. Korey had the clothes, and Jin had the rest of Caver Doe's stuff locked up in his station. All our other evidence was either in the vault or in the police evidence room downtown.'

'That's a blessing,' said Diane. 'Where were the security guards?'

'Brady was in the elevator-side lobby of the crime lab,' said Emery. 'He never saw a thing.'

When the crime lab was put in the west wing on the third floor of the museum, Diane had had an outside elevator and reception room built so the lab could have a separate entrance. In the daytime there was always a guard and a receptionist. The night receptionist stayed in a small glass-walled office on the museum side of the crime lab. The separate entrance had one guard.

'So you think the thief came in through the museum side?'

'Definitely. Joe Rich and Lee Carey were the only people they attacked. Brady never heard or saw a thing.'

'What about the video cameras?' asked Diane.

Emery looked chagrined. 'They managed to disable those too – the museum cameras and the crime lab surveillance. Whoever did it bypassed the security system control box in the basement and used a computer to decode the lock on the bone lab. Someone had to know what they were doing. It's a state-of-the-art system. This has the markings of a professional job.' He said the last statement as if it were a defense – a reason why security was breached.

'Interesting,' said Diane. 'I just got off the phone with the director of the museum in Britain who owns the bones that were stolen. He told me that he expected an attempt to be made to steal them. He gave me the name of the person he suspects, and as it turns out she visited the museum last week with a friend. She's a middle-aged Druid.'

Emery looked startled, as if someone had just shocked *him* with a stun gun. 'A what?' he said.

'A Druid. It's a pagan religion, I think. She didn't strike me as a professional burglar.' Diane had her forearms on the table. She clasped her fingers together and waited for a reaction.

Emery was an ex-marine. He was fit and sported a short haircut. Right now he stared at Diane, dumbfounded.

'Do you have a name for this woman?' asked Garnett.

'Charlotte Hawkins.' She looked at David. 'I assume you processed the labs and the basement.'

David nodded.

'I have a sample of her DNA. I took it to verify that the witch bones were from her ancestor.' Diane turned to David. 'Did you find anything we can use?' she asked.

281

'We found glove prints and some blue wool fibers in the basement. The inside of the keypad on your osteology lab door had powder residue used in medical gloves. We traced the brand of glove to a supplier in Atlanta. That's about it. They didn't leave a whole lot to work with, and so far, nothing that we can use for a DNA comparison.'

The osteology lab, Diane's bone lab, was technically part of the museum, though it was located adjacent to the crime lab and used the crime lab's security. She was thinking about changing that arrangement.

'Why didn't the receptionist see them coming down the hallway and raise the alarm?' Diane asked. 'There's no way he could have missed someone breaking into the lab from the museum side.'

'That's what I thought,' said Emery. He hesitated a moment. Emery still seemed rattled with all the talk of witches. Probably the idea that a middle-aged Druid got by his security system didn't sit too well with him either. 'But the guard said he was coming back from the bathroom and they jumped him from behind. He said he never knew what hit him. I'm thinking they hid in the museum until it closed. That's how they got in. Easier than trying to get access to the lab from outside.'

'They jumped him.' She turned to David. 'Did you . . .'

'We processed his clothes. No transfer,' he said, shaking his head.

'We are still looking at him,' said Garnett.

'I would expect so,' said Diane. 'I'm suspicious when burglars get a lucky break, like him being in the bathroom.'

'Why was the Druid lady – Charlotte Hawkins – here in the museum, and why did your British guy expect the bones to be stolen?' asked Garnett.

'Two factions are laying claim to the set of bones that has been on display in his museum – a woman who says she is a descendant, and the owner of the cave where the bones were originally found. The cave owner is suing for custody of the bones. The woman has made threats. She came here with a Wiccan friend from the United States to ask me to turn the bones over to her. I talked her into giving me a swab so I could check her DNA against the bones to verify whether she truly is a descendant.'

Garnett shook his head as though trying to clear water out of an ear. 'That's strange. Did she want them badly enough to hire professionals?'

'I don't know. Would professionals risk breaking into a crime lab?' asked Diane.

'I've known people who'll go anywhere for enough money,' said Emery.

'Do you know where this Charlotte Hawkins is staying?' asked Garnett.

Diane gave him the card Charlotte Hawkins had given her.

Garnett dropped the card into an evidence envelope and put it in his coat pocket. 'I'll look into it, Diane, we are trying to keep it quiet that the crime lab was burglarized. We don't want any defense lawyers getting the idea that evidence has been compromised. When David called it in he had the good sense to say it was the museum that was broken into. We need to find out what happened as soon as we can. I'm handling this one myself.'

'If you don't need me anymore, I'll be going,' said Emery. 'I want to solve this too. I don't like this happening on my watch. I know a few people I can talk to about who might be for hire.'

Emery stood up, looked around as if searching for something he'd forgotten, then left the lab by way of the elevator. Diane thought she noticed that his shoulders slumped. This was a blow. He had recommended the security system they had.

'I assume he's been been checked out,' said David.

'He will be. We aren't leaving anyone out.' Garnett smiled, and David smiled back at him.

'Is there any news about the stabbings at the funeral?' Diane asked.

Garnett shook his head. 'It's hard to believe, but no one saw a thing.'

'David, did the Odells provide you with anything useful?'

'The Odells?' asked Garnett.

'My neighbors,' Diane explained.

'The Addams Family,' said David.

'They attend all funerals of any interest,' said Diane. 'And take notes.'

CHAPTER 27

Garnett looked from Diane to David, wondering, no doubt, if they were pulling his leg.

'Did the Odells see anything suspicious?' Garnett asked finally.

'Not at the funeral itself,' said David. 'But at the grave there were several people who did not possess the solemnity that they should have. And there was one person who moved around a lot – going from one side of the gathering to the other. At first they thought he might be a reporter. They said he couldn't have been a mourner. He was too mobile, and his long black raincoat was not of good quality – it didn't hang right or something.'

Diane smiled, trying to imagine what went on in the Odells' minds.

'I asked them to describe the person. All I could get was male, medium height, dark hair, and several inches taller than Mavis Hatfield. Veda Odell did notice that he wore a ring with a bloodred stone, and one of his fingers looked like it had something wrong with it. She couldn't see what. She said they were never too near him.'

'Who is Mavis Hatfield, and how tall is she?' asked Garnett.

'One of the mourners,' said David. 'And she's five-foot-three. I told the detective on the case that the perp might have been standing next to her, so maybe he could interview her to see if she saw something.' Diane could tell from the position of David's eyebrows that he didn't believe the detective would follow through.

'How much weight should I give this?' asked Garnett.

'I'm not sure,' said Diane. 'They are familiar with how people act at funerals, and they go there to watch, so they would notice things out of the ordinary in that respect. That's all I can say . . .'

'Oh, they did say that they would never use that funeral home,' David said, grinning.

'Why?' asked Diane.

'They said they didn't do a good job embalming and the casket wasn't sealed right. Seems they got a whiff of an unpleasant odor.'

Diane laughed. 'God, what people.'

'Odell, did you say? I believe one of my detectives tried to interview them because their name was in the guest book. He didn't get very far.'

'I guess he didn't have David's savoir faire,' said Diane.

David scowled at her.

Garnett rose from the table. His tailored suit hung well on his lean body. Diane didn't think she had ever seen him when he wasn't well dressed. He smoothed his hair with a hand.

'At least we have a start. I'm not sure it will lead anywhere, but it's more than we had. I was beginning to think whoever stabbed you and Seger was a ghost.'

When Garnett left, Diane turned to David. 'So the Odells liked you?' David rolled his eyes. 'I told you they were weird folks,' she said.

David shook his head. 'Weird is when Druids and Wiccans come to the museum to demand a box of bones. Weird is enjoying hanging on the end of a rope over a hundred-foot precipice. These folks are several steps beyond weird. I'm telling you, you need to move away from there. Go stay with Frank. If you can't do that, you can stay with me.'

'You propositioning the boss?' Jin had come through the doorway carrying a plastic garbage bag, which he set in the corner.

'I'm trying to get her to move away from her freaky neighbors,' said David.

Jin's face lit up. 'You tell her about your visit?' He pulled out a chair and sat down at the table.

'I was about to. Seriously, Diane. These people are disturbed.'

'I saw Veda Odell this morning. She said she showed you their collections. They seemed to have taken to you.'

David looked somber. 'You don't know how that disturbs me to hear that.' Jin laughed, and David shot him a stern look. 'Do you know what they collect?' he said.

'No, and I'm not sure I want to,' said Diane.

'Go on, tell her,' said Jin.

'The more innocuous of their collections is mourning jewelry – rings, lockets, brooches that people wore in the eighteenth and nineteenth centuries to commemorate dead loved ones. Most of them have the deceased's hair in little compartments. Some of the hair-work jewelry has scenes made from bits of hair. Most of it is actually very good. They had a lock of woven hair that was supposed to have belonged to one of the Hapsburgs – Empress Elizabeth, I think they said.'

'Tell her about the other stuff,' urged Jin, leaning forward on his forearms and grinning at Diane. 'You're not going to believe this, Boss.'

'The jewelry was kind of nice, and I made the mistake of showing an interest. That's when they brought out their other collection.'

'Dare I ask?' said Diane.

'They have a collection of daguerreotypes of dead children.'

Diane opened her mouth and shut it again. 'What?' she said finally.

'Can you believe it?' said Jin.

'Dead children?' repeated Diane. 'Who would take pictures of dead children? You mean like autopsy photos, funeral shots?' She wasn't sure she wanted to hear any more.

'As nearly as I can understand it, it was the rage

in the eighteen hundreds to photograph the dead –
mostly children, but adults too. They would frame
the photos in these velvet-lined gold-and-leather
frames. Sometimes they would set the dead up in
fancy chairs like they were alive. The Odells had
a whole collection of them. I can't tell you how
depressed I was when I left.'

'You didn't tell her the worst part,' said Jin.

'They had albums of their own children's
funerals. Seven of them, and they all died in the
fifties before the age of ten. I'm telling you, Diane,
someone needs to investigate these people.'

'My landlady mentioned something about their
children once. How did they die; did you ask?'

'Some hereditary illness, they said, but jeez,
you'd have thought they would have stopped after,
say' – he made an exaggerated shrug with his
shoulders – 'four.'

'That was the forties and fifties,' said Diane. 'I
imagine birth control wasn't as good.'

'Neither was forensics,' said David.

'Maybe all this death stuff is just their way
of dealing with grief,' said Jin. 'You know, like
making death commonplace so it looks like their
children's dying was just a common part of life.
Supposing they didn't help their children into the
afterlife; it must have hurt big-time to lose so
many. That'd make you go crazy. Maybe that's
their way of being close to them.'

'I still think Diane ought to move,' said David.

Diane shook her head. That was a little more

than she wanted to know about her neighbors. She had thought they were odd before. Now they were downright creepy. 'Okay, let's change the subject. David, you said the bodies were piling up. Fill me in.'

'Jin and Neva worked a crime scene yesterday – two men found drowned in a quarry lake north of here just at the county line. One was a scuba diver. It's Sheriff Canfield's jurisdiction, and he thinks the diver got tangled up underwater in some brush and old fishing line. The other guy tried to help him, fell in and drowned too. Some fishermen found both of them. We don't have the medical examiner's report. We're calling the scuba diver Scuba Doe and the other guy Quarry Doe.'

Jin jumped up, went to his desk and came back with a folder. 'I have photographs and drawings. Like David said, Sheriff Canfield thinks it was an accident.'

Diane pulled the papers over to her. 'What do you think?' She stopped, wrinkled her nose and looked up. 'What is that smell?' Her gaze shifted to the garbage bag that Jin had put in the corner.

'You're not going to like this, Boss,' said Jin, looking like he clearly didn't want to say anything more. Unusual for Jin.

'Give it to me,' she said.

'It's one of the bodies.'

She raised her eyebrows and looked over at the bag. 'One of the drowning victims?'

'No. One of the bodies that David said is piling up. Do you remember Deputy Singer, that guy who was so mad because he had to wait for us to come out of the cave?'

Diane cocked an eyebrow. 'Yes. That's not him, is it?'

Jin laughed. 'You're going to wish it was. Some Boy Scouts out in the woods in Lumpkin County came across some bones – well, not completely bones. They still had some flesh on them – looks like a couple of months' decomposition, maybe. Anyway, they called Sheriff Burns, who sent Deputy Singer. He gathered up the bones and stuffed them in that garbage bag and brought them to the daytime reception desk an hour ago.'

Jin laced his fingers together, apparently waiting for her to react. Diane stared at him for a long moment, hoping that this was some joke of Jin's.

'He *stuffed* them in the garbage bag?' she said slowly.

'I told you that you weren't going to like it, Boss.' He and David exchanged glances. David looked as if he were stifling a chuckle.

'I don't suppose Deputy Singer has had a single course in crime scene protocol?' said Diane.

'Probably thinks they're a waste of his valuable time. It only took him a few minutes to gather them up. Think of how much time he saved,' Jin said sarcastically.

Diane put her head in her hands, then looked

up. 'I'll call Sheriff Burns and tell him to get the deputy to take you and . . .' Diane looked around the lab area. 'Where is Neva?'

'Mike's getting out of the hospital today,' said David. 'She's gone to get him settled in at home.'

'Is she doing okay?'

Jin nodded. 'Since her house was trashed? Yes,' he said. 'But she's been running on anger. The detectives think it was some teenagers in the neighborhood that she had a run-in with, but they can't prove it. We've accounted for all the prints. Whoever it was wore gloves.'

Diane shook her head. 'The MO doesn't sound like teenagers,' she said. 'It was too deliberate.'

'I agree,' said David. He stroked the fringe of dark hair he still had around the sides and back of his head. Diane wondered if he read somewhere that massaging the head made hair grow. 'Unfortunately,' he continued, 'we don't have much to give the detectives. We know the route he took through the house breaking things. We know he came in and left through the back door. He left the front door open, probably so his vandalism would be found, if not by Neva, then by someone noticing the open door. We know the paint was bought at Kmart, but we couldn't trace who bought it. The perp wore rubber gloves that left a powder residue. And we know it's someone who is really pissed off at Neva.'

'Powder residue?' asked Diane.

'Not the same kind as in your lab break-in.

Gloves are from a different company,' said Jin. 'But that's not to say it couldn't be the same guy.'

Diane chewed her lower lip. 'Too bad, though. I'd like to connect some of these things.' She sighed. 'No one in the neighborhood saw anything, I suppose?'

'No,' said David.

Diane sat in silence for a moment, organizing her thoughts on how to proceed. 'Okay. Jin,' she said, 'when Neva returns, I want you and her to go work the crime scene in the woods. I'll call Sheriff Burns and ask him to tell Deputy Singer to take you to where the body was found.'

'Deputy Singer's going to like that,' said Jin.

'I'm sure he will,' said Diane, hoping that Jin and Neva could somehow salvage the crime scene in the woods that Deputy Singer had messed up. 'And, Jin, be careful.'

'Always, Boss.'

'And put that sack in my isolation closet.'

'Sure.' He grabbed the sack and made for her lab.

In Diane's osteology lab she had two small rooms sealed off from the rest of the lab for the purpose of keeping and cleaning bones that still had flesh. They were so small that Diane referred to them as her closets. One room had a dermestarium similar to the one in the faunal lab, an old chest-type freezer converted to house a colony of dermestid beetles – the insects that stripped bones of flesh. The faunal

294

lab used their beetles to clean animal skeletons for the reference collection and museum display; Diane used her colony for cleaning human bones. She preferred dermestid beetles and hydrogen peroxide, rather than boiling, which made a greasier bone.

Diane used one room to keep contaminated remains isolated from the rest of the building and the other to keep the insects confined. Nothing could be more devastating to a museum than to have dermestids get loose. They loved to eat all the things that museum collections were made of. The isolation room also had a sink for washing the finished bones in hot water to kill any beetles hiding in cracks or openings. Diane didn't usually clean bones that had a lot of flesh still attached, like Caver Doe, or decomposing bodies. She let the medical examiner's assistant clean those. She cleaned up only bones that were almost completely skeletonized. She guessed that the bones in Jin's garbage bag were of that type.

Diane turned her attention to the folder that Jin had given her for the quarry bodies. She looked at each of the photographs in turn and placed them on the table along with Jin's drawings and notes of the scene.

Jin returned from the isolation room and sat down. 'Sorry, Boss. I should have put the bones away immediately.'

'That's all right. Tell me about these guys.' She gestured at the array of photographs.

Jin pointed to one of the photographs. Diane picked it up and examined the scene. It showed a body dressed in jeans and a T-shirt lying face-down in the water next to a log. It was labeled QUARRY DOE.

'The fishermen first found the body of just one man,' said Jin. 'When Sheriff Canfield came, they found the scuba diver in the water caught under the brush. The sheriff speculated that the first man slipped and fell trying to help the scuba diver.'

'Who's the ME on this?' she asked.

'Rosewood's ME,' said David. 'Rankin.'

'What does he say about them?'

David looked to Jin. 'He hasn't finished the autopsies, but at the scene he said they'd been dead about three or four days. The skin, hair and nails were loose, and the bodies were that greenish-black-purple color they get. He was talking like he agreed with Sheriff Canfield that it was an accident.'

Diane looked at the photograph labeled SCUBA DOE. The scuba diver's black-and-yellow suit barely showed through the tangle of branches that covered him.

'What do you think, Jin?'

'I have questions. Like where's the other diver?'

'Other diver?'

'Scuba diving is like caving. You don't do it alone. It's very dangerous. There has to be another diver. If the other diver was Quarry Doe, then where's his equipment?'

'You tell this to the sheriff?'

'Yes. He had the deputies search near the lake. But, see, if the other diver had his weight belt on and got into trouble, he may be at the bottom of the quarry. And that's another thing. I asked the sheriff how deep it is and he said a hundred feet or more. In that case, where's the descent line? You go that deep, you have to descend slowly and stop at intervals to adjust for the pressure changes. You use a marked descent line to do that. I looked and didn't find one.'

'What did you get from the crime scene?'

'It's all laid out on the table,' Jin said, pointing to one of the analysis rooms.

'Let's go have a look.' Diane rose, scooped up the papers and put them in the file.

Scuba gear and an assortment of evidence bags were arranged on the metal table. The room had the aroma of death from pieces of the victims stuck to their clothes. Diane had never really gotten used to that aroma.

'I checked out the tank,' said Jin. 'Nothing hinky about it. No tampering. It's out of air, and one of the hoses was punctured. There was a small twig stuck in it. That may have been what punctured it. Part of the wood is still lodged in the hose. I haven't examined the hole itself yet.

'I checked his goggles for prints. Found one set,' Jin added. 'David ran them and they didn't show up. The ME's going to try to get prints from the body.'

'I have Scuba Doe's prints.' Neva walked through the door and waved a large envelope at them. 'I just came from the ME's, where I got to wear the skin from the dead scuba guy's fingers. I can't tell you how much fun that was. I think this Halloween I'm going to borrow one of his cadavers and wear a cadaver suit.' She wrinkled up her face – so did Diane. Jin and David laughed. 'Quarry Doe – he's the floater by the log – had his fingertips nibbled off. No prints there.'

'Neva,' said David, 'I thought you were with Mike.'

'I was. I got him into his apartment, fixed him something to eat, made him promise to rest and went to the ME's office.' She handed the envelope to David. 'Grist for your algorithm machines.' Neva looked happy and rested. Her camel-colored slacks and wine silk blouse looked new. She and Star must have gone shopping to replace some of her clothes. Diane liked seeing her in good spirits.

'I'll go run these right now,' said David, heading out the door.

Neva pushed her hair behind her ears. 'Dr Fallon, it's good to have you back. I had a lot of fun at Frank's house. His daughter, Star, is a hoot. We played Monopoly, ate ice cream and looked at fashion magazines. Frank's a really nice guy.'

'He's pretty decent, I have to admit,' Diane said with a smile.

'That's nice what you're doing for Star. Makes me want to go to the university. Of course, you're going to be broke by then. You should see the things Star is looking at.'

Diane rolled her eyes. 'I always say, if you're going to resort to bribery, make it good.' She shook her head thinking of Star, then refocused her attention on work. 'I'm glad you're here. We need you.'

Neva grinned. The last time she saw Neva she had been crying over the shambles the vandal had made of her home.

'You're going to have to change clothes. I need you and Jin to go to the woods.'

'You know that deputy we had the pleasure of meeting when we brought Caver Doe out of the cave?' said Jin. She nodded, and he told her about the garbage bag of bones.

Neva cocked her head to one side. 'Why am I not surprised?'

'I'm sure he didn't get all the bones,' said Diane.

David stuck his head in the door.

'Found a match already?' asked Diane.

'No, not yet. It's still running. But you're not going to believe this.' He jerked his thumb back toward his desk. 'I called Sheriff Burns to get Deputy Duck to take Jin and Neva out to the woods, and found out that he's in the hospital.'

'What happened?' they all asked together.

'After delivering the bones, he was driving back and had an accident. He told the sheriff that a swarm of bugs crawled all over him as he drove down the road.'

CHAPTER 28

Jin and Diane looked each other, then at David, with their mouths agape.

'A swarm of bugs?' Neva wrinkled her nose. 'In his car?'

'That's what Sheriff Burns told me. Said it was right out of a horror movie.'

'I believe our deputy must have been drinking,' said Neva.

'That's not what I'm thinking,' said David.

'Ah,' said Jin. 'It's a good thing we put the bag in isolation.'

'We need to make sure none escaped,' said Diane, horrified. 'Dermestids are terrible museum pests. If they get into the taxidermy displays or the insect collection . . . or, God forbid, the mummy . . .'

'Maryanne downstairs told me the deputy came in and handed her the garbage bag with a smirk. It smelled so bad, she tied off the top of the bag with string. It was plenty tight. As I brought it up the elevator, I checked for holes. There weren't any, so I think we're safe.'

'I'll make sure Maryanne has a bonus in her

300

next paycheck,' muttered Diane. 'What else do we have here?'

Diane picked up and examined each evidence bag. One contained the clothes of Quarry Doe. Another had the scuba diver's underclothes. Others held assorted things found at the scene – one spent shotgun shell casing . . .

'Were they shot?' asked Diane.

'No,' said Jin. 'At least, the medical examiner on the scene said they weren't, but we don't have an autopsy yet.'

There were also two cigarette boxes and thirteen cigarette butts.

'This is interesting,' said Diane. She held up a clear plastic bag containing a soiled photograph. The picture was a blur.

'I thought we might get some prints from it,' said Jin.

All Diane could see were murky shapes and shades of a nondescript gray-green color. 'Can you tell what it is?' she asked.

'Bad photograph. Whoever took it probably threw it away,' said Jin.

Diane stared at the picture, squinting her eyes, looking at the shapes in the foreground.

'You see something, Boss?' asked Jin.

'I don't know.' Diane paused, studying the print through the plastic, turning it different directions. The others looked over her shoulder. 'You know, I think this is a photo taken underwater.'

'You think so?' said Jin. 'Maybe.'

Diane turned to David. 'Okay, Mr I-love-a-good-algorithm, you think you can clear this up?'

David took the evidence bag and studied the photograph. 'The various pieces of software I use essentially reverse the blurring process, so the formula for sharpening it depends on how the image was blurred. For example, in simple out-of-focus pictures, the blurring is equal in all directions.' He made an oval of his hands, touching the tips of his fingers together.

'On a pixel level that means one pixel expands into a circle of pixels of a different color value. But if the blur is caused by motion, like a moving car, then the blurring is in only one direction, hence pixel expansion is in one direction. And, of course, digitizing and scanning have their own formulas, which can cause a blurred image of a different pixel pattern.'

'TMI,' said Neva, swiping her hand over the top of her head.

'Can you clear it up?' repeated Diane.

'Well, it may be that underwater shots simulate out-of-focus shots in the directionality of the blurring effect. I have some new NASA software that does well with hazy—'

'David, can you do it?' said Diane.

'I'll give it a try.'

'Good, thank you.'

David took the photograph to his workstation.

Diane spread the photos of the quarry crime scene out on the table and looked them over again, this time paying more attention to the woods that surrounded the quarry, looking for anything that her crew or the sheriff's people might have missed.

'Did you notice that this is an old roadway?' She put her finger on a less-dense avenue through the woods, with trees shorter than their neighbors on either side.

'No, I didn't notice that,' said Jin.

'Is it relevant?' said David. 'It's overgrown now.'

'Not through here.' She pointed to a place that, if one looked closely, might have been a deer trail.

'How are you seeing this?' said Jin.

'Something my archaeologist friend Jonas Briggs taught me,' said Diane. Archaeologists are good at finding old house sites and roadways after they are all grown over.

'Want me to go back and take a look?' said Jin.

Diane nodded. 'Interview the deputy and the Scouts. Get them to draw how the bones were positioned.'

'Okay, Boss.'

'I want you to do something else, too.' She pulled out the photo showing the scuba diver's body underwater. 'I want a sample of the underwater twigs and tree limbs in which the diver was entangled. Bring them to the lab, and have Korey examine them. He's an expert in submerged and waterlogged wood.'

'Oh, so you're thinking that maybe he didn't get tangled and run out of air,' said Jin. 'You're thinking that the wood was put on top of him after he was dead?'

'I don't know. I'd like to examine the possibility. Okay, everyone has their assignments. Jin and Neva, find out where in the woods the bones were discovered and work the scene. Deputy Singer pretty much messed it up, but look for more bones. After that, go to the quarry, take a look along the trail and get samples of submerged wood. Maybe the perp came from that direction and dropped something. David, you said you want to collect a bug or two from the deputy's car?'

'Neva and I can stop by and do that too,' said Jin. 'I'll find out where they took his car.'

'Then David, you start on the evidence here,' said Diane. 'I'm going to examine the bones in the garbage bag. Caver Doe will have to wait for a while.'

Diane headed for her lab, and David stayed and watched the computer screen as the AFIS software looked for a match between fingerprint from the quarry crime scene and fingerprints from the AFIS databases.

'Diane, wait,' David said just as she reached the door. 'I have a possible match on our scuba diver – Scuba Doe.' She walked back to the computer and looked over his shoulder.

'Okay,' he said, 'let me see if this really matches.' David examined each print, overlaid them, then separated them back out. 'It's only a six-point match, but it's a place for the sheriff to start. It's a Jake Stanley – arrested five years ago for vandalism. He would be twenty-two right now. I'll give Sheriff Canfield a call.'

'This is good. We're making progress.' Diane shrugged her shoulders. 'Is it just me, or are we suddenly overwhelmed with work?'

David put a hand on the telephone. 'It's not just you. I'm having a hard time figuring out which sheriff to call for what crime scene. Are we in a full moon or something?'

'Or something,' she said as she walked back to the door.

'After I call Canfield, I'll come over and brief you on the other investigations,' said David.

With all the dead bodies, Diane had momentarily forgotten about his investigations of Dr Lymon and Alan Delacroix. 'Like I said, too many things going on.'

Diane changed to lab clothes in her office. The last thing she wanted was the smell of death clinging to her good clothes. She put a disposable cap over her hair, donned a pair of latex gloves and went into the isolation room.

She cut the string and opened the garbage bag the deputy had delivered. An unpleasant aroma wafted out of it. She looked in, frowned and swore at Deputy Singer under her breath. Bones with black flesh clinging to them stuck out through a bag filled with leaves and other forest litter.

Diane pulled a long sheet of butcher paper off

the roll, put it on the table and placed the garbage sack on it. She turned down the top of the sack, like rolling down a pair of socks. Several bugs scurried among the leaves.

The first bone she pulled from the jumble was a femur – a thigh bone. There was a fresh cut in the shaft. She would bet Deputy Singer had shoveled the bones up and deposited them in the bag. She swore at him again.

There was also another cut, shallower, a scratch partway down the bone. But that one was not fresh. Examination under her hand lens showed it not to be a continuous line. There were gouges, like hesitations or missteps, followed by slices. A knife, she thought. She forced herself to think of the bone, not the victim. Impossible, but she always tried.

The ilium of a pelvis peeked out from behind a clump of dirt and leaves. As she took it out of the bag, the other half hung by a thread of skin. She saw immediately that it was a female pelvis.

Removing the pelvis had uncovered the dome of the skull. She lifted it out with both hands and set it on the table. Dried skin held on to the lower jaw and clung to the cheeks, in the eye sockets, and on part of the skullcap. Several clumps of gray-white hair stuck to the skin on the skull. Enough of the top of the skull was exposed that she could see the sutures were almost gone. This was an old individual.

Other marks were visible where the bones of the

face showed through the remnants of flesh – striations cut into the bone on the forehead, cheeks and chin, as though someone had sliced her face with a knife.

Diane dipped her hand in the sack, recovering bone after bone, placing them in position on the table. Even with the brief inspection of the bones as she laid them out, several characteristics stood out. The bones were thin and brittle, exhibiting signs of arthritis and osteoporosis. In addition they had been damaged by animals – and sliced by a knife. The ends of the long bones showed the identifiable destructive pattern left by the gnawing of dogs. The shaft had been cut by something sharp, probably a knife. The ribs on each side, the femora, tibias, humeri, and radii and two cervical vertebrae all showed the same marks.

She caught a glimpse of a bit of pink fabric among the leaves in the bag. She gently moved the leaves and dirt away, uncovering a larger and larger piece. It was cotton, faded pink and stained by the body fluids from the decomposing corpse. The dress was thin and handmade and buttoned up the front with small white buttons. She hadn't been a large woman at all. Diane put the remains of the dress in a paper evidence bag and labeled it.

David opened the door and came into the room, sporting a disposable cap, gloves and a glass container. 'Thought I would help you with the insects. Good heavens,' he said, looking into the sack filled with litter. 'What did he do, shovel the body in?'

'From some of the markings I'm seeing, yes, that is exactly what he did.'

'I called Sheriff Canfield. He was happy we were able to tentatively identify one of the quarry victims. I told him we will process the evidence as soon as we can.'

Diane nodded. 'What did you find out about Dr Lymon?'

'She has an alibi for the time of the graveside attack. I spoke with several of her geology graduate students. I didn't find any hint that she has ever sexually harassed any other student. Most of the gossip was about her teaching methods. She isn't well liked. In fact, Mike seems to be one of the few who got along with her. In her classes she'll zero in on a particular student and verbally quiz them during the lecture. The more they don't know, the more she focuses in on them. Geology has lost several students because of her.'

David stopped to scoop up several bugs and put them in his container. '*Dermestes maculatus*. Nice little scavengers,' he said.

'We need to be sure we get them all. I don't want any infesting the museum colony of beetles,' said Diane, staring at the dark beetles running around in David's jar.

'I'll get them all. You know, there are a lot of them,' he said as he peeked into the bag. 'And I'm seeing a lot of bug parts.'

'What do you mean?'

David shook his head. 'I don't know. It just looks like more beetles than usual, if you think about all the bugs left behind and the ones that scared the deputy.'

Diane pulled another bone out of the sack and held it in her hand. It was cleaner than the others, a long bone, a humerus, but not human.

'What is this?' She said out loud and put paper out on another table and set the bone on it. 'I'll get Sylvia Mercer in here to identify this. Go ahead with what you were saying about Lymon.'

'Not a lot more. The students were aware that Mike lost his assistantship, but no one knew why. They thought maybe it was because she was angry over his changing his dissertation research to crystallography, which is out of her field. But she apparently encouraged him and helped him pick someone in crystallography to replace her on his committee. That doesn't sound like anger. I'm thinking maybe this harassment was a onetime thing, and her anger came later.' He stopped talking a moment and stared at the bones Diane was laying out on the table.

Diane turned to look at him. 'You look like you have something else to say.'

'Just trying to think it out. From what I can find out, her husband's leaving hit her hard. I think she wanted to get some self-esteem back and thought Mike would be receptive.'

'Because he worked for her?'

'Because she knew he was attracted to another older woman.'

'You mean me. Is there something I should know about that?'

David looked up at her, surprised. 'About you? No. I'm just thinking out loud. You said she thought you and Mike were having an affair. Everyone knows you and Mike go caving and that you're friends. Some even know Mike would have liked to go out with you. She probably thought that Mike would be a safe place for her pride to land. She was wrong, and that's why she got so angry.'

Diane noticed that David was tiptoeing around calling her an older woman, like Dr Lymon – they were about the same age. She smiled. 'You may be right. I guess the question is, how angry was she? If she didn't stab us, could she have gotten one of her students to do it?'

David leaned with his back against the wall and folded his arms. 'I don't think so. Not the ones I talked to. I didn't find evidence of any students who liked her well enough to carry her briefcase, much less kill for her.'

'How did you get all this information, if I may ask?' said Diane, looking in the garbage bag again and finding a foot bone.

David grinned. 'The students were pretty easy to talk to. I pretended to be a father checking out the department for his kid.'

She looked up at him. 'The students didn't think

that was funny?' Diane remembered when she was a young student, and she would have thought that strange.

'I'm sure they did, but what was really funny was that several of them seemed to like the idea that I would care enough to do it.'

'I'm relieved about Dr Lymon. Thanks, David.' She let out a deep breath. 'What about Alan?' She really didn't want to talk about Alan, but she needed to find out if David had discovered anything.

'You know, I'm having trouble visualizing you married to someone like that,' said David.

Diane didn't like to think about their marriage either. He now made her shiver, and not in a good way. 'Yeah, me too.'

'I think he's in the clear. He had a dental appointment that day. I talked to his dentist.'

'That's a relief, too. Frankly, I didn't want the complications his guilt would bring.'

'How's your mother?'

'I'm not sure. As you can imagine, this had quite an effect on her. She's usually strong and opinionated, but she was cowed when we brought her back. I think it will take time.'

Diane pulled out a cluster of bones with a long tail. 'Got any idea what this is?' She put the bones on the table with the other animal bone.

'From the tail it looks like an opossum.'

'Why, David, I didn't know you knew animal bones.'

'I've seen enough roadkill to be able to ID the tail.'

'It looks like we have several animals mixed in with Jane Doe.' She pulled out another animal long bone and a cheap walking shoe.

David picked out the beetles as Diane fished around in the leaves. She found several more bones of some kind of mammal.

Most of the human hand and foot bones were missing, as was her left femur. Oddly enough, the hyoid bone, which was often missing in decomposed corpses because it was so small, was there, but only because it was stuck to flesh. It was broken.

'The hyoid is a bone in the neck that is often broken in strangulation,' said Diane. 'It looks like someone strangled her, slit her throat and sliced her up – and I'm not sure in that order.'

'Overkill?'

'Maybe. The woman was old, weak and vulnerable. Why do this – and why do I keep asking questions like that?'

'Looking for a rational killer, I guess. You think it may be a serial? The way she was killed suggests a pattern.'

'Maybe. Have a look at the database. I'm not sure Sheriff Burns has the access or the manpower to do the searches we do.'

David collected all the live bugs he could find, as well as several bug parts. 'Quite a collection,' he said.

'I'll put the rest of the bag contents on the screen, spray out the dirt and pick out the leaves. I'll let you have a look at the detritus to see if there are any other kinds of bugs.'

David nodded. He took his jar of bugs and left Diane alone with her bones. In the screen she found three bones of the hand and a thin gold wedding band. Unfortunately, it wasn't engraved.

CHAPTER 29

Diane took the scope and viewer into the isolation room to examine the bones for telltale fibers and any other small thing that might be revealed. She ran the scope along the bones and dried flesh and watched the magnified image on the monitor. She found several fibers, lifted them out with tweezers and placed each one in an envelope and labeled it.

The magnified image showed several cuts on the ribs similar to the cuts on the long bones. The killer had sliced down her torso, leaving nicks on both sides of her rib cage. *God*, thought Diane, *how do people get disturbed enough to do this to a person?*

Diane left the room and came back with the handheld metal detector from the crime lab. She moved it slowly a couple of inches above Jane Doe's bones. It would be a long shot, but— The detector went off in the middle of her thought. The area was the upper part of the left femur, the greater trochanter, a prominence where the gluteals, iliopsoas, and piriformis muscles attached to the bone. The bone was covered with dark dried

314

skin. When she put the scope over it, she could see it was sliced.

With a scalpel she gently cut the dried flesh away. In the scope image she saw something embedded in the exposed bone. She grasped it with a pair of forceps and pulled. It came out easily and was what she had expected and hoped for – the tip of a knife blade. With this, if they found the knife, they could identify it as the weapon. She put the metal fragment in an evidence bag and labeled it.

She used the scope again and examined the face, the teeth and the eye sockets for the minutiae that criminalists looked for – something caught in the teeth, a shred of something that had taped her mouth shut or her eyes closed – anything that might provide a clue to who she was and what had happened to her.

Jane Doe had most of her teeth, and they were in good condition – just a few old fillings. The pattern of wear on the adjacent teeth said that she'd had a bridge anchored to her upper back molars. But the bridge wasn't present. Perhaps Jin and Neva would find it.

Something in the left eye socket caught Diane's attention – a very small, light-colored object stuck to the dried skin. Diane pulled gently on it with her tweezers until it came free. The object had a piece of something else attached to it. Diane put it in a tray and gently rinsed it.

She stepped out of the small room, taking the tray containing the tiny something with her.

Mounting the object on a glass slide, she slipped it on the microscope stage and looked through the eyepieces, moving the focus until she could see it. It looked plastic and translucent – almost like a head with a tail. She moved it with her tweezers. It was some kind of tube with a rounded something attached to one end. Diane turned it over, trying to figure out what it could be. The other side was marred by an imperfection. She twisted the focus knob. Not an imperfection, but something stamped or engraved into it. She increased the magnification and refocused. It was a string of digits – a number.

Diane wrote down the numbers, then attached the digital camera to the microscope and photographed the tiny object. When she finished taking several shots on each side and at different magnifications, she took the memory stick from the camera to the vault where her computers were.

The vault was a secure, environmentally controlled room where she stored skeletal remains. It was also where she kept her special computer equipment and software. With her forensic software, using a few bone measurements from a skeleton she could make accurate predictions about a victim's race, sex and a host of other variables. She could enter skull and facial measurements into another program and it would predict with a fair degree of accuracy what country or demographic region the individual came from.

She also had three-D facial-reconstruction

equipment – a laser scanner that mapped skulls, and a dedicated computer with software for building a face from the data. When she discovered that Neva was an artist, she had taught her how to use the equipment, and they had been able to get identification of several victims from Neva's artistic reconstructions. Neva had also given a face to the mummy that the museum inherited – all with the help of the equipment. It was a pretty high-tech room.

The vault also had a plain, ordinary office computer. As she entered the room she saw Caver Doe on a table in the corner, waiting for his examination to be finished. She looked at her watch. Not today, maybe tomorrow.

Diane booted up the computer, put in the memory stick and looked at the pictures she had taken of the object from Jane Doe's eye socket. She sat back in the chair and stared at the image – a tube attached to something round, with a number, and found in the eye socket. Something medical? What medical thing would be in the eye?

She logged on to the Internet and ran a Google search on medical devices and eyes. As she browsed through the hits, several words and phrases kept appearing dealing with glaucoma, eye pressure and drainage devices. She searched on those terms, and the first hit contained a diagram of a device that looked remarkably like what she had found – a tube shunt. She searched again using the terms *eye shunts* and *glaucoma* and came

317

up with over eight hundred hits. She clicked the Images button in Google, and pictures of eye shunts scrolled across the screen. She didn't even have to enlarge the pictures to see that she was right. What she was looking at were many variations on the device she had found – an eye shunt, a treatment for glaucoma. If the number on the shunt was a serial number, could it be traced? Diane smiled to herself with satisfaction. She loved unexpected discoveries.

Diane turned off the computer. As she locked the vault behind her, the thought of the thieves crossed her mind, and she shivered with a combination of fear and relief that they hadn't broken into the vault containing all that expensive equipment – and data.

She secured the shunt in an evidence bag and took it to the lab, along with the gold ring and pieces of clothing. David was there looking for fingerprints on the photograph.

'I found something interesting,' she said as she put the memory stick in the lab computer and called up the pictures.

'What is that?' said David. 'Looks sort of like a robotic sperm, or perhaps an android tadpole.'

'It's an eye shunt. It's used in glaucoma patients to drain the eye fluid and relieve pressure.'

'Where did you find it?'

'In Jane Doe's eye socket. The best part is, this little deal has a serial number.' Diane looked at him and grinned broadly.

'Well, damn, I wonder if we can track her from the number?'

'We can try.'

'I'll get on it when I finish here. I took a swab of the photograph before I dusted it for prints. Besides dirt, there was some other stuff on it.'

'Work's piling up, isn't it?'

'Have you thought about hiring an extra person?' said David.

'I've thought about it. What I haven't thought about is how to approach Chief Garnett. Let's get through this. We'll do a time audit on ourselves and I'll make a proposal to him. When he finds out we all have to work overtime just to get the normal work done, perhaps he'll let me hire additional criminalists.'

'It would be good. You're only supposed to be part-time. If I'm not mistaken, you work full-time in both your jobs. Not much time for a life away from the office.'

'Frank has to work long hours too, so we're well suited in that respect.'

'Why don't you two get married?'

'Why don't you mind your own business?' she said without rancor. 'Things are good the way they are.' Diane wondered why everyone wanted her to marry. Things were just fine.

David opened his mouth and shut it again. 'You and Frank seem like a good match to me,' he said finally. 'You are always happy together. At least move away from those neighbors.' He looked at the photograph. 'No prints, just smears.'

'I *have* been thinking about a house,' said Diane.

'It's good to have goals outside of work,' said David. 'Dead bodies can start weighing on your psyche . . . as you know.'

'How about you? What would you like to do?'

'I've been considering teaching some photography courses at the tech school.'

'We have workshops at the museum. Why don't you work up a plan and submit it to me – like bird photography?' suggested Diane. 'You can make an exhibit of your bird photographs.'

David looked up from his work, surprised. 'That's a good idea. I'd like that. I would. There are a lot of nice places on the nature trail to get pictures. Thanks. I'll do that.' He nodded his head up and down. 'Yeah. Good idea.'

'Unless you have any more suggestions about my private life, I need to finish Mrs Doe.'

'Mrs?'

'A guess. There's a wedding band among the detritus. No engraving.' Diane put the evidence in one of the drawers and labeled it JANE DOE.

Diane went back to the lab and worked on Jane Doe. *A sad-sounding name,* she thought. *Jane Doe lying dead in the woods, and no one knowing where you are or who you are.*

She examined the pelvis and discovered that Jane had probably given birth. She had arthritis in the knees, hands, shoulders and back. Her pelvis was

320

thin, and so were several of her vertebrae. Her left radius was broken, and there was no sign of healing. Deputy Singer hadn't done it with his shovel. It had happened around the time she died. The deputy had broken two of her ribs, however.

Jane Doe was Caucasoid, in her eighties, and was about five feet, two inches tall and stooped when she walked. She was left-handed. She was a small, elderly woman, and someone broke her arm, strangled her, cut her with a knife from head to toe and dumped her body in the woods for Deputy Singer to come along and violate with his shovel.

Diane hoped it wasn't a serial killer. She didn't want to think about more anonymous people lying alone in the woods waiting to be found. She took Jane Doe's bones in the other room, where she had a colony of dermestid beetles. Nothing could clean bones like they could. Their mouth parts were enormously strong for their small size, and they loved dried flesh. The dermestarium was kept separate from the room where the bodies were examined to reduce the chance the colony would be contaminated by mites that lived on beetles from the wild. A mite infestation could wipe them out. The museum's colony came from a supply house and were free of pests.

In just a few days Jane Doe's bones would be rendered almost white, clean and unaltered – the beetles didn't damage even the smallest bones. Then Diane would check again for stray marks she might have missed from things like knives or bullets.

Diane changed out of her lab clothes. Her museum clothes felt good, and it was a relief to get away from the smell. After she was dressed she walked down to the lab, where she found David hard at work on the quarry crime scene.

'How is it going?'

'Sure but slow. Right now I'm collecting all the trace from the evidence. When I'm finished I'll start analyzing. How about you? You must be finished if you changed clothes.'

'I put Mrs Doe with the dermestids.'

David laughed. 'Every time I see a beetle now I'm going to think of Deputy Singer.'

'That must have been frightening for him.'

'I'm sure it was. Sheriff Burns told me Singer loves those horror movies about insects and spiders out of control. Talks about them all the time. Says his favorite is one called *They Crawl*. Can you believe it? There's got to be thousands of those B-grade movies, and apparently he's seen every one. Then suddenly he's in one. God, I almost feel sorry for him.'

'Did anyone else get hurt?'

'No, and he wasn't hurt badly. He ran into a fire hydrant. They're keeping him overnight for observation. He'll be going home tomorrow.'

'From the insects you found on her, can you give me a time line for Jane Doe?' asked Diane.

'I need to know more about the place where she was found. From the look of the forest litter it was damp. I'll talk to Jin when he returns. I may have to go out there myself.'

'Keep me informed. I'm going to grab something to eat.' Diane left David working in the lab and took the elevator down to the first floor. She intended to go to the restaurant, but she decided to go to her office and check in with Andie first.

'Dr Fallon. Just in time. You've got a phone call. He's called a couple of times. I didn't want to disturb you in the lab. He won't say who he is.'

Probably someone wanting access to their Egyptian mummy. There was a steady stream of scientists who wanted tissue samples, X-rays, body parts or MRIs for their research ever since the museum had inherited him, and they would usually speak only with Diane herself.

Diane sighed. 'I'll take it in my office. Andie, could I get you to run down to the restaurant and get me a sandwich?'

'Sure. What kind?'

'Oh, how about a BLT and a glass of iced tea.'

'You got it.'

Andie went off to the restaurant. Diane sat down at her desk and picked up the phone.

'Diane Fallon.'

'Diane, what the hell are you trying to do to me? Just what the hell are you playing at?'

Diane didn't say anything. For a second she didn't recognize his voice. 'Alan, is that you?' *Great*, she thought. *I'd rather speak to the mummy researchers.*

323

CHAPTER 30

'Yes, it's me. Who the hell do you think it is?'

Well, I didn't know, thought Diane. *There could be any number of people this pissed off at me.*

'Alan, what's the matter?'

'What's the matter! How can you ask that? Dammit, are you trying to ruin me?'

'What are you talking about?' she asked, even though she knew. He didn't like being investigated.

'This guy from the Rosewood police called me and wanted to know my whereabouts when you were stabbed. God, how could you think I would do such a thing?'

'When you creep into my room at night and sniff my clothes, you make yourself a suspect.'

There was dead silence on the other end of the phone. It stretched out so long, Diane was about to say something when he finally spoke.

'How did you . . .' He didn't finish.

'It doesn't matter. What in God's name were you doing?' she asked.

'I wanted to talk to you,' he said.

What do we have to talk about? she thought. 'Why didn't you knock?'

'I didn't know if you were awake. I wanted to see first.'

Diane rolled her eyes. 'Alan, do you know how lame that sounds?'

'I wasn't going to hurt you.'

'It was not appropriate. We aren't married. My bedroom is private.'

'God, Diane, what's the big deal? For that you turn me in to the police?'

'The act made you a suspect, and I had to check you out.'

'I told them you invited me and then got cold feet.' His voice sounded smug.

David hadn't told her that. She smiled grimly. Alan didn't know that the policeman who called was actually one of her employees. David probably introduced himself as a criminalist from the Rosewood Police Department. Alan probably didn't know what a criminalist was.

'I doubt he believed you, Alan.'

He gave a derisive snort. 'You don't think so? I told him you've always had a hard time accepting our divorce. It's your word against mine, and I am very convincing.' His voice had regained its confidence.

'Alan, let me clue you in. You are the one who moved to the town where my parents live and kept up a relationship with them. I'm the one who lives a state away and hardly ever visits. Who does it look like won't let go?'

Alan was silent again for a long moment. 'Why are you doing this?'

'I'm not doing anything. Believe it or not, I wanted to rule you out as a suspect. I asked that they be discreet.'

'Well, when the police guy talked to my dentist he told him he thought I was witness to a car accident in Atlanta,' he admitted.

'See? That doesn't make you look like a deranged killer.'

'The policeman wasn't so nice when he talked to me.'

Diane smiled and tried not to laugh. 'Don't take it personally. They talk that way to everyone.'

'How else should I take it?'

'Look, if Mother can get though Tombsberg, you can take a little questioning. Alan, what's happening to you? You didn't used to be . . . well, mean.' *Self-centered, maybe, but not deliberately mean.*

'Mean? What are you talking about?'

'I'm talking about what you did to Gerald and Susan. They have always supported you.'

'They told you about that, did they? Gerald was trying to make me look bad to the partners in my firm.'

'As I understand it, he was just trying to tell the truth.'

'What would it have hurt to go along with me? They aren't his employers.'

'I don't know the details, but presumably you

did something wrong with the firm's accounts and he had to straighten them out. Gerald wouldn't go along with your lie, so you tried to destroy his marriage. What kind of friend are you?'

'You don't know it was a lie.'

'Alan, you just told me you lied to the police about me. What am I supposed to think about your veracity?'

'You always did like to play with words, twist them around in your favor.'

'Alan, I have to go.'

He was silent again. He never used to have so hard a time searching for a comeback. Diane wondered if she should just hang up, but she was starting to pity him. *God, where did that come from?* she thought. *Don't start feeling sorry for him.*

'Alan, please fix things with Susan and Gerald. I don't know why you are separated from your wife, but it might be good to work on that. You have two kids. They should be a joy in your life. Nothing else should matter.'

'I was hoping we could start talking again,' he said.

'No. That's not a good idea. You have so many things going for you. Don't self-destruct.'

'It was good seeing you again. I . . . I wasn't being a pervert. I was just smelling your perfume,' he said, then abruptly hung up the phone.

As if my life isn't complicated enough, Diane thought as she closed her eyes and rubbed her temples. God, the last thing she wanted to do was to feel sorry for Alan. She heard Andie's office door open and close.

Andie peeked her head in. 'One BLT and cold iced tea, coming up.' She walked in and set the sandwich and glass on Diane's desk.

Diane was hungry now. The sandwich looked good. 'Thanks, Andie. Anything going on that I should know about?'

'We have several more letters from researchers insisting on access to the mummy.'

'You send them the standard reply we crafted? No access, but we'll share the data we've collected?'

'With some of them that isn't working. They have research needs that we didn't cover in our own research, apparently.'

'If it becomes a problem, take their number and I'll call them and say no.'

'Aquatics and Insects want to change the curators' meeting to next Friday.' Andie always referred to the curators by their subject names when she spoke to Diane about museum business. Diane didn't know if it was to keep things organized in her mind or it tickled her sensibilities. 'Avians, Mammals and Dinosaurs said they don't care. Archaeology said it isn't convenient, but he'll go with the majority. As usual, Reptiles is afraid to voice an opinion, and I can't get hold of Rocks.'

'You know we have a new geology curator,' said Diane.

'Yes,' Andie replied, nodding her head excitedly. 'Is that immediate?'

328

Diane was glad to see that everyone she talked to was enthusiastic about Mike's coming on board as curator. That would certainly make it an easy transition for him.

'For the purpose of museum business, yes. But while Mike is recovering, work around him.'

'There are some proposals and acquisition requests for you to look at in your in box, and the velociraptors are due to arrive next week. Paleontology wants to know if he can shut down the dinosaur room while they're being assembled.'

Diane knew they wanted to work on the velociraptors without the constant clamor of visitors, but visitors to the museum loved seeing dinosaurs being put together. Besides that, she really couldn't afford to close down the most popular attraction for as long as it took to put the raptors together.

Diane thought a moment. 'We'll temporarily reroute people to the overlooks. That way they can watch them being assembled, but not be too close.'

'That's everything. I'm glad Mike'll be curator. Lymon was always hard to reach and difficult to deal with.'

'So am I. Mike has a lot of interesting ideas for special exhibits.'

Diane had gone through a handful of papers from her in box by the time she finished her sandwich and tea. The rest she put in her briefcase to take home. She took the elevators to the third floor and walked to the exhibit-preparation room to check on the progress of the Journey to the Center of the Earth exhibit and on the text for the velociraptors. After getting an update, she walked to the west wing and the crime lab.

David was at the computer. Diane looked over his shoulder. He had the mystery photo from the quarry on the screen.

'Trying out different filters,' he said. 'Jin's back. He and Korey are working on the wood samples from the quarry. Neva will be back soon. She went to check on Mike.'

Jin and Korey were in one of the rooms making slices of wood. Korey's back was to her, his dreadlocks tied together in a low ponytail. Away from machinery, she thought. Jin turned off the saw when she entered.

Korey shifted his safety glasses to the top of his head. 'Hello, Dr F. We were just making some thin sections, but I can tell you right now, the wood hasn't been in the water long at all.'

'Months, weeks?' asked Diane.

'Days,' said Korey. 'It's hardly wet, really – no more than from several days of hard rain.'

'Thank you, Korey. Jin, photograph the sections, and, if you will, Korey, write up your findings. We need to show that they aren't waterlogged.'

'Sure thing. Glad to help.'

Diane turned to Jin. 'Did you find anything else at the quarry?' she asked.

'Went down the deer trail like you said and

followed it for about a quarter of a mile. Just beyond where the trail ends is an old residential section. Neva and I drove by and had a look. Most of the houses are old, but they're being fixed up by some real estate developer. Some of them look kind of nice now. Anyway, thought the sheriff might want to canvass the area. Somebody may have seen something. You never know. Other than the sample of branches, we didn't find anything new.'

Just as well, thought Diane. They had enough to process already.

Diane left Korey and Jin and went back out to where David was working with the photograph.

'That tangle of wood that was on top of Scuba Doe has only been in the water a few days at most,' she said.

'The bodies had been in the water only a few days,' David responded. 'So what are you thinking, the brush was used to hold him down?'

'Or stage the crime scene. Have you looked at the hose on the tanks yet? Do we know if it was really a twig that punctured it?'

'No. Jin checked the tanks, but I don't think he's looked at the hose yet. I've checked for trace evidence, but that's all. Let's go have a look. I need to take a break from this.'

The evidence for the quarry victims was laid out neatly on a table. The number of evidence bags had grown as David collected trace from the objects found at the scene. He put the air hose under a dissecting microscope and examined the hole in it.

'It's a puncture,' he said, 'but not from a stick.' He stepped aside and gave Diane a look.

She looked through the dual eyepieces at the compromised air hose, turned it over and examined the side opposite the puncture. The edge of the cut was smooth, probably made by a small knife that had gone through and pierced the other side of the hose.

'The air hose is small. A slice with any size knife at all would have cut the hose completely in two. This had to be done carefully. I think maybe he was already knocked out when they cut the hose.'

'It looks to me as if the scene was staged to look like an accident,' said Diane.

'I agree,' said David.

The elevator doors to the crime lab opened. Diane looked up through the several glass windows between the lab and the entrance. It was Sheriff Canfield. The sheriff of Rose County was a large man in his late fifties with a full head of brown hair and a warm smile. Diane buzzed him in. David went back to the photograph.

'Howdy,' he said in a friendly manner. 'You know, I don't believe I've had the tour. Sheriff Braden tells me you have a fine facility here, though he says you lack a DNA lab.'

Jin came out with Korey, and for a moment Diane thought he was going to tell the sheriff they were thinking about getting one. He had been pushing Diane for it, and she hadn't decided.

'We use the GBI's DNA lab. They have a good one,' said Diane. 'What brings you here? A tour?'

'No. I wish. It's about those bodies at the quarry lake. The ME's not ready to call this an accident or natural causes. Although he said the scuba guy died of a heart attack, he has concerns about some bruises on his back, and something about his teeth being broken.'

He tapped an envelope he was holding. 'I have his report here. The other dead guy also had some bruises that concerned the ME. On the back of his neck, like someone was holding him down. So I came to see what you people found. The scuba diver was Jake Stanley. Rankin was able to confirm his identity from his dental records when he had a name. Frankly, I thought Jake was kind of young for a heart attack – just twenty-two.'

'We haven't analyzed all the trace evidence yet, but we don't believe it was an accident either,' said Diane. She explained to him about the twigs and branches that had been in the water only as long as the two victims, and the air hose that was punctured with a knife.

'I was afraid of that. You know, Rankin is pretty good. When he says something is suspicious, he means it.'

'The teeth often get broken when the regulator's forcibly pulled out,' said Korey. He looked suddenly embarrassed.

'I mean, if you're looking for foul play, that's a clue.'

Diane looked at Korey a moment before she spoke. He was obviously enjoying being on the other side of the building – the dark side, as she had heard some of the museum staff call it. Korey knew something about scuba diving and wanted to share.

'This is Korey Jordan, my head conservator at the museum. Among other things he's an expert on waterlogged wood, and we're using that expertise on the quarry case.'

'Expert on waterlogged wood. They got an expert on everything nowadays, don't they?' The sheriff held out his hand. 'Glad to meet you, son.'

'Likewise.' Korey looked at Diane. 'I've worked with divers. That's how I know about the regulators.'

'Find much work in waterlogged wood?' the sheriff asked, grinning, showing an even row of tobacco-stained teeth.

'Between museums, archaeology and recovery of ancient logs, and the fact that there aren't that many of us, I get a lot of consulting.'

'Ancient logs?'

'Like those hundred-year-plus old-growth logs discovered at the bottom of Lake Superior. When they're dried out they're some sweet wood.'

Canfield shook his head. 'I'm always amazed at the things I don't know about.'

Jin reached for the autopsy report. 'Korey's right.

You get your mouthpiece jerked out, it can break your teeth.'

He flipped through Rankin's report, reading the findings. Diane looked over his shoulder.

'The ME said something about that – the teeth being broken from the inside out. That must have been what he was talking about,' said the sheriff. 'Now, Jin, didn't you say there might be a second diver?'

'There had to be one, unless the guy was a complete idiot.'

'I've been talking to his relatives, and that would be the consensus,' the sheriff said. 'He took some scuba-diving lessons, but the instructor kicked him out because he wouldn't follow safety protocol.' He pronounced *safety protocol* as if he were quoting the instructor. 'Jake Stanley has never been in bad trouble, but always on the fringes of it. Kind of guy who wants the quick buck, knows everything and won't listen to anyone.'

'And that's why he's dead,' said Jin.

'You see something in the autopsy report, son?' the sheriff asked Jin.

Diane directed Canfield and Jin to the table to sit down. Korey took his leave just as Neva came in carrying a box.

'Have a seat, Neva,' said Diane. 'We're discussing the quarry crime scene.'

Neva nodded to the sheriff and sat down.

'The tests on his tissue samples and blood,' said

Jin, answering Sheriff Canfield's question, 'had a high nitrogen level. He probably at least had nitrogen narcosis, which would have impaired his judgment considerably, plus caused a lot of other physical problems. That may be why, if he was attacked and his hose was cut, he didn't put up much of a fight.'

Diane nodded. 'Some of the bruises are consistent with having those branches pushed down on him, which is what may have happened, rather than his getting tangled up in them.'

The sheriff shook his head. 'His family and friends that me and my deputies have talked with so far haven't a clue as to what he was doing or who he was doing it with. They all said he'd been acting real secretive lately.'

'God, I'm good,' David shouted from his computer.

CHAPTER 31

As if choreographed, all their heads turned toward David, who sat with his hands folded across his chest, looking at his computer screen with the amount of satisfaction that Newton must have had when he discovered gravity, or college freshmen when they discover beer comes in a keg.

'You have something to share?' asked Diane.

'Sure, when I finish enjoying the moment,' said David.

Neva smiled at Jin, who shook his head.

'You've got to understand how difficult this was. You don't just plug it into the software and ask it to make the picture clear. You have to work with it, tweak it, baby it – failing that, write your own algorithm.' He hit a key, which initiated the sound of the printer. 'You see, the problem is, range between color values is different in, for example, the background and the foreground, so one—'

'David,' said Neva. 'We really appreciate the level of intelligence and skill it takes for you to do what you do, but I for one don't understand what the heck you are talking about. Bottom-line it for us. Let's see the picture.'

'That would be the most impressive.' David scooped up the pages coming out of the printer and walked over to the table. 'In case you have forgotten, here is the original.' He tossed it on the table.

'You mean to tell me you made something of this?' said the sheriff. 'There's nothing here.'

'It would seem not, but . . .' He made a flourish with his hand and began dealing the pictures like cards in a deck. 'I printed one for each of you.'

'I'll be damned,' said the sheriff. 'This can't be possible.'

'Wow,' said Neva. 'Now, see, this is impressive.'

'I'll say,' agreed Jin.

Diane examined the photograph. What was once a foggy blur was now something recognizable – not crystal-clear, but it didn't have to be. It showed enough. It was an old car, the kind in old Eliot Ness gangster movies. What was so remarkable about the work that David had done was not that he brought out the car in the photo, but that, on the shelf of the backseat near the rear window, was unmistakably a human skull.

None of them said anything as they studied the photograph. Finally, Jin broke the silence. 'How long you think that's been down there?'

'I have to hand it to you and the lab here,' the sheriff said looking from the original photograph to David's enhancement. 'This is pretty amazing.'

He laid the pictures down on the table. 'So we know what our dead guys were looking for. What we don't know is why anybody would care after all this time – if, of course, that's why they were killed.' He shook his head. 'Now I've got to figure out how I can get that thing up off the bottom.'

'I'd like to go down and photograph it first,' said Jin. 'Maybe even work the crime scene from down there. I scuba-dive.'

The sheriff nodded. 'How do you think we should go about this?'

'We can call a company,' said David. 'They'll probably do something like inflate a balloon inside the vehicle – or tie special balloons to it. That's how they got those enormously heavy antique logs that Korey was talking about off the bottom of Lake Superior. Depending on what condition it's in, they'll try to contain it in some way. Jin can tell us how the process works.'

'Well,' the sheriff, said as he stood up. 'Thanks for finding me another crime scene – one that looks expensive.' He chuckled. Canfield went to the door and Diane buzzed him out.

'Good job, David,' said Diane. 'You did good. More than good. I'm really impressed.'

'We all are,' said Jin. 'I thought the sheriff's eyes were going to drop out of his head.'

'All the praise is appreciated – and deserved.' He made a flourishing bow. 'Thank you.' He turned to Neva. 'So, Neva, what's in the box?' said David.

'I found something at my house.'

'Something that I missed?' cried Jin.

'Sort of. In a way.'

Jin's look was a mixture of amazement and horror.

'What is it?' said Diane.

'You know that the intruder destroyed all my polymer clay figures. He also got into my workplace and messed up my clay, mashing it all together.' She took a twisted and folded piece of red, blue and brown clay and set it on the table with a clunk. She had clearly baked the mass of clay.

'I went by my place before visiting Mike and sort of got to crying over my clay and looking at it. I think the intruder made a mistake. There was an imprint in the clay.'

'Fingerprints?' asked David.

'No, not fingerprints. I think he wore latex gloves.' She tapped the piece she had set on the table. 'I found an imprint in here that looks like the folds of a glove. I baked this piece to make a mold. Then I put another piece of clay in the mold and made a cast. This is what I found.' She put another piece of baked clay on the table. This one was the color of terra-cotta pots.

Diane picked it up and looked at the form in the clay. 'It's an impression of his fingers.'

'I'm thinking that he took my clay and was mashing it together and made the impression with his four fingers. Look at the folds, kind of like the inside of a gloved hand, and the impression itself is sort of muted, as if it had something covering it. You can see the back side of a ring and finger-nails. You can also see that one finger is badly damaged.'

'Very good, Neva,' said Jin. He grinned at her.

'I'll put it in the evidence drawer for my house break-in,' said Neva.

'Call Garnett,' said Diane. 'Tell him what you found.'

'Me?' said Neva.

Neva had always been a little intimidated by Garnett. 'You found it,' said Diane. 'And it's an identifying characteristic.'

Neva nodded, then smiled. 'Sure.'

Diane turned to Jin. 'What did the two of you find at the Jane Doe crime scene?'

'A running shoe, a pair of socks, several small plastic buttons,' said Jin. 'But I may have missed something.'

'Get over it, Jin,' said Diane.

'Yeah, Neva was there,' said David. 'She would have found anything you didn't.'

Jin shrugged and continued. 'We found some of the bones of her hands and feet and a few others we couldn't identify. We photographed the place, but didn't find anything but the bones. The deputy did a number on the site. Oh, I did get a bug out of his car. It's a dermestid, just like we figured.'

'Did you find a femur?' asked Diane. 'Our Jane Doe is missing one.'

Jin and Neva looked at each other. 'No,' they said, shaking their heads.

'Are there any nursing homes in the area?' Diane asked.

'The closest one is ten miles. Sheriff Burns said no one is missing that he's aware of,' said Jin. 'The sheriff took us to the site. He's pretty steamed at Deputy Singer, especially when he saw all the shovel marks in the ground and we told him how the bones arrived. Singer was supposed to have called us to photograph the scene and collect the bones.'

'I got the impression,' said Neva, 'that he won't be having a job when he gets out of the hospital.'

'Whenever that is,' said Jin. 'Sheriff Burns said that besides his injuries, he developed some kind of rash thing.'

'Urticaria, probably,' said David. He rubbed his arm unconsciously. 'It's a skin condition brought on by an allergic reaction to insect bites. He probably looks pretty bad about now.'

'Poor guy. Is that all the crime scenes we have at the moment?' said Diane. She hoped that the murderers in the area would hold off killing anyone until her team got caught up.

'I believe that's it, Boss,' answered Jin. 'Except Caver Doe.'

'Caver Doe has waited fifty years. He can wait a little longer. Let's get the analysis of these cases done as quickly as we can. Neva, when you have time, I'd like to see some sketches of the faces of the victims. First up, get the autopsy photos of Quarry Doe and draw him a presentable face – preferably with his eyes open. We need to identify him. You okay with that?'

Neva wrinkled her nose. 'Sure. If I can slip on their fingers to get a print, I can draw their decaying faces.'

'Jane Doe's skull from the woods will be ready in a couple of days. It's in with the dermestids now. And it looks like we'll be getting another skeleton from the deep.'

CHAPTER 32

Diane spent the next day working only on museum business. Jin and Sheriff Canfield were arranging for a salvage company to raise the car from the bottom of the quarry lake. Most of the evidence from the various crime scenes had been processed. She'd checked Jane Doe's bones. They were nearly ready for her to examine again. Things were going smoothly, and that always made her a little nervous. She went to bed that evening waiting for the other shoe to drop. Frank told her that she was turning into a pessimist.

Early the next morning Diane stood on the bank of the quarry waiting for Jin to surface. A salvage crew was waiting with her. They had their own divers. Once Jin and his team came up, they would begin the job of raising the car from the bottom. The depth had been measured at 120 feet. The divers had to descend and ascend in increments to adapt to the changes in pressure.

The plan in operation was for Jin to work the inside of the car and collect the bones and anything else that could get damaged or lost during the recovery. Diane had brought Korey with her. He stood talking to the salvagers and Sheriff Canfield.

Korey had told Jin that when he put anything in a bag, to make sure he sealed enough water in to protect the evidence inside. Everything wet had to stay wet to prevent decomposition from exposure to the air – at least until they got all the information they needed from it.

'As soon as the bones and artifacts come out of the quarry,' Korey said, 'they'll go into tubs of distilled water. Then we'll dry the bones and prevent them from cracking with a series of alcohol baths, increasing the concentration until we reach a hundred percent alcohol. You can go ahead and analyze the bones if you want to. It won't hurt to take them out of the water for a short amount of time if you keep a spray bottle handy to keep them damp.'

Diane looked at her watch. Jin still had fifteen minutes before he and the other divers had to come up, according to the chart he showed her. She occupied herself by comparing the scene around her with the notes and reports that her team had created. The long-overgrown avenue through the woods was more evident in person. The road that led to the quarry consisted of two parallel dirt tracks with its middle grown up with tall grass.

The quarry lake was a pretty place, a place that would have been a good swimming hole. The water was clear and it was relatively private. A thick wood grew around the whole area. Diane was told by the local historians that a hundred years ago granite had been mined here. She'd probably seen buildings made from its stone and didn't know it.

Rocks made her think of Mike. She wondered how he was getting along. Neva said he had been busy making notes of what he wanted to do in his new job. Her mind wandered to Annette Lymon. Andie had told her that Dr Lymon was looking for her. She dreaded that encounter.

The sun was warm on her face. She closed her eyes. She would like to go swimming right now. She'd been fighting a mild feeling of depression for the past few days, brought on, no doubt, by what had happened to her mother, seeing her ex-husband again, and what he did to Susan and Gerald. And not to mention getting stabbed. She rubbed her arm.

It was as if a dark mist were settling around her. She couldn't see it, but she felt it, and it gave her a sense of dread. Frank was good; he was her anchor. He'd come over the evening before and brought one of her favorite meals – Chinese. And he had made her laugh. She touched the locket around her neck, pushing the heart shape into her chest, feeling the metal, remembering that Ariel had touched it. Yes, a swim right now would be good.

She was brought out of her reverie by a splash and voices. She opened her eyes. Jin was back up, bags and camera tied to his body. One after another, minutes apart, divers popped up after him. Four in all, each carrying bags. Jin was swimming to shore rather than getting in the boat. The second group of divers started putting on their gear. For them it was time for the real show – bringing up the car.

'Hey, Boss. It's nice down there. A little chilly, but nice. I got some good pictures and a lot of evidence.' He pointed to the bags hanging from his body weighing him down. 'Damn, these weren't so heavy underwater.' He grinned.

'It's an old Plymouth, maybe 1935-ish or something. David will probably know. It's in pretty good condition, considering. No license plates on it. Too bad. That might have helped.' Diane walked with Jin to the museum van, where he took off his diving gear.

The van was one the groundskeepers used and had been stripped of carpeting. Korey came trotting over to help transfer the bones Jin had brought up into tubs of distilled water in the van.

Diane held the dripping skull in her hands. It was almost pearlescent, the way the saturated white bone reflected the sunlight. Right away she knew it would probably be a young female. It was too gracile to be otherwise. The wisdom teeth were just about to erupt. There was nothing on the face that suggested how she died. No broken face bones or broken teeth that suggested a car accident. But at the back of the head there was a depression fracture. She put the skull in the water with the other bones and replaced the cover.

'You know, Boss,' said Jin, stripping off his wet suit. 'When you look at the bones, it doesn't really matter if they dry out too fast and crack. You'll just be burying them after you finish.'

Korey looked scandalized.

'We don't know what we'll find, when we'll find it or how long it will take to identify her,' Diane said. 'We may have to store her for years, and we want her in the best condition possible.'

'Yeah,' agreed Korey. 'Always err on the side of conservation.'

Jin laughed. 'If you'll excuse me, I'm going to climb in the van a minute and close the door to change clothes.' He slammed the door shut after he was inside. 'We searched the bottom for another diver,' he yelled as he was changing clothes. 'Nothing.'

While he put on dry clothes, Diane looked at the special slates he had used for writing under-water. He had made a grid of the scene and a drawing of where everything was found. What had the scuba diver, Jake Stanley, and Quarry Doe been looking for? she wondered, staring at Jin's drawing. What besides an ancient skeleton could be in an old car that probably had been at the bottom of the quarry for who knew how long? For that matter, what was the relationship of Quarry Doe to the diver, Jake Stanley?

Jin had made notes of a few things found outside

the car on the quarry bottom: old tires, cans, bottles, several unidentified pieces of metal. Because the time the divers could spend at that depth was limited, he had concentrated most of his time inside the car itself.

The van door opened and Jin jumped out, dressed in cutoffs and a T-shirt. 'You're not going to believe what we found.'

'Probably not,' said Diane. She half expected them to come up with something of value – like a suitcase full of money.

'Vintage men's magazines.'

'What?' said Korey.

'Really. From the thirties and forties. You know, Boss . . .'

She could see Jin's mind working. 'No, we aren't going to do a museum display of them.'

'How did you know that's what I was going to ask?'

Diane simply looked at him.

'The difference between what people thought was beautiful then and now is really interesting. I mean, with all the plastic surgery and exercise and . . .'

'Jin, move on,' said Diane.

'We can get some dates off the mags.'

'Good.'

The other divers on Jin's team came to the van with their booty – mostly bones. They also brought clothes – a yellow gingham dress, a white apron, black shoes, and a sweater. Diane and Korey placed all of it in containers of distilled water.

349

While Diane and her team were packing up the evidence, the recovery team got to work. Diane heard them calling orders to one another in the background. A large tow truck sat near the edge of the water. Men wearing life jackets stood in the water on the underwater shelf near where Jake Stanley was found. The shelf was about six feet wide and four feet deep. After that, there was a dropoff all the way to the bottom of the lake. The salvagers were letting orange material down into the water, readying the lift bags for the divers to take down to the car.

The museum crew stayed well away from the operation, unlike an Atlanta news crew, who were taking pictures up close. Korey and Jin got on top of the museum van to observe the process. Diane sat in the van and studied Jin's map of the under-water crime scene. After several minutes she put it away to watch with the others.

At the moment there was nothing much to see. The boat that anchored the descent line that Jin and his people used was gone, and the lake was calm and empty. Then, like a whale surfacing and spouting water, the car suddenly surfaced surrounded by orange lift bags, and everybody clapped. That must be one of those things, Diane thought, that you never got tired of seeing if you did this kind of work – large objects suddenly popping up out of the water. She grinned as if she'd just seen a circus act.

The divers tied a line to the car, and the men

on the bank began winching it in. Jin got off the top of the van and retrieved his camera to take more photographs. At the depth the car was submerged, they had been unable to see true colors. Diane could see that the dark gray car had maroon seats. When the recovery team had the car secure on shore, Jin took a picture of the dark gray humpbacked Plymouth that was in remarkably good condition. Diane heard one of the men say he thought it was a 1938. For Diane, looking at the old car brought up from the depth of the lake was like looking back in time.

Plymouth Doe, as Jin had christened their newest skeleton, lay on the table in Diane's osteology lab. The next day Diane had come in early to get started on the skeleton. The bones were wet and shining like pearls that had been molded into the shape of a skeleton. Korey had told Diane to keep the bones wet as she worked, so she had a spray bottle for that purpose. Korey had mixed a bath of fifty percent alcohol and fifty percent distilled water that the bones would be submerged in after Diane's examination of them.

Plymouth Doe was female. Her pelvis was clear on that. It was broad and shallow like a cradle – and it had held at least one infant in her lifetime. Her wisdom teeth were just starting to erupt. The medial end of the clavicle was just beginning to unite with its epiphysis. There was no complete epiphyseal union on her femora or her humeri.

351

Plymouth Doe was young – between sixteen and twenty-two, Diane guessed. Too young to die.

The newest magazine found in the car with her was dated 1942. If, for sake of argument, they could say that was the date Plymouth Doe died, she would now have been around eighty. Plymouth Doe could still be alive had someone not cracked her skull. Diane examined the rod-shaped fracture with a hand lens. The edges were smooth except for one nick in the bone. It looked like whatever object made the fracture had some small protrusion on it, like a burr or imperfection on whatever weapon was used.

There were no healed fractures on any of her bones. One curious characteristic Diane discovered when she was looking for evidence of right- or left-handedness – the beveling on her right glenoid fossa, the right shoulder socket of the scapula, was greater than on her left. This usually indicated that there had been more rotation in the right shoulder socket – a common sign of right-handedness. Greater beveling usually went hand in hand with larger muscle attachments on the dominant arm and shoulder. But Plymouth Doe's left muscle attachments on her arm and shoulder were larger than her right. Her glenoid fossa said she was right-handed, but her muscle attachments said she was left-handed.

One occupation Diane had read about that could cause this was waitressing. Having to balance a heavy tray with the less-dominant hand left the dominant hand free. A right-handed waitress balanced a tray on her left hand. Had Plymouth Doe been a waitress in her relatively short life? She thought about the white apron found with her clothes.

Diane moistened the skull with the spray bottle and began taking the tedious measurements on the face just as Neva entered the lab with a folder tucked under her arm.

'I have some drawings of Quarry Doe – Jake Stanley's partner in death,' she said. Quarry Doe had been dead in the water long enough for his face to become distorted. Diane wanted Neva to try to make his face look alive to help identify him. 'I also scanned Caver Doe's skull,' Neva continued, 'since he was sitting there right beside it. Remember that photo we found with Caver Doe? Even though it had been soaked in Caver Doe's blood and fluids, David got me an image from it by using the computer and some of his fancy lights. It was a photograph of a girl, and I drew her picture too.'

'That photo wasn't stolen?' she asked.

Neva looked a little embarrassed. 'I had taken it from the evidence box and had it in the desk in the vault. That's where I've been working on the drawings.'

'That's a relief. I thought we had lost it in the burglary,' said Diane. She walked over to the table, where Neva laid out the drawings.

The modern body, Quarry Doe, had a seventies

shag haircut. With some guys that cut had never quite gone out of style. To be so young – the ME estimated his age at twenty-five – his face had a rough edge to it. Quarry Doe was aging fast. He had thin lips, wide eyes, black hair and a crooked nose that was slightly pug.

Beside the drawing was an autopsy photograph of Quarry Doe's back. It was covered with tattoos – tigers, snakes, knives, fangs, guns, roses, crosses, swastikas and more – filling every square inch. Some were well-done; others were crude.

'These are prison tattoos,' said Diane. 'That will make it easy for the sheriff to identify him. Did you give Sheriff Canfield a copy of your drawing of his face?' Neva nodded. 'Prison tattoos are forbidden, so having them is a sign of rebellion; the more you have, the more time you had to spend getting them, and the greater the risk of getting caught. It's a kind of prestige to have a lot of them. Probably says something about our vic.'

Diane went to the next set of drawings. Neva had placed the last two portraits together – Caver Doe and the girl in his photograph – possibly his sweetheart? Caver Doe looked young. His bones told her that he was, but his portrait really showed his youthful, graceful face – quite a contrast to the face of Quarry Doe. The face of the woman from the photograph was equally pretty. Short wavy hair, bright eyes, full lips with corners turned into a hint of a smile. Her dress had a crocheted collar. There was something about her that looked vaguely familiar.

'These are good,' said Diane. 'Poignant to put a face on our caver.'

Diane was pleased with the way Neva was able to draw faces from skulls. Diane had taught her what a fleshed-out face would look like given specific underlying bone structures. She'd shown her how to calculate skin depths on the face, how to use the size of the nasal opening to find out the length of the nose, how to define the eyes. Neva picked up forensic art quickly. Diane also showed Neva how to use the sophisticated scanning software to have the computer draw the face. The computer drawing wasn't as life-like as Neva's drawings, but combining Neva's artistic ability and the computer's scanning ability made the work a lot quicker.

'Yes, it is sad. His girlfriend too – I'm guessing it's his girlfriend. I wonder what happened to her. She must not have known what became of him.'

'Probably not.'

'Unless she conspired to leave him in the cave,' said Neva.

Diane laughed. 'You've been in crime too long. You're getting a cynical, suspicious mind.'

'It does come with the territory, doesn't it?'

'When I finish Caver Doe, we'll do a newspaper article and run it with the drawings. Maybe there is someone around who will recognize them or remember them.'

Diane looked over at Plymouth Doe. 'There's another lost soul. When I'm finished with these measurements, you can take this skull to the vault and let the laser scan her features and start building a face. When you finish, put her skull in that tank sitting on the counter.' Diane looked at all the drawings again before walking back to Plymoth Doe's bones. 'Really nice work,' she told Neva. She sprayed them down again with water.

'It's really interesting to listen to Korey tell how he's going to preserve the stuff from the car,' said Neva. 'Do you know he froze all the magazines in a little battery-powered freezer he had in the van at the site?'

Diane nodded. 'That immediately stopped any destructive chemical or biological processes going on. In his lab he's using a process called vacuum freeze-drying. He'll put the frozen magazines in a chamber and pump the air out and form a vacuum – that will dry them at freezing temperatures. It's a method that changes the ice directly into gas so it never goes through a liquid state. The magazines will be dry documents when it's finished.'

'That's amazing.'

'Sometime when we have some downtime – if we ever do – you might enjoy spending some time in the conservation lab. They do interesting work.' Diane measured and recorded all the craniometric points on Plymouth Doe's skull as she and Neva talked. The laser would do the same, but Diane

356

still liked to take the measurements herself – as with caving, she liked to get to know the bones.

'You know,' said Neva, 'I like the older crimes better than the new ones.'

'Less blood and putrid flesh,' said Diane.

'Yeah. And the tragedy is farther away.'

'I know what you mean,' Diane agreed.

Neva gestured toward the skeleton. 'How is Korey handling her clothes?'

'There are several methods for working with water-logged fabric, but I think he's going to use a process that impregnates the material with silicone oil. Jin'll have to look for trace and blood before any processing is done. I think he and Korey have come up with an experiment to see how much these methods affect the ability to do blood analysis. I know Korey wants to go to the fabric store to get different kinds of textiles for the experiment. He and Jin are writing a paper together.'

Diane finished measuring the skull and began her examination of the other bones. She started by feeling along the ribs with her fingers, searching for nicks.

'I can see how that kind of information helps us,' said Neva. 'But what are Korey and the museum going to get out of the experiments?'

Diane looked up from the skull. 'For one thing, archaeologists also look for blood residue. Even after thousands of years, they can still find protein markers from different kinds of animals on arrowheads.

Same thing with ancient textiles they run across. It would be good for them to know how preservation techniques affect blood or other kinds of stains that might be on artifacts.'

'How do you know all this stuff?'

Diane looked up from the rib she was examining and paused a long moment, grinning. 'I've got this really big museum connected to the crime lab and it knows all kinds of stuff.'

Neva hit her forehead with the heel of her hand.

'Speaking of the museum, how's Mike doing?' asked Diane.

'Antsy and a little obnoxious about having to rest, if you can imagine Mike being obnoxious.'

Diane couldn't. 'He's only been out of the hospital, what – two, three days?'

'That's what I keep telling him. He wanted to come in to the museum today. I think I talked him out of it. But he's really excited about his new job.'

'So is Shelly, the collection manager for Geology. She's so glad Dr Lymon is gone that I'm expecting her to be doing cartwheels down the halls. She and Lymon have gotten into it a few times.'

'I wanted to thank you for . . . well, you know, keeping me out of the harassment business. I know I shouldn't have been such a coward.'

'Don't worry about it. Sylvia Mercer's witnessing the incident was all the evidence that mattered. David checked out Dr Lymon, by the way, and she had an alibi for the day of the stabbing at the funeral.'

358

'That's a relief.'

Diane was about to hand Plymouth Doe's skull over to Neva when David called on the intercom.

'Diane, Jin and Korey want us in the conservation lab ASAP. Jin sounds excited.'

CHAPTER 33

'Jin just loves this job.' Neva grinned. 'You know, he's decided he likes caves too. He said he'd like to go with us sometime. I invited him to come to the caver club meeting at the museum.'

'You did tell him we don't always discover bodies?' Diane covered the bones with a special absorbent material that she had saturated with water, hung her white lab coat on a wall peg and washed her hands.

Neva laughed. 'I did. He and Korey came over for dinner last night and Mike showed him his album of caving photos. Have you seen it?'

Diane shook her head. 'No, although I'd like to. I understand he's been to some interesting caves. I just hope Jin doesn't get the idea of cave diving,' said Diane.

'I think Mike was worried about that too. Jin mentioned that it'd be neat to combine his scuba diving with exploring underwater caves. Mike told him that when cave divers die, it's usually from cave diving. That was a real conversation stopper.' Neva pushed the door open and held it for Diane. 'I think it kind of hurt Jin's feelings. He thinks

Mike doesn't like him because of the Luminol incident in the cave.'

'Is it true?' Diane secured the door behind her.

'No. I don't think so. Mike tends to like everybody. He's like that little kid who just knows there has to be a pony in a pile of manure that large . . . He's always such an optimist. In the past few months he's been shot, stabbed, harassed, lost his assistantship, and he still thinks he's the luckiest guy in the world.'

'That does sound like Mike. I'm sure he was only trying to make a point with Jin about just how dangerous cave diving is.' She and Neva headed for the conservation lab.

'What about ice caves? I understand they're dangerous too,' Neva said.

'You thinking about this extremophile collecting job Mike is taking?'

'Yes. I know Mike is good, but . . .'

'It's a very reputable company, and he'll be working with a team. Like stuntmen in movies, they do a lot of work in advance and set everything up so they'll be safe.'

'Still . . .'

'I know, but Mike is very safety conscious. He's one of the best caving partners I've ever had – and that's mainly because he has good sense when it comes to danger.'

They took the stairs down to the second floor and walked across to the conservation lab, where they met David at the door. He shrugged his shoulders as they all entered. He clearly didn't know what this was about either.

The conservation lab was similar to the osteology lab – a room filled with tables and all manner of equipment, with a large environmentally controlled storage vault for special items. It was outfitted with equipment that allowed them to keep at bay the natural tendency for things to disintegrate. The lab mostly worked with bones, fossils, botanical specimens, objects from nature used in exhibits, and documents, but the staff recently had had the opportunity to work with a mummy and Egyptian artifacts. Now they were working with textiles.

Jin was standing, grinning over a table laid out with clothing from Plymouth Doe. Another table contained rows of evidence bags, presumably trace evidence from the clothing. There was a bra – more substantial than what most women wore now – cotton panties, a slip. All the underclothes had been white, but were now badly stained. The yellow gingham dress was laid out with the apron beside it. Plymouth Doe had been a slim woman. Diane already knew from the length of her long bones that she was five-foot-five.

They walked around the table and stood near Jin and Korey. Diane noticed that the apron was scalloped and had RAY'S DINER written in blue embroidery – she had been a waitress.

As interesting as the apron was, however, it was the sweater that Jin and Korey were focused on.

362

Jin looked from David to Diane to Neva, still grinning. Clearly there was something he expected them to notice right away.

It was a woman's sweater, a gray hand-knitted piece, stained from being in water near a decaying body all those years. It had a row of silver buttons down the front. Diane's eyes widened in surprise. David saw it too. He grabbed his hand lens out of his pocket and bent over the sweater.

'I don't believe it,' he muttered.

'Aren't those buttons the same as the one you found in the cave?' asked Neva.

'Yes,' said David. 'Definitely the same.' He straightened up. 'These buttons are rare because they never came into general use. Which means we have a connection between Caver Doe and Plymouth Doe.'

Even though they didn't know that the cave button was actually associated with Caver Doe, the coincidence was too much to ignore.

'Wow,' said Neva, 'If Plymouth Doe was his girlfriend, I apologize for the things I thought about her.' Both David and Jin looked sideways at her. 'We were discussing the photograph found with Caver Doe and I made some suggestions about her possible involvement in his death. But if she's dead too . . .'

'Not all the buttons are attached,' said Diane.

'No, only two,' Jin replied. 'The others were found nearby on the seat and there's the one from the cave.'

'Let me have a look at them first,' said Korey. 'I can stabilize the decomposition. I've noticed the shanks are rusty. Some are eaten away.'

Diane nodded. 'How are you coming with the clothes?'

'Jin's been doing his thing,' said Korey. He jerked his head toward the table of evidence bags. 'When he finishes, I'll work on the fabric. Do you want it cleaned?'

'No,' said Diane. 'Just keep it from falling apart.'

'Sure thing, Dr F.'

'I haven't found any blood so far,' said Jin. 'I'm not sure I would after all that time in the water. But I thought you'd like to see the buttons. Especially David. Your button database is paying off. Who knew?'

'And all of you scoffed,' said David.

Diane shook her head. 'This is just amazing – and unexpected.'

'It surprised the heck out of me,' said Jin.

'Yeah,' said Korey, 'we thought he'd gone nuts.'

'Good work, guys.' She looked at her watch. 'I need to get back to Plymouth Doe. Neva, why don't you get to work on Plymouth Doe's face. See if it's a match with the snapshot found with Caver Doe.'

'Diane. Been looking for you.' Jonas Briggs, the museum's archaeologist, and professor emeritus from Bartram University, came strolling into the conservation lab, his face lit up with his usual smile. 'The archaeology faunal lab at the university thanks you profusely for helping out with its faunal remains.'

Diane looked at him blankly. 'What was it I did for them?'

'Did Dr Mercer not tell you? You were on vacation, so I guess she forgot.'

He handed her an envelope. Diane tore it open and found a thank-you note from the Archaeology Department head for allowing them to use the museum's faunal lab to strip some of their remains. She looked up at Jonas.

'Some idiot stole their dermestid colony about three weeks ago. Probably some fraternity prank. They had fresh carcasses and were in immediate need and appealed to us – actually to me. I asked Sylvia Mercer, and she generously agreed to help.'

Diane stood looking at him for a long moment. She and David looked at each other.

'You don't think . . .' began David.

'It's entirely possible,' said Diane.

'What?' said Jin.

'Not frat boys?' said Jonas.

'Maybe not,' said Diane.

'But you aren't going to tell, are you?' said Jonas. 'This is part of the business of the museum's dark side, isn't it?'

'Yes. Sorry – ongoing case. I suppose it's too late to work the scene,' mused Diane. 'But Jin, go ahead and have a look at the faunal lab sometime today.' He nodded. 'Do they have any leads?' she asked Jonas.

'On the theft? No. It's pretty easy to come and go in the lab. Could have been anyone,' said Briggs.

'I'll check it out,' said Jin.

'What was that about?' asked Neva when she and Diane were out the door.

'David found a lot of beetles with Jane Doe. She had cuts all over her body, and she was found with other animals in various states of decomposition. Just a hunch, but I'm thinking that maybe the killer wanted to hurry the process of decomposition. One way to do that is to cut the body tissue to allow access to insects. I believe he also thought that putting out extra bugs and other carcasses would increase the rate of decomposition.'

'So maybe Jane Doe hasn't been dead as long as we first thought,' said Neva.

'That could be the case. I was thinking maybe a month. But now I'm not so sure.'

On the way back to the stairwell they walked through Earth Science. Through the doorway that led to the rock room, Diane saw Dr Lymon and Mike at the door to the geology lab.

'What is he doing out?' said Neva. She started to go to him when Diane put a hand on her arm.

'Let me handle this,' said Diane. 'You start on Plymouth Doe's face.'

'Is that Dr Lymon?'

'I'll catch up to you later,' said Diane.

'Yes, ma'am,' Neva said, though she hesitated

for a moment before continuing on to the osteology lab.

Diane passed through the rock room, headed for the geology lab. Several people were looking at the igneous rocks, trying not to look like they were listening to the argument that was clearly going on. Dr Lymon's voice was getting progressively higher. Mike was trying to get out of the doorway, but she grabbed his arm.

Diane walked up to the two of them. 'Let's go into the lab. Now.'

'This is none of your damn business.' Dr Lymon's face was red with anger.

'You're making a spectacle in the museum, and that makes it my business. If you don't want to be escorted out by security, take this to the office.'

Annette Lymon looked at Diane as if she didn't understand her. 'I've been trying to get in touch with you,' she said after a moment. 'No one seemed to know where you were.'

Out of the corner of her eye, Diane saw Shelly Cates, the geology collection manager, in her office putting down the phone receiver. She dashed out and came toward them. Diane could tell by her body language that she was angry. Her face was red under her tanned skin, her body rigid.

Shelly Cates was a fit woman in her early forties. Her hair was up in a tight ponytail. She was the type of person who seemed more comfortable in jeans and a T-shirt, but in the museum she always wore nice suits usually topped by a lab coat. She had come to the profession late. After being a stay-at-home mom, she got an undergraduate degree in geology and took courses in museum management. Her job meant a lot to her.

'She has been pitching a fit in front of visitors in the museum,' said Shelly. 'I was just about to call you.'

'Doc,' began Mike. 'I'm sorry.'

'Mike, why don't you and Shelly go talk in her office. I'm going to speak with Dr Lymon.'

Mike hesitated a moment. So did Shelly.

'Now,' said Diane.

The two of them turned and went into Shelly's office. Mike moved slowly and stiffly, favoring one side.

'Dr Lymon, let's go sit down, and you tell me what's going on.'

Diane managed to maneuver Annette Lymon so she could shut the door to the geology lab, cutting off the view and the sound of the unfolding drama from the public. She held the office door open for Dr Lymon, who reluctantly walked through and sat down behind the desk, as if she intended never to get up again.

'Now what's this about?' Diane pulled up a chair and sat opposite her.

'How dare you hire him! I told you he is incompetent, and you gave him my job!'

'Dr Lymon, who I hire isn't your concern. You wrote me several letters telling me of your dissatisfaction and intention to quit. You told me you are severing ties with the museum. I had a position to fill. Mike is qualified. As far as you are concerned, that's the end of the matter. Why were you looking for me?'

'To talk to you about giving him my job.'

'It's not your job. And you can never come into the museum and make a scene. The visitors in the museum don't need to be subjected to whatever problem you have with my hiring practices. Your letter said you are resigning the curatorship.' Diane was exasperated, but tried not to show it. She hoped she sounded matter-of-fact, but firm.

Dr Lymon had a stubborn set to her face. Her chin was thrust out and her mouth was turned down into a frown. 'That's not the point. You didn't have to hire him. Not him. He came on to me; did you know that?'

Diane was starting to get angry. She was glad she had an independent witness to the episode. 'No, he did not come on to you. You came on to him. It was inappropriate, and if you weren't leaving I would fire you. I have no tolerance for that kind of thing here.'

Angry tears sprang up in her eyes. 'He's lying. He's just trying to get my job. He's just trying to make himself look like he's the wronged party.'

'Mike never told me about it. You were observed by another curator.'

Annette Lymon's eyes grew wide. She was silent for a long moment. The tears spilled down onto her cheeks, leaving black mascara tracks. She

369

grabbed a Kleenex from her purse and wiped her eyes.

'He rejected me. Do you know what that feels like? Who was he to reject me after all these years? After everything I've done for him. I put him through school.'

'He was your student. He doesn't owe you sex, Dr Lymon.'

'Doesn't owe me? We were married for sixteen years.'

'What? Who are you talking about? Mike's not your ex-husband.'

Dr Lymon looked puzzled for a moment. 'Not Mike. Ransford. I did everything for that son of a bitch, and he leaves me for that young slut.'

Diane suddenly felt way out of her depth. She hadn't a clue how to treat the woman.

'I understand that your husband betrayed you terribly. But that wasn't Mike's fault; nor was it the museum's. Is there anyone I can call for you? A friend or family member?'

Dr Lymon shook her head.

'Why don't you stay here and collect yourself before you go home.'

'Why did you give him this job?'

'I need a curator, and he had an excellent proposal with several good ideas for the museum.'

'I'll bet that was the reason. I know about you and him.' Her eyes glittered as she stared at Diane.

Stay calm, Diane said to herself. *It doesn't do to exchange barbs with a madwoman. Nor is it a good idea to become defensive.* Diane ignored Lymon's remark and took her own cell phone, dialed the nurses' station on the first floor of the museum and asked them to send a nurse up to the geology lab.

'Dr Lymon, I don't feel comfortable leaving you alone in a state like this, and I'm ill equipped to give you what you need. I've called one of the nurses and she is going to stay with you until you are ready to go home. She'll drive you, and I'm going to ask one of the security guards to follow in your car.'

Dr Lymon didn't say anything. Diane hoped that meant she agreed.

'Can I have your car keys?' Diane held out her hand.

'My keys?' Lymon looked at her as if she'd asked for a frog.

'Your car keys. For the guard. You don't need to be driving home. I'm having someone take you.'

Dr Lymon still had her keys in her hand from when she had arrived and saw Mike. She handed them over without a fuss. When Diane heard the nurse enter the lab, she got up and met her with a great deal of relief. It was Mrs Pierce. She was a very motherly woman with a knack for comforting children. In a low voice, Diane told her the problem.

'It sounds like she's had a break with reality, doesn't it?' said Mrs Pierce. 'I'll stay with her until she's ready to leave, then take her home. Don't you worry.'

'Thank you. I'll have one of the security guards follow in her car.'

Diane led the nurse into the office and introduced her. Glad to be out of there, she walked to Shelly's office to fetch Mike. She felt like taking one of his ears and pulling him down to his car.

'Look, Doc. I'm really sorry. I didn't know she would be here. She hardly ever comes to the museum.'

'One of the nurses is taking her home.'

'One of the nurses?' said Shelly. 'How about the police?'

'She's confusing Mike with her husband at the moment. I'm trying to get her some help right now.'

'You mean she's totally flipped?' said Shelly.

Diane called museum security, explained the situation to Chanell, her head of security, and asked that a guard be sent to escort Dr Lymon when she was ready to leave.

'Damn,' said Mike. 'Did she think I was him when—'

'No. I think it's rejection that's sending her over the edge right now. Anyway, Mike, while she's in the office, I want you to come with me. I don't think it's a good idea for her to see you.'

Mike followed her out, and Diane resisted the urge to grab his ear.

CHAPTER 34

'I've really pissed you off, haven't I, Doc?' said Mike when they were alone in the elevator on the way to the third floor. 'I had no intention of getting into it with Dr Lymon, especially in front of visitors.'

'That wasn't your fault. What I'm concerned about is your being out so soon. Does your doctor know?'

'You're worried? Really?'

'Yes, and so is Neva.'

'If it were up to her, she'd tie me to the bed – not that that doesn't hold a certain appeal – but really, if I'm going to get stronger, I have to be up and about.'

'Driving? Coming to work? Look, Mike, this is really none of my business, but as a friend, I do worry that you are pushing it too soon.'

The elevator doors opened, and they stepped out into the lobby in front of the staff lounge and headed toward the osteology lab.

'I know my limits.'

'No, you don't, Mike. You don't know your limits until you exceed them. And that's what I'm concerned about.'

'It's just that I have so many ideas. Shelly and I have talked about a lot of things, but Dr Lymon never wanted to listen. There are so many ways we can really improve the geology exhibits.'

'And I'm looking forward to hearing those ideas. I'm also looking forward to going caving again, and I'd like you to be well so you can go too. You can't do any of those things if you reinjure yourself.'

'Okay, I take your point,' Mike said. 'I'm really sorry about Dr Lymon. She's not taking her husband's leaving well, is she? Did she really think I was her husband? We don't even look alike.'

'I believe she was mixing up the two rejections. Anyway, have you been to the osteology lab?'

Diane was anxious to get away from Dr Lymon's problems. She kept thinking that she should call the university, but she didn't want to make Lymon's problems any more public than they were.

'No, I haven't,' said Mike.

'Neva is reconstructing a face from one of the skulls; you can watch her if you like. I also have a comfortable couch in my osteology office, and you can rest there if you need to.'

'You are so good to me, Doc.'

Diane unlocked the lab door. Plymouth Doe, covered with the wet cloth and sans head, was lying on the table.

'Yes, I am.'

She unlocked the bone vault. Neva was there. The skull was turning on the stage of the laser scanner, shafts of red lasers measuring the contours of the facial bones.

'Mike,' Neva said. 'You doing okay? Was that Dr Lymon?' She came over to him. He hugged her and kissed the top of her head.

'I'm fine. I'll tell you about Lymon later. Show me what you're doing. Looks high-tech and flashy.'

Diane left them and went back into the outer lab to the bones of Plymouth Doe. She uncovered them and resumed her examination of the ribs. She found no nicks on them; nor did she find anything on the long bones. She did find that the feet showed evidence of bunions. Her toes had a marked deformity where the big toe drifted toward the smaller ones. Diane guessed that Plymouth Doe during her young years had spent a lot of time on her feet in tight shoes.

Neva, followed by Mike, came out of the vault carrying the skull, put it in the alcohol tank and washed her hands. Mike held the picture generated by the software from the laser scan.

'I haven't drawn her yet, but I thought you'd like to see the face generated by the computer.' She took it to the table where the other drawings were still laid out and put it beside the drawing of Caver Doe's snapshot.

The computer image showed Plymouth Doe with a wide jaw and forehead, a straight nose and wide, almond-shaped eyes. Both Plymouth Doe and the woman in the unidentified snapshot were very pretty women, but they were not the same.

'Okay, not Caver Doe's girlfriend,' said Neva. 'So what is the connection? Black-market button seller?'

Diane shrugged. 'Maybe the trace evidence will tell us something. Nice job, Neva.'

'When I do the drawing of her it'll look better. Let's do a newspaper article soon. I'd like to find out who these people were and why they have the same rare button.'

Diane smiled at her. 'That's the first thing we'll ask the next of kin.'

When Neva and Mike left her lab, Diane went back to the bones, examining them one more time under a magnifying glass, making sure she hadn't missed something that might help identify Plymouth Doe or indicate what happened to her. She found nothing more. Diane put the Plymouth Doe bones in the alcohol bath and walked to the crime lab.

David was on the phone and taking notes. Neva was at the light table working on her drawing. Jin came bouncing in, still elated over the buttons.

'We have a name,' said David, waving a piece of paper. 'That was the eye surgeon who implanted the shunt you found in Jane Doe. I traced him from the number on the shunt. Her real name is Flora Martin. I was about to call Sheriff Burns.'

'Do we have all of her evidence processed?' said Diane.

'Yes. I have a report ready to fax him.'

'Excellent. When the dermestids are finished

with her bones and I have a chance to take one more look at them, that case will be closed for us.' Diane felt a wave of relief go through her, and it surprised her.

'We're making some progress. Look, guys, you all have been working very hard and doing a good job. It's almost quitting time – I realize we often don't pay any attention to that, but why don't we knock off for the evening? I'll stay on call, and if anything comes up, I'll phone you,' Diane said.

'I'd kind of like that,' said Jin. 'The thing about this job is that it's hard to have a love life – of course, I could be like Neva and just bring mine to work with me.'

Neva punched him gently in the arm with her fist.

David looked lost – as if the prospect of going home early were confusing to him.

'David,' said Diane. 'Why don't you go home and work on that proposal we talked about for teaching photography?'

His face brightened. 'I could do that.'

'You could come over to Mike's for dinner,' Neva said to David. 'I'm sure we're having some variation on tofu. Didn't you say you like tofu?'

'Good idea,' said Jin. 'And tomorrow we can work on lesson two of how to have a life.'

'You guys are really funny,' said David.

'I was serious about dinner,' said Neva.

'Get out of here,' said Diane. 'I'll call you if I need you.'

Diane cleared out her team just as the night receptionist came on duty. He was new. Garnett had suspended the former one while the crime lab break-in was being investigated. So far the former receptionist hadn't admitted to anything; nor had any money shown up in his accounts. Maybe he was innocent, but Diane had a gut feeling that the break-in was at least partly an inside job. She called Garnett from her osteology office to get an update. As she expected, he was still at work.

'Just curious about the break-in here,' she said when he answered.

'Not much to tell you. We've questioned the ladies – the Wiccan and the Druid. They indignantly deny having anything to do with it. Their coven members alibi them, but I imagine that's what covens are for. I just don't stand that stuff. In my day, covens were witches, but this woman denies being a witch. I tell you, I don't know what to make of them.'

'And my receptionist?'

'Nothing there either. The little trace evidence you've found hasn't been helpful either. We just don't have a thing. I agree that the women don't seem like the type who could pull off something like this, but I can't think of a reason why anyone else would want the bones that were stolen. Whoever it was is liable to be disappointed – you say they were actually deer bones?'

'That's what the owner says was in the box. We never got a look at them.'

'Well, deer bones or human bones, it doesn't matter. When we catch them they're going to do jail time for breaking into a crime lab. How's your arm doing?'

Diane stretched it out in front of her and moved it around. 'It's gradually getting well.'

'And that student? I hear he's home from the hospital.'

'Yes. Mike's doing fine too. Neva's staying with him while she gets her home in order.'

'Neva?'

'Mike's her boyfriend.'

'Oh, I didn't know that, or did I? I tell you, I feel overwhelmed here some days.'

Diane knew how he felt. She stared at the watercolor of the wolf and wished she were out somewhere in the wild. 'Do you have anything on Neva's break-in?' she asked.

'Not a thing. I guess that's why I'm feeling overwhelmed. I'm not able to clear any of these cases that involve the department. Makes us look pretty incompetent.'

'I know how you feel.'

'That mold of the perp's fingers Neva found was a break. At least if we find a suspect, we can identify him. The mold didn't match any of the young hoodlums in her neighborhood.'

Diane was disappointed. She was hoping for at least a break in Neva's case. The attack on Neva's home worried her. 'Thanks for the update,' she said, and sighed as she cradled the phone.

Diane locked up, said good-bye to the evening receptionist and started to close the door when Korey came down the hall rolling a trolley loaded with several boxes.

'Got your new microscopes,' he said.

Diane opened the door and helped him put them on a counter. 'We'll set them up tomorrow. What else you have there?'

Another box twice as large as the microscopes sat on the trolley.

'A messenger brought it a few minutes ago. The label says it's from Great Britain.'

'Ah, the witch.'

'Another one?'

'The real one. The first one was a decoy.'

Korey shook his head. 'You know, sometimes it's hard to keep up around here.' He carried the witch to the osteology lab.

'It's awfully big,' said Diane.

'The first one, if I remember correctly, had an outer and an inner box.'

Korey cut open the top with his knife. Inside they found a smaller box surrounded by bubble wrap and the words *Moonhater Cave Bones* written on the top. Diane took it out of the bubble wrap and locked it inside the vault.

'Thanks, Korey. I understand you had dinner with Neva and Mike last evening.'

'Yes. Had a good time. Mike seems to be getting along pretty good. I have to tell you, I was worried. That was scary at the funeral.' He shook his head, then smiled. 'I'm glad you hired him. That was a good choice. He works hard around here.'

Diane locked up the lab again and walked down the hall with Korey.

'You going home or back to the lab?'

'Home. I was in Andie's office when the stuff came and I offered to bring them up.'

Diane arched an eyebrow and smiled. Korey laughed out loud.

'I can't pull anything off around you, can I, Dr F.?'

They reached the elevators. 'Spill it, Korey. What is it you want?'

'I'd like to go the International Conference of Museum Conservators.'

'Where is it going to be?'

'Glasgow this year.'

Diane thought for a moment. 'Let me see what we have in the budget for conferences. But assuming we have the money, sure, pack your bags.'

'Thanks, Dr F.' He punched the elevator button. It opened and Frank got off.

'Diane. Just coming to see you. Hello, Korey.'

'Hey, Frank. How's it going?'

They shook hands and all of them rode down in the elevator together. Korey said good-bye, and Diane walked with Frank to her office.

'I was about to go look at some paperwork and then call it a night.'

'Good timing. How about you take your

paperwork home and let me take you to dinner? We can eat here in the restaurant if you like.'

'Actually, I can leave the paperwork. I let the crime staff go home early – well, early for us, anyway. I'll get on it tomorrow. You look happy.'

'I'm celebrating,' Frank said.

'Good.' Lately everything had been about her – all her problems. It would be nice to spend an evening talking about Frank for a change. 'You catch that guy you were looking for?'

'Yes, I did, and I'm celebrating.'

Over a dinner of steak and baked potato in the museum restaurant, Frank told her about the embezzler that everyone, including the FBI, had been looking for.

'He hit some Atlanta companies; that's why my unit was involved. I noticed that in one of his hotel rooms our guys discovered a small glassine envelope. I thought that might mean he was a stamp collector, but that was a long shot. There are lots of uses for glassine envelopes. I gave the info to the FBI. They checked out stamp conventions that corresponded to places he'd visited and didn't find a correlation, so they dropped it.'

His eyes twinkled in the candlelight as he spoke. Diane absolutely loved his eyes. 'But you didn't.' She took a bite of her steak. It occurred to her that she hadn't eaten all day, except for an energy bar for breakfast.

'I'd been studying the guy. He collected Matchbox cars, rocks, coins and comic books as

382

a kid – he was a collector. Stamps are nice for someone who moves around a lot. No, I didn't let it go. The FBI had hacked into some of the places he shopped online and saw that he used the password "ironage" on one site, "lavaroad" and "tigerail" on a few others.'

'Tiger ale? What is that, some kind of drink?'

Frank shook his head. 'The FBI didn't think anything about his passwords, but I got to playing around with them. They're anagrams for Noriega, Alvarado and Galtieri.'

Diane stopped eating and stared at him. 'How did you possibly come up with that?'

'I'm a detective – one who deals with lots of numbers and words. What can I say?'

'So what did you make of these anagrams?'

'The FBI thought it was interesting, but still didn't make anything of it. I was betting that was his stamp interest – dictators of small countries, something like that. I looked again at the places he'd been and got the catalogs of the ones that had stamp conventions. They all had stamps of the kind I thought he might collect if my hunch was right. As a check, I looked at some of the stamp convention catalogs at places he didn't go – sure enough, none of them had the kind of stamps I thought would interest him.'

'Pretty slick,' said Diane. 'How did you find him?'

'The FBI at this point had come to my way of thinking, and they tried to set a few traps, but they couldn't lure him in. Then the thing about Pitcairn Island came up in the news – the mayor and his buddies convicted for multiple rapes. The mayor served as a de facto dictator on the island for years. It turns out, too, that the basis of Pitcairn's economy is stamps. It was a long shot, but I thought maybe it might appeal to him. So I picked out a set of stamps that he would find interesting – and rare – and set my own trap. I put them up for sale – called them a rare collection from the realm of Pitcairn's petty dictator – he bit and we got him.'

Diane laughed and clapped her hands. 'Frank, I'm impressed. I really am.'

'Sometimes it comes down to paying attention to words.'

'You certainly went a long way with a few jumbled words.'

Diane took a bite of her potato and kept her fork in her mouth so long that Frank put his own fork down and looked at her.

'I know that look,' he said. 'You thought of something.'

'I did. It was the word. You're right: Sometimes it comes down to words.'

CHAPTER 35

Frank's eyes sparkled in amusement as he watched Diane.

'Okay, what's the word?'

'Cave. You know about the break-in here?'

'Yes.'

'I've been assuming that the real target of the break-in was the Moonhater Cave witch bones – but it wasn't.'

'It wasn't?'

'No, I don't believe it was. It was a sleight-of-hand kind of thing – you watch one thing while something else is really going on. John Rose sent a decoy box of bones because he expected that an attempt would be made to steal the Moonhater witch bones somewhere in transit or after they arrived here.'

She explained to Frank about the controversy over the Moonhater Cave witch bones and about the Wiccans and Druids.

'He expected the bones to be stolen by the Druids or by someone they hired to do it. The bones were stolen, and that's what fooled me. It was a natural conclusion that his expectation had come true. The thieves also took a couple of microscopes, but I thought that was a distraction meant to hide their real intent. They stole a box of Caver Doe evidence too, and I thought maybe that was also for show.'

Diane punctuated her sentences with her fork. 'The real Moonhater witch bones arrived today. They're in a box packed and labeled identically to the box of bones that was stolen. It was a plain box cushioned with bubble wrap inside the shipping box. On the box containing the bones, John Rose wrote the words 'Moonhater Cave Bones' – didn't say 'Moonhater Witch Bones,' which is the way we've been thinking about them. It said 'Moonhater *Cave Bones.*' You see?'

Frank squinted at her. 'Spell it out.'

'The thieves came looking for the bones we found in a cave. They saw a box lying in plain sight that said "cave bones' and probably thought, 'How many could there be?' They were after Caver Doe. They thought they got him. And that's why they also took the box of evidence labeled Caver Doe.'

'It makes sense,' said Frank. 'But why? Caver Doe's bones are, what . . . about fifty, sixty years old?'

'I don't know yet.' She reached for her cell. 'I need to call David.' She dialed his number and he answered on the first ring.

'Hey, Diane, what's up?' David sounded hopeful.

'Something just occurred to me.' She told him about her theory.

David was silent a moment. 'That makes more sense to me than that the Druids did it.'

'You know what that means, don't you? It means the Caver Doe death, the crime lab break-in and the quarry murders are linked. If Caver Doe is linked to the quarry by the buttons, and the break-in was about Caver Doe, then the break-in and the quarry murders are linked.'

'Interesting,' said David. 'Of course, it depends on your scenario being right.'

'It is right,' she said emphatically and laughed. 'We'll talk about it tomorrow. I just wanted you to be thinking about it.'

'That sounded interesting,' said Frank.

'No more crime. Let's talk about dessert. Let's order something really rich.'

Diane was in early the next morning. After a workout at home, she jogged the museum nature trail and took a shower in her office suite. She felt invigorated. Her arm was healing nicely. She did some museum business and had put all the finished papers on Andie's desk by the time her assistant arrived. They spent a few minutes discussing museum business; then Diane went upstairs to the crime lab.

David was in the lab. So was Jin.

'I thought I was early,' said Diane.

'You are,' said David. 'We're just earlier. I told Jin about your revelation.'

'I think you're right, Boss.'

Jin and David were writing on two whiteboards. On one board, Jin was listing each crime and the evidence they had so far. On the other board, David was making a matrix. The top of the matrix he labeled *Crime Scene* and listed *Cave, Lake Bottom, Quarry, Lab.* The side of the matrix he labeled *Evidence* and listed *Buttons, Picture of Car, Decade, Theft.* He marked an X wherever one of the pieces of evidence was linked to a scene.

When he finished he stood back and looked at his work. An X at one intersection in the matrix indicated that identical buttons were found at the Caver Doe and the Plymouth Doe crime scenes; another showed that both deaths occurred during the same decade. Another X in the matrix confirmed that the picture of the submerged car found near the bodies of Scuba Doe and Quarry Doe linked their deaths with the car containing Plymouth Doe found at the bottom of the quarry. The crime lab break-in and the Caver Doe death were connected by the box of Caver Doe evidence stolen from the lab. Most of the connections were tenuous, but all were suggestive.

Jin looked at the matrix David had constructed. 'It's like a logic problem,' Jin said. 'If A is connected to B, and B is connected to C, then C is connected to A. All the crime scenes could be connected in some way. Isn't that a surprise?'

'Okay, but how?' said Diane. 'What motive or driving force connects a sixty-year-old body in a cave and a sixty-year-old body in the bottom of the lake with the recent quarry murders and the crime lab break-in?'

'My first thought would be money or something valuable,' said David.

'If their deaths weren't so long ago,' said Jin, 'I'd say the murderer was trying to protect himself by keeping Plymouth Doe from being found and by stopping us from analyzing the Caver Doe evidence. But that seems unlikely, because . . . well, everyone who was involved in the original murders, including the perp, is probably dead now.'

'Not necessarily,' said David. 'Diane, didn't you say Caver Doe was in his late teens or early twenties, and that Plymouth Doe was about the same age?'

'Yes,' said Diane.

'So they would be in their eighties or nineties now,' said David.

'What?' Jin laughed. 'You thinking somebody in a nursing home is orchestrating all of this? I know the statute of limitations doesn't run out on murder, but I really can't see them doing hard time now, even if they're caught.'

'And we don't know that Caver Doe was murdered,' said Diane. 'We only know he wasn't rescued.'

The elevator opened and Neva rushed in, out of breath. 'Sorry I'm late. I had a terrible time talking Mike out of taking a run. God, he's going to be the death of me. Between him and that stupid caller.'

'What caller?' asked Diane. They all looked over at her with identical expressions of concern.

'This guy – I think he's a guy; his voice is kind of high-pitched – he's been calling Mike the past couple of weeks and saying he's the top of the food chain.'

Jin and David grinned. 'What does that mean? Who's the top of the food chain?'

'The caller. It's really weird. That's almost all he says. Once he told Mike he wasn't getting his rabbits. I think the guy's on drugs. I wish he'd lose Mike's number.'

'What does the caller ID say?' asked Diane. She didn't find it as humorous as Jin and David.

'Mike doesn't have it. Can you believe it? He doesn't even have a cell phone.'

'Could it be the person who stabbed him?' asked David.

'That's what I thought,' Neva replied. 'But Mike doesn't think so. He said it's just somebody on drugs or somebody who hates vegetarians.'

'Tell the police anyway,' said Diane. 'Get them to put a tap on the phone.'

'I'll try to talk him into it. We first thought it was my uncle Brad – the family clown. Uncle Brad's a stonemason and he has these really strong hands, and he likes to intimidate people with his strength. When he shakes hands, especially with my and my cousin's boyfriends, he likes to squeeze real hard until it hurts.'

Diane could see where this was going.

'Mom and Dad invited Mike over for a family barbecue. When Uncle Brad heard Mike was a vegetarian . . . well, you should have heard him making fun.'

'Ah,' said David, 'Real-men-don't-eat-quiche kind of thing.'

Neva nodded. 'I introduced Mike, and Uncle Brad shook his hand and started his squeeze routine. But Mike's a rock climber. I didn't tell Uncle Brad that Mike often has to lift his body weight up by his fingers. Well, Mike could squeeze harder than Uncle Brad.' Neva grinned. 'They stood there holding hands, Uncle Brad's face getting redder by the second. Finally, Mike said that if they didn't quit holding hands, people were going to start talking. Ever since then, Uncle Brad keeps talking about how he'd hurt his hand at work and it wasn't as strong as it usually was. He's the kind who can dish things out but can't take them.' Neva shrugged. 'But the phone calls are weird even for him.' As she spoke, Neva looked at the board with David's crime scene and evidence chart. 'What's this?'

Jin explained to her about the possibility that Caver Doe was the real focus of the lab theft and the witch bones had been stolen by mistake.

'That makes sense. I have to tell you, I was having a hard time wrapping my brain around the theory that Druids broke in. So are you telling me that all our crime scenes are related?'

'The evidence and the logic say they are,' said Diane. 'It's something to look into. We need to get Detective Garnett, Sheriff Burns and Sheriff Canfield in here together to discuss this. They're going to love that. There's nothing like cross-jurisdictional cases to deal with. Okay, let's finish the trace evidence. I'll go call Garnett and the others.'

'I was just thinking,' said Neva. 'Why don't I use our software and age the girl in the snapshot – the one found with Caver Doe? Show what she might look like today. I could do another drawing. Maybe two drawings. One where she ages well and one where she doesn't.'

'That's a good idea,' said Diane. 'She might still be alive, and people would more likely recognize her face as it is now rather than the way she looked when she was young.'

'Good thinking,' said Jin, gently shoving her. 'You've been doing a lot of that lately.'

Diane went to her office and called Garnett, Burns and Canfield. All were surprised at the connections. Burns was skeptical. They agreed to come and discuss pooling resources. Garnett would like that, thought Diane. That was exactly what he and the mayor wanted – for Rosewood to become the place where all the surrounding counties came to get help solving their crimes.

While Diane was at her desk, she gave Lynn Webber a belated call to thank her for working on Caver Doe.

'Why, you're welcome,' said Lynn. 'It was interesting to work on mummified remains. I hope the bones were nice and clean when you got them. I miss Raymond every day that goes by, but my new assistant, Grover, is just precious. Have you met him?'

'No. I haven't had the pleasure yet. But he did a fine job on the bones. Did you know he put them in separate boxes according to their side? Got it right too.'

'Did he really?' Webber laughed with that mirthful laugh that Diane noticed men just loved, but she found grating. 'Why am I not surprised?' she said.

'He is obviously very conscientious in his work.'

'Next time you're over here, I'll introduce you. He worked as a mortician's assistant before he applied for Raymond's job. He knew Raymond. I think they may even be related, like third cousins. He's a really big guy with a large round face and hands as big as dinner plates. But he has a delicate touch with the cadavers when it's called for. He talks to them too, and is so solemn all the time that I have to make an effort not to laugh. You know how Raymond had that great sense of humor. Grover is completely opposite. But I'm pleased with his work.'

Lynn Webber obviously still grieved for her former assistant, who was murdered not that long ago.

'I'm looking forward to it,' said Diane. 'I won't keep you. I just wanted to thank you for your work on Caver Doe.'

'Anytime – well, not anytime – but I like interesting challenges. How are you? I've been hearing the most alarming things – that you got stabbed at a funeral? That can't be right.'

'I did. Some maniac, I imagine. We don't know who did it. But I'm healing fine. It wasn't serious. Just very annoying. Thanks for asking.'

Diane got off the phone before Lynn started asking about the break-in and other questions she didn't want to answer. When she hung up, she went to finish Caver Doe. She'd put him on the back burner, but if there was a connection among the crimes, he'd just moved himself to the front burner.

She rolled the table with Caver Doe's bones from the vault out into the osteology lab. She read over her notes from her preliminary examination. His right tibia was broken. His right heel bone and ankle bone, the bones in his right wrist and two lumbar vertebrae were also fractured.

Diane examined the bones one by one under the microscope, looking for any minute breaks or marks that she had missed. She found nothing else. Up until the time he died, Caver Doe appeared to have been in good health and well muscled. He was probably right-handed. When he died he was in substantial pain from his broken bones. She packed up Caver Doe's bones and stored him in the vault.

Diane checked in on Jane Doe's bones from the woods site that were being worked on by the dermestid colony. The beetles had made substantial progress. She lifted the skull out of the tank, cleared it of beetles, checking all the orifices, and took it into the vault. Neva was there working on aging the snapshot picture.

'I'm going to do a laser scan of Jane Doe's skull so we can have a picture of her when the sheriffs and Chief Garnett get here,' said Diane.

'If I have time, I'll do a sketch of her,' said Neva.

'If you have time. But don't rush.'

Diane scanned Jane Doe's skull, and Neva downloaded the scan data into the imaging software.

'You say Mike's restless?' asked Diane.

Neva nodded. 'He's a pain in the butt right now.'

'I'm sure he doesn't like being weak.'

'No, he doesn't,' said Neva. 'I think he must have been a hyperactive kid. He absolutely hates sitting still.'

'You're doing a good job taking care of him.'

'I ought to just not say anything and let him do what he wants to do and suffer the consequences. I did talk him into calling his doctor and asking him what kind of activity he can do.'

Diane left her alone with her work. Neva seemed to enjoy the solitude of the vault and the work she did there. Jane Doe's skull went back to the insects. The sheriff and Garnett couldn't come until after lunch, so Diane decided to go to the museum to do some work.

The paleontologists working on the velociraptors wanted to do an exhibit of Jurassic plants in the plant room, but the botanists were balking at having another curator design exhibits in their territory, and furthermore, they had plans of their own. Diane hadn't yet read either proposal, and she was rather looking forward to something that didn't require her to look at the dead – at least, she hoped it didn't come to that.

As Diane left the osteology lab, she saw Lane Emery, head of the crime lab security, at the reception desk talking to the day guard. She waved and crossed the overlook to the dinosaur room. She looked down for a moment, watching the tourists look at the exhibits of the giant animals. She smiled and walked on to the bank of elevators.

The elevator doors opened to a darkened interior. Two young men in museum T-shirts were inside. Docents, she thought. Diane started to back up to let them out when they grabbed her and pulled her in. She tried to scream, but they put a cloth over her mouth. She tried to claw at their faces, but felt suddenly weak. For a brief moment she smelled the chloroform before passing out.

CHAPTER 36

Diane awoke, but didn't move. She listened. She heard audible breathing. It sounded like a broken nose that hadn't healed properly – or a deviated septum. She still smelled the chloroform, but other odors were starting to filter in – paint, glue, pesticide, orange cleaner. They were very familiar smells. She knew where she was – in the basement of the museum. It was being renovated, but the crew was off this week. At least she was in the museum. The knowledge gave her comfort. She was sitting in a chair, her arms bound with what felt like tape. She had a blindfold over her eyes.

'She's got to be awake by now.'

'Dr Fallon, you awake? Just nod.'

Diane concentrated on keeping her breathing even.

'She's awake; she's just playing possum.'

There were two men, probably the two who were in the elevator. Neither wore aftershave or cologne, no aroma to identify. She tried to remember their faces, but they had been turned toward each other, as if one was looking at something the other had.

'Lady, we aren't supposed to hurt you. This is kind of like a board meeting. We just want you to listen. We are going ahead and talking, and you just listen.'

Diane didn't move.

'I'll say this for you: You're good at playing possum. That's okay. We don't need your co-operation, or an answer. We're just delivering a message.'

He was the one with the deviated septum. Probably got it from a fight, she thought. Their voices came from different levels. Deviated Septum was sitting, the other standing. As if verifying it, the first man slid his chair across the tile floor so that he was closer to Diane.

'You control the evidence in the crime lab. All you have to do is get rid of the stuff you took from the cave and the bottom of the lake. That's all. Just get rid of it. It's a sixty-three-year-old crime. It's the past. History. It's not like you can put anybody on trial.'

'If you don't,' said the man standing, 'well, we sort of own you in a way. We own the museum. We can come and go as we please. We can reach your family.' A chill went through Diane. 'We can burn down the museum.'

'So,' said Deviated Septum, 'it sounds like a bargain to me. Some old bones for an entire museum full of all kinds of fascinating things.'

'You don't have to answer. Just know that we can get to anyone. We got to your mother without having to leave our house,' said the other man.

Diane was frightened at first; now she flushed with anger. These were the hackers who had caused her mother to be arrested and put in Tombsberg. 'I can't hear,' whispered Diane through her teeth.

They were silent for a second, as if confused, as if contemplating that the entire speech went unheard.

'My ears. I'm dizzy. What do you want?'

'Well, shit. Do you know how long I've been rehearsing that little speech? Okay, let's do it again.' He got close to her ear and yelled, 'With stereo! You are going to lose the bones found in the cave and in the lake and all the stuff found with them or we are going to burn down the museum. Did you hear that?'

'Yes, I hear you. Why do you want me to do that?'

'Why isn't important. It's just the way things are. Have I made myself clear?'

Diane's left ear reverberated with the sound.

'To a point.'

'Just as long as you know what to do. Do you know what to do?'

'Yes.'

He stood up. 'Now . . .'

'I can't hear you. The chloroform. My head's spinning.'

He got near her ear again. 'We're leaving a knife twenty feet in front of you. You can get yourself loose. Do you understand?'

Diane nodded. Then she got an extra bonus. The other man, not Deviated Septum, bent to where he could yell in her other ear.

'We got to your mother without breaking a sweat. How is she doing, by the way?'

'My mother? That was you? Why?'

'Oh, I think you can figure it out. You seem to be fair at figuring things out. Just know that we did it.'

'Did you stab me? Why?'

'No, we didn't do that. But we could have.'

He rose, and she heard the two of them leave the room. She listened to their footfalls echoing in the empty basement. She heard the key put in the lock to call the elevator to the basement. She heard them as they got on and as the elevator rose.

She stayed there after they left and didn't move until there were no more sounds of movement. Were they gone? Probably. They wanted her co-operation, not to kill her. She tried to rise from the chair, but was tied too tightly to it. She stood as much as she could and half walked and half scooted, feeling with her feet for the knife. She ended up kicking it and heard it bounce off the wall. *Damn.*

She dragged the chair with her in the direction of the sound and felt along the floor with her foot. Several tries and she stepped on it.

Now to pick it up. Briefly she thought about using her toes, but she had very little dexterity in her toes even without panty hose. After half a dozen failed efforts to get to it, she rocked the chair until it fell. She banged her head against the floor and cursed under her breath. Finally she squirmed around until her back was to the knife. Diane grabbed it with her hands and felt the double-edged blade.

It was a dagger. She wondered if it was the one used to stab her and Mike. But why would they have denied doing it and admitted to other things? Avoiding the cutting edges, she grasped the hilt of the dagger and maneuvered it into a position so that she could saw at the tape that bound her. It was a dull knife, not the one used to stab her and Mike. They wanted her to get loose, but to delay her escape, to give them a head start.

She sawed halfway though the tape. The other half yielded more easily. Her hands came free. She wiggled them around until she could maneuver out of the tape around her shoulders, and removed the blindfold from her eyes.

She estimated that it had taken her about fifteen minutes to get free. She picked up the knife and tape, then looked around the room for anything else that might have been left behind by her kidnappers. The chair was all she saw at the moment. She grabbed it too and went for the elevator. They had left the elevator key on the floor. She put it in the lock and rode to the third floor, carrying all the items with her.

She made it to the crime lab. Chief Garnett,

Sheriff Burns and Sheriff Canfield were sitting around the table. David was giving them coffee.

'What you got there, Boss?' said Jin, rushing over to help her. 'What is all this stuff?'

'Don't touch it until you get some gloves on,' she said. She turned to her guests. 'I have an emergency. I'll be with you in just a minute.'

'David, Jin, Neva, you're with me.' She led them to one of the evidence rooms, carrying the items with her, and closed the door. Garnett and the two sheriffs stared after her.

'What's up, Boss?'

'I just escaped from being kidnaped, knocked out with chloroform and tied up in the basement.'

Neva, Jin and David stood with their mouths open.

'Just now? That's where you were all morning?' said David.

'Yes. David, I want you to go to the basement and process Room . . . Room J, I think it's called. There's a temporary paper sign with the letter above the door. Process the far right elevator, the key, the tape, the chair. Look around and see if they've been using the basement as a home base.'

She turned to Jin. 'I need you to process me.'

'You?' said Jin. 'What did they do?' He looked alarmed.

'For one thing, my nails. I tried to scratch them, but I don't think I got anything. I managed to get them to yell at me close to my ear and I'm hoping a good spray of spittle got transferred. One guy was on the left side, the other on the right. The left-side guy had noisy breathing. I'm thinking he might have had a deviated septum. Anyway, Jin, I want you to take the samples to Atlanta and do whatever you have to to get them processed ASAP.'

Jin went to get his kit to collect the samples. Diane turned to David. 'When he gets the DNA results, run them through CODIS and any other DNA database you can get access to. Even if we are not supposed to have access.'

'This is serious.'

'They threatened to burn down the museum unless I get rid of the Caver Doe and Plymouth Doe evidence.'

Neva sucked in her breath.

David's mouth was agape. 'My God. You have to tell Garnett.'

'I will, but I'm not sure who to trust. They didn't say it, but they seemed to know that we're putting things together.' Diane shook her head. 'I think – or they may simply have bungled the break-in and are now trying intimidation.'

Jin returned, and Diane gave him her jacket. 'If you need to cut my hair, go ahead.'

'I'll try not to make you look too bad,' he said. 'How did you get them to yell in your ear?'

'I told them I couldn't hear because of the chloroform.'

'You convinced them the chloroform made you deaf? Way to go, Boss.' Jin took samples of her hair around her ears, then swabbed her skin and other parts of her hair. 'If they left their DNA, I got it,' said Jin. 'You want me to leave now for the lab in Atlanta?'

'Yes.'

'You know, Boss, if we had our own lab . . .'

'You get me some usable DNA and I'll give it serious thought.'

'You got it,' said Jin.

'Send the information directly to David's computer when you get the results.'

'Sure thing. You okay now, Boss?'

'No, I'm not. I am very angry. They also admitted – bragged about – being the ones responsible for what happened to my mother.'

'Good God,' said David. 'I see what happened now. They wanted to steal the bones before you had a chance to look at them, so they went after your mother to get you out of town. Something – or someone – important must be connected to them.'

'Yes, I'm sure you're right. They had me blindfolded and tied up, but here's what I gathered from their conversation. One of them said the bones are sixty-three years old – both Caver Doe and Plymouth Doe. Now we have a firm date. At least one of them is a hacker – he took the time right before they left to brag how he could get to my family. I think it is probably the one without the nose problem. He would be the one who yelled in my right ear.'

404

'I was trying to find you this morning,' said David, 'to tell you that I've filled in more blanks in our chart out there. The powder from the surgeon's gloves that we got from the keypad on your bone lab lock is the same as powder found on the photograph of the submerged car. We also found some navy wool fibers on Quarry Doe like the wool fibers we found in the basement security room. So from what you've told me, I'd say it was these guys who did the crime lab burglary and murdered the two guys at the quarry.'

'Jin, when you process my jacket, check for powder residue. Feel free to cut it up if you need to.'

'Don't you worry, Boss; we've all but got them.'

'You guys are doing a good job.' Diane turned to Neva. 'They've been hanging around the museum, probably wearing museum T-shirts. I want you to check the security videotapes and interview the museum personnel – especially security and the docents – for anyone seen hanging around whom they didn't recognize. That's not going to be an easy task, since the museum is usually full of strangers. The guys were young – in their twenties. Cocky. They have a sense of entitlement. Both were athletic in build. White.'

Diane searched her memory of the two men in the elevator before the lights went out.

'One was just under six feet. The other about six-two or three. I didn't see their faces, but they had tanned complexions. One had dark blond hair, short. The other had brown hair that came below his ears. He was the taller of the two.'

'Wow,' said Neva. 'I wonder what they'd think if they knew how much data you got from them.'

Diane shrugged. 'Neva, if anyone seems to recognize them, draw a picture. I know you haven't had any experience doing that kind of drawing, but here's your chance.'

'I'll get the videotapes from security and start interviewing the docents,' said Neva. 'I'll get right on it.'

'There has to be a third person,' Diane said. 'They were waiting for me in the elevator. How did they know when I was going to the elevator?' She tried to remember if there was someone in the staff lounge when she passed. She thought so, but she passed it so many times during the day. 'I have no idea what this person might look like.'

'If I can get a line on the first two, maybe the third was seen hanging around with them,' said Neva.

'I hope someone remembers them, or at least that the damn security cameras worked this time. David, take a couple of the security guards with you. Do a sweep of the entire basement.'

'Isn't there a subbasement?' said Jin. 'Korey showed me some old plans of the building.'

Diane raised an eyebrow. 'Yes. But it's dank and musty. I didn't get any sense of that aroma from them. And from my times down in the subbasement, they'd definitely come back with a scent.

But we'd better check it.' She sighed, suddenly out of breath.

'I need to know if the stabbings were connected to all these crimes. They denied they did the stabbings, but they don't have a lot of credibility with me. See if you can connect Neva's house break-in with them. Perhaps when we find them, we'll see that one has something wrong with a finger.

'Now, I need to ask if any of you have mentioned anything about the current cases to anyone. This isn't an accusation. I'm having to think about what I might have said to Frank. I was with him when I called David on the cell to discuss my revelation about the cave-witch bones. Someone might have overheard me.'

'I hardly talk about what I do,' said Jin. 'I never discuss anything specific.'

'I don't know anybody,' said David.

'Sometimes I tell Mike about drawings, but only in general terms. He was up here yesterday watching, but he knows not to mention anything about the crime lab, and he wouldn't . . . but I'll check with him about it.'

'Okay, now I have to have the same conversation with the guys out there.' She pointed to Chief Garnett and the two sheriffs, who were waiting in suspense. 'I have a feeling they aren't going to be as nice as you guys about being questioned.'

CHAPTER 37

C hief Garnett, Sheriff Burns and Sheriff Canfield looked slightly put out when Diane sat down across from them. They shifted in their seats and finally leaned forward with their forearms on the table. She looked at each of them in turn, still trying to decide how much to say. She should tell Garnett everything, since he was not only Rosewood's chief of detectives, but technically her boss when it came to the crime lab. The crime scene unit was his baby.

'We have a serious problem,' Diane began.

'You said on the phone that you have evidence that all the crimes are linked,' said Sheriff Canfield, obviously anxious to get on with it. His jurisdiction covered the quarry and the lake because they were in Rose County but outside of Rosewood city limits, where Garnett's jurisdiction ended.

Canfield handed Diane a report that identified Quarry Doe as Donnie Martin – from his prison tattoos. She wrote the name on the chart as she brought the board around to face them. 'This is a chart of the crime scene evidence. Not all the evidence in the cases is represented, by any means. Just the pieces that connect two or more crime scenes. The Xs show the connections.' She watched their eyes to see if they were following.

She guided them through the links formed by the rare buttons, the same estimated date for the two old deaths, the picture of the submerged car, the items stolen from the lab, the blue wool fibers, and the powder residue.

The three stared at the table with wrinkled brows and frowns. Sheriff Canfield squinted his eyes, as if that made everything clearer.

'Logically, as you can see, all the crimes are connected,' Diane finished.

Sheriff Burns's phone rang and Diane felt annoyed. It was stealing the power of the moment, and she needed the impact of the evidence in order to gain their cooperation. Burns grabbed the phone from his belt.

'Yeah?' He listened for a minute before speaking again. 'Are you sure? You don't say? I would've been surprised five minutes ago.' He hung up.

Sheriff Burns got up, took one of the dry markers and added to the chart. He wrote *woods* on the crime scene line and *relatives* over the evidence column and put an X where the relatives column crossed the quarry and woods lines.

They looked at him, puzzled.

'That was one my deputies. They just discovered that Flora Martin – a.k.a. Jane Doe in the woods – is the great-grandmother of Donnie

Martin – a.k.a. Quarry Doe – over in your juris-diction, Canfield.'

'So,' said Garnett, 'all these cases are related. Any idea how?'

'Some,' said Diane, 'but as I said, we – or rather, I – have a problem.' Diane decided to lay most of it on the table.

'I was late because two men chloroformed me in the elevator and took me to the basement, where they tied me up and proceeded to tell me that if I don't destroy evidence, they will burn down the museum and harm my family.'

Like her staff, the three law officers stared at her in disbelief. Garnett's face twisted into anger and he slammed his fist on the table.

'Here? Someone got you here?'

'What evidence do they want you to destroy?' said Sheriff Burns.

'Evidence from the cave and from the lake bottom.'

'For God's sake, why?' said Sheriff Canfield. 'Those are ancient cases.' He tapped the table. 'Didn't you say the lake-bottom victim could have died in 1942?'

'And if they all are connected, why not demand you destroy all the evidence?' asked Sheriff Burns.

'I'm guessing,' said Diane. 'But I think when we find out what happened in the cave and at the bottom of the lake in 1942, the evidence will point directly to someone who, even after all these years, has a great deal to lose. My attackers were cocky.

They think they're too smart to get caught. They don't think we can connect them to the murders of Jake Stanley, Donnie Martin and Flora Martin. And they realize that I can destroy the evidence from the cave without arousing a great deal of suspicion, but I can't destroy evidence from current cases.'

'Do you know who they were?' asked Garnett.

'No. I have my staff looking for trace evidence.' Diane held back that she might have their DNA.

'We'll give the museum extra protection, of course,' said Garnett.

'I'm going to be beefing up security, too. And I'll have the day lighting stay on at night until we sort this out. That will make it easier for security.'

'So you weren't tempted to destroy the evidence?' said Burns. It wasn't an accusation, but simply a comment, something a reasonable person might do, given the alternatives.

'No,' said Diane. 'Destroying evidence of a crime is not an option. Neither is having my museum burned to the ground or having my family harmed. What I'm going to do is get the sons of bitches.'

'We'll help you,' said Burns. 'Let us know.'

Diane gave them a brief description of what happened to her mother and how the two thugs bragged about it. 'They were proud that they could get to anyone without leaving the house.'

'Son of a bitch,' echoed Sheriff Canfield. 'People can do something like that?'

411

'Yes, they can,' said Garnett. 'We have a unit that deals with computer fraud. It's frightening what a hacker can do. So these guys are computer geeks?'

'At least one of them has to be.' Diane took a deep breath. Here she had to be her most diplomatic self. 'One thing you can do,' said Diane. 'I got the impression that the guys knew that we're making progress. I'm checking my staff and phones to see if there is a leak, a bug or any way someone might have overheard a conversation between me and my staff. I'd like you all to do the same.'

They took the suggestion that they might have a leak much better than she had hoped.

'My big leaker is in the hospital,' said Burns. 'Deputy Singer is our county commissioner's brother-in-law and a pain in the butt. I try to keep him on easy things, like serving papers and the like. I understand he shoveled up the bones of Flora Martin and delivered her to you in a garbage bag.'

'Yes, he did.'

Burns shook his head. 'That's not how I taught him. I sent him to Atlanta for training with the GBI. I don't know why he didn't learn anything.'

Having Burns admit – in a manner of speaking – to a potential leak loosened up Canfield to the possibility.

'I'll talk to my secretary and deputies. You know, we talk all the time about a break in this case or that, without giving details.'

'That's the problem,' said Diane. 'So do we, and that's all the information they needed. They didn't need details.'

'It's impossible not to talk at all about a case within earshot of the people you work with,' said Garnett. 'Like Canfield, we don't give out details, just . . . "we're making progress" kind of thing. Frankly, I'm surprised anyone takes that seriously.'

They all laughed.

'I may be all wrong,' said Diane. 'Maybe they just assumed that we'd be making progress by this time.'

'If they've been hanging around the museum,' said Canfield, 'they might have picked up something here.' He was not accusatory, but there was still a slight defensive edge to his voice.

'I agree. That's most likely,' said Diane. She saw Canfield relax, but Garnett frowned. 'That's why I'm checking the phones. We know they have the ability to hack into secure computers. They also bypassed our electronic locks and alarms and disabled the security cameras for the lab break-in. They most likely have other electronic talents, such as tapping phones.'

'We'll check our offices,' said Canfield.

Garnett's frown softened. Diane knew it was important to him that the crime lab seem invincible and infallible, but she wasn't going to get any cooperation from the two sheriffs if she put the burden of a possible leak entirely on their shoulders. In reality, she was concerned that someone overheard her phone call to David when she and Frank were in the restaurant.

'I appreciate all of your cooperation. I've got reports for you on the evidence found at your crime scenes.' Diane passed out papers from a stack David had put on the table in preparation for the meeting. She stood up. 'If you'll excuse me, I need to go talk to my security personnel.'

Garnett stayed after the others left. Clearly he needed more debriefing.

'What are you doing to find these guys?'

'David is working the basement. He'll also be searching the databases for hackers – maybe our guy did time, possibly as a juvenile. We'll be reviewing the videotapes. Neva is interviewing museum personnel to see if anyone remembers seeing them on the third floor. We don't have any exhibits up there. It's all docents, exhibit planners, archives – and us. Jin is processing the evidence we do have.'

'I don't like this at all. Someone thinks they can come in and bully their way out of trouble. We can't allow them to get away with these kinds of tactics. I'm glad you didn't succumb to their threats.'

'That wasn't going to happen. I have very strong feelings about terrorists. I had to deal with a lot of them when I worked for World Accord International in South America. However, I have to protect the museum, and I will.'

'I'll do everything I can. All you have to do is tell me what you need.'

Diane knew he meant it. If for no other reason than that she had the power to break the arrangement with Rosewood about the crime lab and he knew it.

Diane called Kendel, Andie, Chanell Napier, her head of museum security, and Lane Emery, head of crime lab security, into her office, closed the door and told them about the threat to the museum. She was beginning to get accustomed to the bug-eyed, openmouthed look. When they recovered she asked for suggestions about closing the museum.

'Should I close the museum for a while? Say we're putting up exhibits?'

'Can't give in to terroristic threats,' said Chanell.

'I have to think of the safety of the visitors and staff,' said Diane.

'I agree with Chanell,' said Kendel. 'However, we can go to shorter hours and give the same reason – changing our exhibits. God knows, the paleontologists have been wanting us to close so they can assemble the velociraptors without spectators looking over their shoulders. But if we were to close, how would we know how long to stay closed? We couldn't just stay closed indefinitely.'

'What about the restaurant? Closing would cost the owner,' said Diane.

'The restaurant has its own entrance and exit. It can stay open even when the museum is closed,' said Kendel. 'But that doesn't help, does it? They are still in this building.'

'Andie? Any thoughts?' asked Diane.

'I say business as usual. Don't give an inch. Another thing you can do is solve it real fast.'

'You haven't said anything, Mr Emery,' said Diane.

He had been sitting silently, his lips in a thin grim line.

'I don't like to give in to terrorists either, but I say we close down the museum – say for the weekend – so we can give it a thorough search.'

'Search?'

'Burning down a place like this wouldn't be easy; it's not like they can light a match to a set of draperies. From what you said, it sounds like they're confident they can carry out their threats. If they've been able to come and go at will, they may have already planted a device in the building.'

'Device? Like a bomb?' asked Diane.

Emery nodded. 'They could use incendiary bombs loaded with jellied gasoline. There may be more than one. Down deep, I think they're bluffing. But if we shut down just for the weekend – and say something like, "The environmental controls broke down" – we can get dogs in here. If there is a device here, we can find it. But we'll need everybody out of the building.'

Diane closed her eyes and thought about all the options, everything that everyone had said. Her thoughts were churning. Was the threat credible? She had no choice but to treat it as if it were. There

416

was a silence that began to get uncomfortable. Throats were cleared; there was some squirming in the creaking chairs. A decision suddenly came to her in a flash of insight – or paranoia; she didn't know which. She opened her eyes and looked at Emery.

'Mr Emery, I think your points are well-founded. Prudence dictates that we take every reasonable precaution. I want you to organize the search, but let's do it in such a way as to minimize the disruption. This is Friday. When normal quitting time for the day staff arrives at five o'clock, I want the museum closed, and to remain closed for the weekend.'

There were sounds of surprise from some of the staff. Chanell looked taken aback. After all, she was head of security for the museum. For a moment Diane thought Chanell was going to object. She looked at Diane and shook her head, but then gazed down at her hands and said nothing. It probably seemed to her, thought Diane, that she was being taken out of the loop.

'Andie, I need you to see what tour groups and special activities we have scheduled for the weekend. Offer our apologies and ask them to reschedule. Offer them a seventy percent discount if they will.'

Andie nodded.

'I would hope that twenty-four hours is plenty of time to make all preparations for the search. So let's say the search will officially begin

417

tomorrow at six P.M. Mr Emery, can you make arrangements?'

'Yes. I'll get right on it.'

Diane looked at her watch. 'It's three o'clock now. We're locking down at six o'clock today, including the restaurant. The only people who will stay will be museum security personnel and the crime lab crew. Mr Emery, I want your security people fresh when the bomb unit gets here tomorrow, so you and yours can go home now for rest, and Chanell's people can secure the building until tomorrow afternoon. Is that okay with you, Chanell?'

She nodded. 'I'll notify my people and call in a couple of officers on leave to double up until Mr Emery's people come in tomorrow,' she said.

'Okay, all of you tell any of your people who will be affected,' Diane said. 'But do not discuss with anyone what has been said in this room. The official reason for closing is a breakdown of environmental controls, to be repaired over the weekend. Security is extremely important. We can't take the chance that any information might leak out of here about what we're doing. Maybe we'll get lucky and resolve this whole thing in a few days and can get back to normal.'

That was possible, she thought. Sometimes it was like falling dominoes when they got a critical mass of evidence – just one more piece could make them start falling, and suddenly a case was solved.

Maybe that critical evidence would be the DNA. Diane realized that she was counting on their getting DNA that she had tricked her captors into giving her. There was a good chance that the spittle didn't contain any, or there wasn't enough.

She sent the staff away to make plans. Now came the task that she dreaded most – calling her parents and telling them that *she* was the reason for her mother's nightmare.

Diane called Daniel Reynolds first. She told him part of the story – leaving out the danger to the museum. The fewer people who knew about that the better.

'I need you to contact the federal marshals' office, the FBI, and the Bureau of Prison authorities; alert them that the danger might not be over, that someone still may hack into their systems to hurt a member of my family.'

'That must be some kind of case you're working on, to worry someone this much,' he said.

'That's just it – the events that started this whole thing happened in 1942. Most of the people involved would be very old or dead.'

'Their descendants wouldn't.'

Diane was silent for a moment. Of course, she thought, people didn't live out their lives in a vacuum. They had children and grandchildren. And great-grandchildren, just like Jane Doe-Flora Martin had a great-grandchild. People built lives, reputations and fortunes, and their descendants often depended on those reputations and fortunes.

Reynolds's remark put her mind on a new line of inquiry, a new way to look at the problem.

'From the silence, I must have gotten you thinking,' said the lawyer.

'You did, indeed. And it seems so obvious.'

'I'll get on this right away. I suppose you'll be calling your folks.'

'Yes. After I hang up with you.'

'Then I won't keep you. Don't worry about this end. I'll see that the right people get on this.'

She called Gerald first. She caught him at his office and told him essentially what she had told Daniel Reynolds.

'I just wanted you to know, because they are going to be needing support, and they won't want it from me.'

'God, Diane. I'm not sure I understand this. This sounds more like the Russian mob or something.'

'It is extreme, I agree. Are you and Susan doing okay?'

'We're still living under the same roof and being civil to each other, so I guess we're doing fine. Alan took some vacation time, I understand. Apparently, it was a blow to him for you to think he'd stab you.'

'That, and being wrong. He always had a hard time with that.'

'Your dad's been at home all week with your mother, so they should be together. You want me to call Susan and give her a heads-up?'

'Yes, thanks. She might want to go on over there.'

When Diane hung up, she waited with her hand on the phone, dreading what was coming. A knot formed in her stomach, making her nauseated. She thought about calling Gerald back and asking him to tell them. But instead, she dialed her parents' number.

CHAPTER 38

Diane sat alone at her desk, her head down on her arms, sobbing.

'Diane?'

She felt a hand on her shoulder and heard Mike's voice. She didn't remember him ever using her first name. Surprised and embarrassed, she lifted her head. She was still holding the telephone receiver tight in her hand. She put it back in its cradle.

'Mike. Sorry. You caught me at a bad time.'

Diane grabbed a Kleenex and wiped her eyes. Mike stood in front of her desk, a deep crease between his brows, his light brown eyes filled with puzzled concern.

At least he can see me off my pedestal, she thought as she blotted her eyes again.

'Can I help? Is it Frank?'

Diane tried to smile as she met his gaze. 'No. It's my parents. I had to tell them that what happened to Mother was my fault.'

'How was it your fault?'

'Did Neva tell you about any of this?'

'A little. Something about identity theft and

422

someone's hacking into police records causing her to be put in prison for a week.'

'It was really much worse for her than that. It was done to get me out of town, away from the crime scene evidence. Mike, I shouldn't be telling you this. I'm sorry. Did you need something?'

He shook his head and sat down in the stuffed chair across from her desk. 'No. I just dropped by. Andie wasn't at her desk, so I just came in – I'm sorry I disturbed you.'

'It's all right, really. You look better. How is your recovery?'

'Better. The doctor put me on an exercise program that Neva and I can both live with,' he said flashing a brief smile.

'She's just looking out for you.'

'I know, and she's doing a good job of it. I'm a lousy patient. My mother used to say that when I was sick as a kid, she got me well in self-defense.'

'It sounds like you have nice, caring parents.'

'They are. They live way out in the country on a farm. Dad grows grapes, muscadines and scuppernongs. Dad's always been a farmer. Mother's always been a housewife. They're just plain folk.'

Mike's small talk sounded awkward, not like his usual confident, glib self. She'd made him uncomfortable. Tears leaked from her eyes again. She imagined his parents loved their son very much. She envied him.

'What happened couldn't have been your fault,' he said.

'Look at everything, Mike – my daughter is murdered, Frank is shot, you are shot *and* stabbed, my poor, naive mother is thrown in a hellhole of a prison.' *And now the museum*, she thought. 'The common denominator is me. Hell, the break-in at Neva's probably has something to do with me.'

'No. None of it.' He leaned forward. 'I certainly don't hold you responsible, and if I remember right, what happened to Frank wasn't because of you at all; it was to stop *him* and *his* investigation.'

Mike reached out and took her hand. His touch was warm and safe-feeling, and right now human contact felt good. She squeezed back. After a moment, Diane slipped her hand from his.

'My mother told me she hates me for what I did – for what I am.'

Diane didn't mean to blurt it out that way. After complaining about information leaks, she was becoming a faucet.

'I'm sure she didn't mean it.'

In his world he probably couldn't imagine a parent hating her child. But her mother had suffered horribly, and Diane could see her mother's point of view. If she had been the daughter they wanted, if she weren't involved in solving crimes, all that happened wouldn't have happened. And in that, her mother was right. The small headway she had made with her family was now irreparably damaged. Even Susan was angry with her again. She had been with her parents when Diane called and she couldn't resist weighing in with her opinion of Diane's guilt.

'Diane—' he whispered.

'I'm fine.' She cut him off, stopped him from saying anything further.

Frank was right; she could see it in Mike's eyes. He cared very much for her. Diane had no doubt he cared for Neva, too. But right now Diane was vulnerable, and she could see that Mike was ready to step in and try to fix whatever was wrong. She stood up.

'There are some things I need to do.'

'Sure. Let me know if I can help.'

'I will. I'm going to be closing the museum . . . only for a few days, I hope.'

Mike looked startled. She started to give him the reason that she and Kendel had come up with, but she found she couldn't lie to him.

'I can't tell you why. And if you will, please don't mention it to anyone. I'm going to tell the staff.'

'No, of course not. Neva asked me if I ever mention to anyone what goes on in the crime lab. I don't know much, but I never talk about what little I do know.'

'I didn't think you did. We may have a leak, and I had to ask everyone. I'm asking Frank, too. I'm also looking at myself. The wrong people may have overheard me talking.'

'Is everything all right here?'

'No, Mike, it's not. But I intend to make it right.'

'I want to help you.'

'I know you do. But now, though, I must ask you to work at home, since I'm closing the museum for the weekend.'

Mike started to leave. He didn't want to; she could see him hesitate, search for something else to say, make some other offer of help. Finally, he turned and walked out.

She called David and asked him to meet her at the feeding dock on the swan lake – the large pond with a family of swans that was the centerpiece of the nature trail.

The nature trail was a half-mile loop in the midst of a wooded garden in back of the museum. It was part of the museum's exhibits, only outside, growing, and ever changing with each season. It was filled with trilliums, bluet, violets, azaleas, rhododendrons, berries, trees, shrubs, birds, butterflies and more plants than she could remember, and it was always beautiful. She didn't want to imagine it filled with smoke. Damn whoever was behind this.

She stood on the feeding platform and threw the arriving swans bread crumbs she had picked up in the restaurant. She heard footfalls come onto the bridge and looked up to see David approaching. She left the swans and walked with him deeper into the trail.

'Why do I feel like I'm in a James Bond movie?' he said, and sneezed.

'Because I've gone completely paranoid. I don't want to be overheard. David, how do you feel about sleep?'

'I don't need that much. What do you want me to do?' He sneezed again. 'Next time we do cloak-and-dagger, can we meet at McDonald's or some-place like that?'

'Sorry, I didn't know you're allergic.' Diane told him of her suspicions and outlined the plan that had been working in her mind. 'I think Lane Emery is involved in some way. I'm going to ask Garnett to help search the museum tonight and try to catch Emery or the kidnappers in the act tomorrow. Can you stay at the museum a few days?'

'I can do that. Why do you think it's Emery?' said David.

'A hunch really. First of all, there had to be a third person involved in kidnapping me. Going to the elevators, I saw Emery when I left the oste-ology lab. He could have signaled my kidnappers that I was coming.' Diane looked over at David watching the swans. She couldn't tell from his face what he was thinking.

'Do you have any more than that?' he asked, not taking his eyes off a particularly feisty swan.

'I was speaking with Kendal, Andie, Chanell and Emery earlier – asking their advice . . .' Diane hesi-tated for a moment. The reasons for her suspi-cions did sound weak. 'He's the one who suggested we close down for the weekend. There was just something in the way he said it . . . I don't know.' Diane was beginning to feel silly.

'If there's a bomb threat, it makes sense to close down.'

'There's not a bomb threat. The guys who kidnapped me said they would burn the museum down. It was Emery who suggested bombs. He said that was about the only way to effectively burn the building.'

'He has a point,' said David.

'Yes, he does. I said all I really had was a hunch. But it occurred to me that the kidnappers had no real expectation that I would just hand over evidence – they didn't even ask for all the evidence. However, if they made a threat like the one they made, there was a very real expectation that I would close the museum for a couple of days. That way they could just take what they needed without a problem – especially if they had the head of security on their side.'

'Okay, I'm starting to buy into it,' said David. 'But what if you are wrong about him?'

'Then I will apologize profusely and we'll have at least searched the museum for incendiary devices.'

David laughed. 'I'll talk to Garnett and take care of the details,' he said.

'Thanks. I need to tell Vanessa Van Ross what's up.'

David raised his eyebrows. 'Why?'

'I always keep her apprised of anything that affects the museum. People think that I don't answer to anyone, but I do answer to her.'

Diane walked with David back to the museum. He sneezed all the way. Diane felt as though a weight had been lifted from her just to be able to express her suspicions.

Diane drove to Vanessa Van Ross's home. Vanessa lived in the oldest section of Rosewood, where many of the trees were even older than her 114-year-old grandmother had been. Her huge house was at the end of a long, tree-lined, winding drive.

Diane pushed the doorbell and waited. The house was so well insulated she didn't hear footfalls until the door was opened by the housekeeper, Mrs Hartefeld, a fixture who had been with Vanessa for years. She was a tall, straight-backed woman in a dark gray pantsuit that matched her hair and eyes. Diane always thought she looked out of place in modern apparel – she should be wearing Victorian clothes to match her physical appearance. Despite her dour face, Mrs Hartefeld was a friendly, happy person with a good sense of humor. She led Diane into the parlor, a white and gold French Provençal room that made her feel like she was waiting for the queen. Perhaps she was.

'Dr Fallon, I wanted to thank you for giving my granddaughters a personal tour of the museum. They felt so special. They are still talking about it.'

'I was happy to do it. I'm glad they enjoyed themselves.'

'I'll get Mrs Van Ross. She'll be delighted to see you. May I get you something to drink – coffee, tea, soda?'

'No, thank you, Mrs Hartefeld.'

Diane stood by the fireplace looking up at a portrait of Milo Lorenzo staring down at her. His hand was on a Greek Ionic column pedestal. She sensed his disapproval and she felt guilty.

'Diane, dear. What a surprise,' Vanessa Van Ross said.

'I'm sorry I didn't call, but I'm afraid my phones might be tapped.'

Vanessa raised her eyebrows. 'Sit down and tell me about it.'

Diane sat on a white silk chair, hoping that the seat of her pants wasn't soiled from the basement. She told Vanessa about the kidnapping, the threats, what happened to her mother, and how the two thugs claimed responsibility – including what they wanted. She thought Vanessa would give her the now-familiar openmouthed stare of surprise, then chastise her for letting things get so out of control.

Vanessa did neither. She sat very still in her white and gold French sitting room, looking at the portrait of Milo.

'What are you going to do?' she asked.

Diane outlined her suspicions of Emery and her plan. Vanessa looked thoughtful as she spoke. When she finished, Diane blurted out, 'If you want me to resign, I will . . . or I'll resign from the crime lab.' She suddenly felt like a child in the principal's office.

'Don't be silly, girl.' Vanessa did look cross now.

She glanced up at Milo again. 'We can't have people making threats and controlling what we do, and we certainly can't have them threatening the museum. Milo would have hated that. They must be found, rooted out and taken to task. They can't be allowed to get away with it.'

'I'll do everything in my power to see that they are arrested.'

'What both Milo and I liked about you is that we sensed that you would care for the museum more than for your career. We were right. That's what we want for the museum – someone who sees it as their job to take care of it, not just themselves.'

Diane was relieved. 'Right now, I feel like I've put it in danger.'

'No. It's being held hostage.'

'The board is going to be very angry – about the closing in particular,' said Diane.

Vanessa smiled thinly. 'Probably so. You will just have to handle that.'

Diane didn't look forward to it. 'I must ask you not to tell anyone about this until it's over.'

'Of course.'

'I don't quite know how to say this.'

'Say what, my dear?'

'The indications are that something very large is at stake here. Perhaps a great deal of wealth or power. Maybe an organization or a family. Someone had to pay these guys to do what they did. They hurt my family just so I'd leave town

431

and they could steal the bones before I got a chance to identify them. Then they kidnapped me when that didn't work.'

'What are you trying to tell me?'

'I don't yet know who may be involved. I can't anticipate the direction the investigation may take. There are not that many rich and powerful people in the area whom you don't know.'

Vanessa's face became stern. 'Put yourself at ease, Diane. If anyone I know is responsible for this, then I would regard their actions as a betrayal and a threat to all those things I hold dearest to me. I would expect that every effort within your power be made to apprehend and punish them in the most severe way allowed under the law. Anyone who threatens Milo's museum is not a friend of mine.'

'Thank you for that. And thank you for seeing me unannounced.'

'Did you think I was going to have Hattie kick you out? I think you're feeling a little sorry for yourself. It's not like you.'

'I know.' Diane rubbed her temples. 'I'm getting pathetic.'

'It looks like you've been crying.'

Diane looked over at an ornate mirror hanging on the wall. Her eyes did look puffy. 'I had to tell my parents why someone wrecked their lives, destroyed their tranquillity and ruined their reputation. They are very angry with me. My mother blames me for what happened to her.'

'Oh, my dear, I see.'

'She has suffered a lot.'

'No doubt. It was a cruel thing that was done to her. But her blame is misplaced. I know family relationships can be difficult – Lord knows, mine are complicated enough. But you have to keep yourself anchored in reality. The reality is that there are some very bad people out there who are trying to get their way.'

Diane liked talking to Vanessa – she was good at putting things in perspective. She wished she had the same relationship with her family.

'I know that, deep inside. It's just hard to put into practice sometimes.' Diane looked at her watch. 'I need to ask another favor. I couldn't call Frank on my phone at the museum or my cell phone. May I use yours? It's long-distance, to Atlanta.'

Vanessa nodded. 'Of course, dear. You can use the phone on the desk.'

She pointed to a white French Provençal desk with a glass-covered top. The phone matched the decor – white and gold.

'Would you like me to leave you alone?'

'That's not necessary.' Diane sat down at the desk and called Frank's cell. 'Frank, it's me,' she said when he answered.

'Hey, Diane. How are you? I understand you called your parents and they blame you for your mom's arrest. Did you find out what happened?'

Frank caught Diane completely by surprise. 'How did you know?'

'Mike called.'

'Mike called? He shouldn't have.' Diane felt a little annoyed.

'He called about Neva,' said Frank. 'He wants her to stay at my house again.'

Diane's annoyance evaporated. 'Why?' she asked.

'There's some nut who's been calling him – says something about being the top of the food chain and Mike isn't going to get his rabbits.'

'Neva mentioned something about that. They thought it was someone on drugs.'

'He called this morning and told Mike that Neva would make a pretty little rabbit.'

'Oh, my God.' Talking with Vanessa had had a calming effect on her, but now she was scared again.

'It shook him up pretty bad,' said Frank. 'He was going to ask you to ask me, but he said you had a lot on your plate and he didn't want to bother you. What's going on?'

Diane told him the whole story as she fingered the feathered ink pen on the desk. She wondered if anyone ever wrote with it. She could just see him staring at the phone with his mouth open.

'Did they hurt you?'

'They made my arm sore again. Pissed me off royally. But I'm basically all right.'

'So you think one is a hacker?'

'Yes.'

'I have a database of known and suspected hackers.'

Diane smiled. 'David would be envious.'

'Tell me everything you know about him and I'll start looking for possibilities. If Jin can get his DNA, he may be in CODIS. That was good thinking, by the way, getting them to yell into your ear and leave their DNA.'

'Thanks. I think better in a blind panic.'

Diane told Frank everything she could think of about the men. It wasn't much, but maybe he could find something useful.

'I'll come stay with you tonight,' he said.

'That would be a comfort. Bring a bedroll; we'll be sleeping in the museum.'

Diane hung up the phone. 'Thank you, Vanessa. I appreciate your lending me your support and giving me some perspective.'

'I hardly said anything, dear.'

'Just talking it out helped.' Diane looked at her watch. 'I need to get back to the museum. I just wanted you to know what's going on, so you wouldn't be shocked when I close it up.'

'I appreciate your keeping me informed. Take care of yourself.' Vanessa saw Diane to the door.

Diane drove back to the museum and straight to the crime lab, hoping that David had heard from Jin. He hadn't. But he had swept the lab and her office for electronic bugs.

'We're clean,' he said.

'We're probably giving these guys too much credit,' she said. 'At least I know I can talk on the phone now.'

Neva came in from the osteology lab carrying a stack of her drawings of the various victims. She laid them out on the table side by side.

'I have some new drawings,' she said, spreading them out on one of the empty tables.

Diane and David walked over to examine them.

'Frank told me about the phone call. Are you all right, Neva?' Diane asked.

'I'm fine. I think Mike is making too much of it.'

'What phone call? What's going on?' asked David.

'You know how I told you that Mike's been getting a bunch of strange messages?' said Neva. David nodded. 'Whoever it is called again and made it more personal.'

She related the latest thing he said to Mike. Diane could see she was trying to downplay it.

'Mike's not making too much of it,' said David. 'You know, he's looking to me like the guy who stabbed Mike.'

'Well, what if he comes back after him while I'm at Frank's playing Monopoly?'

Neva's voice was getting high-pitched. As much as she tried to hide it, she was scared.

'I'm staying at the museum for a while, so I'll ask Mike to go over to my place,' said David. 'You can go there too, if you like.' David explained to Neva why he would be at the museum.

While they were talking, Diane was examining the photographs.

'This last one – is this Jane Doe . . . I mean Flora Martin?' she asked.

'Yes. The one next to it is the aged version of the woman in Caver Doe's snapshot. I sort of thought she would turn out to be Flora Martin, but they are completely different,' said Neva.

Diane had had the same thought, that the snapshot would turn out to be the older woman found in the woods – she wasn't. But Diane did recognize her, and she could almost hear the dominoes clinking against each other as they started falling.

CHAPTER 39

Diane surprised David and Neva when she told them who the aged version of the woman in the snapshot looked like.

'It could be a coincidence,' said David, 'but her family does have money.' David paused a moment and rubbed his bald head. 'You know, you can publish the drawings in the newspaper or give them to the TV stations in Atlanta. I bet you'd have people coming out of the woodwork who recognize the drawings.'

'I agree, but first, I need to secure the museum.' Diane turned to Neva. 'David and I are staying in the museum for a few days. You are welcome to stay, or—'

'I'll stay here with you. Can Mike stay?'

Diane shook her head. 'I don't want any civilians. No one outside the crime unit staff.'

Neva didn't want to give up. 'But what if whoever it is follows Mike to David's? He would be safest here.'

'I'll ask Frank to pick Mike up. He'll see if anyone is following.'

Neva nodded reluctantly. 'I hate this. It's like somebody is after all of us.'

'Not all of you,' said David. 'Just you guys who found the body in the cave.'

Diane was taken by surprise at David's statement. He was right. Finding the body in the cave was like stumbling over a tripwire. Everything started happening after that event was in the newspapers, including all the current murders.

'He's right,' whispered Neva. 'Why didn't we see that? It's so obvious. I mean, obviously Caver Doe is central. We knew that. But I never quite realized that all of us who were in the cave have become targets. The newspaper article named us all.'

She looked at Diane. 'MacGregor,' they both said simultaneously.

Diane took out her cell, punched up the list of caving buddies and called MacGregor, who was also with them in the cave.

'MacGregor.' Diane was relieved to hear him answer.

'It's Diane Fallon, Mac. How are you?'

'I'm fine. How are you?' He sounded slightly puzzled but glad to hear from her.

'Mac, has anything strange happened to you lately?'

'Strange like what?'

'Has anyone broken into your house?'

'No. But there is something kind of weird going on.'

'What's that?'

'I've been getting these calls for the past couple of weeks – some guy tells me that he's the one who's the top of the food chain and I'm just a bottom-feeder and that I can't have his rabbits.' MacGregor laughed. 'It cracks me up just thinking about it. I asked him what the heck he was talking about and he just hung up. He's called several times. Once in the middle of the night. I told him the calls had to stop, and if it made him feel better, I wouldn't get any of his rabbits.'

'What did your caller ID say?'

'No data. I was hoping to be able to call him back in the middle of the night and tell him I'd changed my mind, that I like rabbit stew.' MacGregor chuckled.

'What was his voice like?' asked Diane. She frowned at Neva and David, who stood watching her closely. The calls were sounding less and less like a prank.

'Kind of high-pitched, like a girl's, but I could still tell it was a guy.'

'Are you at work?' Diane asked.

'Yes, I'm here at my daddy's hardware store.'

'Can you stay at your parents' house for a while?'

'Why?'

'Mike's getting the same calls. In the last one he referred to Neva as a nice little rabbit.'

'Oh, shit, is this some kind of real nutcase?' MacGregor's voice went up several decibels, and Diane had to hold the phone away from her ear.

'I don't know for sure what it is. I can't give you any details, Mac, but there is some serious stuff going on. Why don't you stay with your parents, or at your cousin's?'

'I guess you haven't heard. My cousin's place burned down.'

Diane looked wide-eyed at David and Neva. 'Mac, your cousin's home burning falls under the category of unusual things I was asking about,' she said. Diane's heart beat faster; it was like discovering a danger that she hadn't known existed.

'I didn't think about it. Nobody was hurt, but his trailer was gutted. The thing is, my cousin and his wife and kids are staying with my parents and it's kind of crowded. And frankly, I kind of get on everybody's nerves, if you know what I mean.'

Diane did. 'Is there anyplace else you could stay?'

'You're serious about this, aren't you?'

David was making motions with his fingers to give him the phone. Diane handed it to him.

'Hi, Mac, this is David Goldstein; I work with Jin and Diane at the crime lab. I'm going to have Mike stay at my condo, and you can stay there too until we figure this out.' He paused awhile, listening. 'You'll be fine. I'm a paranoid guy, and I have a steel-reinforced door with four different locks, and bars on my windows.' He paused again for several long moments. 'Good. Why don't you come to the museum and I'll give you directions to my place. Just ask for Diane at the front desk.'

David clicked off the phone and jiggled his ear with his little finger. 'The guy can talk up a storm.'

'He's getting the same calls as Mike?' asked Neva.

'Yes,' said Diane. She squeezed her eyes closed and pinched the bridge of her nose. 'You know, this is not fitting together. The threats I'm getting about the museum are completely different in content and tone from the food-chain threats, or whatever they are.' She shook her head. 'But MacGregor did say his cousin's trailer burned down. His cousin owns the land the cave is on. Was that in the paper too?'

Neva nodded.

'I need to get in touch with Jin. Has anyone heard from him since he left?' Jin was in the cave with them too.

'No,' said David. He took his own phone and punched up Jin's cell. 'Jin, this is David. Call the lab as soon as you get this.' He shook his head. 'It went straight to the answering service.'

'We need to find him,' said Diane. 'Call the DNA lab. If you can't get him, let me know. Kendel's set up a meeting with the museum staff. I've got to send them home.'

Diane met with her staff in the auditorium on the second floor of the museum. When they were all assembled, she told them she was closing the museum for the weekend so that repairs could be made on a critical environmental system that was failing. It was a lame excuse. But most, she believed, would welcome a free vacation. It was the faculty curators who were conducting experiments whom she expected to have trouble with, and she was not disappointed.

'I have to check on my experiment every four hours,' said the botany curator.

'Turn in your schedule to security and they will escort you to your lab. But you will have to do it yourself; you can't send a student.'

'What? What's really going on?' asked the botany curator. Diane could see it was not going to be easy leaving them in the dark.

'This would be a perfect time to work on the velociraptors,' interrupted the paleontology curator, before Diane could answer. 'We've been wanting to close down the dinosaur exhibit so we can work.'

'This might seem like a good time, but it is not. Now, everyone enjoy your long weekend.'

'Wait a minute,' said Botany. 'I can't come every four hours throughout the night.'

'Why?'

'Well, I just can't. I'll be asleep.'

'Who does it for you at night?'

'My graduate student. That's what they're for.' There was a ripple of laughter throughout the room.

'We have a critical and difficult system failing,

and I have worked out the protocol for repairing it. I've tried to accommodate ongoing experiments. However, it will have to be you who takes care of your experiment. I don't want a student doing it. You don't have to understand my reasoning, just my instructions,' Diane said.

The botanist looked at her, stunned. 'I suppose I can set a clock.'

'Good, before you leave today, I want to see your schedule at the front information desk in the lobby. If it's not there, you won't be allowed in.'

'This is ridiculous. I've never been treated this way in my life.'

'I'm sorry, really. But I need cooperation. When I don't get it, I have to enforce it. This is just one weekend. If we get repairs done earlier than expected, I'll call you and you can arrange for your student to do the work.'

'Very well, since I have no choice.'

This was a different botanist than the one she started with. When she had made the arrangements with the university, the departments were unwilling to send faculty to what they considered basically an unpaid position, and ended up sending the newest-hired or their retired faculty. When it was discovered what kind of lab space she was offering, some departments pulled rank and gave the part-time job to tenured professors. This was one of them. If she was lucky, he'd change his mind about the appointment and she'd get back her original curator. Diane stepped down, even though she was flooded with questions from the curators.

When people left today, the museum would be virtually empty, and a search would be conducted for any devices that might be waiting to burn the museum. The possibility of those devices anywhere on the premises chilled her and made her face hot with anger.

'Look, if it's the air-conditioning, I've worked in heat before,' said the paleontologist. 'I've excavated in the desert, for heaven's sake.'

'It's something more she's not telling us,' said Botany.

'Now, gentlemen,' said Jonas Briggs. 'Let's not start treating this like the university. If Diane says she has an environmental problem that needs fixing, then let's take her word and not cause problems.'

'It's just that I don't understand why I have to be escorted to my own research lab.'

'Is it going to alter the outcome of your research if you are escorted to the lab to attend to it?' asked Diane.

'No, of course not.'

'Then I don't see your problem. This is the way it's going to be.' She paused a moment. 'What do you need to do for the experiments? If it's simply recording observations or readings, I can do it. If we're lucky, your graduate student can take it up on Sunday.'

'Yes, that will work. Yes. I'll go write out the

instructions and leave them at the information desk.'

Diane left them calling after her and started for her crime lab office to call Garnett. For several days something had been nagging at the back of her mind, something she had forgotten. She rubbed her eyes. *It'll come to the surface eventually*, she thought. She started up the stairs.

'Diane.' It was Jonas Briggs. 'I think it's obvious to everyone that something is going on. I won't ask you what, but do you need help?'

'Thank you, Jonas. But I have help coming.'

'You look tired, and if I may say, that is just a terrible haircut.'

Diane laughed and ran her fingers through the sides of her hair where Jin had cut samples. She'd forgotten about that.

'Good, I made you laugh. For some women that would have made them cry,' said Jonas.

Diane laughed again at the thought of what she must have looked like up there talking to the curators.

'I have another suggestion,' said Jonas.

'Shoot,' said Diane.

'If it wouldn't offend your sensibilities, I could hint that we may have a serious pest infestation that has gotten out of control and you'll be using some highly toxic chemicals to rid the museum of them. If I can start some gossip in that direction, maybe that will keep their minds occupied. We all know when those pesky dermestids get out, they can reek havoc in a museum,' said Jonas.

Diane nodded. 'That's a good idea. I'll tell you what's really going on when it's over,' she said. 'Have a good vacation. I'll see you next week.'

Diane left Jonas at the foot of the stairwell and climbed up to the third floor. She met David in the crime lab.

'Have you heard from Jin?'

'He's in the GBI lab in Atlanta. They're replicating, reproducing or whatever it is they do with DNA.'

'That's a relief. You told him about the possible danger?'

'Yes. He'll be careful. He's going to be staying the night in Atlanta anyway.'

'Do you have everything you need?'

'I told Garnett about your suspicions of Emery. He was skeptical, but he's bringing his men to search the building tonight.' David paused and put a hand on Diane's shoulder. 'We are going to figure all this out,' he said. 'We know a lot. We've just got to put it together the right way.'

'I know.' Diane put her hand over his. 'I just feel like I've forgotten something. You know that feeling?'

'Yeah, I have it too. Something's nagging at me and I can't remember what it was. It's like an idea that passes through your head too quickly to grasp and aggravates your synapses.'

She heard the phone ringing, and Neva

answered it. She'd sent the receptionists home and put the museum guards on the crime lab. She trusted her handpicked museum guards more than the crime lab guards that Rosewood hired. And she wanted the museum searched and empty by the time Lane Emery's men arrived the following evening. She fully expected either Emory or the two kidnappers to try and steal evidence from the crime lab.

'Diane, it's Sheriff Burns,' Neva called out. 'He has some information on Flora Martin.'

CHAPTER 40

Diane settled in her chair and picked up the phone.

'Sheriff Burns? What have you got?'

'First off, I've talked to all my people. Nobody's given out any information, general or otherwise, about the cases. I went to see Deputy Singer. He's covered in this rash. Your guy said it was urti something.'

'Urticaria,' said Diane.

'That's it.' The sheriff laughed. 'I shouldn't laugh at the poor fellow, but it's some kind of strange justice. Singer likes to scare the ladies by putting bugs on their desk and such. Anyhow, he knows nothing that's been going on, and he can't talk about anything but himself at the moment.'

'I'm sorry he's so miserable,' said Diane. But she agreed with the sheriff: It looked like karmic justice had bitten him in the ass.

'But the reason I called,' said Sheriff Burns, 'is that I've been investigating Flora Martin's murder. Finding out her great-grandson was Donnie Martin, another victim, has been a big help. I talked to Donnie's girlfriend. Up until about a week ago, he'd been in prison for the past three years. Been in some kind of trouble all his life – burglary, bar fights, you name it. His one virtue was that he loved his great-grandma. She visited him every visiting day, and when he got out, he was going to live with her.'

'I suppose everybody has some soft spot,' said Diane, wishing that the sheriff would hurry and get to the point.

'Maybe. That was his only saving grace. By the time he got out, his great-grandmother, Flora Martin, had already gone missing.'

'Why didn't he report it?' asked Diane.

'It turns out, he did. But he was still a prisoner at the time, and Flora lived way over in Gilmer County, and the sheriff there didn't take it real seriously. He said he looked for her. Told me he thought she knew Donnie was getting out soon and moved away. Frankly . . . Well, I won't say anything about a fellow sheriff. The point is, Donnie's girlfriend said she got a big envelope in the mail before he was released. Inside it was a smaller envelope addressed to Donnie and one to her. Hers was a letter from Flora Martin asking her to keep Donnie's letter safe until he got out. Which is what she did. He read it and told his girlfriend that he had a family inheritance after all. Wouldn't tell her what it was and kept his letter close to him all the time. We found no sign of it among his things.'

Diane perked up. So Flora Martin's – formerly Jane Doe's – great-grandson expected to come into money. 'Did you get a look at their house?' she asked.

'By the time I got there somebody had ransacked it and the landlord had thrown everything out on the street.'

Diane was disappointed. 'That's too bad.'

'There were some old diaries, but they were ruined. Got rained on. I had a look; the pages were sopping wet and muddy and stuck together and the ink had run.'

'Where are they now?'

'My deputy put them in a sack. I'll see what she did with them. But they were ruined.'

'We have people at the museum who specialize in bringing ruined items back to life. My conservator can dry out and clean the diaries and separate the pages.'

'Can he unrun the blurred ink?'

'The conservation lab and the crime lab have an ESDA.'

'What's that?'

'Electrostatic detection apparatus. We can read what was indented on the page.'

'I think I saw something like that on TV. I'll see what Sally did with them. That's about all I've found out.'

'That's a lot, Sheriff. Thanks for calling.'

'Sure thing. Tell me, is Singer going to get over that urti-whatever?'

'It can last a long time, and it can come back in spots and itch. It's a nuisance, but he'll be fine.'

'I think he's going to rethink his attitude on bugs from now on. My secretary's baking him a bug-shaped cake. She's kind of looking forward to getting even.'

'Oh, how old was Flora, exactly?' Diane had estimated the bones as putting her between seventy and eighty.

'She was seventy-seven.'

'Do you know where she lived when she was a little girl?'

'No idea. I'll see if I can dig that up.'

'Thanks.'

Diane sat thinking about what the sheriff had told her and did some figuring on her notepad. It seemed pretty evident to her that when Flora Martin was fourteen years old in 1942 she saw something, and whatever it was had to do with the submerged Plymouth. That was why her great-grandson Donnie was at the quarry with a scuba diver looking for it. Considering how things turned out, Diane guessed that Flora's knowledge of what happened was the family inheritance, and it seemed likely that blackmail was how Donnie was going to collect that inheritance – unless there was something valuable at the bottom of the lake, he got it, and it was taken from him when he was killed.

Before Diane left her office, she called Mike's number. She was about to hang up when he answered, out of breath. 'Neva?' he said.

'No. It's me, Diane.'

452

'Hey, Doe. How's everything going?'

'Going well. I need a favor.'

'Sure,' he said.

'Don't be so quick to agree. You aren't going to like it.'

'I'll do it anyway.'

Diane smiled at his eagerness to please her. 'We called MacGregor. He's been getting the same crazy phone calls about rabbits and the food chain.'

'You're kidding. What you think that's about?'

'I think it has something to do with the cave, but I have no idea what. It's just that a lot of things have been happening since we found that body in the cave.' She paused and took a breath. 'MacGregor's cousin's trailer burned down.'

'Damn. Was anybody hurt? Is that connected with the calls, you think?'

'No one was hurt, but I understand they lost everything. I don't know if that is connected to the calls, but I told MacGregor to stay in David's condo for a few days.'

'Oookay.' Mike was sounding cautious now.

'I told him you would be staying there too. Presumptuous of me, I know.'

'Sure. I'll do it. Is Neva staying at Frank's?'

'She's decided to stay in the museum. All the crime unit are. I've sent the rest of the staff home until next week.'

There was silence on the other end of the phone for several moments. 'Look, Doc, I need to know if Neva is in danger. I should be with her.'

'Neva is a police officer, as well as a criminalist, and she's doing her job. She'll be fine. We have an army of security, I assure you.'

'Are you expecting a raid or something? What the hell is going on?'

Diane could hear the frustration in Mike's voice. She was tempted to confide in him. But she thought it better that as few people as possible know what she was up to. 'Mike, I need you to trust me.'

'I do, Doc, but you know, this sounds like it involves me too.'

'It does. I won't lie to you. I'm not giving you the cover story that I gave the rest of the staff. The danger is why I'm trying to get you and Mac both out of harm's way. Please, Mike, trust me.'

'When you put it that way . . .'

'Thank you.'

'Either Frank or David will be by to pick you up. As I understand it, David's condo's a fort. He's inclined toward paranoia.'

'It sounds like an exciting evening. I'll collect some books and some DVDs. He does have a player, doesn't he?'

'Oh, yes. I think you and Mac will enjoy his entertainment system.'

'You know this is weird, don't you?'

'Yes, I do. Just try to make the best of it.'

The museum was clearing out. The restaurant owner was not happy when Diane told him he had to close for two of his busiest days. Fortunately, the contract with them specified that sometimes the museum would have to close and so would the restaurant. When she had had that clause put in, she'd thought of things like fumigating, but nothing like this.

In a few minutes, the museum would be completely empty except for her security personnel and her crime scene crew. Diane sat down to collect her thoughts. Neva was digitizing her drawings. She looked up from the scanner and smiled at Diane.

'David's gone to take care of MacGregor and Mike. I talked to Mike. He says you owe him big-time for making him room with Mac.' Her grin turned into a chuckle. 'Poor Mike.' Neva seemed much happier now that Mike was taken care of.

Diane looked at her watch. It would be about an hour before Garnett and his crew arrived. She decided to pass the time by looking at the Moonhater Cave bones.

'I'll be back in the osteology lab seeing what the witch has to say.'

'I thought I'd get my drawings ready to transfer to the newspaper when we decide to advertise them. When I finish, I'll come back and map the witch's skull.'

'I think John Rose will be tickled to see what she looked like.'

In her lab, Diane opened the box from the Rose Museum of Antiquities. The bones were carefully

455

protected in bubble wrap. The small pieces were in separate boxes. Diane took the fragile bones from the box and laid them out on the table the way they would have been in her body. If it was a *her*. Diane never took on faith what people said about a skeleton's gender until she could verify it. Diane looked at the pelvis as she put it in position on the table. She was indeed female.

An amazing number of the bones were present. More than Diane expected from a set of bones handed down with only an oral provenance that could be mythical. There were a couple of vials of dirt packed with them. Diane smiled as she thought of Gregory and his wife surreptitiously collecting the dirt from the cave. She took the dirt samples and set them aside. She'd ask Mike to analyze them when the museum opened again.

She surveyed the bones laid out on the table. They were fragile but in good condition. She'd ask John Rose if he wanted her to have Korey stabilize them. They were an amber color – a sort of mottled gold-red-brown – and had a patina that, though it wasn't shiny exactly, did have a vague sheen. Around the skull and some of the bones was a crust of minerals – probably salt.

The first thing Diane did was to take samples. She scraped the mineral deposit into a separate vial and labeled it. She looked inside the skull and other orifices and found samples of dirt, which she put in another labeled vial.

Rose had given her permission to take samples

of the bone and teeth for testing. She would take a piece out of a long bone and a couple of teeth. Isotope analysis of oxygen, nitrogen, carbon, strontium and lead from her teeth could give interesting results about where she was actually from. These elements were taken into the body through the food that was eaten, the air that was breathed, and the water that was drunk as a person was growing, and became a fixed part of their chemical makeup. The proportions of the chemicals deposited in the teeth were different in different locales throughout the world. The chemical analyses would tell where she grew up.

Diane could see the appeal of archaeology. There was something satisfying and calming about looking at the bones of the ancient dead, trying to figure out not just how they had died, but what their lives were like.

I really should have Jonas Briggs here with me while I'm doing this, she thought. *When the museum is cleared, I'll bring him in on the analysis.*

Time was short, so Diane decided to look over the bones quickly and go back for a more thorough examination later. She focused on the ribs – on something she had spotted when she laid out the bones.

The right eighth rib was in two pieces that had been glued back together. She would ask Korey the best way to dissolve the glue. The seventh and ninth ribs on the right side were a quarter and a half cut through, respectively. The cut on the seventh was on the bottom of the rib. On the ninth the cut was on the top. She did a quick calculation on her notepad. That would encompass a width of about two inches.

A glance at the sternum – the breastbone – revealed about a half-inch chunk missing on the left side. Diane looked again at the cuts in the seventh and ninth ribs. The cuts were V-shaped, and the bone displacement went from back to front.

It looked like she had been stabbed in the back with a double-edged sword. The blade had cut through the eighth rib, slicing the edges of the two adjacent ribs, passed though and nicked a chunk out of the breastbone. The sword would have gotten the heart and liver, and possibly several other organs. It was a blow that killed instantly.

Diane didn't know much about swords, but a two-inch-wide blade struck her as a rather sizable weapon. She would measure the width of the cuts and other variables that the bones showed and come up with a rough facsimile of the blade. Maybe John Rose could discover what kind of sword it was.

'Finding anything interesting?' Neva came in from the crime lab smiling. 'I just talked to Mike. He says you really owe him.'

'MacGregor wearing thin already?'

'Sort of. He says David has a great home theater system, though.'

'I think Mike's feeling like he should be here protecting you, rather than hiding out in David's condo,' said Diane.

'I know. It doesn't help that I can't tell him what's going on.'

'I feel bad about that too, but hopefully it'll all be over soon.' Diane looked at her watch. 'Garnett should be arriving any minute now. I'm going down to meet him. Why don't you stay here and work on our witch's face?'

CHAPTER 41

David ushered Garnett from the loading dock into the Pleistocene room. Behind them followed men from the bomb squad with their dogs. Each officer had a map of the museum from subbasement to attic.

The dogs, German shepherds and Labrador retrievers, stood quietly and looked around the room expectantly, wagging their tails. If they were surprised at the sight of the huge Pleistocene animals, they didn't show it.

'I appreciate this, Chief Garnett,' she said.

'It's important that we get this settled. We can't have this kind of threat to the crime lab – or the museum. However, I think you're dead wrong about Emery. He's a decorated marine. I know him.'

'I hope I am wrong,' said Diane. 'I don't want it to be anyone connected to the crime lab or the museum.'

Garnett nodded curtly. 'Okay,' he said, 'let's get started.'

'Don't you worry, Miss Fallon; if there's something here, the dogs will find it.'

'Thank you, Sergeant . . .'

'Remington, ma'am.'

'Good name for a police officer.'

'I think so, ma'am.'

'Everyone should be gone except for my crime lab staff.'

'And they will be going shortly?'

'We thought we would stay.'

'No, ma'am. No one can be here except us. That's the rules. If we have to get out in a hurry, we can't be hunting for civilians.'

'I understand. But we—'

He was shaking his head. 'No, ma'am.'

'There's an experiment that has to be attended to every four hours.'

'I'm real sorry about that. I hope it wasn't one that was going to cure cancer.'

'No.'

'Good.'

Sergeant Remington was good-natured throughout, but Diane could see he was going to win this argument. And he was absolutely right.

'I have to get a few things. It should take about twenty minutes. Is that okay?'

'That'll be fine. After that, I want everyone out.'

One of the security guards came in, escorting Frank Duncan. Diane smiled when she saw him.

'Detective Duncan,' said Garnett, holding out his hand. 'Good to see you. Come to offer assistance?'

'It looks like your men have everything under

461

control. I borrowed my neighbor's RV. I thought we could watch the grounds a safe distance away.' Diane looked at him, amazed. He smiled at her. 'You thought they were going to let you stay and work, didn't you?'

'Yes.'

'Now see, this guy has the right idea,' said Remington.

'I'm working on a set of bones. I need to get them from my lab,' said Diane. 'I also need to get my computer and a few tools. It won't take long.'

She left Garnett and the others to do their work and walked with Frank up to her lab.

'How are things going here?'

'I'm hoping the dominoes are falling.'

'Closing in, are you?'

'Maybe. I also may be completely wrong and we have nothing. Jin is in Atlanta. They did get some usable DNA. If I'm lucky, the two thugs will be in a database. I've been toying with the idea of asking the prosecutor to get a John Doe indictment based on the DNA. Striking at a crime lab . . .' She shook her head. 'It's too lawless. It has to be stopped.'

'I agree completely.' Frank put an arm around her shoulders and squeezed. It felt good. 'You said you're working on some bones?' he said.

'Yes. The witch – I think you were there when Gregory called.'

'Ah, yes, the witch that was supposed to be stolen, but was really a roe.'

'That's the one, only this is the real one.'

Neva was busy working on the face of the Moonhater Cave skeleton when Diane got back to the lab. She'd finished with the skull and had replaced it on the table.

'Neva, pick up your things. We have to get out of the museum.'

Neva turned around in her seat. 'Oh, no, they found something?' She looked more disappointed than frightened.

'No. They just don't want anyone here while they search. Frank brought an RV.'

She looked up at Frank. 'You think of everything. I'll gather up my stuff and go out to the parking lot. I guess they're running David out too.'

'Yes, everyone.'

Diane packed up the bones, her measuring devices and her field computer. When she had everything, she left the building, with Frank helping her carry her things. It would be like doing forensic anthropology out in the bush again. They met David and Garnett at the door.

'Remington seems like a really competent officer,' said Diane.

'He is,' said Garnett. 'Very serious and safe. He's also my godson, so I'm partial.'

'We'll be in the RV at the edge of the woods if you need me,' said Diane. Garnett nodded. He still wasn't pleased about her suspicions of Emery.

David helped them carry their boxes of equipment and bones.

Diane looked at the huge RV as they approached. This would be much more comfortable than camping in the jungle, she thought.

'Thanks, Frank. This is great.'

'I knew you would want to stay, and I knew they would run you out of the building.'

Diane looked around the grounds and saw the distant flashlights of her museum guards as they patrolled the grounds, two at a time, watching for anyone who might be sneaking up to set fire to the museum. She looked back at the huge Gothic structure and tried to think whether she had done everything she could do to protect it. She wished she didn't feel so guilty for putting it in danger.

Diane invited Garnett to share the RV with them, but he said he needed to go to the office and that he might drop by later. David, Neva, Frank and Diane climbed into the luxury vehicle and settled in for the evening.

The inside was a combination of oak cabinets and gray and blue textiles. Everything was compact and efficient. On one side was a small kitchen, on the other side a dining table and couch. The motor home had a small bedroom and a bathroom on one end and a bunk over the cab on the other. All the comforts of home.

'This is great,' said David. 'You Atlanta guys know how to do a stakeout.'

'I wish,' said Frank. 'This belongs to my neighbor. He's trying to sell it, and I'm thinking about buying it. I thought it'd be good to take my son Kevin and Star on vacation sometime.'

'You can take me too,' said David. 'I don't suppose it came with food?'

'I'm sure Frank brought enough for a week,' said Diane.

'We can start with Chinese and go from there,' said Frank.

Diane didn't realize she was so hungry until she smelled the hot food. After they ate, she claimed the bedroom, spread butcher paper on the bed and laid the bones out. Neva sat at the table and worked on the drawings. David sat in the cab, watching the museum and listening to music. Frank watched Diane work with the bones. She showed him the sword wound.

'Poor girl,' said Frank.

'Girl is right. She was young. No wisdom teeth; her epiphyses have just started to unite. Some have been glued on by the people who've had the bones. The pattern pubis symphysis is very rough, sternal end of the ribs barely scalloped – everything points to between fourteen and eighteen.'

'How old are the bones?' Frank asked.

'I don't know. I'll have to sample a piece of bone and have it dated.'

'Her teeth look pretty good,' he said.

'They are. I see only one cavity and it's very small. Not like our poor mummy, who probably died of bad teeth. Our girl was healthy too. I don't see any sign in her bones that she was undernourished or

465

suffered from any disease, at least none that affects the bones.'

Diane began the measurements of the skull. She liked this part, particularly feeding the data into the computer. She set her laptop up on a tiny table in the corner of the bedroom.

When the measuring started, Frank lost interest and went in to watch Neva draw.

Diane finished all her measurements, and repacked the skeleton before putting the data into the computer. 'Okay, let's see what the database says about where she's from,' she said aloud to no one in particular.

Frank and Neva came to watch. Neva perched on the bed; Frank stood behind her and rubbed her shoulders.

'What you doing now?' he asked.

'I've got a couple of databases that I can plug information into, and it will give me a probability of her ancestry, among other things.'

'Really, it'll tell you where she's from in the world?'

'To a point. It's only as good as the sample contained in the database, but yes, it's pretty good. I back it up with other kinds of tests – oxygen and strontium isotope analysis, for example. Different regions of the world have various oxygen isotope ratios in the water. That same ratio will be in the teeth and bones of a person who grew up there.'

Frank looked at Neva and grinned.

466

'I know,' said Neva. 'Mike talks like that too – only about rocks. You know you can use the same damn test to find out where rocks come from? Who knew?'

Diane gave them a look that was halfway between a grimace and a smile. 'Let's see what it says.' She looked at the data that showed up on the screen. 'Female. That's good. Five feet tall, that's what I estimated. Caucasoid, that's good. Okay, now this is interesting – good thing I'm backing this up with other tests.'

'What does it say?' asked Neva.

'Mediterranean. I was expecting England.' Diane thought a moment, picturing a map of the Mediterranean countries in her head. 'I bet she's Roman.'

'Roman?' said Neva.

'I'll have to look at the other tests, including dating the bones, but she could be. Romans were in England for a time. I don't think Mr Rose was expecting this.' Diane liked the unexpected – at least in bones. Unexpectedness in the museum was another matter.

'Interesting,' said Frank. 'A young Roman girl stabbed through with a sword. I wonder what her story is.'

'Do you have a drawing?' Diane asked Neva.

'I just finished building the computer face when we left the building. I've been working on the drawing.' She went back to the dinette table and grabbed the picture and handed it to Diane. 'I didn't know what to do with her hair, so I made it dark and long. If it turns out she was Roman, I could look up how they wore their hair back then.'

Diane looked into the heart-shaped face of a young girl with wide-spaced eyes and a small, straight nose. She looked so young.

'Did I hear you say she was killed with a sword?' asked Neva.

'A rather large sword.'

Neva grimaced. 'Well, didn't the story say that her husband killed her with a sword after luring her to the cave? I guess that part of the story is true.'

'According to Charlotte Hawkins. John Rose's version has her being killed by the boyfriend of the maiden whom she turned to salt.'

'So she was either the good witch of the north or the wicked witch of the east,' said Neva.

Diane shook her head. 'She was such a small thing, I can't see her being a threat. Her bones don't show that she was particularly muscular. And the thrust came from the back.'

'So you're thinking they called her a witch to cover up a murder?' said Neva.

'I'm not saying anything now. I don't even know yet that she is from the same cave.'

'So you won't be able to tell if she's a witch?' asked Neva.

'There are no osteological characteristics that I am aware of that indicate witchiness in an individual – so no, I won't be able to do that,' Diane said with a smile.

'But then,' said Neva, 'her body wasn't found for hundreds of years, right? So they didn't need a story. Besides, it wouldn't have worked anyway, since the Romans were in charge. Witch or not, the Romans would have arrested them . . . or worse.'

'We'll probably never know what really happened,' said Diane. 'But we'll know something about her. And at least the general height of her killer.' She handed the drawing back to Neva. 'You did a good job. I'm anxious for Gregory and Mr Rose to see your drawing.'

Just as Diane spoke she heard someone knocking on the door. As Frank was about to answer, David entered the RV with Garnett.

'Do you know if they have found anything?' asked Diane.

Garnett shook his head. 'Nothing yet. I really don't think there's anything there. I know you're on the wrong track about Emery. I'm betting he won't show up tomorrow night to steal the evidence, and I don't believe he is in league with those guys who kidnapped you.'

Diane didn't address her hunch about Emery. There was a good chance she *was* wrong about him. 'I'll be just glad to clear the museum and crime lab of any threats.' She shook her head. 'They knew just how to scare me.'

In the wee hours of morning just before dawn, Diane heard a telephone ringing. She reached for

469

her cell, then realized that it wasn't hers that was ringing. She and Neva were on the bed. Frank was on the sofa, and David was in the bunk. The phone sounded like it came from the bunk.

Diane raised herself up and slipped out of bed, trying not to wake Neva. She heard David answer it in a sleepy voice. She went over to his bunk.

'Jin's ready to upload the DNA profiles,' said David. 'Can we do that here?'

Frank roused to wakefulness and stretched. He was much more of a morning person and was wide-awake by the second stretch. Diane was still trying to focus her eyes. Sometimes she envied Frank.

'You can plug it in here,' he said. He and David set up the laptop on the dining table and connected via wireless network to the museum server. Diane was glad Frank was here to lend his expertise. She resolved to learn more about her own computer – not only the software.

David sent an instant message to Jin to start the download. It took several minutes. When it finished, he sat down at the computer and logged on to his system in the lab. He started the search on the DNA sample taken from Diane's left ear, hair and the left side of her jacket – Deviated Septum. Diane was surprised when he got a hit. She realized that she hadn't expected either of them to be in the system – she didn't know why, just that she wasn't feeling particularly lucky.

'Neil Valentine. The name doesn't ring a bell,

but I'm not surprised,' she said. Diane looked at his face. She didn't recognize it. 'Let's try the other one.' She was feeling luckier now. But there wasn't a match.

'I have other databases I can look in,' said David, 'but I'd like to reserve those as a last resort, if you know what I mean.'

Diane did. They were databases that they didn't legally have access to, and therefore any information they got from them couldn't be used in court.

'Let's look up Valentine's record again,' said Frank. 'Look for known associates.' He took a piece of paper from his pocket. 'This is a list of hackers – some were juveniles when they were caught, so their records would be sealed, but we can find the arresting officer and talk to him.'

They looked at the Neil Valentine record again. He'd served eighteen months in prison for assault. David pulled up a list of five known associates on the screen. None matched Frank's list.

'Go to each of Valentine's associates and pull up their associates,' said Frank.

They got nothing on the first one, but the second had a name that was on Frank's hacker list.

'Randy MacRae,' said Frank. 'He was busted for hacking into some corporate systems when he was a teenager. I'll contact the arresting officer and get the info for you.'

'Okay, we're getting somewhere,' said Diane, rubbing her hands together.

She looked at Frank and saw how fresh he

looked. She ran her hands through her hair. 'I don't suppose I can get a shower?' she asked.

'If it's very – and I mean *very* – quick. There's not much water.'

'I can do quick. I had to take quick showers in the jungle all the time.'

'Oh,' said Frank. 'I thought those jungle waterfalls ran day and night.'

'Cute,' she said.

Diane got in the shower, let the water run over her for a second, then shut it off. She lathered up her body and hair and rinsed almost as quickly. She dried off and put on fresh clothes that she'd gotten from her car. Neva was just waking when Diane finished touching up her face.

'Hey. Are they finished?' Neva sat up and yawned.

'I'm about to find out. I'm going over to see what they turned up,' said Diane.

'Wait. Do you have some scissors?' asked Neva, grinning at her.

'In my purse. They're small; will that do?'

'Yes. Jin's not real good at hairstyling. Let me kind of trim you up. Good thing you wear your hair short anyway.'

Neva took the scissors and evened up the sides of Diane's hair. She stepped back to take a look, then made a few more snips. 'There. That's better.'

Diane looked in the mirror. 'Yes, that does look better. Thanks, Neva. I must have looked a fright all day yesterday.'

Neva didn't say anything, and Diane laughed. Neva started giggling. Her staff probably thought she was nuts for sure.

'Neva, I'd like to get these cases finished up. Let's go ahead and send your drawings of Caver Doe and Plymouth Doe to the newspaper and the TV stations. Ask Canfield and Burns first; we can't cut them out. On second thought. I've already told them that's what I might do, and they okayed it. Let's not give them a chance to say no.'

'Why would they?'

'I don't think they would, but I'm just feeling a little paranoid. Go down and take care of it this morning, will you?'

David cleared his throat. 'If you don't mind a little helpful advice,' he said.

Diane stared at him with a question on her face. 'What?'

'There is no need in this modern day and age to actually *go down* to the newspaper,' he said, pointing to his computer.

Diane and Neva looked at each other. Both of them started to laugh again. Diane was starting to feel giddy. That happened when she didn't get much sleep.

David and Frank looked at each other and shrugged.

'We must all be very, very tired,' said Neva.

'Of course. Neva, scan your drawings of Caver Doe and Plymouth Doe as soon as we can get back into the lab.'

'I've already scanned them. They're on my computer in the crime lab.'

'I can get them through the network connection from here,' said David. 'Why don't I write a press release, then e-mail it and Neva's drawings to the Rosewood paper, the *AJC*, and all the Atlanta TV stations? It'll probably get picked up by the AP and be on every TV screen in the state by noon, and every newspaper in the country by tomorrow. You'll be famous, Neva.'

'And,' said Diane, 'if there is anyone alive who knows these victims from so many years ago, there is a strong chance they'll see the drawings and make the connection. Good thinking, David.'

'Oh, nothing special,' he said. 'Am I getting paid extra now for being the crime lab publicist?'

Diane started to respond when her cell phone rang. It was Garnett telling her they were finished.

Diane had a chill in her gut as she walked to the Pleistocene room to meet Garnett and his team. He was waiting by the mammoth, still looking well dressed in his tailored suit, even after being up all night. She'd have to ask him how he did it. She ran a hand through her own hair, glad Neva had trimmed it for her.

Sergeant Remington and his shepherd stood beside Garnett. Remington was playing with his dog. Some of the search teams were there; others were just coming through the doors. Diane walked over to the mammoth. At least they all looked happy.

'Good news,' said Remington. 'We didn't find a thing. And we gave the place a thorough search.'

Diane closed her eyes and let out a breath. 'That felt good. I'd been holding my breath all night. Thank you. Sergeant, please give me the names of your men. I'm going to give each of them and their families passes to the museum.'

'That'd be just real nice. I'd kind of like to see it when I have time to stop and look.'

'I appreciate all of your hard work.'

'Glad we didn't find anything.'

As the bomb sniffers were packing up to leave, Diane turned to Garnett. She started to tell him about the DNA results when her cell phone rang. It was David.

'I checked Randy MacRae. It's his DNA. You can't use this ID, if you know what I mean. You'll have to get a known sample from him to compare to the sample Jin got from your clothes to make it official.'

'I gotcha. Thanks.'

Diane handed Garnett a card with Neil Valentine's and Randy MacRae's names on it.

'These are the two who kidnapped me. The DNA matched Valentine, although we need to get a legal sample of MacRae's to test against, since he wasn't in CODIS. MacRae's a hacker and is an associate of an associate of Valentine. I will also recognize their voices when I hear them.'

Garnett looked surprised as he took the card

475

and looked at the names. He tapped the index card on his hand.

'Good work. I'll have them picked up. You want to be in on the interrogation?'

'You couldn't drag me away. Will you let me have a gun?'

CHAPTER 42

G arnett leaned against the wall. He was doing the questioning. Diane sat across the interrogation table from Randy MacRae. He probably had been a pimply faced runt of a teen, because he was now an acne-scarred adult. He was buffed up, but he still had the look of a runt about him. He wasn't wearing the museum T-shirt, and she wasn't blindfolded, but she recognized his arrogant voice. He sat smirking at her with his arms folded – still cocky.

'You got nothin' on me. I'm not saying anything without my lawyer. That means this is over.'

'You don't have to say anything,' said Diane. 'We have you and Valentine. How else could we have found you? And when I say we have you, let me assure you I mean we have you. We have your code of life.'

'What's that supposed to mean?'

'She means your DNA, you stupid little twit,' said Garnett. 'We also know you did time as a juvenile.'

'Juvi records are sealed.'

'Not from me,' said Diane. 'You were caught

477

hacking into people's computer files, changing information, trying to mess their lives up. You didn't learn, did you?'

He was having to force his smirk now. 'I'm not talking without my lawyer.'

'Fine by me,' Garnett said. 'You want to wait for your lawyer, that's your legal right. Maybe you think your lawyer can cut you some kind of deal. We don't need a deal. We've got everything we need to put you away for the rest of your natural life. Your lawyer can't even get you out on bail. Not after you made terroristic threats.'

'You can't prove nothin'.'

Garnett banged his hand on the desk. Randy jumped.

'You can't talk without your lawyer. You have to shut up now.'

'I don't think he'll talk even with his lawyer,' said Diane. 'I think he and Valentine have what they think is job security. All they have to do is a little jail time and they get a lot of money. It's like a job, except instead of going to work every day, they stay in jail every day. They were probably told they'd serve only a couple of years if they got caught. These aren't the kind of guys who keep up with current events.'

'No,' said Garnett. 'They don't know that the kind of threats made against you, the museum and the crime lab will put them away for twenty-five to life. Before they get out, we'll have them for the murders. We'll turn them over to the Feds for kidnapping you, and they'll get another twenty-five years under federal mandatory sentencing.'

'Besides,' said Diane, looking Randy in the eyes. 'You really think the Taggart family is going to pay you, knowing you gave them up?'

Randy's fake smirk vanished, his eyes widened and he looked from Diane to Garnett, clearly surprised, clearly scared. She'd made a hit, all of it. He was promised money if he kept his mouth shut, and it was the Taggart family. *Shit.* She had followed her instinct and she was right. But proving the connection was going to be a problem unless Randy MacRae or Neil Valentine folded.

'Well, I suppose I'll be going now,' said Diane. 'When his lawyer comes, I wonder who he'll be working for, this skinny little twit or the Taggarts.'

Diane rose and left the room. Garnett followed on her heels.

'Okay.' Garnett was almost in a frenzy. 'You want to tell me what that was about? The Taggarts? The ones who own Taggart Industries? The guy running for senator? The best-known do-gooder in the state?'

'The same,' said Diane.

'You have some kind of proof the Taggarts are involved? Because if you don't, I'm not going to stick my neck out. Why didn't you tell me ahead of time?'

'I don't have proof. We aged a snapshot of a young woman we found with Caver Doe – it looks amazingly like Rosemary Taggart. I saw her at the funeral of Vanessa Van Ross's grandmother. It all just came together for me.'

'That's it?'

'I was playing a hunch.'

'That's what we do,' said Garnett. 'We play hunches. You find the evidence.'

'When the crime scene unit processed Valentine's and MacRae's apartments, they found navy wool caps that match the fibers from the lab break-in and from the quarry murders of Jake Stanley and Donnie Martin. They also found a box of surgeon's gloves containing the same type of powder present at both of those scenes. It's circumstantial, but put that with their DNA on my clothes and the same powder on the duct tape that bound me, and the evidence is more than coincidental.' Diane let out a breath. 'I know – without a confession I have nothing against the Taggarts, but you saw his face.'

Garnett raked his hands through his hair. 'Dammit. Yes, I saw his face.'

'I don't know which family member. It's a large family. And you don't have to interrogate them until we have substantially more evidence to go on.'

'And I won't.' He paused and gave her a long look. 'Okay, let's see what the other one has to say. Go ahead and play your game on him and we'll see how he reacts.'

They didn't get much more information from Neil Valentine. He started out just like MacRae, cocky, calling for a lawyer, and ended up with the same surprised look on his face. He'd done jail time before. Diane was betting he didn't want to do any more without the payoff he had been promised. She had hoped that putting a wedge of doubt in might get one of them to talk. But the bottom line was, neither said anything.

The only plus was that they came away with a cup Randy MacRae had drunk from. Now she had a legitimate sample of his DNA the crime lab could compare with the sample they had from her abduction. She had also gotten a good look at their hands. Neither had the badly damaged finger that showed up in the clay from Neva's break-in.

As Diane was leaving the Rosewood police station, she heard her name called out.

It was Police Officer Janice Warrick, with whom Diane had a bumpy history. Officer Warrick was dividing her attention between motioning to Diane and watching the TV monitor. Diane walked across to the TV area.

'Have you seen this?'

Janice Warrick was all smiles, without a trace of any unpleasantness between them. Diane looked at the TV screen where Janice was looking, along with eight or ten other police officers.

'Those are Neva's drawings, aren't they?' Janice said. 'Look, Bud,' she said to a fellow officer, 'Neva did those.'

All of Neva's drawings were on the TV screen. The news anchor was basically reading the press release sent to them by David, urging anyone who recognized the people in the drawings to contact the Rosewood Police Department.

Diane read the lettering printed on the screen below the portraits: ROSEWOOD 1942 COLD CASES. DO YOU KNOW THESE PEOPLE?

Officer Warrick put her arms around Diane and hugged her. Diane wasn't sure why. Perhaps celebrity hysteria was sweeping Rosewood.

Diane drove back to the museum feeling oddly depressed. She believed the museum was safe, the thugs who threatened to burn it down were in jail and she had solid evidence against them. What nagged her was that she was afraid the real orchestrator was beyond her reach – and would stay out of reach. Even with a mountain of evidence against them, the rich and powerful often weren't convicted – and she had no evidence whatsoever. Even if Valentine and MacRae rolled over on their benefactors, she had no corroborating evidence. The snapshot from the cave didn't mean anything. It was just an old picture Caver Doe had in his pocket, and the resemblance to Mrs Taggart could be a coincidence.

She pulled into the parking lot of the museum. Few cars were there – mostly her crime lab people. She recognized Mike's SUV. The RV was gone. She smiled to herself. That was a nice thing Frank had done.

As she entered the building a woman who looked

to be in her forties and an older man somewhere between sixty and seventy were arguing with the security guard. The woman was dressed in an inexpensive dark blue pantsuit that fit snugly on her slightly overweight frame. The man wore jeans, a plaid short-sleeved shirt, and a cap that hadn't been conditioned to put a curve in the bill. The woman was shaking a large manila envelope she held in her hand.

'We don't want to see the museum; we want to see this Fallon woman. It's about the people they're asking about on TV,' the woman almost shouted at the security guard.

Diane's spirits lifted. Already there was a bite.

'I'll see them.'

They turned toward her.

'I'm Diane Fallon.'

'I'm Lydia Southwell. This is my father, Earl Southwell,' said the woman. 'We think the woman they're asking about may be my grandmother Jewel Southwell.'

'Come inside, please,' said Diane.

She led them inside to her office lounge and sat them down at the table. She offered coffee, tea or a soda. Each took a Coke. Diane took one as well from the small refrigerator.

'You recognize someone in these drawings?' Diane had copies of the originals lying on the table.

The woman touched the drawing of Plymouth Doe with her fingertips.

'That looks like my mother,' Earl said. 'The TV said she worked at Ray's Diner. My mother worked there a long time ago before she disappeared.'

The woman still held the large brown envelope in her lap. 'We have these pictures.' She pulled the photographs out and they spilled over the table.

'Lydia,' said her father sharply, 'you didn't need to bring all our pictures.'

'I didn't want to take the time to hunt through them.'

Lydia picked out a large portrait of her grandmother. One corner was singed.

'My daddy tried to burn the pictures,' said Earl Southwell, 'but my granny – Mama's mother – pulled them out of the fire.'

'Do you have any dental records or X-rays?'

'No. That was a long time ago,' said Lydia. 'I don't think they had that stuff then.'

Diane looked at the photograph. It was a woman smiling into the camera. She looked very much like Neva's drawing of Plymouth Doe.

'Can you tell me about her?' said Diane. 'What happened to her?'

'We thought she left us,' said Mr Southwell. 'I was just a little bit of a thing, only five years old. My daddy was working in Atlanta, coming home on weekends. Those days it took longer to get from here to there. Mama was a pretty woman and kind of forward, if you know what I mean.'

He paused and took a long drink of Coke. 'My

daddy was angry. I remember that more than anything. He wanted to burn everything that had anything to do with Mama.'

'Why did he think she left?'

'The story was, she ran off with Dale Wayne Russell,' he said. 'That was a cussword at our house. The two of them just up and left. Mama left my daddy and me when I was just a young'un, and Dale left a sweetheart.' Mr Southwell was quiet for a moment. 'You think she's been dead all these years?'

Tears welled up in Lydia Southwell's eyes. 'Grandpa was a bitter man because of it – so was Daddy.' She looked at her father almost accusingly. She turned back to Diane. 'Can you tell us if it's really her?'

Diane nodded.

'Right now? Can we know right now? Please, we need to know.'

'Come with me.' Diane helped Lydia gather up her photographs and she led them up to her osteology unit office.

As they walked through the museum, Diane got whiffs of an unpleasant odor. It wasn't strong, like something that had lingered, a little like something rotting, or decaying tissue. *I hope it's not that damn snake, crawled up and died in the wall*, Diane thought. Maybe it was something in a garbage bin. She'd have to ask janitorial services to check.

'Grandma was a hard worker,' said Lydia. 'My great-granny said Grandma worked at the diner and took in laundry and sewing to give Daddy a better life. Great-granny never believed she'd run off and left him.'

'Sit right here. I'll be back,' said Diane. She stopped at the door. 'Sewing? Did you have a relative in the military – a quartermaster?'

They looked at her, puzzled. 'Her daddy was a quarter-master in the army,' said Earl Southwell.

'Thank you,' said Diane, smiling. 'Please wait here. This won't take long.'

Diane almost skipped her way to the crime lab. David, Jin and Neva were there packing up the evidence to move it to the vault in the archives to keep it out of harm's way.

'We may have someone who knows Plymouth Doe.'

'Already?' said David.

Diane showed them the photograph of Jewel Southwell.

'Wow, Neva, you nailed it,' said Jin.

'I looked at her dress,' said Neva. 'The way it was sewn, where the darts were. It was hand-stitched and made to fit real well. I thought she might be someone who would look right into a camera and smile at whoever was looking.'

'That's good, Neva,' said Diane. 'Very intuitive.'

Neva had taken to heart the lessons on facial reconstruction Diane had given her.

'David,' she said, 'Did we do an X-ray of Plymouth Doe's skull?'

'Yes. I took all the skeletal remains to Korey and

he X-rayed everyone.' David went to the filing cabinets, pulled open a drawer and found a file with the X-ray, which he gave to Diane.

She carried the X-ray to the copy machine. She measured the head of the woman in the photograph between two craniometric points – the nasion, where the nose met the forehead, and the gnathion, the tip of the chin. She made the same measurements on the X-ray of Plymouth Doe's skull and calculated the percent difference between the photograph and the skull. She put the photo on the copier and increased the size by a small amount and measured the result at the same points.

When she had the heights of the faces the same on the measurement points, she took the X-ray and the copy of the photo to the light table and laid one on top of the other.

'I thought you did that with a projection screen so you could fiddle with it,' said David.

'I do, but right now this is quicker, and if it's the same person, it should fit dead on.'

It did. Plymouth Doe was Jewel Southwell.

Just to make sure, Diane used a loupe and examined Jewel Southwell's teeth in her portrait. Plymouth Doe had an overlapping upper incisor. Jewel Southwell's portrait showed the same overlap, one incisor slightly forward, casting a shadow on the incisor next to it. To compute how far forward, Diane used one of David's esoteric photography databases to provide some of the numbers she needed, based on the shadow length in the photo. She retrieved Plymouth Doe's skull from the vault and took a few tooth measurements. It wouldn't be exact, but the measurements from the offset teeth in the skull should be very close to the computed value from the photograph. Again, dead-on.

She took two DNA sampling kits from the supply cabinet and walked back to the father and daughter waiting in her office.

'Could I ask each of you to give me a DNA sample for comparison with DNA we took from the remains? It's nothing invasive. I just need to take a swab from inside your cheek.'

As Diane talked, she opened the DNA test kits and showed them a swab. Earl and his daughter Lydia both opened their mouths. Diane took the samples and sealed the swabs in their envelopes and labeled them. She sat down across the table from the two and looked into their eyes. Their faces showed a cross between expectation and dread.

'I can tell you that the photograph is a match with the remains. It's her, almost beyond a doubt. The DNA results will give us the final confirmation.'

'It is Grandma then?' asked Lydia.

'Yes.' Diane nodded. 'It is Jewel Southwell.'

Earl Southwell began sobbing. 'All these years, the things we all thought about her, and she was at the bottom of that quarry. I swam there when I was a kid, and my mother was down there.' His shoulders shook with his sobs.

Diane noticed that his daughter didn't reach over to comfort him.

'How did she die?' he asked when his sobs subsided.

'From a blow to the head.'

'You mean, like deliberate, or an accident?' asked Lydia.

'It appears to have been deliberate,' said Diane.

'You think you can find out who killed her, after all this time?'

'There's a good chance.'

'When can we have her for burial?' Earl asked.

'We'll need to wait for the DNA results to confirm the match. That should take about ten days. After that we can release the remains.'

Lydia's face had grown angry. 'I want you to find out who did this. Grandpa could've been happy.' She looked at her father, Earl Southwell. 'We all could've been happy. Bitterness poisoned our family. I want to know who did this to us.'

Earl Southwell didn't say anything. The vacant look in his swollen eyes said that he had lapsed into deep introspection, or grief, or remorse. Probably a combination of all those emotions and more. The two of them, the father and the daughter, each suffering in their own way.

'Is your grandfather still alive?' Diane asked the daughter.

Lydia nodded, her eyes downcast. 'But he has Alzheimer's and don't know anybody anymore.'

Diane put her hand on Lydia's. 'The brain's a

funny thing. Tell him that his wife didn't leave him after all. It might get through to him.'

Lydia looked dubious. Diane wished she could say something comforting.

'When we have DNA confirmation, I'm sure the TV and newspapers would like a follow-up on this story. Tell them your story and the impact this has had on your life. It will make the authorities more interested in pursuing it.'

Lydia nodded. 'You'll let us know when you get the DNA test back?'

'Of course. Give me your phone number and address. When everything is done, I'll return the photograph and all the effects we found with your grandmother's remains. There are some clothes and things.'

Lydia wrote down the information for Diane.

'Did you happen to recognize anyone else in the drawings?'

'No.' Both shook their heads.

'When did she disappear?' asked Diane.

'June fourteenth, 1942,' said Earl Southwell, as if the date were branded on his brain. It probably was.

'Did she own an automobile?' asked Diane.

'No, she didn't,' said Earl. 'Daddy's Ford pickup was all the car we had.'

Diane made some notes in her notebook.

'Do you have a photograph of Dale Wayne Russell?'

'Are you kidding?'

★　　★　　★

Diane walked them to the museum exit and let them out. She watched them as they slowly made their way to their vehicle, an old pickup, keeping their distance from each other. Each might as well have been alone.

There was no doubt in Diane's mind that the DNA would be a match. She turned and walked back toward the lab to fill out her report and send the samples to the GBI lab.

CHAPTER 43

Diane and her crew sat around the table in her museum office waiting for their pizza. She told them about the father and daughter and their story about Jewel Southwell.

'Jewel's father was a quartermaster,' said Diane.

'So the buttons came from her, probably,' said David. 'You think Caver Doe is Dale Wayne Russell, the guy Jewel Southwell was supposed to have run off with?'

'Maybe. She did sewing for people. Whoever left the button in the cave could be someone she did sewing for, or someone who knew her father. Or it may all be coincidental and the two deaths may be totally unconnected.'

'Too many coincidences,' said David.

'That's my feeling too,' said Diane. 'But we still don't have anything that ties it all together, so that it all makes sense.'

'Still, we're making progress,' said Neva. She was very pleased with herself for the drawing she had made of Plymouth Doe.

'Yes, we are,' said Diane. 'The identification of

Plymouth Doe as Jewel Southwell is a big step forward.'

She told them about the interviews with Valentine and MacRae and their reaction to the mention of the Taggart name.

'The Taggarts have always been associated with good things,' said Neva. 'I really find it hard to believe any of them is involved in' – she threw up her hands – 'all of this.'

'I don't know that they are involved,' said Diane. 'But someone is behind it. Valentine and MacRae don't have the intellectual talent to think it up by themselves. And look at their ages. They weren't even born when Caver Doe died, so what interest would they have in wanting Caver Doe's crime scene evidence destroyed? Do we have anything that points to the involvement of anyone besides the two of them?'

'You going for a unified field theory, Boss?' asked Jin. 'Everything is connected to everything?'

'I agree with David,' Diane said. 'Too many coincidences. Let's follow the evidence. What key evidence do we have that is not matched to a suspect?'

'We have Valentine and MacRae linked to the Donnie Martin crime scene,' said David. 'But we don't have anyone directly linked to the Flora Martin murder. We do have the knife tip you found in Flora Martin's bone. If we find the knife, we can match it. That might point to Valentine and MacRae, or it might point to someone else.'

'We have the unknown fingerprint in the bug terrarium,' said Jin.

Diane looked at him for a moment, puzzled. 'Oh, the break-in at the dermestarium on the university campus?'

'Yeah, that,' said Jin. 'We got that one fingerprint inside the bug box that doesn't match any of our known exemplars. But that could be a long shot. Lots of people come and go from a university lab. The print could have come from almost anyone.'

Diane looked at David. 'I don't suppose you can match the stolen bugs with the Flora Martin crime scene?'

David shook his head. 'They're all *Dermestes maculatus,* wild and domestic. I can't tell the wild ones from the others. I don't really know if the dermestids stolen from the university are the same ones found on Flora Martin's remains – just that she had more beetles than are usually found with a body in the wild. And speaking of bodies and beetles, has anybody noticed a smell in the museum?' asked David. 'Kind of bad.'

'I did,' said Diane.

'Me, too,' said Neva. 'I think a couple of the dogs took a dump somewhere.'

'More like that snake crawled up somewhere and died,' said Jin.

Diane laughed. 'That's the first thing that came to mind to me too.'

'I just get a whiff and then it's completely gone,' said David.

'I'll have the custodial staff go through the place when this is over,' said Diane. 'And I hope it's over soon.' She looked at her watch.

'We have a bet going,' said Jin. 'I say your suspicions about the museum break-in are wrong. David says you're right – but he's paranoid and doesn't trust anybody. Neva's with you, only because you have a good track record of being right. So I hope you're wrong about Emery and I win a lot of money.'

'So do I, Jin,' said Diane. 'Is that all the information we have on any of this? Have we exhausted all leads?'

'The sheriff brought diaries that belonged to Flora Martin and I took them to Korey,' said Jin. 'He said it would take a while. They're pretty bad off. Saturated with mud.'

'Speak of the devil,' said David. 'Here he comes in dreadlocks.'

Korey came in carrying a folder, followed by Mike carrying several flat boxes.

'Anybody order pizza?' said Mike.

Korey and Mike pulled up chairs. Diane got everyone soft drinks from her refrigerator and they passed slices of pizza around the table.

'I ran your samples, Doc,' said Mike. Diane looked blank for a moment. 'The ones Neva gave me. She said they're from England.'

'The dirt samples, yes. What did you find out?'

'Sample one, the dirt from the cave, and sample two, the dirt from the bones, are the same.

Sample three, the mineral deposits on the bones, is sodium chloride.'

'Salt?'

'Salt.'

'So the bones did come from the cave,' mused Diane.

'According to the dirt,' said Mike.

'I appreciate your analyzing them so quickly.'

'As a show of your appreciation, can I stay here tonight, Doc? Don't get me wrong, David; I really like your condo, and it was good of you to let me stay there. But I'm going to get a concussion banging my head against the wall,' said Mike.

'MacGregor?' said Diane.

'I like Mac, I really do, but in smaller doses. When we were cleaning David's kitchen, he sang "Ninety-nine Bottles of Beer on the Wall' – all the way to the end. And then started over again.'

Neva collapsed into giggles with the others and patted him on the back. 'Poor baby.'

'Okay, you can stay here,' said Diane.

'Oh, thank you, Doc. You don't know how I appreciate it. Does your evidence tell you who's been making the prank calls to us?'

'No.' Diane didn't say she wasn't sure the police were looking. She was suddenly filled with guilt. She hadn't thought about the crank calls since she heard about them. 'Did the police tap your phone?'

'I don't know. I don't think so.'

'I'll check into it.'

496

'Someone want to tell me what's going on?' said Korey. 'Why did you empty out the museum? Nobody believes we have a critical environmental system failing. I mean, what exactly would that be?'

'I'll tell you about it tomorrow,' said Diane.

'Does it have something to do with what happened to you and Mike?'

'I don't know.' She didn't. They had not been able to match any of the evidence of the knifing or Neva's break-in to the murders they were working on. Valentine and MacRae had a whole boxful of those surgeon's gloves they used. Why would they have used another brand to break into Neva's apartment?

'So it's a maybe,' said Korey.

'Possibly, but that's all I'm going to say right now. I know this is terribly inconvenient for you and all the curators.' *Especially for botany*, she thought. All in all, she had missed three readings on their experiment because of the search.

'I don't mind the inconvenience.' He shrugged. 'Is everything going to be all right?' Both Korey and Mike were looking intensely at her; both wanted reassurance.

'Yes,' said Diane. 'That's my job.'

Korey nodded and smiled. He set down his slice of pizza and grabbed up the folder he had laid on the desk behind him.

'I don't know why you even bothered to build a crime lab. I can do everything in my conservation lab that you all can do.' He opened the folder

497

and took out a piece of paper that looked like a photograph of an electrostatic copy of . . . something.

Diane craned to see the page. 'What is it?'

Korey held it to his chest out of her sight. His dreadlocks fell forward, shielding his face.

'All in good time. You know those magazines found in the submerged Plymouth?'

'Yes,' said Diane cautiously. 'This had better not be Miss October, 1942.'

'Just wait,' Korey said, motioning with his hand. 'Most of them were pretty much pulp. When we dried them, what we got was very thick handmade paper . . . impossible to separate into pages.'

Jin looked disappointed.

'But,' continued Korey, 'it was good practice for my technicians.'

'You got something, though?' said David.

'On one of the magazines that we could separate from the rest, there was a shape just under the cover, which was translucent by this time. It looked like a piece of paper – something I recognized – was stuck in the magazine. I used various lighting, even X-rayed the thing. That didn't work, by the way. But light did, and by slicing the magazine paper off what was under it, I was able to bring out writing on the piece of paper inside the magazine.'

'You're going to stretch this out, aren't you?' said David.

'As long as I can,' said Korey.

He handed the photograph to Diane. She was audibly startled when she looked at the page.

'What is it?' said Jin.

'It's a receipt,' said Diane. 'From Cash or Casher General Store, made out to D. W. Russell for a carbide lantern, forty feet of rope, and two Moon Pies – three dollars and sixty cents.'

Neva's eyes grew wide and she sucked in her breath. 'You have got to be kidding.'

'Well, I'll be damned,' said David.

'Way to go, Korey.' Jin pounded the table with the flat of his hand. 'You're right: What do we need the crime lab for?'

'When I read the list,' said Korey, 'it rang a bell, since I'd seen all of Caver Doe's things. It was the Moon Pie wrappers that cinched it for me. You think maybe this D. W. Russell is Caver Doe?'

'The probability is high,' said Diane.

'Has to be,' said David. 'Jewel Southwell and Dale Wayne Russell disappeared at the same time, supposedly ran off together. Here is a receipt made out to D. W. Russell in the car with Jewel Southwell for the very items we found with the body of Caver Doe, which we know to have been there since that time period. Caver Doe has to be Dale Wayne Russell.'

Diane could still hear the dominoes clicking against one another as they fell. 'Korey, this is excellent work. I don't know what to say. I'm just amazed.'

★   ★   ★

A scenario was forming in Diane's mind. Actually, several, but she kept weeding them out when one or the other piece of evidence didn't fit. But what it looked like to her was that a crime of opportunity had led to a crime of premeditation.

Diane sent the others home for a breather. David went to check his condo. Neva went to help Mike pack a few clothes. Jin and Korey went to the conservation lab so that Korey could show Jin how he had revealed the writing on the receipt.

She looked at her watch. In just three hours, security of the museum would be turned over from Chanell's personnel to Emery's people. In the woods the police were watching the building. Everything was calm. She went up to her lab with Mike's notes. She had just enough time to call John Rose and give him a preliminary report on his bones.

She entered her osteology lab to find it dark, but not so dark that she couldn't see a gun in her face.

CHAPTER 44

'Lane Emery,' said Diane in a voice that was far calmer than she felt. 'Jin's not going to be happy. He bet a lot of money that you weren't going to do this tonight. You're early, you know. I expected you much later.'

Even in the relative darkness of the night lighting in the lab, she could see that Lane Emery held a Glock 20 five feet from her chest. Diane didn't doubt that he knew how to use it. There was no way she could outrun it or dive for cover, even in the dim light. She thought she saw his hand shake, and that sight made her heart beat harder. The sound of blood pulsing in her ears was already deafening. The only thing she could think of was that the Glock held lots of bullets. She closed her eyes and opened them again, trying to regulate her breathing. From the sweat on his brow and upper lip, he wasn't happy either.

'You really took me by surprise, setting a trap for me,' he said, 'bringing in the bomb squad last night. How did you know? What tipped you off?'

'Just my own paranoia. I never believed that Valentine and MacRae could gain access to the museum past your security system and have free run of the place without some inside help. The only question was, Who on the inside was helping them? When we were in the staff meeting discussing what to do, hearing you talk about shutting down the museum – that just didn't sound like you. Your record is of a man of action and courage who would secure and protect, not someone who would take cover at the first sign of threat. And you introduced the prospect of an incendiary bomb, almost as if you were trying to scare the staff. I just thought to myself, If the museum is shut down, what an opportunity to destroy the evidence the two bunglers didn't.'

As Diane spoke, she tried to think of what to do. She hadn't a clue.

'How did you know about the museum security sweep last night?' she said.

'One of my men told me. That kind of thing is hard to keep secret. I was trying to avoid your trap. If I came early tonight before the changeover of security, I just might get away with the evidence.'

'Are you really going to kill me?'

'This isn't something I enjoy, but I'll do what it takes. I have a museum van parked by the outside elevator. All I need to do is load the evidence into it and drive away. Your security people won't stop a museum van. But then I discovered that you've moved all the evidence. Where is it? In your vault?'

'I can't tell you that. Were you in with Valentine and MacRae?'

'No, you were wrong about that. I wasn't even approached until after they failed. They're buffoons. All they know is computers and electronics. It wasn't me who helped them. But your paranoia served you well.'

'Why are you doing this? You've always had a good record – an exemplary record. No one – including me, really – believed you'd do this.'

'That's a fair question. I want you to know: It's for my family. I got a bad diagnosis from my last physical. I want to leave them something. A large bank account in the Cayman Islands is too good to pass up.'

'How about leaving them a history of being a good man?'

'One of the things I've discovered is that there's no reward for being a good man. It's never bothered me until recently, you know, goodness being its own reward and all, but this happened . . .'

He tapped his abdomen as if that was where the offending illness was seated.

'I had to take a good hard look at things – at what I had to leave my kids. No offense, but after all my years of hard, honest work in the military, I end up guarding a museum?'

'A crime lab, actually. It's something we value. That's why we tried to get the best person we could for the job. And even if it were the museum, it's something worth protecting. It's history and learning, a repository of good things that should not be lost or destroyed.'

503

'Please spare me. Are you trying to flatter me into believing that this job has some real merit?'

'No. I suppose I'm trying to save you. Is this what you want your kids to remember you by?'

That may not have been the right thing to say either. From the hardening of his face, she saw that she had hit a nerve.

'I told you I'm doing it to help my children. They wouldn't have known about this if you hadn't figured out my plan.'

'What, did you think you would steal the evidence, turn it over to the Taggarts, collect your money and it would all just be forgotten? We'd have figured it out sooner or later. It's what we do.'

'So you know who it is,' he said.

Her suspicion had been confirmed again, but naming the Taggarts was probably a mistake, she thought.

'They were right; they figured there might be something that points to them.'

'They told you about their involvement in the murders?'

'Not much. Just enough. They were probably confident that I would accept their offer. Desperation has a smell all its own.'

I ought to be getting ripe then, thought Diane. *If I keep him talking long enough, won't someone eventually come looking for me? He's not going to let me go.*

'Is there any way I can buy myself out of this?

What if I paid you more than the Taggarts are paying you?'

'They offered me' – he shook his head as if amazed by their offer – 'a lot of money. I told them that they should offer the money to the museum, that you'd probably take it. I told them everyone knows you're devoted to the museum.'

'Really? What did they say?'

Diane wondered if it would do any good to ease away in some direction. He would just track her with the gun and it would probably make him nervous. She didn't want that – a nervous trigger finger. In the back of her mind she thought she knew that Glocks didn't go off with a nervous shake; it took a deliberate action. But she didn't really know that much about guns.

Shit, what am I going to do? She couldn't think of anything. She felt sweat running from her hairline down her forehead. Sweat stung her armpits. She had to concentrate to keep her breathing normal.

'They said they sized you up at that old gal's funeral and decided you wouldn't go for it.'

'Really,' Diane said again. 'What was it they saw that caused them to make such a major decision in so short a time?'

'I don't know. Now, will you tell me where you moved the evidence? Is it your idea that you can keep me talking until help arrives? All your help is outside and, frankly, your crime scene people aren't up to it.'

She could see in his eyes and his body tension

that he was approaching a decision point, and it didn't look like a change of heart, but she kept trying. A man who loved his children must still have a soft spot somewhere inside. Maybe just soft enough to let her off the hook if she could offer him what he really wanted.

'I was hoping to offer you more money. That way you could save your reputation, get rich, I'd keep my evidence and we'd all be happy.'

'You don't have that kind of money. We're talking about a lot.'

'I have access to a lot of resources. I know people with a lot of money. Isn't your reputation worth at least thinking about it?'

'You know, Dr Fallon, I wish I believed you, because I would like to take you up on your offer. It does appeal to me, but there's just no way that can work out. Once I leave here, all deals are off. I know that, and so do you.' He waved the gun at her. 'Now quit stalling and tell me where you moved the evidence.'

Diane said nothing.

'Okay, let's look in your vault. Open it up,' he said, advancing on her.

Diane started for the vault. 'Can we at least turn on the lights?'

'I tried. They're out.'

'Out? Are you sure?'

'Yes, I'm sure. Quit stalling.'

Diane was confused. Her eyes had grown accustomed to the dim light, so it wasn't really a problem, but the night lighting shouldn't be on at this time. She wondered if it was that way all over the museum. She wondered if it was a harbinger of a fire to come – someone tampering with the electricity. Diane punched the first three codes into the door security pad.

'Don't burn down the museum.' She felt her voice crack as she spoke. 'You don't have to do that.' Her voice sounded pleading to her ears. She wondered if she sounded weak and pathetic to him.

'I hadn't planned to.'

'What's the thing with the lights, then?'

He was showing exasperation and impatience now. 'I told you, I don't have anything to do with the lights. Why are you going on—'

Emery abruptly stopped speaking, and Diane looked at him. He stood motionless, holding the gun on her, looking bewildered. There was something familiar about the expression. As he dropped to the floor she saw the same expression on Emery's face that she had seen on Mike's when he was stabbed.

CHAPTER 45

Diane was paralyzed with confusion and fear. Her six-foot-four-inch head of crime lab security lay limp, facedown on the floor. There was a wet, dark stain on the back of his jacket. In his place stood a much smaller man. In his right hand was a long knife dripping with Emery's blood. The bad aroma she'd detected earlier wafted through the air. Not for even a moment did she believe she had been rescued.

A cold fear clutched at Diane's heart, worse than what she'd felt with Emery. It was a primal fear that choked her in its grip. The thought passed through her mind that he wasn't a man at all, but some demon rooted up from the bowels of the museum subbasement.

He was dirty. She could see that and smell it, but it wasn't just body odor. Another smell clung to his dark, mangy clothing. His coat, perhaps at one time a wool suit coat, too warm for their weather, had been on his body so long it had merged and transformed and become a part of him, like scales or a molting skin. But it wasn't his odor, the filthy clothes or his short, ratty hair, but his eyes that frightened her the most. They were flat-black, almost dead eyes devoid of humanity – or any emotion found in the human world.

She had once looked into the eyes of Ivan Santos, the man who slaughtered her daughter and her mission friends and hundreds of others during his horrific reign. In his eyes she thought she had seen the devil. But as she looked at this man, she realized that what she had seen in Santos's eyes that one time was arrogant, self-centered hatred and anger. He was evil, but this man before her now was something different, something beyond that. Looking into his eyes was looking into a dull, black . . . nothing.

'Who are you?' Diane found a fragment of her voice. It was shaky, but audible.

He kept staring for a long moment. Diane looked at the knife in his hand. His fingers. The tips of his fingers on his left hand were deformed, curved in some funny way, and the nails were thick and split, some of them missing. One finger on his right hand was severely deformed, and on that hand he wore a ring with a red stone.

In a flash, Diane put it together, the thing that had been nagging at her that she couldn't remember – the blood-red ring and injured finger of the man the Odells had seen at the graveside service, the impression in the clay from Neva's break-in showing a deformed finger. The evidence had pointed to the same person, but she had missed

509

it until now. He was the one who had wrecked Neva's house. He was the one who had stabbed her and Mike at the cemetery. But who was he, and what possible motive could he have for the brutal and murderous things he was doing?

Diane moved her fingers slowly to punch the remaining numbers to her vault, hoping to rush in, lock the vault door and call for help. He slashed out at her hand. She pulled back quickly, his blade just missing her fingers. She backed away, looking for a table to put between them. But the tables were too far away.

'Who are you?' she repeated.

Again he said nothing, just stared at her with his blank eyes, easing toward her with the knife tip pointed at her, making little jabbing motions. She saw his eyes dart to the tables, and a little smile crept onto his thin lips and he parted them slightly. His eyes lit up suddenly.

What? she thought, but she dared not take her eyes off him. She tried to back up more quickly. If she could reach the table, at least she would have a barrier. She wanted to try for the Glock, but he was too close. *Get to the table, and at least you'll have time to think.*

'What do you want?' she asked, trying to pull his attention to her, away from the table.

It startled her when he answered in a high-pitched voice, 'Rabbits. I want rabbits.'

Rabbits? He was the one who had been calling MacGregor and Mike.

'What does that mean exactly?' said Diane. 'Why did you stab me?'

'It's what you do with rabbits.'

'And Mike. Is he a rabbit too?' If she could get him talking, maybe she could get some sense out of him.

He frowned; his eyes went dark again. 'Tried to steal my rabbits.'

'You know, fella,' said Diane, 'you aren't making a lot of sense.'

'You don't have to make sense to a rabbit.'

'For the sake of argument, pretend for a moment that I'm not a rabbit. What the hell are you talking about?'

She made a dash for the nearest table and stood at one end. To her good luck, the brakes were off and it rolled easily. She held on to it as if it were a weapon.

He crouched and began easing around the table. She moved so that it stayed between the two of them. She backed up then and ran at him, pushing the table into him, knocking him onto his back on the slick floor. His knife bounced into the corner.

She ran for Emery's gun, but the man jumped to his feet with an inhuman swiftness and ran at her, screaming. She tried to get away, but he knocked her sprawling against a table, overturning it with a bang. The table just missed falling on her. She tried to scramble up, but he caught her foot and dragged her to him. She kicked and he twisted her foot. She cried out in pain.

'Gotcha, rabbit.'

She looked for any kind of weapon, but there was nothing. She tried to scramble away from him, grabbing at the table for leverage, something to hold on to to keep from sliding in his direction. She kicked as she scrambled, freed herself and almost made it to her feet before he caught her legs again and pulled her toward him. Damn, he was strong. He hit her across the jaw, stunned her and picked up his knife from the floor.

'You'll mind what I tell you,' he hissed. 'Get on the table.'

'The hell I will.' Diane punched him in the throat with her fist.

He squealed and raised his knife over his head.

The shot was deafening in the enclosed room. The specter paused, knife in midair. Diane didn't wait to scramble away from him. He fell forward.

She looked over to see Emery half propped up with his gun aimed in her direction.

'I hope you don't intend to shoot me after all this,' she said.

He lowered the gun. Diane went to him. He collapsed again into a pool of his own blood on the floor.

'Don't tell my family, please. I'm sorry.'

'I'll tell them you're a hero,' said Diane.

He closed his eyes and Diane ran for the phone. It had been pulled out of the wall. She ran to her office phone. It was dead. She opened the vault. The phone in there was working. She dialed 911.

When she came out of her office, she expected to see the wild man gone, vanished the way demons did. But he lay on his face still, his blood spilling into an expanding puddle.

She felt for a pulse in Emery. There was none. His life had been shorter than he thought. In some odd way, his fall from grace may have saved her life. If Emery hadn't been there, the madman would have killed her. She shivered at the thought. The smell that clung to her clothes sickened her. She went to the sink and threw up.

Her crew, including Mike and Korey, came in with the paramedics. They stood in the doorway like a startled Greek chorus and stared at Diane and the bloody scene. Garnett appeared soon after, looking equally as baffled.

'What happened here?' He went over to look at Emery, then at the stranger. 'Who is he?'

'I have no idea. Emery saved my life. The other man was trying to kill me.'

Garnett looked at her and they locked gazes for several moments. 'Okay, that works for me,' he whispered. 'You have no idea who this other man is?'

'He's the one who stabbed me and Mike.'

'Him?' said Mike, and started to walk toward the body. A policeman held him back. 'Why?'

'I don't know. He babbled something about you trying to steal his rabbits.'

Neva slid her arm around Mike's waist and he put his arm around her. Anchoring each other from evil, it seemed to Diane.

'That's him too?' said Mike. 'Who is he? Damn. What is he?'

'A demon from hell, as near as I can tell,' said Diane.

'We now know where that strange smell came from,' said David.

Neva's face blanched. 'How long do you think he's been in the museum?'

'And why didn't someone see him?' asked Garnett. 'Guess we'll never know the answer to that.'

Neva was staring at Diane. She said, 'Should you go to the doctor? Your face.'

Diane found a mirror and looked into it. A large bruise spread across her jaw, and her lip was split and bleeding. One of the paramedics came to look at it.

'Can you move it? Does this hurt?'

'It's fine. Just a little sore,' she said.

He pronounced her jaw unbroken, but told her to put ice on it. She nodded absently.

'Neva, he's also the one who trashed your house. If you look at his hands, you'll see they fit the mold you made. And David, you know that thing we couldn't think of?'

'The Odells,' he said, and Diane nodded. 'They saw him at the funeral.'

'I'm not sure why you guys didn't smell him,' said Jin, waving his hand in front of his face. 'This guy was rotting before he even died.'

'He's putrid,' said Diane. 'David, Jin, will you

514

two process my clothes, please? I've got to get out of them and get a shower before I die from nausea.'

'Of course,' said David. 'Let's take you into the conference room, so as not to contaminate this crime scene.'

'When you're done, get some rest,' said Garnett. 'I'll do a report later. Do put some ice on that jaw. It looks terrible.'

Diane sat in her museum office in clean jogging clothes with an ice pack on her jaw and her feet up on a chair, her hair still wet from the shower. A crime scene cleanup crew was working in her lab removing the residue of the human carnage that had occurred there. Chanell was overseeing the installation of a new and better surveillance system that had arrived to replace the one sabotaged by Valentine and MacRae. Korey was still working on the diaries.

Things were working toward normal, but nothing felt right. Someone in the Taggart family had caused all this mess, and she wanted them brought to justice. She'd been over and over the evidence looking for something, anything that would definitively point to them.

'Boss?' Jin was at the door holding a piece of paper, waving it at her.

Diane put her feet on the floor and the ice pack down on her desk. 'What have you got?'

Jin collapsed in a chair in front of her desk. 'I

like this office. I think you need to spiff up your bone office some more.'

'Did you come to recommend a decorator?'

Jin grinned and brushed his hair back from his eyes. 'No. Korey and I were talking about the diaries, and Korey wondered why Caver Doe – I can't get used to calling him Dale Wayne Russell – anyway, Korey was wondering why he didn't write down what happened, since he didn't die right away – and had nothing to do but sit in that cave and wait. He at least had time to eat a couple of Moon Pies.'

'And you said?' prompted Diane.

'That he didn't have anything to write on. Then I remembered that he had a pencil in his pocket, and I thought about it, and there it was . . . the money. What if he wrote on the money? Remember the roll of bills we found in his shirt pocket?'

Diane nodded.

'I didn't do anything with them.' He shrugged. 'It was money covered in blood and cadaver juice. I didn't think. But I went back and did the ESDA thing. Did you know that Korey has an electrostatic detection apparatus too?'

'Yes, Jin, I did.'

'We have lots of redundancies,' said Jin.

'No, we don't. The museum and the crime scene unit are separate.'

'Oh, yeah, I forget sometimes.'

'What did you find on the bills?'

'He wrote down what happened. Sort of.'

Diane leaned forward and took the paper from Jin. The photograph of the electrostatic image was difficult to read, but she could make out words. The handwriting grew progressively worse – probably as he had grown sicker.

'I kind of translated it on the back,' said Jin.

Diane turned it over and read.

Fell. Broke lots of bones. Hurt. Emmett gone for help.
Water gone. Food gone. Emmett should be back. Hurt.
Rosemary. I love you, Rosemary.
Emmett, where are you? Accident?
Emmett not coming back. I'm dead.
Whoever tell Rosemary I love her.
Dale.

'That's a sad story,' said Diane. 'It's signed "Dale." We were right; it's Dale Wayne Russell.'

'Poor fellow. Waiting for someone named Emmett to come back for him. And in love with Rosemary. Isn't this like a dying declaration?' said Jin.

'Yes, it is. Garnett's been trying to find out something about the identity of Dale Wayne Russell. I haven't talked with him about it since yesterday. He's having a hard time overcoming his political survivalist tendencies. This might light a fire under him.'

517

Diane was about to pick up the phone when it rang.

'Diane Fallon.'

'Dr Fallon, this is Emmett Taggart. We met at Helen Egan's funeral.'

'Yes, Mr Taggart, I know who you are.'

Jin's eyes grew wide. Diane pointed to the phone in Andie's office, and Jin nodded and went in to pick up.

She watched Jin. When he was ready to pick up she said, 'Hold on just a moment, please, Mr Taggart. Let me go to my other phone.'

She motioned to Jin and he picked up the receiver to listen. There was the momentary sound of another phone on the line until Jin pressed the mute button.

'What can I do for you, Mr Taggart?' she said.

'It's what I can do for you. I've been thinking about that mummy exhibit of yours and how much I like the museum. I was considering making a sizable donation.' Emmett Taggart's voice reflected a man accustomed to being in control, to having his wishes fulfilled, to having people ingratiate themselves to him.

'Kendel Williams takes care of donations,' said Diane in an attempt to disarm him. 'She's not in her office at the moment. I've had to clear out the museum because of some unfortunate events. Our lives are very much disrupted.'

There was a pause during which Diane imagined Taggart enjoying the contribution he had

518

made to that disruption. She looked at Jin and held up her legal pad on which she had written the word *Emmett* in big letters for Jin to see. Jin's face registered astonishment.

The tone of Emmett Taggart's voice now reflected a noticeably more insistent quality but with a varnish of civility. 'I understand what you are saying, but for the kind of donation I'm thinking about, I'd rather speak to the director.'

'And you would want what in return for this donation? For large donors, we usually name a room after them.'

Distaste was now evident in his voice as he was actually having to ask for something, to justify himself. 'I wasn't thinking of a room. I was thinking of consideration for all the years of good I have done, all the charities I have given to, all the people I have helped.'

'You want acknowledgment?' Diane was almost enjoying this. Rubbing his face in his own arrogance and his guilt. And it had its desired effect. He came back at her on the offensive, with less caution.

'Let's stop this. You know exactly what I want, and I have enough money to pay for it. You may think I did something in the past that I should be punished for, but anything I might have done has been balanced several times over by all the good I've done.'

But Diane was just warming to the challenge. 'I've just spoken to the family of Jewel Southwell.

They have been devastated by her disappearance sixty-three years ago, and are still feeling the effects today.'

'Jewel.' He said the name as if he had just now remembered. Perhaps he had forgotten her name. 'She was a waitress with an illegitimate child.'

'No, the child was not illegitimate. Jewel's husband worked out of town.'

'You wouldn't have known she was married by the way she acted.'

'She loved life, and her family loved her. I also have a last letter from Dale Wayne Russell. Let me read it to you.' Diane read the poignant last words of Caver Doe. 'He expected you to come back for him.'

There was a long, drawn-out silence, but Diane could still hear the old man breathing. When he spoke again, he was not contrite, but he was calmer and sounded sincere, almost pleading.

'Dale was hurt too bad. My cousin was a careless boy. He was going to die anyway. You have to understand. I loved Rosemary too.'

'He was your cousin?'

'I thought you knew that. Yes, he was my cousin. Don't presume to judge me until you know everything.' His calm had not lasted long, and was replaced by a return of his arrogance and self-justification.

'I know we have three recent murders,' said Diane.

'Blackmailers!' he spit. 'Blackmailers!'

'Nothing they did justifies your taking the lives of Jake Stanley, and Flora and Donnie Martin,' said Diane, her own temper now raised. 'My mother was thrown in a black hole of a prison as a result of your criminal activities. There is nothing you can do to undo her suffering or to repair my ruined relationship with my family. No amount of money will change any of the evil you have done. You've hurt me and people I love and you want my goodwill?'

'About your mother, that wasn't—'

The blast that exploded through the phone was so loud it hurt Diane's ear.

'Mr Taggart? Are you there? Mr Taggart?' Diane heard the phone click.

CHAPTER 46

Jin rushed into her office as Diane was calling 911.

'That was a gunshot!' he shouted.

'Yes, it was . . .'

'Nine-one-one. What is the nature of your emergency?' the calm, businesslike voice of the dispatch operator said.

Diane identified herself and gave her phone number and a description of what had just happened. In talking to 911, she realized that all she knew for certain was that she had been called by a man who claimed to be Emmett Taggart, and that the earsplitting sound she'd heard sounded like a gunshot. She couldn't even give the caller's number because her caller ID had been blocked.

'Can you be reached at this number?' the dispatcher asked.

'Yes,' replied Diane.

'Stay on the line, please.'

Diane and Jin looked at each other, not knowing exactly what to think or do. The operator came back on.

'An officer has been dispatched to the scene. He may be back in touch with you later.'

'Thank you,' said Diane.

When she put the phone down she was still stunned.

'What do you reckon?' said Jin.

'I don't know.'

Neither moved for several moments, as if waiting for something. So much had just happened. Emmett Taggart had confirmed his complicity in the deaths of how many people? Five? What was he saying about her mother? Diane was brought out of her thoughts by the throbbing of her aching jaw. She picked up the ice pack and held it to her face.

Jin stood up and headed toward his lab area. 'I'll fax Caver Doe's – I mean Dale Wayne Russell's – letter to Garnett.'

Diane nodded. Her mind went back to worrying about what effect the coming publicity surrounding two violent deaths inside the crime lab would have on the museum. She relived in her mind the events and wondered what she could have done differently.

She tried to get some work done, but gave up. She started to go see how the cleanup was coming when the phone rang. It was Garnett.

'Emmett Taggart has been shot. We have his wife, Rosemary, in custody.'

'I thought he lived in Atlanta. How did the Rosewood police get involved?'

'He and his wife are staying with their grandson, Robert Lamont, who has a farm that lies inside the Rosewood city limits. Mrs Taggart's not saying anything. She, uh, only wants to talk to you.'

'Me? I don't even know the woman. I met her only briefly at Helen Egan's funeral.'

'I don't know why, but that's what she says.'

'You need us to work the crime scene?' asked Diane.

'Get David and Neva to do the work – you and Jin are witnesses.'

'Should I be talking to Mrs Taggart?'

'She says she won't talk to anyone else.'

'Okay. Get a search warrant for the entire premises – outbuildings and grounds. Jin can do the outside search.'

'Very well. What are you thinking?'

'I'm just being thorough.'

'How's your jaw?'

'Hurts like hell. Looks worse.'

Before she left her office Diane checked her appearance in the mirror. Her face was now swollen and badly discolored. She could already hear what Frank was going to say when he saw this. He had been threatening to quit work just to be able to watch after her well-being. She was beginning to think she did need a keeper.

Diane remembered Robert Lamont when she saw him. He was the auburn-haired man who was at the funeral with his running-for-senator uncle,

Steve Taggart, and his grandparents, Rosemary and Emmett Taggart. Lamont's farm was larger than Diane had expected. It reminded her of Tara in *Gone with the Wind* – the run-down Tara, not Tara in her prime. Not that Lamont's place was dilapidated. It was more shabby chic. The Greek Revival two-story columned house needed fresh paint, as did all the outbuildings. However, the yard was freshly mowed, the fields looked well-kept, and the black-and-white cows looked contented.

When their crime van pulled to a stop in the circular driveway, Garnett was already there. He informed them that the search warrant covered only the room in which Emmett had been shot.

'Damn,' said Diane. 'Why?'

'The victim's son, Steven Taggart, already had lawyers in the judge's chambers when I went to get the warrant. They were very persuasive.'

'I think someone here helped Emmett Taggart orchestrate everything,' said Diane. 'He couldn't have done it by himself. I doubt he would have known how to find people like Valentine and MacRae.'

'That may be true. But the only crime scene we are working is the one in the study. That's all we can do. No search of the rest of the house, no search of the grounds or outbuildings.' Garnett shook his head in disapproval.

'Jin, you wait in the van,' said Diane. 'They pulled a fast one on us.'

He nodded. 'Sure. We brought a computer. I'll just entertain myself.'

'David and Neva, you two work the study,' Diane told them.

Emmett Taggart had not died but was in critical condition and had been removed from the scene by the time Diane entered the study where he had been shot. The room had a leather, wood and tobacco-stand ambience that said it was for men only.

Taggart had been sitting behind a mahogany desk when he was shot. There wasn't much blood, just spots on the desk and chair and some high-velocity spatter almost invisible to the naked eye on the rug and desk.

Garnett ushered Diane into the parlor, where Mrs Taggart was sitting on a love seat. She looked much the same as she had at the funeral, but wore a mauve pantsuit and a light pink silk scarf tucked around her throat, rather than mourning black. She was fidgeting with a piece of old yellowed lace, gathering it up with her fingers.

When Diane sat down across from her, she saw that the material in Mrs Taggart's hand was a lace collar. It was a moment before Diane realized that it was the same lace collar worn by the very young Mrs Taggart in the snapshot found with Caver Doe.

Garnett seemed completely clueless as to the purpose of this meeting, but Diane thought she understood.

'Thank you for coming.' Mrs Taggart's voice was almost cordial.

Diane thought that odd. But she didn't respond to her first impulse and say, *That's all right; I had to do the crime scene anyway.* The woman was not as cold as she had been at the funeral. Diane dug deeper into herself to come up with more compassion. Sometimes sympathy fled her in the wake of everything she had to deal with.

'Why did you want to see me?' asked Diane.

'I want you to tell me what happened.'

'I don't know for sure . . .'

'All right, this stops right here,' a man in a dark, expensive-looking suit said as he walked into the room. The lawyer had arrived. He was followed by Robert Lamont. It was then that Diane noticed Lamont scratching, and the bandages on his arms. 'Mrs Taggart, you don't have to say another word.'

'Get out,' said Rosemary Taggart, her mouth set and her eyes downcast.

'You heard the lady,' said the lawyer.

'I was talking to you, you sycophant.' She glared at him. 'You aren't my lawyer and I don't want you here.'

The lawyer looked shocked, then sympathetic. 'You don't understand. I'm here to help.'

'You are here to do no such thing. And stop treating me like I'm senile. I have a lawyer and she's on her way. Until she gets here, I'm talking privately to this woman. Now get out. I know enough about the law to know that when I say you aren't my lawyer, you have to get out.'

'Grandma,' said Robert, 'he only wants to make sure you are okay and don't say anything to incriminate yourself.'

'Just last week I had a thorough annual physical that included mental acuity. I am certifiably fit in mind and body. If you don't leave, then I will leave with this woman so I can talk in private. You don't know what business I have with her, so don't presume that you are competent to take care of my needs.'

'I think we need to do as she says,' said Garnett. He seemed to take a great deal of pleasure in ushering the two men out of the room.

Rosemary Taggart smiled grimly. 'I always include a mental checkup when I get a physical, for just such an occasion. I don't trust my family – God help me.'

She bowed her head for a moment. Diane didn't know if she was praying, falling asleep, or just organizing her thoughts. She brought her head up sharply.

'Tell me about Dale. Tell me what you think happened to him. You've seen him, touched his bones.'

'Mrs Taggart . . .'

'Call me Rosemary. I'm never going by the name Taggart again.'

'Okay, Rosemary. It's a guess, but it is based on what we have discovered. Dale Wayne Russell and

Emmett Taggart were caving together. Through a mishap – I believe it was an accident, but I don't know for sure – the railroad spike that anchored his rope pulled out of the rocks. Dale fell into a cavern from a considerable height and broke several bones.' Diane hesitated.

'Don't leave anything out on my account, please.'

'One break, his shinbone, was a compound fracture. It broke through the skin and caused bleeding and later became infected. He also broke his ankle and wrist and had some internal injuries. We know that because of . . . We know that he did.'

Rosemary put a hand to her face and whimpered. 'Please don't stop. I need to hear this.'

'There was no way for Dale to climb out, and no way for Emmett to carry him out without help. Emmett got him situated and left him with water and a couple of Moon Pies.'

Rosemary smiled. 'Dale loved his Moon Pies.'

'It is my belief that sometime while making preparations to go for help, Emmett hatched a plan to abandon Dale. He took Dale's wallet so Dale wouldn't be identified if anyone found him. But he and Dale had stopped in that morning at Ray's Diner on their way to the cave. Jewel Southwell, a waitress at Ray's Diner, was the only person who could tie them together that day. In order for Emmett's plan to work, he had to get rid of Jewel Southwell.'

'Jewel was the woman Emmett said Dale ran off with. At first I didn't believe it. I didn't think Dale would do it, and I didn't think she would leave her child. But as more and more people believed it, I just fell in with them.'

'Emmett took Dale's Plymouth.'

Rosemary looked at the lace she caressed with her fingers and nodded. 'I remember that car like it was yesterday. He was always polishing that car and working on it. He was proud of it.'

'Emmett somehow got Jewel out of the diner and into the car. I don't know if he hit her on the head then, or waited until he got to the quarry. But at some point he struck her, probably with a tire iron, and killed her. The quarry lake was deep, and he knew that whatever was at the bottom of it would likely never be found. He pushed the car with Jewel's body inside into the lake. He was probably the one who then started the rumor that Dale and Jewel had run off together. Jewel had a reputation around town that made it easier for people to believe.

'What Emmett didn't know at the time was that a little fourteen-year-old girl saw him push the car into the quarry. She also may have seen him kill Jewel. Her name, her married name, was Flora Martin. All these years later, when my caving partners and I went into the cave and found' – Diane almost said Caver Doe – 'and found Dale Russell and it came out in the paper, it started a chain of events in motion.

530

'Emmett, of course, recognized whose body it was and tried to have the bones and other evidence stolen. At the same time, a much older Flora Martin remembered what she had seen as a little girl and tried to blackmail Emmett, and Emmett had her killed.

'But Flora had left a letter with information in it for her grandson, Donnie Martin. Donnie tried to find the sunken car with Jewel in it, but he and his partner, Jake Stanley, were murdered by Randy MacRae or Neil Valentine, who were hired for the job.' Diane explained who all the various people were as she mentioned them.

'My museum was burglarized and threatened with arson by MacRae and Valentine in an attempt to destroy the bones of Dale and Jewel and the evidence that went with them. When those attempts failed, Emmett called me on the phone and tried to buy me off. And here we are.'

Rosemary nodded her head. 'Dale and I were going to be married. I was pregnant. When Dale disappeared, Emmett offered to marry me and pass the baby off as his. Things are different now, but back then that was a godsend. But Emmett never let me forget what he did for me. Every argument we had, he threw it in my face that Dale left me pregnant and he had saved me. The swine, the lying, murdering swine.'

She shook her head. 'It wasn't just for me that he killed Dale.' She cast a shrewd glance at Diane. 'I was listening in on the telephone conversation with you. I heard everything. With Dale's disgrace and disappearance, Emmett became his grandfather's heir. That's how he built all this fortune. You see, Dale was the favorite in his grandfather's eyes. And there was my fortune. Emmett made out well.'

'Mrs . . . Rosemary, I have to tell you that I can't hold anything you say in confidence.'

Rosemary looked into Diane's eyes and smiled a smile that looked to be born more from deviousness than kindness.

'Dear, I want a trial. I want a very public trial. Your testimony is what I want. I don't care what you repeat about our conversation. Dale Russell was the love of my life.' Her eyes filled with tears that spilled down her cheeks. 'My life could have been so different. I want the world to know what happened to him and what Emmett Taggart really was, what he really is.'

'Grandma, you wouldn't do that to Granddad.' Robert Lamont had come into the room carrying a tray with two cups of coffee and set it down on the coffee table. 'Mom and Uncle Steve are on their way.'

'Robert, dear,' said Rosemary. She patted the seat beside her. He complied. He looked to Diane like he had spent years doing what he was told. 'You should have been told a long time ago. Emmett isn't your real grandfather. I was carrying your mother when I married Emmett. Your grandfather was Dale Wayne Russell, Emmett's cousin.

Emmett killed your real grandfather and tried to cover it up. I didn't know when I married him that he had killed Dale. All I knew was that Dale had disappeared.'

'No, that's not true.' Robert Lamont was visibly shaken.

'Yes, it is true, Robert. Emmett has confessed it. Why do you think he treated your uncle Steve and his children with such favoritism? Steve is his child. Your mother is not his child. Look at that auburn hair of yours. No one on Emmett's side of the family has that hair.' She smiled. 'That's Dale's hair. Dale would have loved you. You look so much like him.'

Diane hadn't realized it, but Robert did favor the reconstruction of Dale Russell that Neva had drawn. Rosemary's words so stunned Robert that Diane thought he was going to faint. He stared at his grandmother and scratched his arms. Diane wondered how Rosemary's resolve for the truth would hold up when she discovered the depth of Robert's involvement.

Diane was willing to bet that the rash on his arms was urticaria – caused by dermestid bites. Unfortunately, there was no evidence to prove it. But she'd bet the fingerprint found in the university dermestarium would be his. She believed he was the one who'd stolen the dermestid beetles and used them to try to throw off calculations of the time of death for Flora Martin. Was he the one who killed Flora? Sliced her open to speed the access of the beetles in order to hasten her decomposition? If Jin could find the knife with the missing tip, that would be a slam dunk, but she suspected that it was in a landfill somewhere.

Robert looked sick. 'I . . . I just wanted to tell you that Mom and Uncle Steve are here, and your lawyer.'

Diane saw it clearly now. Robert had become the man Emmett used to be – the unfavored grandchild who would do anything to gain favor.

Diane and Rosemary stood and she walked with the elder woman to the entryway to meet her children. They were talking to the family lawyer, ignoring Rosemary's lawyer, who had just arrived. Garnett came in, and all of them started talking to him at once.

'I don't like the way this was handled,' said Steven Taggart. 'You'll be hearing from the commissioner.'

'Shut up, Steven,' Rosemary said. 'They have behaved fine, and I don't want you being a bully. Chief Garnett, do you think we could dispense with the handcuffs? I promise I won't run or try to hurt myself. As my doctors can attest, I am perfectly sane.'

Rosemary picked up her purse on the hall table and smiled at her children. 'You'll have to excuse me. Ms Talbot and I have to go and plan my defense.'

She took Garnett's arm and they walked out

the door. Her children gaped and scurried after her.

Diane spotted David from the hallway. He was peeking out the door of the study. He gave her a thumbs-up.

CHAPTER 47

Diane went to the study before Rosemary's relatives could return and question her. Neva was taking photographs of the bloodstains. David was taking samples.

'How's it going?' she asked.

'I'm not sure why they restricted the search,' he said in a low voice, 'but we have everything we need here.'

Diane raised her eyebrows. 'What have you found?' She laid a hand on his arm, shook her head after seeing a reflection in the ornate mirror on the wall. She turned toward the doorway. 'Can we help you, Mr Lamont?'

'We were wondering when you will be finished.'

'Sir,' said Diane, walking over to him, leading him out into the hallway, 'I'm sorry, but you can't be here while we are processing the scene. My team is working as quickly as they can.'

His eyes darted around the hallway. He appeared to her as if he was looking for an escape hatch.

'If my grandmother confessed . . . I mean, do you really have to continue?'

'We are required to collect the evidence from

536

the scene of the crime, regardless. But she didn't confess.'

'What? I thought that was what you were discussing,' Robert Lamont said.

'What were you talking about?' Steven Taggart came in, his brows knitted together, a polished look of concern on his face. 'I know you are just doing your jobs, but my attorney tells me that anything my mother said to you is not admissible. She is an elderly woman . . . This has been hard on her.'

'That's true,' said Steven's lawyer, coming in behind him. 'You can't use any of it in court.'

Rosemary's daughter, Dahlia Lamont, appeared in the large hallway. She looked like her mother – same bone structure, same build. Diane knew she was sixty-three, based on what Rosemary had told her about being pregnant when Dale Russell disappeared, but she looked older, too old to have a son in his thirties. Being the bastard daughter hadn't been easy on her, even if she hadn't known that she wasn't Emmett's biological daughter. Emmett knew and Diane guessed he made her feel it, if not know it.

'What is this about?' asked Dahlia. 'What did Mother—'

'Don't say anything,' said Steven through his teeth. 'Just shut up.'

'Uncle Steven,' said Robert. He could clench his teeth as well as his uncle.

'Of course, I'm just distraught,' Steven said. 'I'm

sorry, Dahlia. I'm sure you are distraught too. I just didn't want you to say anything the police technicians might misunderstand. We can have a family meeting when they are out of here.' He looked at Diane as if she were a houseguest who couldn't take a hint.

'Mr Taggart, your mother said little to me. She isn't a stupid woman. She knew exactly what she wanted: information. She may be elderly, but she is not frail, nor is her mind diminished in any way, so you needn't worry about what she may have said. We'll get out of your house as soon as we can.'

A young woman dressed in a suit and carrying a briefcase came in holding an official-looking document. Garnett came in with her. He shrugged at Diane.

Steven's lawyer looked briefly at the document. 'You'll leave now,' he said. 'I have a court order stopping this invasion of privacy. You have your photographs and the samples you need. Get out and leave the family alone.'

Diane read over the document. It said that once they had inspected the scene in the immediate vicinity around the desk where the victim was found, they had to leave in a reasonable time. She had never seen anything like this. She wasn't even sure it was legal, but in the time it would take her to challenge it, the family would have a chance to get rid of anything incriminating. Her cheeks flushed with anger. *Amazing*, she thought, *what money will buy*. She looked at the judge's name and noted it for future reference.

'Very well. David, Neva.' Diane motioned toward the door. They came walking out of the study with a camera and an evidence bag.

'I need to see that,' the lawyer said.

Neva pulled the evidence bag back away from the lawyer's reach. 'It's a sample of blood spatter,' she said.

'That's evidence of the crime, collected under legal authority,' said Diane. 'It has to remain in the chain of custody. No one but members of the crime scene unit can touch it until it is processed. I'm sure you know that.'

'What about the case?' said the lawyer, indicating the forensic kit.

'What about it?' said David. He opened it and showed the various collection paraphernalia. 'What's going on?'

'Just making sure you follow the warrant,' the lawyer said. 'The new one that restricts your collection of evidence to what you find around the desk.'

David raised a hand. 'That's all we had time to search – around the desk and the area of the rug immediately where Mr Taggart was shot. But is it not proper procedure to search the room?' he said.

'There are private matters in the filing cabinets and other places that are none of your business,' said Robert. 'We have suffered a tragedy, and you barge in here like you own the place.'

'An attempted murder, which may become a murder, was committed in this room,' said Garnett. 'We are just doing our job as is required under the law. I read something about that in your law-and-order political platform. I would have thought we would have your support.'

'This is not some crack house,' Steven said.

'The law does not specify that we are to investigate only those felony crimes that occur in crack houses,' said Garnett. 'However, we obey the orders of the court. We have done what the law demands of us, and will be on our way.'

David closed up the forensic case and they all walked out of the house.

'I can't believe those people,' said Diane on the way back to the crime lab. She sat in the front seat of the van. David drove, and Neva and Jin were in the back. 'I can't believe the judge.'

'A billion dollars buys a lot,' said David.

'Except brains,' said Neva, who broke up in a fit of laughter. Jin and David joined her.

'What?' asked Diane.

'We found one of those fancy fantasy knives sticking up in a stone on the desk where Taggart was shot,' said Neva. 'Guess what?'

'It has the tip missing?' said Diane.

David nodded. 'That's probably why it broke – wasn't made out of good steel – unlike the knife of our mystery stranger who stabbed you and Mike. His knife was top-of-the-line.'

'Thanks for reminding me.' Diane rubbed her arm.

'So, even with that restricted search, you found the knife?'

'Yeah, you'd think they would talk to each other,' said David. 'You know, coordinate their criminal activities.'

'I bet somebody moved it and they didn't know,' said Jin. 'But that's not all we got.'

'Wait a minute,' said Diane. 'You didn't come out with anything but the camera and blood samples. And Jin, how do you know what they found?'

'David's paranoia,' said Jin. 'You know, I'm going to have to get some of that myself. It's sure working for you and David.'

'Neva overheard the lawyer talking on the phone,' said David. 'I had a feeling they might try to pull something, so I called Jin on the cell and handed him the evidence out the window. However' – he held up his hand – 'everything we found' – he started laughing again – 'everything we found was right inside the limits of the new warrant.'

'I thought you were fairly unruffled when you showed him your case,' said Diane.

'Just part of the show.'

'What else did you find?' said Diane.

'Neva found it under the desk. The old man must have had it in his hand. It was the letter that Flora Martin wrote to her grandson Donnie. We're hoping for Donnie's fingerprints.'

Diane was speechless the rest of the way to the lab.

'You are sure this was around the desk – all of it?' said Garnett. He sat across from Diane at the table in the crime lab looking at the report they had written up. 'I mean, this guy's running for senator.'

Diane showed him a photograph. 'David took this from the doorway before we even entered the room. It shows Robert Lamont standing by the window with his head in his hands. It shows the desk with the fantasy knife in the stone. Look at this blowup of the area beneath the desk. You can just see the corner of an envelope. The envelope contained Flora Martin's letter and it had Emmett Taggart's blood spatter on it. All this is in line with the very – and may I say criminally – restrictive search warrant.'

'Yes, but sneaking the evidence outside . . .'

'That's not against the law. Just my crew saving themselves from going back and forth through the house.'

'The prints?'

'David saw Robert Lamont touch the desk and lifted his prints from there. Steven Taggart was in the military, and they had his prints on file,' said Diane.

'I'll go pick them up and let Mr Steven Taggart explain what his prints are doing on a letter written by a murder victim. Mr Robert Lamont can explain what he was doing with a knife whose point was embedded in that same murder victim, and what his prints are doing inside the – what did you call it?'

'Dermestarium. The container where the missing colony of dermestid beetles were kept.'

'And people keep these beetles . . . why?'

'To strip bones cleanly and quickly of tissue.'

'Okay, I'll pick them up – with pleasure.' Garnett rose and started for the door. He turned and looked at her. 'You know, I was going to vote for the law-and-order son of a bitch.'

He hesitated and then said, 'I suppose I should tell you, we've identified the dead stranger.' He came back to the table and sat down.

Like a swarm of flies at a picnic, the three members of her crew appeared out of nowhere and sat down. It was obvious they had been listening.

Diane leaned forward. 'You found him in the *Book of the Dead*, I'll bet.'

'Do we need to hire an exorcist for the bone lab?' asked Jin.

'I almost decided not to tell you,' said Garnett. 'It makes me sick to think about it.'

Diane and her crew exchanged glances. 'Who was he?'

'His name was Dr Jermen Sutcliff. He was a gynecologist.'

Diane drew in a breath and put her hands over her mouth. The others were similarly horrified.

'Oh, God. Who would go to him?' said Diane.

'Poor people. He worked at a free clinic in Atlanta,' said Garnett.

'That's sick,' said Neva. 'That's really sick.'

Diane shook her head. 'Look, this guy was seriously demented. There's no way he could hold down a job. He couldn't carry on a coherent conversation.'

'They said he wasn't the most popular doctor there, and he was a little strange, but he worked long hours for little money. Maybe he was schizophrenic or something and could switch it on and off,' said Garnett. 'I've seen really crazy people pass for normal when they have to.'

'No, he was something different. You need to investigate that place,' said Diane. She would never be able to get that face out of her mind – the deranged look he'd had when he saw the metal lab tables and the way he demanded that she get on the table. 'I'm serious. You need to talk to his patients.'

'I put a bug in the ear of an Atlanta detective I know. I told him that this guy was disturbed.'

'You need to put more than a bug in his ear; put a whole colony,' said Diane. 'I'm serious. There needs to be a follow-up on his patients.'

Garnett nodded and stood up again. 'There are other things, but I don't think I'll share. Some things it's best not to know. You are right: This guy had something seriously wrong with him.'

'You can't leave us with that,' said David. 'What other things?'

Jin nodded in agreement. 'What, man? Tell us.'

'The ME said he was a necrophiliac,' said Garnett. 'And recently . . .'

'Oh, God,' said Diane and Neva together.

'Okay,' said David. 'I'm sorry I asked that question.'

'I told you he was disturbed,' said Diane.

Garnett left through the museum entrance to the crime lab. Diane had noticed him doing that more and more lately. She believed that like the rest of them, he had discovered that the museum had a soothing charm that washed away the dark stains of the evil side of life.

She stood up. 'How about going to the museum restaurant? My treat.'

'I'd like that,' said David.

Jin nodded.

'I'll ask Mike to join us,' said Neva. 'If I can pull him away from the rocks.'

'I have the proposal for the photography class,' said David. 'You can read it while we wait for dinner.'

Diane agreed. The museum had a way of soothing all their souls.

EPILOGUE

Charlotte Hawkins, the Druid from England and claimant to the Moonhater Cave bones, and Charlotte's friend Caitlin Shanahan, the Wiccan from the United States, sat in front of Diane's desk in the museum. Caitlin unconsciously fingered the meditation fountain near Diane's desk, moving her fingers in and out of the clear water.

'I hope you've been having a good time in the U.S.,' Diane said to Charlotte.

'A wonderful time. Caitlin has been a most gracious host. You've found out something about the bones, haven't you? Are you going to give them to me?'

'I have indeed found out something about the bones. We performed several analyses – one dating the bones and another to establish their origin.'

'We know where they're from,' said Caitlin. She was still ready for a fight. Charlotte patted her arm gently.

'You know partly where they're from,' said Diane. 'It's a young girl.'

'Woman,' said Caitlin.

Even Charlotte rolled her eyes at that one.

Diane smiled. 'She was between fourteen and eighteen. She was healthy and well nourished. Her bones had indeed been in the cave, probably since the second century, and she was run through from back to front with a sword.'

Caitlin almost jumped out of her chair. 'It's her, it's Annwn. That's what happened to Annwn.'

Charlotte's eyes glittered, but she said nothing.

'And,' said Diane, 'she was Roman.'

They both looked dumbfounded. 'Roman?' they said together.

'She can't be,' said Caitlin. 'She's Celtic . . .'

Charlotte sighed and looked at her hands. 'So she isn't my ancestor after all.'

'I didn't say that,' said Diane.

Both of them looked up sharply.

'You mean she is?' said Charlotte.

Diane nodded. 'We were able to get DNA from her tooth, and matched her mitochondrial DNA to yours. You both are descended from the same female ancestor.' Diane reached beside her desk and handed Charlotte a beautiful painting done by Neva. 'This is a reconstruction of her face. Neva, the artist, researched the hairstyle and fashion of the times for the painting.'

'Well . . .' whispered Charlotte, 'she looks a bit like my granddaughter Brenna.' She shook her head and frowned. 'I always thought we were descended from the Celts.'

'You are,' said Diane, running her fingers through her hair as a gesture to Charlotte.

'Oh, of course, how silly of me,' said Charlotte, touching her own red hair. She caressed the face in the painting, stroking the face. 'I wonder what her story is?'

'Maybe there are other families around the area with stories that can shed some light on hers,' said Diane. 'John Rose would love to sit down and talk with you about trying to research her history. He only wants to know who she is and what happened to her. Whatever happened to her is the history of the whole region. He was very excited to find out that you are related.'

Charlotte nodded. 'She was a pretty little thing.'

'Yes, she was,' said Diane.

'I'll go see John again. We'll talk. I would like to know what happened to her.'

Caitlin stood up abruptly. 'In light of everything, I'll take the curse off the museum,' she said.

'Caitlin!' admonished Charlotte. 'You didn't. What a naughty girl you are.'

'Woman.'

Charlotte clucked. 'You're a girl, dear. You'll see when you get to my age.'

'It's all right,' said Diane. 'The museum is immune to curses. She has a goodness all her own, and it usually rubs off on people. You are welcome to visit while you are here.'

It had been three months since Mike's stabbing. He was now fit and raring to go. Diane and her caving buddies were on their first outing since

549

finding Caver Doe, and she was thrilled to be here. Among all the other things to celebrate, she and Mike were celebrating the negative results from the blood tests they'd had to take because of their stabbings. She had told Andie that if there was any crisis, to tell the perpetrators to wait until she returned.

Diane stood in the cave tunnel by the passage entrance where she had first heard the waterlike noise, waiting for the others. MacGregor was with them. He had lost weight so that he could fit through the squeeze.

'He doesn't look half-bad,' Neva had told her. 'He's real proud.'

The others came down the tunnel shortly, catching up.

'This is fun,' said Jin, who this time was dressed in clothes that fit and had a reasonably sized backpack picked out for him by Mike.

'Okay, Diane has point,' said Mike. 'I'll take up the rear.'

The flashing, bobbing lights from their five headlamps lit the tunnel walls. The surface was gritty under Diane's touch, the texture of sandstone. Rocks of all sizes filled the passage. They looked stable, but Diane tested them before she committed herself. The only egress for several of the large boulders was to climb over them. It was exhilarating. Halfway down the passage, Diane smelled damp soil, and she could hear a waterfall. A waterfall! The thought excited her. She watched the rocks around her and the ground under her, alert for the unexpected.

The tunnel was like a round rabbit hole going gently downward to a wonderland. Just ahead she spotted an off-shoot tunnel. Another temptation. This was a great cave.

She arrived at the new tunnel entrance – and suddenly a strong and distinctive odor hit her. She stopped and stared, seeing nothing but the upward-sloping passage filled with rocks. The others stopped and looked in.

'What is that smell?' said MacGregor. 'It's not bat dung.'

'No,' said Mike. 'I don't know what it is.'

But Diane knew. So did Jin. They looked at each other. Diane felt sick, as though someone had desecrated a church or the museum.

'Wait here,' she told the others. 'Jin and I will go.'

But they didn't wait for her and Jin. They followed close behind them into the tunnel. The smell increased until all of them had trouble controlling their gag reflex. The tunnel suddenly widened into a room, littered with storage, or . . .

'Oh, my God,' cried Neva.

MacGregor ducked away and leaned against a wall, heaving. Mike grabbed Neva and held her.

Diane and Jin stared at what was before them. She understood now. It was as clear as bright daylight. When they had entered the cave and found Caver Doe, it was like stumbling over a tripwire that set in motion all the events that culminated in the shooting of Emmett Taggart. What they didn't realize at the time, what Diane saw now with lightning clarity, was that they had touched off another tripwire completely unknown to them. The first time in the cave they had almost stumbled upon what they had now discovered: The other entrance to the cave and the lair of a serial killer.

Sunlight filtered in through the cracks of an ancient wooden door to one side. Metal tables lined the stone walls of the room. Chained on top of the tables were rotting dismembered female corpses. These were Jermen Sutcliff's rabbits.